The Great Pursuit

By the same author

RIOTOUS ASSEMBLY
INDECENT EXPOSURE
PORTERHOUSE BLUE
BLOTT ON THE LANDSCAPE
WILT

THE GREAT PURSUIT

Tom Sharpe

SECKER & WARBURG
LONDON

First published in England 1977 by
Martin Secker & Warburg Limited
14 Carlisle Street, London W1V 6NN

SBN: 436 45806 3

Printed in Great Britain by
Cox & Wyman Limited
London, Fakenham and Reading

Chapter 1

When anyone asked Frensic why he took snuff he replied that it was because by rights he should have lived in the eighteenth century. It was, he said, the century best suited to his temperament and way of life, the age of reason, of style, of improvement and expansion and those other characteristics he so manifestly possessed. That he didn't, and happened to know that the eighteenth century hadn't either, only heightened his pleasure at his own affectation and the amazement of his audience and, by way of paradox, justified his claim to be spiritually at home with Sterne, Swift, Smollett, Richardson, Fielding and other giants of the rudimentary novel whose craft Frensic so much admired. Since he was a literary agent who despised nearly all the novels he handled so successfully, Frensic's private eighteenth century was that of Grub Street and Gin Lane and he paid homage to it by affecting an eccentricity and cynicism which earned him a useful reputation and armoured him against the literary pretensions of unsaleable authors. In short he bathed only occasionally, wore woollen vests throughout the summer, ate a great deal more than was good for him, drank port before lunch and took snuff in large quantities so that anyone wishing to deal with him had to prove their hardiness by running the gauntlet of these deplorable habits. He also arrived early for work, read every manuscript that was submitted to him, promptly returned those he couldn't sell and just as promptly sold the others and in general conducted his business with surprising efficiency. Publishers took Frensic's opinions seriously. When Frensic said a book would sell, it sold. He had a nose for a bestseller, an infallible nose.

It was, he liked to think, something he had inherited from his father, a successful wine-merchant whose own nose for a palatable claret at a popular price had paid for that expensive education which, together with Frensic's more metaphysical nose, gave him the edge over his competitors. Not that the connection between a good education and his success as a connoisseur of commercially rewarding literature was direct. He had arrived at his talent circuitously and if his admiration for the eighteenth century, while real, nevertheless concealed an inversion, it was by exactly the same process that he had arrived at his success as a literary agent.

At twenty-one he had come down from Cambridge with a second-class degree in English and the ambition to write a great novel. After a year behind the counter of his father's wine shop in Greenwich and at his desk in a room in Blackheath the 'great' had been abandoned. Three more years as an advertising copywriter and the author of a rejected novel about life behind the counter of a wine shop in Greenwich had completed the demolition of his literary ambitions. At twenty-four Frensic hadn't needed his nose to tell him he would never be a novelist. The two dozen literary agents who had refused to handle his work had said so already. On the other hand his experience of them had revealed a profession entirely to his taste. Literary agents, it was obvious, lived interesting, comfortable and thoroughly civilized lives. If they didn't write novels, they met novelists, and Frensic was still idealistic enough to imagine that this was a privilege; they spent their days reading books; they were their own masters, and if his own experience was anything to go by they showed an encouraging lack of literary perspicacity. In addition they seemed to spend a great deal of time eating and drinking and going to parties, and Frensic, whose appearance tended to limit his sensual pleasures to putting things into himself rather than into other people, was something of a gourmet. He had found his vocation.

At twenty-five he opened an office in King Street next to Covent Garden and sufficiently close to Curtis Brown, the largest literary agency in London, to occasion some profitable postal confusion, and advertised his services in the *New Statesman*, whose readers seemed more prone to pursue those literary ambitions he had so recently relinquished. Having done that he sat down and waited for the manuscripts to arrive. He had to wait a long time and he was beginning to wonder just how long his father could be persuaded to pay the rent when the postman delivered two parcels. The first contained a novel by Miss Celia Thwaite of The Old Pumping Station, Bishop's Stortford and a letter explaining that *Love's Lustre* was Miss Thwaite's first book. Reading it with increasing nausea, Frensic had no reason to doubt her word. The thing was a hodgepodge of romantic drivel and historical inaccuracy and dealt at length with the unconsummated love of a young squire for the wife of an absent-bodied crusader whose obsession with his wife's chastity seemed to

2

reflect an almost pathological fetishism on the part of Miss Thwaite herself. Frensic wrote a polite note explaining that *Love's Lustre* was not a commercial proposition and posted the manuscript back to Bishop's Stortford.

The contents of the second package seemed at first sight to be more promising. Again it was a first novel, this time called *Search for a Lost Childhood* by a Mr P. Piper who gave as his address the Seaview Boarding House, Folkstone. Frensic read the novel and found it perceptive and deeply moving. Mr Piper's childhood had not been a happy one but he wrote discerningly about his unsympathetic parents and his own troubled adolescence in East Finchley. Frensic promptly sent the book to Jonathan Cape and informed Mr Piper that he foresaw an immediate sale followed by critical acclaim. He was wrong. Cape rejected the book. Bodley Head rejected it. Collins rejected it. Every publisher in London rejected it with comments that ranged from the polite to the derisory. Frensic conveyed their opinions in diluted form to Piper and entered into a correspondence with him about ways of improving it to meet the publishers' requirements.

He was just recovering from this blow to his acumen when he received another. A paragraph in *The Bookseller* announced that Miss Celia Thwaite's first novel, *Love's Lustre*, had been sold to Collins for fifty thousand pounds, to an American publisher for a quarter of a million dollars, and that she stood a good chance of winning The Georgette Heyer Memorial Prize for Romantic Fiction. Frensic read the paragraph incredulously and underwent a literary conversion. If publishers were prepared to pay such enormous sums for a book which Frensic's educated taste had told him was romantic trash, then everything he had learnt from F. R. Leavis and more directly from his own supervisor at Oxford, Dr Sydney Louth, about the modern novel was entirely false in the world of commercial publishing; worse still it constituted a deadly threat to his own career as a literary agent. From that moment of revelation Frensic's outlook changed. He did not discard his educated standards. He stood them on their head. Any novel that so much as approximated to the criteria laid down by Leavis in *The Great Tradition* and more vehemently by Miss Sydney Louth in her work, *The Moral Novel*, he rejected out of hand as totally unsuitable for publication while those books they would have dismissed as beneath contempt he pushed for all he was worth. By virtue of this remarkable reversal Frensic prospered. By the time he was thirty he had established an enviable reputation among publishers as an agent who recommended only those books that would sell. A novel from Frensic could be relied upon to need no alterations and little editing. It would be exactly eighty thousand words long or, in the case of historical romance where the readers were more voracious, one hundred and fifty thousand. It would start with a bang, continue with more bangs and end happily with an even bigger bang. In short, it would contain all those ingredients that public taste most appreciated.

But if the novels Frensic submitted to publishers needed few changes, those that arrived on his desk from aspiring authors seldom passed his scrutiny without fundamental alteration. Having discovered the ingredients of popular success in *Love's Lustre*, Frensic applied them to every book he handled so that they emerged from the process of rewriting like literary plum puddings or blended wines and incorporated sex, violence, thrills, romance and mystery, with the occasional dollop of significance to give them cultural respectability. Frensic was very keen on cultural respectability. It ensured reviews in the better papers and gave readers the illusion that they were participating in a pilgrimage to a shrine of meaning. What the meaning was remained, necessarily, unclear. It came under the general heading of meaningfulness but without it a section of the public who despised mere escapism would have been lost to Frensic's authors. He therefore always insisted on significance, and while on the whole he lumped it with insight and sensibility as being in any large measure as lethal to a book's chances as a pint of strychnine in a clear soup, in homeopathic doses it had a tonic effect on sales.

So did Sonia Futtle, whom Frensic chose as a partner to handle foreign publishers. She had previously worked for a New York agency and being an American her contacts with US publishers were invaluable. And the American market was extremely profitable. Sales were larger, the percentage from authors' royalties greater, and the incentives offered by Book Clubs enormous. Appropriately for one who was to expand their business in this direction, Sonia Futtle had already expanded personally in most others and was of distinctly unmarriageable proportions. It was this as much as anything that had persuaded Frensic to change the agency's name to Frensic & Futtle and to link his impersonal fortune with hers. Besides, she was an enthusiast for books which dealt with interpersonal relations and Frensic had developed an allergy to interpersonal relationships. He

4

concentrated on less demanding books, thrillers, detective stories, sex when unromantic, historical novels when unsexual, campus novels, science fiction and violence. Sonia Futtle handled romantic sex, historical romance, liberation books whether of women or negroes, adolescent traumas, interpersonal relationships and animals. She was particularly good with animals, and Frensic, who had once almost lost a finger to the heroine of *Otters to Tea*, was happy to leave this side of the business to her. Given the chance he would have relinquished Piper too. But Piper stuck to Frensic as the only agent ever to have offered him the slightest encouragement and Frensic, whose success was in inverse proportion to Piper's failure, reconciled himself to the knowledge that he could never abandon Piper and that Piper would never abandon his confounded *Search for a Lost Childhood*.

Each year he arrived in London with a fresh version of his novel and Frensic took him out to lunch and explained what was wrong with it while Piper argued that a great novel must deal with real people in real situations and could never conform to Frensic's blatantly commercial formula. And each year they would part amicably, Frensic to wonder at the man's incredible perseverance and Piper to start work in a different boarding-house in a different seaside town on a different search for the same lost childhood. And so year after year the novel was partially transformed and the style altered to suit Piper's latest model. For this Frensic had no one to blame but himself. Early in their acquaintance he had rashly recommended Miss Louth's essays in *The Moral Novel* to Piper as something he ought to study and, while Frensic had come to regard her appreciations of the great novelists of the past as pernicious to anyone trying to write a novel today, Piper had adopted her standards as his own. Thanks to Miss Louth he had produced a Lawrence version of *Search for a Lost Childhood*, then a Henry James; James had been superseded by Conrad, then by George Eliot; there had been a Dickens version and even a Thomas Wolfe; and one awful summer a Faulkner. But through them all there stalked the figure of Piper's father, his miserable mother and the self-consciously pubescent Piper himself. Derivation followed derivation but the insights remained implacably trite and the action non-existent. Frensic despaired but remained loyal. To Sonia Futtle his attitude was incomprehensible.

'What do you do it for?' she asked. 'He's never going to make it and those lunches cost a fortune.'

'He is my *memento mori*,' said Frensic cryptically, conscious that the death Piper served to remind him of was his own, the aspiring young novelist he himself had once been and on the betrayal of whose literary ideals the success of Frensic & Futtle depended.

But if Piper occupied one day in his year, a day of atonement, for the rest Frensic pursued his career more profitably. Blessed with an excellent appetite, an impervious liver and an inexpensive source of fine wines from his father's cellars, he was able to entertain lavishly. In the world of publishing this was an immense advantage. While other agents wobbled home from those dinners over which books are conceived, publicized or bought, Frensic went portly on eating, drinking and advocating his novels *ad nauseam* and boasting of his 'finds'. Among the latter was James Jamesforth, a writer whose novels were of such unmitigated success that he was compelled for tax purposes to wander the world like some alcoholic fugitive from fame.

It was thanks to Jamesforth's itinerantly drunken progress from one tax haven to the next that Frensic found himself in the witness box in the High Court of Justice, Queen's Bench Division in the libel case of Mrs Desdemona Humberson *versus* James Jamesforth, author of *Fingers of Hell*, and Pulteney Press, publishers of the said novel. Frensic was in the witness box for two hours and by the time he stepped down he was a shaken man.

Chapter 2

'Fifteen *thousand* pounds plus costs,' said Sonia Futtle next morning, 'for inadvertent libel? I don't believe it.'

'It's in the paper,' said Frensic handing her *The Times*. 'Next to the bit about the drunken lorry driver who killed two children and got fined a hundred and fifty pounds. Mind you he did lose his licence for three months too.'

'But that's insane. A hundred and fifty pounds for killing two children and fifteen thousand for libelling a woman James didn't even know existed.'

'On a zebra crossing,' said Frensic bitterly. 'Don't forget the zebra crossing.'

'Mad. Stark staring raving mad,' said Sonia. 'You English are out of your minds legally.'

'So's Jamesforth,' said Frensic, 'and you can forget him as one of our authors. He doesn't want to know us.'

'But we didn't do anything. We aren't supposed to check his proofs out. Pulteney's should have done that. They'd have spotted the libel.'

'Like hell they would. How does anyone spot a woman called Desdemona Humberson living in the wilds of Somerset who grows lupins and belongs to the Women's Institute? She's too improbable for words.'

'She's also done very nicely for herself. Fifteen grand for being called a nymphomaniac. It's worth it. I mean if someone called me a raving nymphomaniac I'd be only too glad to accept fifteen—'

'Doubtless,' said Frensic, forestalling a discussion of this highly unlikely eventuality. 'And for fifteen thousand I'd have hired a drunken lorry driver and had her erased on a zebra crossing. Split the difference with the driver and we would have still been to the good. And while I was about it I would have had Mr Galbanum slaughtered too. He should have had more sense than to advise Pulteneys and Jamesforth to fight the case.'

7

'Well it was innocent libel,' said Sonia. 'James didn't mean to malign the woman.'

'Oh quite. The fact remains that he did and under the Defamation Act of 1952 designed to protect authors and publishers from actions of this sort, innocent libel demands that they show they took reasonable care—'

'Reasonable care? What does that mean?'

'According to that senile old judge it means going to Somerset House and checking to see if anyone called Desdemona was born in 1928 and married a man called Humberson in 1951. Then you go through the Lupin Growers Association Handbook looking for Humbersons and if they're not there you have a whack at the Women's Institute and finally the telephone directory for Somerset. Well, they didn't do all that so they got lumbered for fifteen thousand and we've got the reputation of handling authors who libel innocent women. Send your novels to Frensic & Futtle and get sued. We are the pariahs of the publishing world.'

'It can't be as bad as all that. After all, it's the first time it's happened and everyone knows that James is a souse who can't remember where he's been or who he's done.'

'Can't they just. Pulteneys can. Hubert rang up last night to say that we needn't send them any more novels. Once *that* word gets round we are going to have what is euphemistically called a cash flow problem.'

'We're certainly going to have to find someone to replace James,' said Sonia. 'Bestsellers like that don't grow on trees.'

'Nor lupins,' said Frensic and retired to his office.

All in all it was a bad day. The phone rang almost incessantly. Authors demanded to know if they were likely to end up in the High Court of Justice, Queen's Bench Division, because they had used the names of people they were at school with, and publishers turned down novels they would previously have accepted. Frensic sat and took snuff and tried to remain civil. By five o'clock he was finding it increasingly difficult and when the Literary Editor of the *Sunday Graphic* phoned to ask if Frensic would contribute an article on the iniquities of the British libel laws he was downright rude.

'What do you want me to do?' he shouted. 'Stick my head in a bloody noose and get hauled up for contempt of court? For all I know that blithering idiot Jamesforth is going to appeal against the verdict.'

'On the grounds that you inserted the passage which libelled Mrs Humberson?' the editor asked. 'After all it was suggested by the defence counsel—'

'By God, I'll have you for slander,' shouted Frensic. 'Galbanum had the gall to say that in court where he's protected but if you repeat that in public I'll institute proceedings myself.'

'You'd have a hard time,' said the editor. 'Jamesforth wouldn't make a good witness. He swears you advised him to jack Mrs Humberson up sexwise and when he wouldn't you altered the proofs.'

'That's a downright lie,' yelled Frensic. 'Anyone would think I wrote my authors' novels for them!'

'As a matter of fact a great many people do believe just that,' said the editor. Frensic hurled imprecations and went home with a headache.

If Wednesday was bad, Thursday was no better. Collins rejected William Lonroy's fifth novel *Seventh Heaven* as being too explicit sexually. Triad Press turned down Mary Gold's *Final Fling* for the opposite reason and Cassells even refused *Sammy The Squirrel* on the grounds that it was preoccupied with individual acquisition and lacked community concern. Cape rejected this, Secker rejected that. There were no acceptances. Finally there was a moment of high drama when an elderly clergyman whose autobiography Frensic had repeatedly refused to handle, explaining each time that there wasn't a large reading public for a book that dealt exclusively with parish life in South Croydon, smashed a vase with his umbrella and only consented to leave with his manuscript when Sonia threatened to call the police. By lunchtime Frensic was bordering on hysteria.

'I can't stand it,' he whimpered. The phone rang and Frensic shied. 'If it's for me, tell them I'm not in. I'm having a breakdown. Tell them—'

It was for him. Sonia put her hand over the mouthpiece.

'It's Margot Joseph. She says she's dried up and doesn't think she can finish—'

Frensic fled to the safety of his own office and took his phone off the hook.

'For the rest of the day I'm not in,' he told Sonia when she came through a few minutes later. 'I shall sit here and think.'

9

'In that case you can read this,' said Sonia and put a parcel on his desk. 'It came this morning. I haven't had time to open it.'

'It's probably a bomb,' said Frensic gloomily and undid the string. But the package contained nothing more threatening than a neatly typed manuscript and an envelope addressed to Mr F. A. Frensic. Frensic glanced at the manuscript and noted with satisfaction that its pages were pristine and its corners unthumbed, a healthy sign which indicated that he was the first recipient and that it hadn't gone the rounds of other agents. Then he looked at the title page. It said simply PAUSE O MEN FOR THE VIRGIN, A Novel. There was no author's name and no return address. Odd. Frensic opened the envelope and read the letter inside. It was brief and impersonal and mystifying.

Cadwalladine & Dimkins
Solicitors
596 St Andrew's Street
Oxford

Dear Sir,

All communications concerning the possible sale, publication and coypright of the enclosed manuscript should be addressed to this office marked for the Personal Attention of P. Cadwalladine.

The author, who wishes to remain strictly anonymous, leaves the matter of terms of sale and choice of a suitable *nom de plume* and related matters entirely in your hands.

Yours faithfully,
Percy Cadwalladine.

Frensic read the letter through several times before turning his attention to the manuscript. It was a very odd letter. An author who wished to remain strictly anonymous? Left everything concerning sale and choice of *nom de plume* and related matters entirely in his hands? Considering that all the authors he had ever dealt with were notoriously egotistical and interfering there was a lot to be said for one who was so self-effacing. Positively endearing, in fact. With the silent wish that Mr Jamesforth had left everything in his hands Frensic turned the title page of *Pause O Men for the Virgin* and began to read.

He was still reading an hour later, his snuff box open on the desk and his waistcoat and the creases of his trousers powdered with snuff. Frensic reached unthinkingly for the box and took another large pinch and wiped his nose with his third handkerchief. In the next office the phone rang. People climbed the stairs and knocked on Sonia's door. Traffic rumbled outside in the street. Frensic was oblivious to these extraneous sounds. He turned another page and read on.

It was half past six when Sonia Futtle finished for the day and prepared to leave. The door of Frensic's office was shut and she hadn't heard him go. She opened it and peered inside. Frensic was sitting at his desk staring fixedly through the window over the dark roofs of Covent Garden with a slight smile on his face. It was an attitude she recognized, the posture of triumphant discovery.

'I don't believe it,' she said standing in the doorway.

'Read it,' said Frensic. 'Don't believe me. Read it for yourself.' His hand flicked dismissively towards the manuscript.

'A good one?'

'A bestseller.'

'Are you sure?'

'Positive.'

'And of course it's a novel?'

'One hopes so,' said Frensic, 'fervently.'

'A dirty book,' said Sonia, who recognized the symptoms.

'Dirty,' said Frensic, 'is hardly adequate. The mind that penned – if minds can pen – this odyssey of lust is of a prurience indescribable.' He got up and handed her the manuscript.

'I will value your opinion,' he said with the air of a man who had regained his authority.

But if it was a jaunty Frensic who went home to his flat in Hampstead that night, it was a wary one who came back next morning and wrote a note on Sonia's scratch pad. 'Will discuss the novel with you over lunch. Not to be disturbed.' He went into his office and shut the door.

For the rest of the morning there was little to indicate that Frensic had anything more important on his mind than a vague interest in the antics of the pigeons on the roof opposite. He sat at his desk staring out of the window, occasionally reaching for the phone or jotting something on a piece of paper. For the most part he just sat. But external appearances were misleading. Frensic's mind was on the move, journeying across the internal landscape which he knew so well and in which each publishing house in London was a halt for

11

bargaining, a crossroads where commercial advantages were exchanged, favours given and little debts repaid. And Frensic's route was a devious one. It was not enough to sell a book. Any fool could do that, given the right book. The important thing was to place it in precisely the right spot so that the consequences of its sale would have maximum effect and ramify out to advance his reputation and promote some future advantage. And not his alone but that of his authors. Time entered into these calculations, time and his intuitive assessment of books that had yet to be written, books by established authors which he knew would be unsuccessful and books by new writers whose success would be jeopardized by their lack of reputation. Frensic juggled with intangibles. It was his profession and he was good at it.

Sometimes he sold books for small advances to small firms when the very same book offered to one of the big publishing houses would have earned its author a large advance. On these occasions the present was sacrificed to the future in the knowledge that help given now would be repaid later by the publication of some novel that would never sell more than five hundred copies but which Frensic, for reasons of his own, wished to see in print. Only Frensic knew his own intentions, just as only Frensic knew the identities of those well-reputed novelists who actually earned their living by writing detective stories or soft porn under pseudonyms. It was all a mystery and even Frensic, whose head was filled with abstruse equations involving personalities and tastes, who bought what and why, and all the details of the debts he owed or was owed, knew that he was not privy to every corner of the mystery. There was always luck and of late Frensic's luck had changed. When that happened it paid to walk warily. This morning Frensic walked very warily indeed.

He phoned several friends in the legal profession and assured himself that Cadwalladine & Dimkins, Solicitors, were an old, well-established and highly reputable firm who handled work of the most respectable kind. Only then did he phone Oxford and ask to speak to Mr Cadwalladine about the novel he had sent him. Mr Cadwalladine sounded old-fashioned. No, he was sorry to say, Mr Frensic could not meet the author. His instructions were that absolute anonymity was essential and all matters would have to be referred to Mr Cadwalladine personally. Of course the book was pure fiction. Yes, Mr Frensic could include an extra clause in any contract exonerating the publishers from the financial consequences of a libel action. In any

12

case he had always assumed such a clause to be part of contracts between publishers and authors. Frensic said they were but that he had to be absolutely certain when dealing with an anonymous author. Mr Cadwalladine said he quite understood.

Frensic put the phone down with a new feeling of confidence, and returned less warily to his interior landscape where imaginary negotiations took place. There he retraced his route, stopped at several eminent publishing houses for consideration, and travelled on. What *Pause O Men for the Virgin* needed was a publisher with an excellent reputation to give it the imprimatur of respectability. Frensic narrowed them down and finally made up his mind. It would be a gamble but it would be a gamble that was worth taking. He would have to have Sonia Futtle's opinion first.

She gave it to him over lunch in a little Italian restaurant where Frensic entertained his less important authors.

'A weird book,' she said.

'Quite,' said Frensic.

'But it's got something. Compassionate,' said Sonia, warming to her task.

'I agree.'

'Deeply insightful.'

'Definitely.'

'Good story line.'

'Excellent.'

'Significant,' said Sonia.

Frensic sighed. It was the word he had been waiting for. 'You really think that?'

'I do. I mean it. I think it's really got something. It's good. I really do.'

'Well,' said Frensic doubtfully, 'I may be an anachronism but . . .'

'You're role-playing again. Be serious.'

'My dear,' said Frensic, 'I am being serious. If you say that stuff is significant I am delighted. It's what I thought you'd say. It means it will appeal to those intellectual flagellants who can't enjoy a book unless it hurts. That I happen to know that, from a genuinely literary standpoint, it is an abomination is perhaps beside the point but I am entitled to protect my instincts.'

'Instincts? No man had fewer.'

'Literary instincts,' said Frensic. 'And they tell me that this is a bad,

13

pretentious book and that it will sell. It combines a filthy story with an even filthier style.'

'I didn't see anything wrong with the style,' said Sonia.

'Of course you didn't. You're an American and Americans aren't burdened by our classical inheritance. You can't see that there is a world of difference between Dreiser and Mencken or Tom Wolfe and Bellow. That's your prerogative. I find such lack of discrimination invaluable and most reassuring. If you accept sentences endlessly convoluted, spattered with commas and tied into knots with parentheses, unrelated verbs and qualifications of qualifications, and which, to parody, have, if they are to be at all comprehended, to be read at least four times with the aid of a dictionary, who am I to quarrel with you? Your fellow-countrymen, whose rage for self-improvement I have never appreciated, are going to love this book.'

'They may not go such a ball on the story line. I mean it's been done before you know. *Harold and Maude.*'

'But never in such exquisitely nauseating detail,' said Frensic and sipped his wine. 'And not with Lawrentian overtones. Besides that's our trump. Seventeen loves eighty. The liberation of the senile. What could be more significant than that? By the way when is Hutch-meyer due in London?'

'Hutchmeyer? You've got to be kidding,' said Sonia. Frensic held up a piece of ravioli in protest.

'Don't use that expression. I am not a goat.'

'And Hutchmeyer's not the Olympia Press. He's strictly middle-brow. He wouldn't touch this book.'

'He would if we baited the trap right,' said Frensic.

'Trap?' said Sonia suspiciously. 'What trap?'

'I was thinking of a very distinguished London publisher to take the book first,' said Frensic, 'and then you sell the American rights to Hutchmeyer.'

'Who?'

'Corkadales,' said Frensic.

Sonia shook her head. 'Corkadales are far too old and stodgy.'

'Precisely,' said Frensic. 'They are prestigious. They are also broke.'

'They should have dropped half their list years ago,' said Sonia.

'They should have dropped Sir Clarence years ago. You read his obituary?' But Sonia hadn't.

'Most entertaining. And instructive. Tributes galore to his service to Literature, by which they meant he had subsidized more unread

14

poets and novelists than any other publisher in London. The result: they are now broke.'

'In which case they can hardly afford to buy *Pause O Men for the Virgin.*'

'They can hardly afford not to,' said Frensic. 'I had a word with Geoffrey Corkadale at the funeral. He is not following in his father's footsteps. Corkadales are about to emerge from the eighteenth century. Geoffrey is looking for a bestseller. Corkadales will take *Pause* and we will take Hutchmeyer.'

'You think Hutchmeyer is going to be impressed?' said Sonia. 'What the hell have Corkadales got to offer?'

'Distinction,' said Frensic, 'a most distinguished past. The mantelpiece against which Shelley leant, the chair Mrs Gaskell was pregnant in, the carpet Tennyson was sick on. The incunabula of, if not *The Great Tradition*, at least a very important strand of literary history. By accepting this novel for free Corkadales will confer cultural sanctity on it.'

'And you think the author will be satisfied with that? You don't think he'll want money too?'

'He'll get the money from Hutchmeyer. We're going to sting Mr Hutchmeyer for a fortune. Anyhow, this author is unique.'

'I got that from the book,' said Sonia. 'How else is he unique?'

'He doesn't have a name, for one thing,' said Frensic and explained his instructions from Mr Cadwalladine. 'Which leaves us with an entirely free hand,' he said when he finished.

'And the little matter of a pseudonym,' said Sonia. 'I suppose we could kill two birds with one stone and say it was by Peter Piper. That way he'd see his name on the cover of a novel.'

'True,' said Frensic sadly, 'I'm afraid poor Piper is never going to make it any other way.'

'Besides, it would save the expense of his annual lunch and you wouldn't have to go through yet another version of his *Search for a Lost Childhood*. By the way, who is the model this year?'

'Thomas Mann,' said Frensic. 'One dreads the thought of sentences two pages long. You really think it would put an end to his illusions of literary grandeur?'

'Who knows?' said Sonia. 'The very fact of seeing his name on the cover of a novel and being taken for the author . . .'

'It's the only way he's ever going to get into print, I'll stake my reputation on that,' said Frensic.

'So we'll be doing him a favour.'

That afternoon Frensic took the manuscript to Corkadales. On the front under the title Sonia had added 'by Peter Piper'. Frensic spoke long and persuasively to Geoffrey Corkadale and left the office that night well pleased with himself.

A week later the editorial board of Corkadales considered *Pause O Men for the Virgin* in the presence of that past upon which the vestige of their reputation depended. Portraits of dead authors lined the panelled walls of the editorial room. Shelley was not there, nor Mrs Gaskell, but there were lesser notables to take their place. Ranged in glass-covered bookshelves there were first editions, and in some exhibition cases relics of the trade. Quills, Waverley pens, pocket-knives, an ink-bottle Trollope was said to have left in a train, a sandbox used by Southey, and even a scrap of blotting paper which, held up to a mirror, revealed that Henry James had once inexplicably written 'darling'.

In the centre of this museum the Literary Director, Mr Wilberforce, and the Senior Editor, Mr Tate, sat at an oval walnut table observing the weekly rite. They sipped Madeira and nibbled seed-cake and looked disapprovingly at the manuscript before them and then at Geoffrey Corkadale. It was difficult to tell which they disliked most. Certainly Geoffrey's suede suit and floral shirt did not fit the atmosphere. Sir Clarence would not have approved. Mr Wilberforce helped himself to some more Madeira and shook his head.

'I cannot agree,' he said. 'I find it wholly incomprehensible that we should even consider lending our name, our great name, to the publication of this . . . thing.'

'You didn't like the book?' said Geoffrey.

'Like it? I could hardly bring myself to finish it.'

'Well, we can't hope to please everyone.'

'But we've never touched a book like this before. We have our reputation to consider.'

'Not to mention our overdraft,' said Geoffrey. 'And to be brutally frank, we have to choose between our reputation and bankruptcy.'

'But does it have to be this awful book?' said Mr Tate. 'I mean have you read it?'

Geoffrey nodded. 'As a matter of fact I have. I know that my father didn't make a habit of reading anything later than Meredith but . . .'

'Your poor father,' said Mr Wilberforce with feeling, 'must be turning in his grave at the very thought—'

'Where, with any luck, he will shortly be joined by the so-called heroine of this disgusting novel,' said Mr Tate.

Geoffrey rearranged a stray lock of hair. 'Considering that papa was cremated I shouldn't have thought that his turning or her joining him would be very easy,' he murmured. Mr Wilberborce and Mr Tate looked grim. Geoffrey adjusted his smile. 'Your objection then I take it is based on the fact that the romance in this novel is between a seventeen-year-old boy and an eighty-year-old woman?' he said.

'Yes,' said Mr Wilberforce more loudly than was his wont, 'it is. Though how you can bring yourself to use the word "romance" . . .'

'The relationship then. The term doesn't matter.'

'It's not the term I'm worried about,' said Mr Tate. 'It's not even the relationship. If it simply stuck to that it wouldn't be so bad. It's the bits in between that get me. I had no idea . . . oh well never mind. The whole thing is so awful.'

'It's the bits in between,' said Geoffrey, 'that will sell the book.'

Mr Wilberforce shook his head. 'Personally I'm inclined to think we would run the risk, the gravest risk of being prosecuted for obscenity,' he said, 'and in my view quite rightly.'

'I agree,' said Mr Tate. 'I mean, take the episode where they use the rocking horse and the douche—'

'For God's sake,' squawked Mr Wilberforce. 'It was bad enough having to read it. Do we have to hold a post-mortem?'

'The term is applicable,' said Mr Tate. 'Even the title . . .'

'All right,' said Geoffrey, 'I grant you that it's a bit tasteless but—'

'Tasteless? What about the part where he—'

'Don't, Tate, don't, there's a good fellow,' said Mr Wilberforce feebly.

'As I was saying,' continued Geoffrey, 'I'm prepared to admit that that sort of thing isn't everyone's cup of tea . . . oh for goodness sake, Wilberforce . . . well anyway I can think of half a dozen books like it . . .'

'I can't, thank God,' said Mr Tate.

'. . . which in their time were considered objectionable but—'

'Name me one,' shouted Mr Wilberforce. 'Just name me one to equal this!' His hand shook at the manuscript.

'*Lady Chatterley*,' said Geoffrey.

17

'Pah,' said Mr Tate. 'By comparison *Chatterley* was pure as the driven snow.'

'Anyway *Chatterley*'s banned,' said Mr Wilberforce.

Geoffrey Corkadale heaved a sigh. 'Oh God,' he muttered, 'someone tell him that the Georgians aren't around any longer.'

'More's the pity,' said Mr Tate. 'We did rather well with some of them. The rot set in with *The Well of Loneliness*.'

'And there's another filthy book,' said Mr Wilberforce, 'but we didn't publish it.'

'The rot set in,' Geoffrey interrupted, 'when Uncle Cuthbert took it into his woolly head to pulp Wilkie's *Ballroom Dancing Made Perfect* and published Fashoda's *Guide to the Edible Fungi* in its place.'

'Fashoda was a bad choice,' Mr Tate agreed. 'I remember the coroner was most uncomplimentary.'

'Let's get back to our present position,' said Geoffrey, 'which from a financial point of view is just as deadly. Now Frensic has offered us this novel and in my view we ought to accept it.'

'We've never had dealings with Frensic before,' said Mr Tate. 'They tell me he drives a hard bargain. How much is he demanding this time?'

'A purely nominal sum.'

'A nominal sum? Frensic? That doesn't sound like him. He usually asks the earth. There must be a snag.'

'The damned book's the snag. Any fool can see that,' said Mr Wilberforce.

'Frensic has wider views,' said Geoffrey. 'He foresees a Transatlantic purchase.'

There was an audible sigh from the two old men.

'Ah,' said Mr Tate, 'an American sale. That could make a considerable difference.'

'Exactly,' said Geoffrey, 'and Frensic is convinced that the book has merits the Americans might well appreciate. After all it's not all sex and there are passages with Lawrentian overtones, not to mention references to many important literary figures. The Bloomsbury group for instance, Virginia Woolf and Middleton Murry. And then there's the philosophy.'

Mr Tate nodded. 'True. True,' he said. 'It's the sort of pot of message Americans might fall for but I don't see what good that is going to do us.'

'Ten per cent of the American royalties,' said Geoffrey. 'That's what good it's going to do us.'

'The author agrees to this?'

'Mr Frensic seems to think so and if the book makes the best-seller lists in the States it will consequently sell wildly over here.'

'If,' said Mr Tate. 'A very big if. Who has he in mind as the American publisher?'

'Hutchmeyer.'

'Ah,' said Mr Tate, 'one begins to see his drift.'

'Hutchmeyer,' said Mr Wilberforce, 'is a rogue and a thief.'

'He is also one of the most successful promoters in American publishing,' said Geoffrey. 'If he decides to buy a book it will sell. And he pays enormous advances.'

Mr Tate nodded. 'I must say I have never understood the work-ings of the American market but it's true they often pay enormous advances and Hutchmeyer is flamboyant. Frensic could well be right. It's a chance I suppose.'

'Our only chance,' said Geoffrey. 'The alternative is to put the firm up for auction.'

Mr Wilberforce poured some more Madeira. 'It seems a terrible comedown,' he said. 'To think that we should have sunk to this . . . this pseudo-intellectual pornography.'

'If it keeps us financially solvent . . .' said Mr Tate. 'Who is this man Piper anyway?'

'A pervert,' said Mr Wilberforce firmly.

'Frensic tells me he's a young man who has been writing for some time,' said Geoffrey. 'This is his first novel.'

'And hopefully his last,' said Mr Wilberforce. 'Still I suppose it could have been worse. Who was that dreadful creature who had herself castrated and then wrote a book advertising the fact?'

'I should have thought that was an impossibility,' said Geoffrey. 'Castrated herself. Now himself I—'

'You're probably thinking of *In Cold Blood* by someone called McCullers,' said Mr Tate. 'Never did read the book myself but people tell me it was foul.'

'Then we are all agreed,' said Geoffrey to change the subject from one so close to the bone. Mr Tate and Mr Wilberforce nodded sadly.

Frensic greeted their decision without overt enthusiasm.

'We can't be sure of Hutchmeyer yet,' he told Geoffrey over lunch at Wheelers. 'There must be no leaks to the press. If this gets out Hutchmeyer won't bite. I suggest we simply refer to it as *Pause*.'

'It's appropriate,' said Geoffrey. 'It will take at least three months to get the proofs done.'

'That will give us time to work on Hutchmeyer.'

'And you really think there's a chance he will buy?'

'Every chance,' said Frensic. 'Miss Futtle exercises enormous charms for him.'

'Extraordinary,' said Geoffrey with a shudder. 'Still, having read *Pause* there's obviously no accounting for tastes.'

'Sonia is also an excellent saleswoman,' said Frensic. 'She makes a point of asking for very large advances and that always impresses Americans. It shows we have faith in the book.'

'And this fellow Piper agrees to our ten per cent cut?'

Frensic nodded. He had spoken to Mr Cadwalladine. 'The author has left all the terms of the negotiations and sale entirely in my hands,' he said truthfully. And there the matter rested until Hutchmeyer flew into London with his entourage in the first week of February.

Chapter 3

It was said of Hutchmeyer that he was the most illiterate publisher in the world and that having started life as a fight promoter he had brought his pugilistic gifts to the book trade and had once gone eight rounds with Mailer. It was also said that he never read the books he bought and that the only words he could read were those on cheques and dollar bills. It was said that he owned half the Amazon forest and that when he looked at a tree all he could see was a dustjacket. A great many things were said about Hutchmeyer, most of them unpleasant, and, while each contained an element of truth, added together they amounted to so many inconsistencies that behind them Hutchmeyer could guard the secret of his success. That at least no one doubted. Hutchmeyer was immensely successful. A legend in his own lifetime, he haunted the insomniac thoughts of publishers who had turned down *Love Story* when it was going for a song, had spurned Frederick Forsyth and ignored Ian Fleming and now lay awake cursing their own stupidity. Hutchmeyer himself slept soundly. For a sick man, remarkably soundly. And Hutchmeyer was always sick. If Frensic's success lay in outeating and outdrinking his competitors, Hutchmeyer's was due to his hypochondria. When he hadn't an ulcer or gallstones, he was subject to some intestinal complaint that necessitated a regime of abstinence. Publishers and agents coming to his table found themselves obliged to plough their way through six courses, each richer and more alarmingly indigestible than the last, while Hutchmeyer toyed with a piece of boiled fish, a biscuit and a glass of mineral water. From these culinary encounters Hutchmeyer rose a thinner and richer man while his guests staggered home wondering what the hell had hit them. Nor were they allowed time to recover. Hutchmeyer's peripatetic schedule – London today, New York tomorrow, Los Angeles the day after – had a dual purpose. It provided him with an excuse to insist on speed and avoided prolonged negotiations, and it kept his sales staff on their toes. More than one contract had been signed by an author in the throes of so awful a hangover that he could hardly put pen to paper, let alone read the small print. And the small print in Hutchmeyer's contracts was exceedingly small. Understandably so, since it contained clauses that invalidated almost everything set out in bold type. To add to the hazards of doing business with Hutchmeyer, most of them legal, there was his manner. Hutchmeyer was gross, partly by nature and partly as a reaction to the literary aestheticism he was exposed to. It was one of the qualities he appreciated about Sonia Futtle. No one had ever called her aesthetic.

'You're like a daughter to me,' he said hugging her when she arrived at his suite in the Hilton. 'What's my baby got for me this time?'

'One humdinger,' said Sonia disengaging herself and climbing on to the bicycle exerciser that accompanied Hutchmeyer everywhere. Hutchmeyer selected the lowest chair in the room.

'You don't say. A novel?'

Sonia cycled busily and nodded.

'What's it called?' asked Hutchmeyer for whom first things came first.

'*Pause O Men for the Virgin.*'

'*Pause O Men for the* what?'

'*Virgin,*' said Sonia and cycled more vigorously than ever.

Hutchmeyer glimpsed a thigh. 'Virgin? You mean you've got a religious novel that's hot?'

'Hot as Hades.'

'Sounds good, a time like this. It fits with the Jesus freaks and Superstar and Zen and how to mend automobiles. And it's women's year so we got The Virgin.'

Sonia stopped peddling. 'Now don't get carried away, Hutch. It's not that kind of virgin.'

'It's not?'

'No way.'

'So there's different kinds of virgin. Sounds interesting. Tell me.' And Sonia Futtle, seated on the bicycle machine, told him while her legs moved up and down with a delicious lethargy that lulled his critical faculties. Hutchmeyer made only token resistance. 'Forget it,' he said when she had finished. 'You can deepsix that crap. Eighty years old and still fucking. That I don't need.'

Sonia climbed off the exerciser and stood in front of him. 'Don't be a dumbcluck, Hutch. Now you listen to me. You're not going to throw this one out. Over my dead body. This book's got class.'

Hutchmeyer smiled happily. This was Fuller Brush talking. The sales pitch. No soft sell. 'Convince me.'

'Right,' said Sonia. 'Who reads? Don't answer. I'll tell you. The kids. Fifteen to twenty-one. They read. They got the time. They got the education. Literacy rate peak is sixteen to twenty. Right?'

'Right,' said Hutchmeyer.

'Right, so we've got a seventeen-year-old boy in the book with an identity crisis.'

'Identity crisises is out. That stuff went the way of all Freud.'

'Sure, but this is different. This boy isn't sick or something.'

'You kidding? Fucking his own grandmother isn't sick?'

'She isn't his grandmother. She's a woman a—'

'Listen baby, I'll tell you something. She's eighty, she's no goddam woman no more. I should know. My wife, Baby, is fifty-eight and she's drybones. What the beauty surgeons have left of her. That woman has had more taken out of her than you'd believe possible. She's got silicon boobs and degreased thighs. She's had four new maidenheads to my knowledge and her face lifted so often I've lost count.'

'And why?' said Sonia. 'Because she wants to stay all woman.'

'All woman she ain't. More spare parts than woman.'

'But she reads. Am I right?'

'Reads? She reads more books than I sell in a month.'

'And that's my point. The young read and the old read. You can kiss the in-betweens goodbye.'

'You tell Baby she's old and you can kiss yourself goodbye. She'd have your fanny for a dishcloth. I mean it.'

'What I'm saying is that you've got literacy peak sixteen to twenty, then a gap and another LP sixty on out. Tell me I'm lying.'

Hutchmeyer shrugged. 'So you're right.'

'And what's this book about?' said Sonia. 'It's—'

'Some crazy kid shacked up with Grandma Moses. It's been done some place else. Tell me something new. Besides, it's dirty.'

'You're wrong, Hutch, you're so wrong. It's a love story, no shit. They mean something to one another. He needs her and she needs him.'

'Me, I need neither of them.'

'They give one another what they lack alone. He gets maturity, experience, wisdom, the fruit of a lifetime . . .'

'Fruit? Fruit? Jesus, you want me to throw up or something?'

'. . . and she gets youth, vitality, life,' Sonia continued. 'It's great. I mean it. A deep, meaningful book. It's liberationist. It's existentialist. It's . . . Remember what *The French Lieutenant's Woman* did? Swept America. And *Pause* is what America's been waiting for. Seventeen loves eighty. Loves, Hutch, L.O.V.E.S. So every senior citizen is going to buy it to find out what they've been missing and the students will go for the philosophomore message. Pitch it right and we can scoop the pool. We get the culture buffs with significance, the weirdos with the porn and the marshmallows with romance. This is the book for the whole family. It could sell by the—'

Hutchmeyer got up and paced the room. 'You know, I think maybe you've got something there,' he said. 'I ask myself "Would Baby buy this story?" and I have to say yes. And what that woman falls for the whole world buys. What price?'

'Two million dollars.'

'Two million. . . . You've got to be kidding.' Hutchmeyer gaped.

Sonia climbed back on to the bicycle machine. 'Two million. I kid you not.'

'Go jump, baby, go jump. Two million? For a novel? No way.'

'Two million or I go flash my gams at Milenberg.'

'That cheapskate? He couldn't raise two million. You can hawk your pussy all the way to Avenue of the Americas it won't do you no good.'

'American rights, paperback, film, TV, serialization, book clubs . . .'

Hutchmeyer yawned. 'Tell me something new. They're mine already.'

'Not on this book they're not.'

'So Milenberg buys. You get no price and I buy him. What's in it for me?'

'Fame,' said Sonia simply, 'just fame. With this book you're up there with the all-time greats. *Gone With The Wind, Forever Amber, Valley of The Dolls, Dr Zhivago, Airport, The Carpetbaggers.* You'd make the *Reader's Digest Almanac*.'

'The *Reader's Digest Almanac*?' said Hutchmeyer in an awed voice. 'You really think I could make that?'

'Think? I know. This is a prestige book about life's potentialities. No kitsch. Message like Mary Baker Eddy. A symphony of words. Look who's bought it in London. No fly-by-night firm.'

'Who?' said Hutchmeyer suspiciously.

'Corkadales.'

'Corkadales bought it? The oldest publishing—'

'Not the oldest. Murrays are older,' said Sonia.

'So, old. How much?'

'Fifty thousand pounds,' said Sonia glibly.

Hutchmeyer stared at her. 'Corkadales paid fifty thousand pounds for this book? Fifty grand?'

'Fifty grand. First time off. No hassle.'

'I heard they were in trouble,' said Hutchmeyer. 'Some Arab bought them?'

'No Arab. It's a family firm. So Geoffrey Corkadale paid fifty grand. He knows this book is going to get them out of hock. You think they'd risk that sort of money if they were going to fold?'

'Shit,' said Hutchmeyer, 'somebody's got to have faith in this fucking book . . . but two million! No one's ever paid two million for a novel. Robbins a million but . . .'

'That's the whole point, Hutch. You think I ask two million for nothing? Am I so dumb? It's the two million makes the book. You pay two million and people know, they've got to read the book to find out what you paid for. *You* know that. You're in a class on your own. Way out in front. And then with the film. . . .'

'I'd want a cut of the film. No single-figure percentage. Fifty-fifty.'

'Done,' said Sonia. 'You've got yourself a deal. Fifty-fifty on the film it is.'

'The author . . . this Piper guy, I'd want him too,' said Hutchmeyer.

'Want him?' said Sonia, sobering. 'Want him for what?'

'To market the product. He's going to be out there up front where the public can see him. The guy who fucks the geriatrics. Public appearances across the States, signings, TV talk shows, interviews, the whole razzamattaz. We'll build him up like he's a genius.'

'I don't think he's going to like that,' said Sonia nervously, 'he's shy and reserved.'

'Shy? He washes his jock in public and he's shy?' said Hutchmeyer. 'For two million he'll chew asses if I tell him.'

'I doubt if he'd agree—'

'Agree he will or there's no deal,' said Hutchmeyer. 'I'm throwing my weight behind his book, he has to too. That's final.'

'OK, if that's the way you want it,' said Sonia.

'That's the way I want it,' said Hutchmeyer. 'Like the way I want you . . .'

Sonia made her escape and hurried back to Lanyard Lane with the contract.

She found Frensic looking decidedly edgy. 'Home and dry,' she said, dancing heavily round the room.

'Marvellous,' said Frensic. 'You are brilliant.'

Sonia stopped cavorting. 'With a proviso.'

'Proviso? What proviso?'

'First the good news. He loves the book. He's just wild about it.'

Frensic regarded her cautiously. 'Isn't he being a bit premature? He hasn't had a chance to read the bloody thing yet.'

'I told him about it . . . a synopsis and he loved it. He sees it as filling a much-needed gap.'

'A much-needed gap?'

'The generation gap. He feels—'

'Spare me his feelings,' said Frensic. 'A man who can talk about filling much-needed gaps is deficient in ordinary human emotions.'

'He thinks *Pause* will do for youth and age what *Lolita* did for . . .'

'Parental responsibility?' suggested Frensic.

'For the middle-aged man,' said Sonia.

'For God's sake, if this is the good news can leprosy be far behind.'

Sonia sank into a chair and smiled. 'Wait till you hear the price.'

Frensic waited. 'Well?'

'Two million.'

'Two million?' said Frensic trying to keep the quaver out of his voice. 'Pounds or dollars?'

Sonia looked at him reproachfully. 'Frenzy, you are a bastard, an ungrateful bastard. I pull off—'

'My dear, I was merely trying to ascertain the likely extent of the horrors you are about to reveal to me. You spoke of a proviso. Now if your friend from the Mafia had been prepared to pay two million pounds for this verbal hogwash I would have known the time had come to pack up and leave town. What does the swine want?'

'One, he wants to see the Corkadales contract.'

'That's all right. There's nothing wrong with it.'

'Just that it doesn't mention the sum of fifty thousand pounds

Corkadales have paid for *Pause*,' said Sonia. 'Otherwise it's just dandy.'

Frensic gaped at her. 'Fifty thousand pounds? They didn't pay—'

'Hutchmeyer needed impressing so I said . . .'

'He needs his head read. Corkadales haven't fifty thousand pennies to rub together, let alone pounds.'

'Right. Which he knew. So I told him Geoffrey had staked his personal fortune. Now you know why he wants to see the contract?'

Frensic rubbed his forehead and thought. 'I suppose we could always draw up a new contract and get Geoffrey to sign it *pro tem* and tear it up when Hutchmeyer's seen it,' he said at last. 'Geoffrey won't like it but with his cut of two million . . . What's the next problem?'

Sonia hesitated. 'This one you won't like. He insists, but insists, that the author goes to the States for a promotional tour. Senior citizens I have loved sort of stuff on TV and signings.'

Frensic took out his handkerchief and wiped his face. 'Insists?' he spluttered. 'He can't insist. We've got an author who won't even sign his name to a contract, let alone appear in public, some madman with agoraphobia or its equivalent and Hutchmeyer wants him to parade round America appearing on TV?'

'Insists, Frenzy, insists. Not wants. Either the author goes or the deal is off.'

'Then it's off,' said Frensic. 'The man won't go. You heard what Cadwalladine said. Total anonymity.'

'Not even for two million.'

Frensic shook his head. 'I told Cadwalladine we were going to ask for a large sum and he said money didn't count.'

'But two million isn't money. It's a fortune.'

'I know it is, but . . .'

'Try Cadwalladine again,' said Sonia and handed him the phone. Frensic tried again. At length. Mr Cadwalladine was emphatic. Two million dollars was a fortune but his instructions were that his client's anonymity meant more to him than mere . . .

It was a dispiriting conversation for Frensic.

'What did I tell you,' he said when he had finished. 'We're dealing with some sort of lunatic. Two lunatics. Hutchmeyer being the other.'

'So we're just going to sit back and watch twenty per cent of two million dollars disappear down the plughole and do nothing about it?' said Sonia. Frensic stared miserably across the roofs of Covent Garden and sighed. Twenty per cent of two million came to four hundred thousand dollars, over two hundred thousand pounds. That would have been their commission on the sale. And thanks to James Jamesforth's libel action they had just lost two more valuable authors.

'There must be some way of fixing this,' he muttered. 'Hutchmeyer doesn't know who the author is any more than we do.'

'He does too,' said Sonia. 'It's Peter Piper. His name's on the title page.'

Frensic looked at her with new appreciation. 'Peter Piper,' he murmured, 'now there's a thought.'

They closed the office for the night and went down to the pub across the road for a drink.

'Now if there were some way we could persuade Piper to act as understudy . . .' said Frensic after a large whisky.

'And after all it would be one way of getting his name into print,' said Sonia. 'If the book sells . . .'

'Oh it will sell all right. With Hutchmeyer anything sells.'

'Well then, Piper would have got his foot in the publishing door and perhaps we could get someone to ghost *Search* for him.'

Frensic shook his head. 'He'd never stand for that. Piper has principles I'm afraid. On the other hand if Geoffrey could be persuaded to agree to publish *Search for a Lost Childhood* as part of the present contract . . . I'm seeing him tonight. He's holding one of his little suppers. Yes I think we may be on to something. Piper would do almost anything to get into print and a trip to the States with all expenses paid . . . I think we'll drink to that.'

'Anything is worth trying,' said Sonia. And that night before setting out for Corkadales Frensic returned to the office and drew up two new contracts. One by which Corkadales agreed to pay fifty thousand for *Pause O Men for the Virgin* and the second guaranteeing the publication of Mr Piper's subsequent novel, *Search for a Lost Childhood*. The advance on it was five hundred pounds.

'After all, it's worth the gamble,' said Frensic as he and Sonia locked the office again, 'and I'm prepared to put up five hundred of our money if Geoffrey won't play ball on the advance to Piper. The main thing is to get a copperbottomed guarantee that they will publish *Search*.'

'Geoffrey has ten per cent of two million at stake too,' said Sonia as they separated. 'I should have thought that would be a persuasive argument.'

'I shall do my level best,' said Frensic as he hailed a taxi.

Geoffrey Corkadale's little suppers were what Frensic in a bitchy moment had once called badinageries. One stood around with a drink, later with a plate of cold buffet, and spoke lightly and allusively of books, plays and personalities, few of which one had read, seen or known but which served to provide a catalyst for those epicene encounters which were the real purpose of Geoffrey's little suppers. On the whole Frensic tended to avoid them as frivolous and a little dangerous. They were too androgynous for comfort and besides he disliked running the risk of being discovered talking glibly on a subject he knew absolutely nothing about. He had done that too often as an undergraduate to relish the prospect of continuing it into later life. And the very fact that there were never any women of marriageable propensity, they were either too old or unidentifiable – Frensic had once made a pass at an eminent theatre critic with horrifying consequences – tended to put him off. He preferred parties where there was just the faintest chance that he would meet someone who would make him a wife and at Geoffrey's gatherings the expression was taken literally. And so Frensic usually avoided them and confined his sex life to occasional desultory affairs with women sufficiently in their prime not to resent his lack of passion or charm, and to passionate feelings for young women on tube trains, which feelings he was incapable of expressing between Hampstead and Leicester Square. But this evening he came with a purpose, only to find that the rooms were crowded. Frensic poured himself a drink and mingled in the hope of cornering Geoffrey. It took some time. Geoffrey's elevation to the head of Corkadales lent him an appeal he had previously lacked and Frensic found himself subjected to a scrutiny of his opinion of *The Prancing Nigger* by a poet from Tobago who confessed that he found Firbank both divine and offensive. Frensic said those were his feelings too but that Firbank had been remarkably seminal, and it was only after an hour and by the unintentional stratagem of locking himself in the bathroom that he managed to corner Geoffrey.

'My dear, you are too unkind,' said Geoffrey when Frensic after hammering on the door finally freed himself with the help of a jar of skin cleanser. 'You should know we never lock the boys' room. It's so unspontaneous. The chance encounter . . .'

'This isn't a chance encounter,' said Frensic, dragging Geoffrey in and shutting the door again. 'I want a word with you. It's important.'

'Just don't lock it again . . . oh my God! Sven is obsessively jealous. He goes absolutely berserk. It's his Viking blood.'

'Never mind that,' said Frensic, 'we've had Hutchmeyer's offer. It's substantial.'

'Oh God, business,' said Geoffrey, subsiding on to the lavatory seat. 'How substantial?'

'Two million dollars,' said Frensic.

Geoffrey clutched at the toilet roll for support. 'Two million dollars?' he said weakly. 'You really mean two *million* dollars? You're not pulling my leg?'

'Absolute fact,' said Frensic.

'But that's magnificent! How wonderful. You darling—'

Frensic pushed him roughly back on the seat. 'There's a snag. Two snags, to be precise.'

'Snags? Why must there always be snags? As if life wasn't complicated enough without snags.'

'We had to impress him with the amount you paid for the book,' said Frensic.

'But I hardly paid anything. In fact . . .'

'Exactly, but we have had to tell him you paid fifty thousand pounds in advance and he wants to see the contract.'

'Fifty thousand pounds? My dear chap, we couldn't—'

'Quite,' said Frensic, 'you don't have to explain your financial situation to me. You're in . . . you've got a cash-flow problem.'

'To put it mildly,' said Geoffrey, twisting a strand of toilet paper between his fingers.

'Which Hutchmeyer is aware of which is why he wants to see the contract.'

'But what good is that going to do. The contract says . . .'

'I have here,' said Frensic fishing in his pocket, 'another contract which will do some good and reassure Hutchmeyer. It says you agree to pay fifty thousand . . .'

'Hang on a moment,' said Geoffrey, getting to his feet, 'if you think I'm going to sign a contract that says I'm going to pay you fifty thousand quid you're labouring under a misapprehension. I may not be a financial wizard but I can see this one coming.'

30

'All right,' said Frensic huffily and folded the contract, 'if that's the way you feel about it bang goes the deal.'

'What deal? You've already signed the contract for us to publish the novel.'

'Not your deal. Hutchmeyer's. And with it goes your ten per cent of two million dollars. Now if you want . . .'

Geoffrey sat down again. 'You really mean it, don't you?' he said at last.

'Every word,' said Frensic.

'And you really promise that Hutchmeyer has agreed to pay this incredible sum?'

'My word,' said Frensic with as much dignity as the bathroom allowed, 'is my bond.'

Geoffrey looked at him sceptically. 'If what James Jamesforth says is . . . All right. I'm sorry. It's just that this has come as a terrible shock. What do you want me to do?'

'Just sign this contract and I'll write out a personal IOU for fifty thousand pounds. That ought to be a guarantee . . .'

They were interrupted by someone hammering on the door. 'Come out of there,' shouted a Scandinavian voice, 'I know what you're doing!'

'Oh Christ, Sven,' said Geoffrey and struggled with the lock. 'Calm yourself dearest,' he called, 'we were just discussing business.'

Behind him Frensic prudently armed himself with a lavatory brush.

'Business,' yelled the Swede, 'I know your business . . .'

The door sprang open and Sven glared wild-eyed into the bathroom.

'What is he doing with that brush?'

'Now, Sven dear, do be reasonable,' said Geoffrey. But Sven hovered between tears and violence.

'How could you, Geoffrey, how could you?'

'He didn't,' said Frensic vehemently.

The Swede looked him up and down. 'And with such a horrid baggy little man too.'

It was Frensic's turn to look wild-eyed. 'Baggy I may be,' he shouted, 'but horrid I am not.'

There was a moment's scuffle and Geoffrey urged the sobbing Sven down the passage. Frensic put his weapon back in its holder

31

and sat on the edge of the bath. By the time Geoffrey returned he
had devised new tactics.

'Where were we?' asked Geoffrey.

'Your *petit ami* was calling me a horrid baggy little man,' said
Frensic.

'My dear, I'm so sorry but really you can count yourself lucky.
Last week he actually struck someone and all the poor man had come
to do was mend the bidet.'

'Now about this contract. I'm prepared to make a further con-
cession,' said Frensic, 'you can have Piper's second book, *Search for
a Lost Childhood* for a thousand pounds advance . . .'

'His *next* novel? You mean he's working on another?'

'Almost finished it,' said Frensic, 'much better than *Pause*. Now
you can have it for practically nothing just so long as you sign this
contract for Hutchmeyer.'

'Oh all right,' said Geoffrey, 'I'll just have to trust you.'

'If you don't get it back within the week to tear up you can go to
Hutchmeyer and tell him it's a fraud,' said Frensic. 'That's your
guarantee.'

And so in the bathroom of Geoffrey Corkadale's house the two
contracts were signed. Frensic staggered home exhausted and next
morning Sonia showed Hutchmeyer the Corkadale contract. The deal
was on.

Chapter 4

In the Gleneagle Guest House in Exforth Peter Piper's nib described neat black circles and loops on the forty-fifth page of his notebook. Next door Mrs Oakley's vacuum cleaner roared back and forth making it difficult for Piper to concentrate on this his eighth version of his autobiographical novel. The fact that his new attempt was modelled on *The Magic Mountain* did not help. Thomas Mann's tendency to build complex sentences and to elaborate his ironic perceptions with a multitude of exact details did not transfer at all easily to a description of family life in Finchley in 1953 but Piper persisted with the task. It was, he knew, the hallmark of genius to persist and he knew just as certainly that he had genius. Unrecognized genius to be sure but one day, thanks to his capacity for taking infinite pains, the world would acclaim it. And so, in spite of the vacuum cleaner and the cold wind blowing from the sea through the cracks in the window, he wrote.

Around him on the table were the tools of his trade. A notebook in which he put down ideas and phrases which might come in handy, a diary in which he recorded his deepest insights into the nature of existence and a list of each day's activities, a tray of fountain pens and a bottle of partially evaporated black ink. The latter was Piper's own invention. Since he was writing for posterity it was essential that what he wrote should last indefinitely and without fading. For a while he had imitated Kipling in the use of Indian ink but it tended to clog his pen and to dry before he could even write one word. The accidental discovery that a bottle of Waterman's Midnight Black left open in a dry room acquired a density surpassing Indian ink while still remaining sufficiently fluid to enable him to write an entire sentence without recourse to his handkerchief had led to his use of evaporated ink. It gleamed on the page with a patina that gave substance to his words, and to ensure that his work had infinite longevity he bought leather-bound ledgers, normally used by old-fashioned firms of accountants or solicitors, and ignoring their various vertical lines, wrote his novels in them. By the time he had filled a ledger it was in its own way a work of art. Piper's handwriting was small and extremely regular and flowed for page after page with hardly a break. Since there was very little conversation in any of his novels, and that only of the meaningful and significant kind requiring long sentences, there were very few pages with broken lines or unfilled spaces. And Piper kept his ledgers. One day, perhaps when he was dead, certainly when his genius was recognized, scholars would trace the course of his development through these encrusted pages. Posterity was not to be ignored.

On the other hand the vacuum cleaner next door and the various intrusions of landladies and cleaners had to be ignored. Piper refused to allow his mornings to be interrupted. It was then that he wrote. After lunch he took a walk along whatever promenade he happened to be living opposite at the time. After tea he wrote again and after supper he read, first what he had written during the day and second from the novel that was serving as his present model. Since he read rather more quickly than he wrote he knew *Hard Times*, *Nostromo*, *The Portrait of A Lady*, *Middlemarch* and *The Magic Mountain* almost off by heart. With *Sons and Lovers* he was word-perfect. By thus confining his reading to only the greatest masters of fiction he ensured that lesser novelists would not exercise a malign influence on his own work.

Besides these few masterpieces he drew inspiration from *The Moral Novel*. It lay on his bedside table and before turning out the light he would read a page or two and mull Miss Louth's adjurations over in his mind. She was particularly keen on 'the placing of characters within an emotional framework, a context as it were of mature and interrelated susceptibilities, which corresponds to the reality of the experience of the novelist in his own time and thus enhances the reality of his fictional creations'. Since Piper's own experience had been limited to eighteen years of family life in Finchley, the death of his parents in a car crash, and ten years of boarding-houses, he found it difficult in his work to provide a context of mature and interrelated susceptibilities. But he did his best and subjected the unsatisfactory marriage of the late Mr and Mrs Piper to the minutest examination in order to imbue them with the maturity and insightfulness Miss Louth demanded. They emerged from this emotional exhumation with feelings they had never felt and insights they had never had. In real life Mr Piper had been a competent plumber. In *Search* he was an insightful one with tuberculosis and a great number of startlingly ambiguous feelings towards his wife. Mrs Piper came out, if anything, rather worse. Modelled on Frau Chauchat out of Isabel Archer she was given to philosophical disquisitions, to slamming doors, to displaying bare shoulders and to private sexual feelings for her son and the man next door which would have horrified her. For her husband she had only contempt mixed with disgust. And finally there was Piper himself, a prodigy of fourteen burdened by a degree of self-knowledge and an insight into his parents' true feelings for one another that would, had he in fact possessed them, have made his presence in the house utterly unbearable. Fortunately for the sanity of the late Mr and Mrs Piper and for the safety of Piper himself, he had at fourteen been a singularly dull child and with none of the perceptions he subsequently claimed for himself. What few feelings he had were concentrated on the person of his English mistress at school, a Miss Pears, who, in an unguarded moment, had complimented little Peter on a short story he had in fact copied almost verbatim from an old copy of *Horizon* he had found in a school cupboard. From this early derived promise Piper had gained his literary ambitions – and from the fatigue of a tanker driver who, four years later, had fallen asleep at the wheel of his lorry, crossed a main road at sixty miles an hour and obliterated Mr and Mrs Piper who were doing thirty on their way to visit friends in Amersham, he had acquired the wherewithal to pursue them. At eighteen he had inherited the house in Finchley, a substantial sum from the insurance company, and his parents' savings. Piper had sold the house, had banked all his capital and, to provide himself with a pecuniary motive to write, had lived off the capital ever since. After ten years and several million unsold words he was practically penniless.

He was therefore delighted to receive a telegram from London which said URGENT SEE YOU RE SALE OF NOVEL ETC ONE THOUSAND POUNDS ADVANCE PLEASE PHONE IMMEDIATELY FRENSIC.

Piper phoned immediately and caught the midday train in a state of wild anticipation. His moment of recognition had arrived at last.

In London Frensic and Sonia were also into a state of anticipation, less wild and with sombre overtones.

'What happens if he refuses?' asked Sonia as Frensic paced his office.

'God alone knows,' said Frensic. 'You heard what Cadwalladine said, "Do what you please but in no way involve my client." So it's Piper or bust.'

'At least I managed to squeeze another twenty-five thousand dollars out of Hutchmeyer for the tour, plus expenses,' said Sonia. 'I should have thought that was a sufficient inducement.'

Frensic had doubts. 'With anyone else,' he said, 'but Piper has principles. For God's sake don't leave a copy of the proofs of *Pause* around where he can see what he's supposed to have written.'

'He's bound to read the book sometime.'

'Yes, but I want him signed up for the tour first and with some of Hutchmeyer's money in his pocket. He won't find it so easy to back out then.'

'And you really think the Corkadales offer to publish *Search For a Lost Childhood* will grab him?'

'Our trump card,' said Frensic. 'What you've got to realize is that with Piper we are treating a subspecies of lunacy known as *dementia novella* or bibliomania. The symptoms are a wholly irrational urge to get into print. Well, I'm getting Piper into print. I've even got him one thousand pounds which is incredible considering the garbled rubbish he writes. He's being paid twenty-five thousand dollars to make the tour. Now all we've got to do is play our cards right and he'll go. The Corkadales contract is our ace. I mean, the man would murder his own mother to get *Search* published.'

'I thought you said his parents were dead,' said Sonia.

'They are,' said Frensic. 'To the best of my knowledge the poor fellow has no living relatives. I wouldn't be at all surprised if we aren't his nearest and dearest.'

'It's amazing what twenty per cent commission on two million dollars will do to some people,' said Sonia. 'I've never thought of you in the role of a foster-father.'

It was amazing what the prospect of having his novel published had done to Piper's morale. He arrived in Lanyard Lane wearing the blue suit he kept for formal visits to London and an expression of smug self-satisfaction that alarmed Frensic. He preferred his authors subdued and a little depressed.

'I'd like you to meet Miss Futtle, my partner,' he said when Piper entered. 'She deals with the American side of the business.'

'Charmed,' said Piper bowing slightly, a habit he had derived from Hans Castorp.

'I just adored your book,' said Sonia, 'I think it's marvellous.'

'You did?' said Piper.

'So insightful,' said Sonia, 'so deeply significant.'

In the background Frensic stirred uncomfortably. He would have chosen less brazen tactics and Sonia's accent, borrowed, he suspected, from Georgia in 1861, disturbed him. On the other hand it seemed to affect Piper favourably. He was blushing.

'Very kind of you to say so,' he murmured.

Frensic asserted himself. 'Now, as to the matter of Corkadales contract to publish *Search*,' he began and looked at his watch. 'Why don't we go down and discuss the whole thing over a drink?'

They went downstairs to the pub across the road and while Frensic bought drinks Sonia continued her assault.

'Corkadales are one of the oldest publishing houses in London. They are terribly prestigious but I just think we've got to do everything to see your work reaches a wide audience.'

'The thing is,' said Frensic, returning with two single gin and tonics for himself and Sonia and a double for Piper, 'that you need exposure. Corkadales will do for a start but their sales record is none too good.'

'It isn't?' said Piper who had never thought of such mundane things as sales.

'They're naturally old-fashioned and if they do take *Search* – and that's still not entirely certain – are they going to be the best people to push it? That's the question.'

'But I thought you said they'd agreed to buy?' said Piper uncomfortably.

'They've made an offer, a good offer, but are we going to accept it?' said Frensic. 'That's what we have to discuss.'

'Yes,' said Piper. 'Yes, we are.'

Frensic looked questioningly at Sonia. 'The US market?' he asked. Sonia shook her head.

'If we're going to sell to a US publisher we need someone bigger than Corkadales over here first. Someone with get-up-and-go who's going to promote the book in a big way.'

'My feelings exactly,' said Frensic. 'Corkadales have the prestige but they could kill it stone dead.'

'But . . .' began Piper, by now thoroughly disturbed.

'Getting a first novel off the ground in the States isn't easy,' said Sonia. 'And with a new British author it's like . . .'

37

'Trying to sell fireworks in hell?' suggested Frensic, doing his best to avoid Eskimos and icecream.

'The words from my mouth,' said Sonia. 'They don't want to know.'

'They don't?' said Piper.

Frensic bought another round of drinks. When he returned Sonia was into tactics.

'A British author in the States needs a gimmick. Thrillers are easy. Historical romance better still. Now if *Search* were about Regency beaux, or better still Mary, Queen of Scots, we'd have no problem. That sort of stuff they lap up but *Search* is a deeply insight—'

'What about *Pause O Men for the Virgin*?' said Frensic. 'Now there's a book that is going to take America by storm.'

'Absolutely,' said Sonia. 'Or would have done if the author could go to promote it.'

They relapsed into gloomy silence.

'Why can't he go?' asked Piper.

'Too ill,' said Sonia.

'Too reserved and shy,' said Frensic. 'I mean he insists on using a *nom de plume*.'

'A *nom de plume*?' said Piper amazed that an author didn't want his name on the cover of his book.

'It's tragic really,' said Sonia. 'He's having to throw away two million dollars because he can't go.'

'Two million dollars?' said Piper.

'And all because he's got osteo-arthritis and the American publisher insists on his making a promotional tour and he can't do it.'

'But that's terrible,' said Piper.

Frensic and Sonia nodded more gloomily than before.

'And he's got a wife and six children,' said Sonia. Frensic started. The wife and six children weren't in the script.

'How awful,' said Piper.

'And with terminal osteo-arthritis he'll never write another book.' Frensic started again. That wasn't in the script either. But Sonia ploughed on. 'And maybe with that two million dollars he could have taken a new course of drugs . . .'

Frensic hurried away for some more drinks. This was really laying it on with a trowel.

'Now if we could only get someone to take his place,' said Sonia looking deeply and significantly into Piper's eyes. 'The fact that he is prepared to use a *nom de plume* and the American publisher doesn't know . . .' She left the implications to be absorbed.

'Why can't you tell the American publisher the truth?' he asked.

Frensic, returning this time with two singles and a triple for Piper, intervened. 'Because Hutchmeyer is one of those bastards who would take advantage of the author and drop his price,' he said.

'Who's Hutchmeyer?' asked Piper.

Frensic looked at Sonia. 'You tell him.'

'He just happens to be about the biggest publisher in the States. He sells more books than all the publishers in London and if he buys you you're made.'

'And if he doesn't it's touch and go,' said Frensic.

Sonia took up the running. 'If we could get Hutchmeyer to buy *Search* your problems would be over. You'd have guaranteed sales and enough money to go on writing for ever.'

Piper considered this glorious prospect and sipped his triple gin. This was the ecstasy he had been waiting so many years for, the knowledge that at last he was going to see *Search* in print and if Hutchmeyer could be persuaded to buy it . . . ah bliss! An idea grew in his befuddled mind. Sonia saw it dawning and jogged it along.

'If there was only some way of bringing you and Hutchmeyer together,' she said. 'I mean, supposing he thought you had written *Pause* . . .'

But Piper was there already. 'Then he'd buy *Search*,' he said and was smitten by immediate doubts. 'But wouldn't the author of the other book mind?'

'Mind?' said Frensic. 'My dear fellow, you would be doing him a favour. He's never going to write another book and if Hutchmeyer refuses to go ahead with the deal . . .'

'And all you would have to do is go and take his place on the promotional tour,' said Sonia. 'It's as simple as that.'

Frensic put in his oar. 'And you would be paid twenty-five thousand dollars and all expenses into the bargain.'

'It would be marvellous publicity,' said Sonia. 'Just the sort of break you need.'

Piper absolutely agreed. It *was* just the sort of break he needed. 'But wouldn't it be illegal? Me going around pretending I'd written a book I hadn't?' he asked.

'You'd naturally have the real author's permission. In writing.

39

There would be nothing illegal about it. Hutchmeyer wouldn't have to know, but then he doesn't read the books he buys and he's simply a businessman in books. All he wants is an author to go round signing books and putting in an appearance. In addition to which he has taken an option on the author's second novel.'

'But I thought you said the author couldn't write a second book?' said Piper.

'Exactly,' said Frensic, 'so Hutchmeyer's second book from the same author would be *Search for a Lost Childhood.*'

'You'd be in and made,' said Sonia. 'With Hutchmeyer behind you, you couldn't go wrong.'

They went round the corner to the Italian restaurant and continued the discussion. There was still something bothering Piper. 'But if Corkadales want to buy *Search* isn't that going to make things difficult. They know the author of this other book.'

Frensic shook his head. 'Not a chance. You see we handled his work for him and he can't come to London so it's all between the three of us. No one else will ever know.'

Piper smiled down into his spaghetti. It was all so simple. He was on the brink of recognition. He looked up into Sonia's face. 'Oh well. All's fair in love and war,' he said, and Sonia smiled back. She raised her glass. 'I'll drink to that,' she murmured.

'To the making of an author,' said Frensic.

They drank. Later that night in Frensic's flat in Hampstead Piper signed two contracts. The first sold *Search for a Lost Childhood* to Corkadales for the advance sum of one thousand pounds. The second stated that as the author of *Pause O Men for the Virgin* he agreed to make a promotional tour of the United States.

'On one condition,' he said as Frensic opened a bottle of champagne to celebrate the occasion.

'What's that?' said Frensic.

'That Miss Futtle comes with me,' said Piper. There was a bang as the champagne cork hit the ceiling. On the sofa Sonia laughed gaily. 'I second that motion,' she said.

Frensic carried it. Later he carried a very drunk Piper through to his spare room and put him to bed.

Piper smiled happily in his sleep.

Chapter 5

Piper awoke next morning and lay in bed with a feeling of elation. He was going to be published. He was going to America. He was in love. Suddenly everything he had dreamt of had come true in the most miraculous fashion. Piper had no qualms. He got up and washed and looked at himself in the bathroom mirror with a new appreciation of his previously unrecognized gifts. The fact that his sudden good fortune was derived from the misfortune of an author with terminal arthritis no longer disturbed him. His genius deserved a break and this was it. Besides, the long years of frustration had anaesthetized those moral principles which so informed his novels. A chance reading of Benvenuto Cellini's Autobiography helped too. 'One's duty is to one's art,' Piper told his reflection in the bathroom mirror as he shaved, adding that there was a tide in the affairs of men which taken at its flood led on to fortune. Finally there was Sonia Futtle.

Piper's dedication to his art had left him little time for real feelings for real people and that little time he had devoted to avoiding the predatory advances of several of his landladies or to worshipping at a distance attractive young women who stayed at the boarding-houses he frequented. And those girls he had taken out had proved, on acquaintance, to be uninterested in literature. Piper had reserved himself for the great love affair, one that would equal in intensity the affairs he had read about in great novels, a meeting of literary minds. In Sonia Futtle he felt he had found a woman who truly appreciated what he had to offer and one with whom he could enter into a genuine relationship. If anything more was needed to convince him that he need have no hesitation in going to America to promote someone else's work it was the knowledge that Sonia was going with him. Piper finished shaving and went out into the kitchen to find a note from Frensic saying he had gone to the office and telling Piper to make himself at home. Piper made himself at home. He had breakfast and then, taking his diary and bottle of evaporated ink through to

41

Frensic's study, settled down at the desk to write his radiant perceptions of Sonia Futtle in his diary.

But if Piper was radiant, Frensic wasn't. 'This thing could blow up in our faces,' he told Sonia when she arrived. 'We got the poor sod drunk and he signed the contract but what happens if he changes his mind?'

'No way,' said Sonia. 'We make a down-payment on the tour and you take him round to Corkadales this afternoon and get him to sign for *Search*. That way we sew him up good and tight.'

'Methinks I hear the voice of Hutchmeyer speaking,' said Frensic. 'Sew him up good and tight. Tight being the operative word. Good I have doubts about.'

'It's for his own,' said Sonia. 'Name me some other way he's ever going to see *Search* in print.'

Frensic nodded his agreement. 'Geoffrey is going to have a fit when he sees what he's agreed to publish. *The Magic Mountain* in East Finchley. The mind boggles. You should have read Piper's version of *Nostromo*, likewise set in East Finchley.'

'I'll wait for the reviews,' said Sonia. 'In the meantime we'll have made a cool quarter of a million. Pounds, Frenzy, not dollars. Think of that.'

'I have thought of that,' said Frensic. 'I have also thought what will happen if this thing goes wrong. We'll be out of business.'

'It isn't going to go wrong. I've been on the phone to Eleanor Beazley of the "Books To Be Read" programme. She owes me a favour. She's agreed to squeeze Piper into next week's—'

'No,' said Frensic. 'Definitely not. I won't have you rushing Piper—'

'Listen, baby,' said Sonia, 'we've got to strike while the iron's hot. We get Piper on the box saying he wrote *Pause* and he ain't going to back out nohow.'

Frensic regarded her with distaste. 'He ain't going to back out nohow? Charming. We're really getting into Mafia-land now. And kindly don't "baby" me. If there is one expression I abominate it's being called "baby". And as for putting the poor demented Piper on the box, have you thought what effect this is going to have on Cadwalladine and his anonymous client?'

'Cadwalladine has agreed to the substitution in principle,' said Sonia. 'What's he got to complain about?'

'There is a difference between "in principle" and "in practice",' said Frensic. 'What he actually said was that he would consult his client.'

'And has he let you know?'

'Not yet,' said Frensic, 'and in some ways I rather hope he turns the idea down. At least it would put an end once and for all to the internecine strife between my greed and my scruples.'

But even that relief was denied him. Half an hour later a telegram was delivered.

'CLIENT AGREES TO SUBSTITUTION STOP ANONYMITY OVERRIDING CONSIDERATION CADWALLADINE.'

'So we're in the clear,' said Sonia. 'I'll confirm Piper for Wednesday and see if the *Guardian* will run a feature on him. You get on to Geoffrey and arrange for Piper to exchange contracts for *Search* this afternoon.'

'That could lead to misunderstandings,' said Frensic. 'Geoffrey happens to think Piper wrote *Pause* and since Piper hasn't read *Pause*, let alone written the thing...'

'So you take him out to lunch and liquor him up and...'

'Have you ever considered,' asked Frensic, 'going into the kidnapping business?'

In the event there was no need to liquor Piper up. He arrived in a state of euphoria and installed himself in Sonia's office where he sat gazing at her meaningfully while she telephoned the literary editors of several daily papers to arrange pre-publication interviews with the author of the world's most expensively purchased novel, *Pause O Men for the Virgin*. In the next office Frensic coped with the ordinary business of the day. He phoned Geoffrey Corkadale and made an appointment for Piper in the afternoon, he listened abstractedly to the whining of two authors who were having difficulties with their plots, did his best to assure them that it would all come right in the end and tried to ignore the intimations of his own instincts which were telling him that with the signing up of Piper the firm of Frensic & Futtle had bitten off more than they could chew. Finally when Piper went downstairs to the washroom Frensic managed to have a word with Sonia.

'What gives?' he asked, a lapse into transatlantic brevity that indicated his disturbed state of mind.

43

'The *Guardian* have agreed to interview him tomorrow and the *Telegraph* say they'll let me—'

'With Piper. Whence the fixed smile and the goggle eyes?'

Sonia smiled. 'Has it ever occurred to you that he might find me attractive?'

'No,' said Frensic. 'No it hasn't.'

Sonia's smile faded. 'Get lost,' she said.

Frensic got lost and considered this new and quite incomprehensible development. It was one of the fixed stars in his firmament of opinions that no one in his right mind could find Sonia Futtle attractive apart from Hutchmeyer and Hutchmeyer had evidently perverse tastes both in books and in women. That Piper should be in love with her, and at such short notice, intruded a new dimension into the situation – which in his opinion was sufficiently crowded already. Frensic sat down behind his desk and wondered what advantages could be gained from Piper's infatuation.

'At least it gets me off the hook,' he muttered finally and went next door again. But Piper was back in his chair gazing with adoring eyes at Sonia. Frensic retreated and phoned her.

'From now on, he's your pigeon,' he told her. 'You dine, wine him and anything else that pleases you. The man's besotted.'

'Jealousy will get you nowhere,' said Sonia smiling at Piper.

'Right,' said Frensic, 'I want no part of this corruption of the innocent.'

'Squeamish?' said Sonia.

'Extremely,' said Frensic and put down the phone.

'Who was that?' asked Piper.

'Oh just an editor at Heinemann. He's got a crush on me.'

'Hm,' said Piper disgruntledly.

And so while Frensic lunched at his club, a thing he did only when his ego, vanity or virility (such as it was) had taken a bashing in the real world, Sonia swept the besotted Piper off to Wheeler's and fed him on dry Martinis, Rhine wine, salmon cutlets and her own brand of expansive charm. By the time they emerged into the street he had told her in so many words that he considered her the first woman in his life to have possessed both the physical and mental attractions which made for a real relationship and one who moreover understood the true nature of the creative literary act. Sonia Futtle was not used to such ardent confessions. The few advances she had had in the past had been expressed less fluently and had largely

44

consisted of enquiries as to whether she would or wouldn't and Piper's technique, borrowed almost entirely from Hans Castorp in *The Magic Mountain* with a bit of Lawrence thrown in for good measure, came as a pleasant surprise. There was an old-fashioned quality about him, she decided, which made a nice change. Besides, Piper, for all his literary ambitions, was personable and not without an angular charm and Sonia could accommodate any amount of angular charm. It was a flushed and flattered Sonia who stood on the pavement and hailed a taxi to take them to Corkadales.

'Just don't shoot your mouth off too much,' she said as they drove across London. 'Geoffrey Corkadale's a fag and he'll do the talking. He'll probably say a whole lot of complimentary things about *Pause O Men for the Virgin* and you just nod.'

Piper nodded. The world was a gay, gay place in which anything was possible and everything permissible. As an accepted author it became him to be modest. In the event he excelled himself at Corkadales. Inspired by the sight of Trollope's inkpot in the glass case he launched into an explanation of his own writing techniques with particular reference to the use of evaporated ink, exchanged contracts for *Search*, and accepted Geoffrey's praise of *Pause* as a first-rate novel with a suitably ironical smile.

'Extraordinary to think he could have written that filthy book,' Geoffrey whispered to Sonia as they were leaving. 'I had expected some long-haired hippie and my dear, this one is out of the Ark.'

'Just shows you can never tell,' said Sonia. 'Anyway you're going to get a lot of excellent publicity for *Pause*. I've got him on the "Books To Be Read" programme.'

'How very clever you are,' said Geoffrey. 'I'm delighted. And the American deal is definitely on?'

'Definitely,' said Sonia.

They took another taxi and drove back towards Lanyard Lane.

'You were marvellous,' she told Piper. 'Just stick to talking about your pens and ink and how you write your books and refuse to discuss their content and we'll have no trouble.'

'Nobody seems to discuss books anyway,' said Piper. 'I thought the conversation would be quite different. More literary.'

He got out in Charing Cross Road and spent the rest of the afternoon browsing in Foyle's while Sonia went back to the office and reassured Frensic.

'No problems,' she said. 'He had Geoffrey fooled.'

'That's hardly surprising,' said Frensic, 'Geoffrey is a fool. Wait till Eleanor Beazley starts asking him about his portrayal of the sexual psyche of an eighty-year-old woman. That's when the fat's going to be in the fire.'

'She won't. I've told her he never discusses his past work. She's to stick to biographical details and how he works. He's really convincing when he gets on to pens and ink. Did you know he uses evaporated ink and writes in leatherbound ledgers? Isn't that quaint?'

'I'm only surprised he doesn't use a quill,' said Frensic. 'It's in keeping.'

'It's good copy. The *Guardian* interview with Jim Fossie is tomorrow morning and the *Telegraph* wants him for the colour supplement in the afternoon. I tell you this bandwagon is beginning to roll.'

That night, as Frensic made his way back to his flat with Piper, it was clear that the bandwagon had indeed begun to roll. The newstands announced BRITISH NOVELIST MAKES TWO MILLION IN BIGGEST DEAL EVER.

'Oh what a tangled web we weave when first we practise to deceive,' murmured Frensic and bought a paper. Beside him Piper nursed the large green hardback copy of Thomas Mann's *Doctor Faustus* which he had bought at Foyle's. He was thinking of utilizing its symphonic approach in his third novel.

46

Chapter 6

Next morning the bandwagon began to roll in earnest. After a night spent dreaming of Sonia and preparing himself for the ordeal, Piper arrived at the office to discuss his life, literary opinions and methods of work with Jim Fossie of the *Guardian*. Frensic and Sonia hovered anxiously in the background to ensure discretion but there was no need. Whatever Piper's limitations as a writer of novels, as a putative novelist he played his role expertly. He spoke of Literature in the abstract, referred scathingly to one or two eminent contemporary novelists, but for the most part concentrated on the use of evaporated ink and the limitations of the modern fountain pen as an aid to literary creation.

'I believe in craftsmanship,' he said, 'the old-fashioned virtues of clarity and legibility.' He told a story about Palmerston's insistence on fine writing by the clerks in the Foreign Office and dismissed the ball-pen with contempt. So obsessive was his concern with calligraphy that Mr Fossie had ended the interview before he realized that no mention had been made of the novel he had come to discuss.

'He's certainly different from any other author I've ever met,' he told Sonia as she saw him out. 'All that stuff about Kipling's note-paper, for God's sake!'

'What do you expect from genius?' said Sonia. 'Some spiel about how brilliant his novel is?'

'And how brilliant is this genius's novel?'

'Two million dollars worth. That's the reality value.'

'Some reality,' said Mr Fossie with more percipience than he knew.

Even Frensic, who had anticipated disaster, was impressed. 'If he keeps that up we'll be all right,' he said.

'We're going to be fine,' said Sonia.

After lunch the *Daily Telegraph* photographer insisted, thanks to a chance remark by Piper that he had once lived near the scene of the explosion in *The Secret Agent* in Greenwich Park, on taking his photographs as it were on location.

'It adds dramatic interest,' he said evidently supposing the explosion to have been a real one. They went down on the river boat from Charing Cross, Piper explaining to the interviewer, Miss Pamela Wildgrove, that Conrad had been a major influence on his work. Miss Wildgrove made a note of the fact. Piper said Dickens had also been an influence. Miss Wildgrove made a note of that fact too. By the time they reached Greenwich her notebook was crammed with influences but Piper's own work had hardly been mentioned.

'I understand *Pause O Men for the Virgin* deals with the love affair between a seventeen-year-old boy and . . .' Miss Wildgrove began but Sonia intervened.

'Mr Piper doesn't wish to discuss the content of his novel,' she said hurriedly. 'We're keeping the book under wraps.'

'But surely he's prepared to say . . .'

'Let's just say it is a work of major importance and opens new ground in the area of age differentials,' said Sonia and hurried Piper away to be photographed incongruously on the deck of the *Cutty Sark*, in the grounds of the Maritime Museum and by the Observatory. Miss Wildgrove followed disconsolately.

'On the way back stick to ink and your ledgers,' Sonia told Piper and Piper followed her advice. In the end Miss Wildgrove returned to her office to compose an article with a distinctly nautical flavour while Sonia shepherded her charge back to the office.

'You did very well,' she told him.

'Yes, but hadn't I better read this book I'm supposed to have written? I mean, I don't even know what it's about.'

'You can do that on the boat going over to the States.'

'Boat?' said Piper.

'Much nicer than flying,' said Sonia. 'Hutchmeyer is arranging some big reception for you in New York and it will draw bigger crowds at the dockside. Anyway we've done the interviews and the TV programme isn't till next Wednesday. You can go back to Exforth and pack. Get back here Tuesday afternoon and I'll brief you for the programme. We're leaving from Southampton Thursday.'

'You're wonderful,' said Piper fervently, 'I want you to know that.' He left the office and caught the evening train to Exeter. Sonia sat on in her office and thought wistfully about him. Nobody had ever told her she was wonderful before.

. . . . .

48

Certainly Frensic didn't next morning. He arrived at the office in a towering rage carrying a copy of the *Guardian*.

'I thought you told me all he was going to talk about was inks and pens,' he shouted at the startled Sonia.

'That's right. He was quite fascinating.'

'Well then kindly explain all this about Graham Greene being a second-rate hack,' Frensic yelled and thrust the article under her nose. 'That's right. Hack. Graham Greene. A hack. The man's insane!'

Sonia read the article and had to admit that it was a bit extreme.

'Still, it's good publicity,' she said. 'Statements like that will get his name before the public.'

'Get his name before the courts more like,' said Frensic. 'And what about this bit about *The French Lieutenant's Woman* . . . Piper hasn't even written one single publishable word and here he is castigating half a dozen eminent novelists. Look what he says about Waugh. Quote a very limited imagination and an overrated style unquote. Waugh just happens to have been one of the finest stylists of the century. And "limited imagination" coming from a blithering idiot who hasn't got any imagination at all. I tell you Pandora's box will be a teaparty by comparison with Piper on the loose.'

'He's entitled to his opinions,' said Sonia.

'He isn't entitled to have opinions like these,' said Frensic. 'God knows what Cadwalladine's client will say when he reads what he's supposed to have said, and I shouldn't think Geoffrey Corkadale is too pleased to know he's got an author on his list who thinks Graham Greene is a second-rate hack.' He went into his office and sat miserably wondering what new storm was going to break. His nose was playing all hell with him.

But the storm when it did break came from an unexpected direction. From Piper himself. He returned to the Gleneagle Guest House in Exforth madly in love with Sonia, life, his own newly established reputation as a novelist and his future happiness to find a parcel waiting for him. It contained the proofs of *Pause O Men for the Virgin* and a letter from Geoffrey Corkadale asking him if he would mind correcting them as soon as possible. Piper took the parcel up to his room and settled down to read. He started at nine o'clock at night. By midnight he was wide awake and half-way through. By two o'clock he had finished and had begun a letter to Geoffrey Corkadale stating very precisely what he thought of *Pause O Men for the Virgin* as a novel, as pornography, as an attack on established values both sexual and human. It was a long letter. By six o'clock he had posted it. Only then did he go to bed, exhausted by his own fluent disgust and harbouring feelings for Miss Futtle that were the exact reverse of those he had held for her nine hours earlier. Even then he couldn't sleep but lay awake for several hours before finally dozing off. He woke again after lunch and went for a haggard walk along the beach in a state bordering on the suicidal. He had been tricked, conned, deceived by a woman he had loved and trusted. She had deliberately bribed him into accepting the authorship of a vile, nauseating, pornographic . . . He ran out of adjectives. He would never forgive her. After contemplating the ocean bleakly for an hour he returned to the boarding-house, his mind made up. He composed a terse telegram stating that he had no intention of going through with the charade and had no wish to see Miss Futtle ever again. That done he confided his darkest thoughts to his diary, had supper and went to bed.

The following morning the storm broke in London. Frensic arrived in a good mood. Piper's absence from his flat had relieved him of the obligation to play host to a man whose conversation had consisted of the need for a serious approach to fiction and Sonia Futtle's attractions as a woman. Neither topic had been at all to Frensic's taste and Piper's habit at breakfast of reading aloud passages from *Doctor Faustus* to illustrate what he meant by symbolic counterpoint as a literary device had driven Frensic from his own home even earlier than was his custom. With Piper in Exforth he had been spared that particular ordeal but on his arrival at the office he was confronted with fresh horrors. He found Sonia, whitefaced and almost tearful, clutching a telegram, and had been about to ask her what the matter was when the phone rang. Frensic answered it. It was Geoffrey Corkadale. 'I suppose this is your idea of a joke,' he said angrily.

'What is?' said Frensic thinking of the *Guardian* article about Graham Greene.

'This bloody letter,' shouted Geoffrey.

'What letter?'

'This letter from Piper. I suppose you think it's funny to get him to write abusive filth about his own beastly book.'

It was Frensic's turn to shout. 'What about his book?' he yelled.

'What do you mean "What about it?" You know damned well what I mean.'

'I've no idea,' said Frensic.

'He says here he considers it one of the most repulsive pieces of writing it's ever been his misfortune to have to read—'

'Shit,' said Frensic frantically wondering how Piper had got hold of a copy of *Pause*.

'Yes, that too,' said Geoffrey. 'Now where does he say that? Here we are. "If you imagine even momentarily that for motives of commercial cupidity I am prepared to prostitute my albeit so far unknown but not I think inconsiderable talent by assuming even remotely and as it were by proxy responsibility for what in my view and that of any right-minded person can only be described as the pornographic outpourings of verbal excreta . . ." There! I knew it was embedded somewhere. Now what do you say to that?'

Frensic stared venomously at Sonia and tried to think of something to say. 'I don't know,' he muttered, 'it sounds odd. How did he get the blasted book?'

'What do you mean "How did he get the book"?' yelled Geoffrey. 'He wrote the thing, didn't he?'

'Yes, I suppose so,' said Frensic edging towards the safety of admitting he didn't know who had written it and that he had been hoodwinked by Piper. It didn't seem a very safe position to adopt.

'What do you mean "You suppose so"? I send him proofs of his own book to correct and I get this abusive letter back. Anyone would think he'd never read the damned thing before. Is the man mad or something?'

'Yes,' said Frensic for whom the suggestion came as a God-send, 'the strain of the past few weeks . . . nervous breakdown. Very highly strung you know. He gets into these states.'

Geoffrey Corkadale's fury abated a little. 'I can't say I'm at all surprised,' he admitted. 'Anyone who can go to bed with an eighty-year-old woman must have something mentally wrong with him. What do you want me to do with these proofs?'

'Send them round to me and I'll see he corrects them,' said Frensic. 'And in future I suggest you deal with Piper through me here. I think I understand him.'

'I'm glad someone does,' said Geoffrey. 'I don't want any more letters like this one.'

Frensic put the phone down and turned on Sonia. 'Right,' he

yelled, 'I knew it. I just knew it would happen. You heard what he said?'

Sonia nodded sadly. 'It was our mistake,' she said. 'We should have told them to send the proofs here.'

'Never mind the bloody proofs,' snarled Frensic, 'our mistake was coming up with Piper in the first place. Why Piper? The world is full of normal, sane, financially motivated, healthily commercial authors who would be glad to stick their name to any old trash, and you had to come up with Piper.'

'There's no need to go on about it,' said Sonia, 'look what he's said in this telegram.'

Frensic looked and slumped into a chair. ' "Yours ineluctably Piper"? In a telegram? I wouldn't have believed it . . . Well at least he's put us out of our misery though how the hell we're going to explain to Geoffrey that the Hutchmeyer deal is off . . .'

'It isn't off,' said Sonia.

'But Piper says—'

'Screw what he says. He's going to the States if I have to carry him. We've paid him good money, we've sold his lousy book and he's under obligation to go. He's not going to back out on that contract now. I'm going down to Exforth to talk with him.'

'Leave well alone,' said Frensic, 'that's my advice. That young man can—' but the phone rang and by the time he had spent ten minutes discussing the new ending of *Final Fling* with Miss Gold, Sonia had left.

'Hell hath no fury . . .' he muttered, and returned to his own office.

Piper took his afternoon walk along the promenade like some late migrating bird whose biological clock had let it down. It was summer and he should have gone inland to cheaper climes but the atmosphere of Exforth held him. The little resort was nicely Edwardian and rather prim and served in its old-fashioned way to help bridge the gap between Davos and East Finchley. Thomas Mann, he felt, would have appreciated Exforth with its botanical gardens, its clock golf, its pier and tesselated toilets, its bandstand and its rows of balustraded boarding houses staring south towards France. There were even some palm trees in the little park that separated the Gleneagle Guest House from the promenade. Piper strolled beneath them and climbed the steps in time for tea.

Instead he found Sonia Futtle waiting for him in the hall. She had driven down at high speed from London, had rehearsed her tactics on the way and a brief encounter with Mrs Oakley on the question of coffee for non-residents had whetted her temper. Besides, Piper had rejected her not only as an agent but as a woman, and as a woman she wasn't to be trifled with.

'Now you just listen to me,' she said in decibels that made it certain that everyone in the guest-house would. 'You can't get out of this so easily. You accepted money and you—'

'For God's sake,' spluttered Piper, 'don't shout like that. What will people think?'

It was a stupid question. In the lounge the residents were staring. It was clear what they thought.

'That you're a man no woman can trust,' bawled Sonia pursuing her advantage, 'that you break your word, that you . . .'

But Piper was in flight. As he went down the steps and into the street Sonia followed in full cry.

'You deliberately deceived me. You took advantage of my inexperience to make me believe—'

Piper plunged wildly across the road into the park. 'I deceived you?' he counter-attacked under the palms. 'You told me that book was—'

'No I didn't. I said it was a bestseller. I never said it was good.'

'Good? It's disgusting. It's pure pornography. It debases . . .'

'Pornography? You've got to be kidding. So you haven't read anything later than Hemingway you've got this idea any book deals with sex is pornographic.'

'No I don't,' protested Piper, 'what I meant was it undermines the foundations of English literature . . .'

'Don't give me that crap. You took advantage of Frenzy's faith in you as a writer. Ten years he's been trying to get you published and now when we finally come up with this deal you throw it back at us.'

'That's not true. I didn't know the book was that bad. I've got my reputation to think of and if my name is on—'

'Your reputation? What about our reputation?' said Sonia as they skirmished past a bus queue on the front. 'You ever thought what you're doing to that?'

Piper shook his head.

'So where's your reputation? As what?'

'As a writer,' said Piper.

Sonia appealed to the bus queue. 'Whoever heard of you?'

Clearly no one had. Piper fled down on to the beach.

'And what is more no one ever will,' shouted Sonia. 'You think Corkadales are going to publish *Search* now? Think again. They'll take you through the courts and break you moneywise and then they'll blacklist you.'

'Blacklist me?' said Piper.

'The blacklist of authors who are never to be published.'

'Corkadales aren't the only publishers,' said Piper now thoroughly confused.

'If you're on the blacklist no one will publish you,' said Sonia inventively. 'You'll be finished. As a writer *finito*.'

Piper stared out at the sea and thought about being *finito* as a writer. It was a terrible prospect.

'You really think . . .' he began but Sonia had already changed her tactics.

'You told me you loved me,' she sobbed sinking on to the sand close to a middle-aged couple. 'You said we would . . .'

'Oh Lord,' said Piper, 'don't go on like that. Not here.'

But Sonia went on, there and elsewhere, combining a public display of private anguish with the threat of legal action if Piper didn't fulfil his part of the bargain and the promise of fame as a writer of genius if he did. Gradually his resolve weakened. The blacklist had hit him hard.

'I suppose I could always write under another name,' he said as they stood at the end of the pier. But Sonia shook her head.

'Darling, you're so naïve,' she said. 'Don't you see that what you write is instantly recognizable. You can't escape your own uniqueness, your own original brilliance . . .'

'I suppose not,' said Piper modestly, 'I suppose that's true.'

'Of course it's true. You're not some hack turning books out to order. You're you, Peter Piper. Frenzy has always said there's only one you.'

'He has?' said Piper.

'He's spent more time on you than any other author we handle. He's had faith in you and this is your big opportunity, the chance to break through into fame . . .'

'With someone else's awful book,' Piper pointed out.

'So it's someone else's, it might have had to be your own. Like Faulkner with *Sanctuary* and the rape with the corncob.'

'You mean Faulkner didn't write that?' said Piper aghast.

'I mean he did. He had to so he'd get noticed and have the breakthrough. Nobody'd bought him before *Sanctuary* and afterwards he was famous. With *Pause* you don't have to do that. You keep your artistic integrity intact.'

'I hadn't thought of it like that,' said Piper.

'And later when you're known as a great novelist you can write your autobiography and set the world straight about *Pause*,' said Sonia.

'So I can,' said Piper.

'Then you'll come?'

'Yes. Yes, I will.'

'Oh, darling.'

They kissed on the end of the pier and the tide, rising gently under the moon, lapped below their feet.

Chapter 7

Two days later a triumphant if exhausted Sonia walked into the office to announce that she had persuaded Piper to change his mind.

'Brought him back with you?' said Frensic incredulously. 'After that telegram? Good Lord, you must have positively Circean charms for the poor brute. How on earth did you do it?'

'Made a scene and quoted Faulkner,' said Sonia simply.

Frensic was appalled. 'Not Faulkner again. We had him last summer. Even Mann's easier to move to East Finchley. Every time I see a pylon now I . . .'

'This was *Sanctuary*.'

Frensic sighed. 'That's better I suppose. Still the thought of Mrs Piper ending up in some brothel in Memphis-cum-Golders Green . . . And you mean to say he's prepared to go on with the tour? That's incredible.'

'You forget I'm a salesperson,' said Sonia. 'I could sell sunlamps in the Sahara.'

'I believe you. After that letter he wrote Geoffrey I thought we were done for. And he is quite reconciled to being the author of what he chose to call the most repulsive piece of writing it had ever been his misfortune to have to read?'

'He sees it as a necessary step on the road to recognition,' said Sonia. 'I managed to persuade him it was his duty to suppress his own critical awareness in order to achieve—'

'Critical awareness my foot,' said Frensic, 'he hasn't got any. Just so long as I don't have to put him up again.'

'He's staying with me,' said Sonia, 'and don't smirk. I just want him where I can reach him.'

Frensic stopped smirking. 'And what is the next event on the agenda?'

'The "Books To Be Read" programme. It will help get him ready for the TV appearances in the States.'

'Quite so,' said Frensic. 'Added to which it has the advantage of getting him committed to the authorship of *Pause* with what is termed the maximum exposure. One can hardly see him backing out after that.'

'Frenzy dear,' said Sonia, 'you are a born worrier. It's going to work out all right.'

'I just hope you're right,' said Frensic, 'but I shall be relieved when you leave for the States. There's many a slip 'twixt cup and lip, and—'

'Not this cup and these lips,' said Sonia smugly, 'no way. Piper will go on the box . . .'

'Like a lamb to the slaughter?' suggested Frensic.

It was an apt simile and one that had already occurred to Piper who had begun to have qualms.

'Not that I doubt my love for Sonia,' he confided to his diary which, now that he had moved into Sonia's flat, had taken the place of *Search* as his main mode of self-expression. 'But it is surely arguable that my honesty as an artist is at stake whatever Sonia may say about Villon.'

And in any case Villon's end didn't commend itself to Piper. To calm his conscience he turned once again to the Faulkner interview in *Writers at Work*. Mr Faulkner's view on the artist was most reassuring. 'He is completely amoral,' Piper read, 'in that he will rob, borrow, beg or steal from anybody and everybody to get the work done.' Piper read right through the interview and came to the conclusion that perhaps he had been wrong to abandon his Yoknapatawpha version of *Search* in favour of *The Magic Mountain*. Frensic had disapproved on the grounds that the prose had seemed a bit clotted for the story of adolescence. But then Frensic was so commercial. It had come as a considerable surprise to Piper to learn that Frensic had so much faith in him. He had begun to suspect that Frensic was merely fobbing him off with his annual lunches but Sonia had reassured him. Dear Sonia. She was such a comfort. Piper made an ecstatic note of the fact in his diary and then turned on the television set. It was time he decided what sort of image he wanted to present on the 'Books To Be Read' programme. Sonia said image was very important and with his usual gift for derivation Piper finally adopted Herbert Herbison as his model. Sonia came home that night to find him muttering alliterative clichés to his reflection in her dressing-table mirror.

57

'You've just got to be yourself,' she told him. 'It's no use trying to copy other people.'

'Myself?' said Piper.

'Natural. Like you are with me.'

'You think it will be all right like that?'

'Darling, it will be fine. I've had a word with Eleanor Beazley and she'll go easy on you. You can tell her all about your work methods and pens and things.'

'Just so long as she doesn't ask me why I wrote that bloody book,' said Piper gloomily.

'You'll be great,' said Sonia confidently. She was still insisting that everything would be just fine when three days later at Shepherd's Bush Piper was led away to be made up for the interview.

For once she was wrong. Even Geoffrey Corkadale, whose authors seldom achieved a circulation sufficient to warrant their appearance on 'Books To Be Read' and who therefore tended to ignore the programme, could see that Piper was, to put it mildly, not himself. He said as much to Frensic who had invited him over for the evening in case the need should arise for a fresh explanation as to who had actually written *Pause O Men for the Virgin*.

'Come to think of it, I don't suppose he is,' said Frensic staring nervously at the image on the screen. Certainly Piper had a stricken look about him as he sat opposite Eleanor Beazley and the title faded.

'Tonight I have in the studio with me Mr Peter Piper,' said Miss Beazley addressing the camera, 'the author of a first novel, *Pause O Men for the Virgin*, which will shortly be published by Corkadales, price £3.95, and which has been bought for the unheard-of sum of . . .' (there was a loud thump as Piper kicked the microphone) 'by an American publisher.'

'Unheard-of is about right,' said Frensic. 'We could have done with that bit of publicity.'

Miss Beazley did her best to make good the erasure. She turned to Piper. 'Two million dollars is a very large sum to be paid for a first novel,' she said, 'it must have come as a great shock to you to find yourself . . .'

There was another thump as Piper crossed his legs. This time he managed to kick the microphone and spill a glass of water on the table at the same time.

'I'm sorry,' he shouted. Miss Beazley continued to smile expectantly as water dribbled down her leg. 'Yes, it was a great shock.'

'You hadn't expected it to be such a great success?'

'No,' said Piper.

'I wish to God he'd stop twitching like that,' said Geoffrey. 'Anyone would think he'd got St Vitus dance.'

Miss Beazley smiled solicitously. 'I wonder if you'd care to tell us something about how you came to write the book in the first place?' she asked.

Piper gazed stricken into a million homes. 'I didn't . . .' he began, before jerking his leg forward galvanically and knocking the microphone on to the floor. Frensic shut his eyes. Muffled voices came from the set. When he looked again Miss Beazley's insistent smile filled the screen.

'*Pause O Men* is a most unusual book,' she was saying. 'It's a love story about a young man who falls in love with a woman much older than himself. Was this something you had had in mind for a long time? I mean was it a theme that had occupied your attention?'

The face of Piper appeared again. Beads of perspiration were visible on his forehead and his mouth was working uncontrollably. 'Yes,' he bawled finally.

'Christ, I don't think I can stand much more of this,' said Geoffrey. 'The poor fellow looks as though he's going to burst.'

'And did it take you long to write?' asked Miss Beazley.

Again Piper struggled for words, looking desperately round the studio as he did so. Finally he took a sip of water and said 'Yes.'

Frensic mopped his brow with a handkerchief.

'To change the subject,' said the indefatigable Miss Beazley whose smile had a positively demented gaiety about it now, 'I understand that your working methods are very much your own. You were telling me earlier that you always write in longhand?'

'Yes,' said Piper.

'And you grind your own ink?'

Piper ground his teeth and nodded.

'This was an idea you got from Kipling?'

'Yes. *Something Of Myself*. It's in there,' said Piper.

'At least he's warming up,' said Geoffrey only to have his hopes blighted by Miss Beazley's ignorance of Kipling's autobiography.

'Something of yourself is in your novel?' she asked hopefully. Piper glared at her. It was obvious he disliked the question.

'The ink,' he said, 'it's in *Something Of Myself*.'

Miss Beazley's smile took on a bemused look. 'Is it? The ink?'

'He used to grind it himself,' said Piper, 'or rather he got a boy to grind it for him.'

'A boy? How very interesting,' said Miss Beazley searching for some way out of the maze. Piper refused to help.

'It's blacker if you grind your own Indian ink.'

'I suppose it must be. And you find that using a very black Indian ink helps you to write?'

'No,' said Piper, 'it gums up the nib. I tried diluting it with ordinary ink but it still wouldn't work. It got in the ducts and blocked them up.' He stopped suddenly and stared at Miss Beazley.

'Ducts? It blocks the ducts?' she said, evidently supposing Piper to be referring to some strange conduit of inspiration. 'You mean you found your . . .' she groped for a less old-fashioned alternative but gave up the struggle to remain contemporary, 'you found your muse wouldn't . . .'

'Daemon,' said Piper abruptly, still in the role of Kipling.

Miss Beazley took the insult in her stride. 'You were talking about ink,' she said.

'I said it blocked the ducts of the fountain pen. I couldn't write more than one word at a time.'

'That's hardly surprising,' said Geoffrey. 'It would be bloody odd if he could.'

It was evidently a thought that had occurred to Piper too. 'I mean I had to keep stopping and wiping the nib all the time,' he explained. 'So what I do now is I . . .' He stopped. 'It sounds silly.'

'It sounds insane,' said Geoffrey but Miss Beazley would have none of it.

'Go on,' she said encouragingly.

'Well, what I do now is I get a bottle of Midnight Black and let it dry out a bit and then when it's sort of gooey if you see what I mean I dip my nib in and . . .' Piper faltered to a stop.

'How very interesting,' said Miss Beazley.

'Well at least he's said something even if it wasn't very edifying,' said Geoffrey. Beside him Frensic stared at the set forlornly. He could see now that he should never have allowed himself to be persuaded to agree to the scheme. It was bound to end in disaster. So was the programme. Miss Beazley tried to get back to the book.

'When I read your novel,' she said, 'I was struck by your understanding of the need for a mature woman's sexuality to find expression physically. Would I be wrong to suppose that there is an autobiographical element in your writing?'

Piper goggled at her vindictively. That he should be supposed to have written *Pause O Men for the* beastly *Virgin* was bad enough, to be taken for the main protagonist in the drama of perversion was more than he could bear. Frensic felt for him and cringed in his chair.

'What did you say?' yelled Piper reverting to his earlier explosive mode of expression. This time he combined it with fluency. 'Do you really think I approve of the filthy book?'

'Well naturally I thought . . .' Miss Beazley began but Piper swept her objections aside.

'The whole thing's disgusting. A boy and an eighty-year-old woman. It debases the very foundations of English literature. It's a vile monstrous degenerate book and it should never have been published and if you think—'

But viewers of the 'Books To Be Read' programme were never to hear what Piper supposed Miss Beazley to have thought. A figure interposed itself between the camera and the couple in the chairs, a large figure and clearly a very disturbed one that shouted 'Cut! Cut!' and waved its hands horribly in the air.

'God Almighty,' gasped Geoffrey, 'what the hell's going on?'

Frensic said nothing. He shut his eyes to avoid the sight of Sonia Futtle hurling herself about the studio in a frantic attempt to prevent Piper's terrible confession from reaching its enormous audience. There was an even more startling crackle from the TV set. Frensic opened his eyes again in time to catch a glimpse of the microphone in mid-air and then in the silence that followed watched the ensuing chaos. In the understandable belief that a lunatic had somehow got into the studio and was about to attack her, Miss Beazley shot out of her chair and dived for the door. Piper stared wildly round while Sonia, catching her foot in a cable, crashed forward across the glass-topped table and sprawled revealingly on the floor. For a moment she lay there kicking and then the screen went blank and a sign appeared. It said OWING TO CIRCUMSTANCES BEYOND OUR CONTROL TRANSMISSION HAS BEEN TEMPORARILY SUSPENDED. Frensic regarded it balefully. It seemed gratuitous. That circumstances were now beyond anyone's control was perfectly obvious. Thanks to Piper's high-mindedness and Sonia Futtle's ghastly intervention his career as a

61

literary agent was done for. The morning papers would be filled with the exposé of The Author Who Wasn't. Hutchmeyer would cancel the contract and almost certainly sue for damages. The possibilities were endless and all of them awful. Frensic turned to find Geoffrey looking at him curiously.

'That *was* Miss Futtle, wasn't it?' he said.

Frensic nodded dumbly.

'What on earth was she doing hurling herself about like that for? I've never seen anything so extraordinary in my life. A bloody author starts lambasting his own novel. What did he say it was? A vile monstrous degenerate book debasing the very foundations of English literature. And the next thing you know is his own agent behaving like a gargantuan banshee, yelling "Cut!" and hurling mikes about the place. Something out of a nightmare.'

Frensic sought frantically for an explanation. 'I suppose you could call it a happening,' he muttered.

'A happening?'

'You know, a sort of random, inconsequential occurrence,' said Frensic lamely.

'A random . . . inconsequential . . .?' said Geoffrey. 'If you think there aren't going to be any consequences . . .'

Frensic tried not to think of them. 'It certainly made it a very memorable interview,' he said.

Geoffrey goggled at him. 'Memorable? I should think it will go down in history.' He stopped and regarded Frensic open-mouthed. 'A happening? You said a happening. Good Lord, you mean to say you put them up to it?'

'I what?' said Frensic.

'Put them up to it. You deliberately stage-managed that shambles. You got Piper to say all those extraordinary things about his own novel and then Miss Futtle bursts in and goes berserk and you've pulled the biggest publicity stunt . . .'

Frensic considered this explanation and found it better than the truth. 'I suppose it was rather good publicity,' he said modestly. 'I mean most of those interviews are rather tame.'

Geoffrey helped himself to some more whisky. 'Well I must take my hat off to you,' he said. 'I wouldn't have had the nerve to dream up a thing like that. Mind you, that Eleanor Beazley has had it coming to her for years.'

Frensic began to relax. If only he could get hold of Sonia before she was arrested or whatever they did to people who burst into TV studios and disrupted programmes, and before Piper could do any more damage with his literary high-mindedness, he might be able to save something from the catastrophe.

In the event there was no need. Sonia and Piper had already left the studio in a hurry followed by Eleanor Beazley's shrill voice uttering threats and imprecations and the programme producer's still shriller promise to take legal action. They fled down the corridor and into an elevator and shut the door.

'What did you mean by—' Piper began as they descended.

'Drop dead,' said Sonia. 'If it hadn't been for me you'd have landed us all in it up to the eyeballs, shooting your mouth off like that.'

'Well, she said—'

'The hell with what she said,' shouted Sonia, 'it was what *you* were saying that got to me. Looks great, an author telling half a million viewers that his own novel stinks.'

'But it isn't my own novel,' said Piper.

'Oh yes it is. It is now. Wait till you see tomorrow's papers. They're going to have headlines to make you famous. AUTHOR SLAMS OWN NOVEL ON TV. You may not have written *Pause* but you're going to have a hard time proving it.'

'Oh God,' said Piper. 'What are we to do?'

'Get the hell out of here fast,' said Sonia as the lift doors opened. They crossed the foyer and went out to the car. Sonia drove and twenty minutes later they were back at her flat.

'Now pack,' she said. 'We're moving out of here before the press get on to us.'

Piper packed, his mind racing with conflicting emotions. He was saddled with the authorship of a dreadful book, there was no backing out, he was committed to a promotional tour of the States and he was in love with Sonia. When he had finished he made one last attempt at resistance.

'Look, I really don't think I can go on with this,' he said as Sonia lugged her suitcases to the door. 'I mean my nerves can't stand it.'

'You think mine are any better – and what about Frenzy? A shock like that could have killed him. He's got a heart condition.'

'A heart condition?' said Piper. 'I had no idea.'

. . . . . .

63

Nor had Frensic when she phoned him from a call box an hour later.

'I have a what?' he said. 'You wake me in the middle of the night to tell me I've got a heart condition?'

'It was the only way to stop him backing out. That Beazley woman blew his mind.'

'The whole programme blew mine,' said Frensic, 'and to make matters worse I had Geoffrey gibbering beside me all the time too. It's a fine experience for a reputable publisher to watch one of his authors describe his own book as a vile degenerate thing. It does something to the soul. And to cap it all Geoffrey thought I'd put you up to rushing on like that screaming "Cut".'

'Put me up to it?' said Sonia. 'I had to do that to stop—'

'*I* know all that but *he* didn't. He thinks it's some sort of publicity stunt.'

'But that's great,' said Sonia. 'Gets us off the hook.'

'Gets us on it if you ask me,' said Frensic grimly. 'Anyway where are you? Why the call box?'

'We're going down to Southampton,' said Sonia. 'Now, before he changes his mind again. There's a spare berth on the *QE2* and she's sailing tomorrow. I'm not taking any more chances. We're sailing with her if I have to bribe my way on board. And if that doesn't work I'm going to keep him holed up in a hotel where the press can't get at him until we have him word-perfect on what he's to say about *Pause.*'

'Word-perfect? You make him sound like a performing parrot—'

But Sonia had rung off and was back in the car driving down the road to Southampton.

The next morning a bemused and weary Piper walked unsteadily up the gangway and down to his cabin. Sonia stopped at the Purser's Office. She had a telegram to send to Hutchmeyer.

Chapter 8

In New York MacMordie, Hutchmeyer's Senior Executive Assistant, brought him the telegram.

'So they're coming early,' said Hutchmeyer. 'Makes no difference. Just got to get this ball moving a bit quicker is all. Now then, Mac-Mordie, I want you to organize the biggest demonstration you can. And I mean the biggest. You got any angles?'

'With a book like that the only angle I've got is Senior Citizens mobbing him like he's the Beatles.'

'Senior Citizens don't mob the Beatles.'

'Okay, so he's Valentino come to life. Whoever. Some great star of the twenties.'

Hutchmeyer nodded. 'That's more like it,' he said. 'The nostalgia angle. But that's not enough. Senior Citizens you don't get much impact.'

'Absolutely none,' said MacMordie. 'Now if this guy Piper was a gay liberationist Jew-baiter with a nigger boyfriend from Cuba called O'Hara I could really call up some muscle. But with a product that screws old women . . .'

'MacMordie, how often have I got to tell you what the product is and what the action is are two separate things? There doesn't have to be any connection. You've got to get coverage any way you can.'

'Yes but with a British author nobody's ever heard of and a first-timer who wants to know?'

'I do,' said Hutchmeyer. 'I do and I want a hundred million TV viewers to know too. And I mean know. This guy Piper has to be famous this time next week and I don't care how. You can do what you like just so long as when he steps ashore it's like Lindbergh's flown the Atlantic first time. So you get yourself a pussy posse and every pressure group and lobby you can find and see he gets charisma.'

'Charisma?' said MacMordie doubtfully. 'With the picture we've got of him for the cover you want charisma too? He looks sick or something.'

'So he's sick! Who cares what he looks like? All that matters is he becomes the spinster's prayer overnight. Get Women's Lib involved, and that's a good idea of yours about the fags.'

'We get a lot of little old ladies and the Ms brigade and the gays down on the docks could be we'd have a riot on our hands.'

'That's right,' said Hutchmeyer, 'a riot. Throw the lot at him. A cop gets hurt is good. And some old lady has a coronary, that's good too. She gets pushed in the drink is better still. By the time we've finished with his image this Piper's going to be like he was pied.'

'Pied?' said MacMordie.

'With rats for Chrissake.'

'Rats? You want rats too?'

Hutchmeyer looked at him dolefully. 'Sometimes, MacMordie, I think you've just got to be goddam illiterate,' he snarled. 'Anyone would think you'd never heard of Edgar Allan Poe. And another thing. When Piper's finished stirring the shit publicitywise down here I want him put on the plane up to Maine. Baby wants to meet him.'

'Mrs Hutchmeyer wants to meet this jerk?' said MacMordie.

Hutchmeyer nodded helplessly. 'Right. Like she was crazy for me to get her that guy who wrote about cracking his whip all the time. What the fuck was his name?'

'Portnoy,' said MacMordie. 'We couldn't get him. He wouldn't come.'

'Was that surprising? It was a wonder he could walk after what he'd done to himself. That stuff saps you.'

'We didn't publish him either,' said MacMordie.

'Well there's that too,' Hutchmeyer agreed, 'but we publish this Piper and if Baby wants him she's going to have him. You know something, MacMordie, you'd think at her age and all the operations she's had and being on a diet and all she'd have laid off a bit. I mean, can you do it twice a day every goddam day of the year? Well, me neither. But that woman is insatiable. She's going to eat this cunt-lapper Piper alive.'

MacMordie made a note to book the company plane for Piper.

'Could be there won't be so much of him to eat by the time the reception committee down here is finished with him,' he said morosely. 'The way you want it things could get rough.'

'The rougher the better. By the time my fucking wife is through with him he's going to know just how rough things can get. You know what that woman's been into now?'

'No,' said MacMordie.

'Bears,' said Hutchmeyer.

'Bears?' said MacMordie. 'You don't mean it. Isn't that a little dangerous? I'd have to be fucking desperate to even think of bears. I knew a woman once who had this German Shepherd but—'

'Not that way,' shouted Hutchmeyer, 'Jesus, MacMordie, we're talking about my wife, not some crazy bitch dog lover. Have some respect please.'

'But you said she was into bears and I thought—'

'The trouble with you, MacMordie, is you don't think. So she's into bears. Doesn't mean the bears are into her for Chrissake. Whoever heard of a woman into anything sexual? It isn't possible.'

'I don't know. I knew a woman once with this—'

'You want to know something, MacMordie, you know some fucking horrible women no kidding. You should get yourself a decent wife.'

'I got a decent wife. I don't go messing no longer. I just don't have the energy.'

'Should eat Wheatgerm and Vitamin E like I do. Helps get it up better than anything. What were we talking about?'

'Bears,' said MacMordie avidly.

'Baby's got this thing about ecology and wildlife. Been reading about animals being human and all. Some guy called Morris wrote a book . . .'

'I read that too,' said MacMordie.

'Not that Morris. This Morris worked in a zoo and had a naked ape and writes this book about it. Must have shaved the fucking thing. So Baby reads it and the next thing you know she has bought a lot of bears and things and let them loose round the house. Place is thick with bears and the neighbours start complaining just when I'm applying to join the Yacht Club. I tell you, that woman gives me a pain in the ass all the problems she manages to come up with.'

MacMordie looked puzzled. 'If this Morris guy went in for apes how come Mrs Hutchmeyer is into bears?' he asked.

'Whoever heard of a fucking naked ape in the Maine woods? It's impossible. The thing would freeze to death first snowfall and it's got to be natural.'

'Isn't natural having bears in your backyard. Not any place I know.'

'First thing I said to Baby. I said you want an ape it's okay with me but bears is into another ballgame. Know what she said? She said she'd had a naked fucking ape round the house forty years and bears needed protecting. Protecting? Three hundred fifty pounds they weigh and they need protection? Anyone round the place needs protection it's got to be me.'

'What did you do then?' asked MacMordie.

'Got myself a machine-gun and told her the first bear I saw coming into the house I'd blow its fucking head off. So the bears got the message and took to the woods and now it's all fine up there.'

It was all fine at sea too. Piper woke the next morning to find himself in a floating hotel but since his adult life had been spent moving from one boarding-house to another, each with a view of the English Channel, there was nothing very surprising about his new circumstances. True, the luxury he was now enjoying was better than the amenities offered by the Gleneagle Guest House in Exforth, but surroundings meant little to Piper. The main thing in his life was his writing and he continued his routine on the ship. In the morning he wrote at a table in his cabin and after lunch lay with Sonia on the sundeck discussing life, literature and *Pause O Men for the Virgin* in a haze of happiness.

'For the first time in my life I am truly happy,' he confided to his diary and that band of future scholars who would one day study his private life. 'My relationship with Sonia has added a new dimension to my existence and extended my understanding of what it means to be mature. Whether this can be called love only time will tell but is it not enough to know that we interrelate so personally? I can only find it in myself to regret that we have been brought together by so humanly debasing a book as *POMFTV*. But as Thomas Mann would have said with that symbolic irony which is the hallmark of his work "Every cloud has a silver lining", and one can only agree with him. Would that it were otherwise!!! Sonia insists on my re-reading the book so that I can imitate who wrote it. I find this very difficult, both the assumption that I am the author and the need to read what can only influence my own work for the worse. Still, I am persevering with the task and *Search for a Lost Childhood* is coming along as well as can be expected given the exigencies of my present predicament.'

There was a great deal more in the same vein. In the evening

Piper insisted on reading what he had written of *Search* aloud to Sonia when she would have preferred to be dancing or playing roulette. Piper disapproved of such frivolities. They were not part of those experiences which made up the significant relationships upon which great literature was founded.

'But shouldn't there be more action?' said Sonia one evening when he had finished reading his day's work. 'I mean nothing ever seems to happen. It's all description and what people think.'

'In the contemplative novel thought is action,' said Piper quoting verbatim from *The Moral Novel*. 'Only the immature mind finds satisfaction in action as an external activity. What we think and feel determines what we are and it is in the essential areness of the human character that the great dramas of life are enacted.'

'Ourness?' said Sonia hopefully.

'Areness,' said Piper. 'Are with an A.'

'Oh.'

'It means essential being. Like *Dasein*.'

'Don't you mean "design"?' said Sonia.

'No,' said Piper, who had once read several sentences from Heidegger, '*Dasein*'s got an A too.'

'You could have fooled me,' said Sonia. 'Still, if you say so.'

'And the novel if it is to justify itself as a mode of inter-communicative art must deal solely with experienced reality. The self-indulgent use of the imagination beyond the parameter of our personal experience demonstrates a superficiality which can only result in the unrealization of our individual potentialities.'

'Isn't that a bit limiting?' said Sonia. 'I mean if all you can write about is what has happened to you you've got to end up describing getting up in the morning and having breakfast and going to work . . .'

'Well, that's important too,' said Piper, whose morning's writing had consisted of a description of getting up and having breakfast and going to school. 'The novelist invests these events with his own intrinsic interpretation.'

'But maybe people don't want to read about that sort of thing. They want romance and sex and excitement. They want the unexpected. That's what sells.'

'It may sell,' said Piper, 'but does it matter?'

'It matters if you want to go on writing. You've got to earn your bread. Now *Pause* sells . . .'

'I can't imagine why,' said Piper. 'I read that chapter you told me to and honestly it's disgusting.'

'So reality isn't all that nice,' said Sonia, wishing that Piper wasn't quite so highminded. 'We live in a crazy world. There are hijackings and killings and violence all over and *Pause* isn't into that. It's about two people who need one another.'

'People like that shouldn't need one another,' said Piper, 'it's unnatural.'

'It's unnatural going to the moon and people still do it. And there are rockets with nuclear warheads pointing at one another ready to blow the world apart and just about everywhere you look there's something unnatural going on.'

'Not in *Search*,' said Piper.

'So what's that got to do with reality?'

'Reality,' said Piper reverting to *The Moral Novel*, 'has to do with the realness of things in an extra-ephemeral context. It is the reestablishment in the human consciousness of traditional values . . .'

While Piper quoted on Sonia sighed and wished that he would establish traditional values like ask her to marry him or even just climb into bed with her one night and make love in a good oldfashioned way. But here again Piper had principles. In bed at night his activities remained firmly literary. He read several pages of *Doctor Faustus* and then turned to *The Moral Novel* as to a breviary. Then he switched off the light and resisted Sonia's charms by falling fast asleep.

Sonia lay awake and wondered if he was queer or she unattractive, came to the conclusion that she was closeted with some kind of dedicated nut and, hopefully, a genius and decided to postpone any discussion of Piper's sexual proclivities to a later date. After all the main thing was to keep him cool and collected through the publicity tour and if chastity was what Piper wanted chastity was what he was going to get.

In fact it was Piper himself who raised the issue one afternoon as they lay on the sundeck. He had been thinking about what Sonia had said about his lack of experience and the need for a writer to have it. In Piper's mind experience was equated with observation. He sat up and decided to observe and was just in time to pay close attention to a middle-aged woman climbing out of the swimming bath. Her thighs, he noted, were dimpled. Piper reached for his ledger of Phrases and wrote down, 'Legs indented with the fingerprints of ardent time,' and then as an alternative, 'the hallmarks of past passion.'

'What are?' said Sonia looking over his shoulder.

'The dimples on that woman's legs,' Piper explained, 'the one that's just sitting down.'

Sonia examined the woman critically.

'They turn you on?'

'Certainly not,' said Piper, 'I was merely making a note of the fact. It could come in useful for a book. You said I needed more experience and I'm getting it.'

'That's a hell of a way to get experience,' said Sonia, 'voyeurizing ancient broads.'

'I wasn't voyeurizing anything. I was merely observing. There was nothing sexual about it.'

'I should have known,' said Sonia and lay back in her chair.

'Known what?'

'That there was nothing sexual about it. There never is with you.'

Piper sat and thought about the remark. There was a touch of bitterness about it that disturbed him. Sex. Sex and Sonia. Sex with Sonia. Sex and love. Sex with love and sex without love. Sex in general. A most perplexing subject and one that had for sixteen years upset the even tenor of his days and had produced a wealth of fantasies at variance with his literary principles. The great novels did not deal with sex. They confined themselves to love, and Piper had tried to do the same. He was reserving himself for that great love affair which would unite sex and love in an all-embracing and wholly rewarding totality of passion and sensibility in which the women of his fantasies, those mirages of arms, legs, breasts and buttocks, each particular item serving as the stimulus for a different dream, would merge into the perfect wife. With her because his feelings were on the highest plane he would be perfectly justified in doing the lowest possible things. The gulf that divided the beast in Piper from the angel in his truly beloved would be bridged by the fine flame of their passion, or some such. The great novels said so. Unfortunately they didn't explain how. Beyond love merged with passion there stretched something : Piper wasn't sure what. Presumably happiness. Anyway marriage would absolve him from the interruptions of his fantasies in which a predatory and beastly Piper prowled the dark streets in search of innocent victims and had his way with them which, considering that Piper had never had his way with anyone and lacked

71

any knowledge of female anatomy, would have landed him either in hospital or in the police courts.

And now in Sonia he seemed to have found a woman who appreciated him and should by rights have been the perfect woman. But there were snags. Piper's perfect woman, culled from the great novels, was a creature who combined purity with deep desires. Piper had no objection to deep desires provided they remained deep. Sonia's didn't. Even Piper could tell that. She emanated a readiness for sex which made things very awkward. For one thing it deprived him of his right to be predatory. You couldn't very well be beastly if the angel you were supposed to be beastly to was being even beastlier than you were. Beastliness was relative. Moreover it required a passivity that Sonia's kisses proved she lacked. Locked occasionally in her arms, Piper felt himself at the mercy of an enormously powerful woman and even Piper with his lack of imagination could not see himself being predatory with her. It was all extremely difficult and Piper, sitting on the sundeck watching the ship's wake widening towards the horizon, was struck once again by the contradiction between Life and Art. To relieve his feelings he opened his ledger and wrote, 'A mature relationship demands the sacrifice of the ideal in the interests of experience and one must come to terms with the Real.'

That night Piper armed himself to come to terms with the Real. He had two large vodkas before dinner, a bottle of Nuits St Georges, which seemed to be appropriately named for the encounter, during the meal, followed this with a Benedictine with his coffee and finally went down in the elevator breathing alcohol and endearments over Sonia.

'Look, you don't have to,' she said as he fondled her on the way down. Piper remained determined.

'Darling, we're two mature people,' he mumbled and walked unsteadily to the cabin. Sonia went inside and switched on the light. Piper switched it off again.

'I love you,' he said.

'Look, you don't have to appease your conscience,' said Sonia. 'And anyhow ...'

Piper breathed heavily and seized her with dedicated passion. The next moment they were on the bed.

'Your breasts, your hair, your lips ...'

'My period,' said Sonia.

'Your period,' murmured Piper. 'Your skin, your ...'

'Period,' said Sonia.

Piper stopped. 'What do you mean, your period?' he asked vaguely aware that something was amiss.

'My period period,' said Sonia. 'Get it?'

Piper had got it. With a bound the author by proxy of *Pause O Men for the Virgin* was off the bed and into the bathroom. There were more contradictions between Life and Art than he had ever dreamt of. Like physiological ones.

In the big house overlooking Freshman's Bay in Maine, Baby Hutchmeyer, née Sugg, Miss Penobscot 1935, lay languorously on her great waterbed and thought about Piper. Beside her was a copy of *Pause* and a glass of Scotch and Vitamin C. She had read the book three times now, and with each reading she had felt increasingly that here at last was a young author who truly appreciated what an older woman had to offer. Not that Baby was, in most aspects, older. At forty, read fifty-eight, she still had the body of an accident-prone eighteen-year-old and the face of an embalmed twenty-five. In short she had what it takes, the It in question having been taken by Hutchmeyer in the first ten years of their married life and left for the last thirty. What Hutchmeyer had to give by way of attention and bovine passion he bestowed on secretaries, stenographers and the occasional stripper in Las Vegas, Paris or Tokyo. In return for Baby's complaisancy he gave her money, indulged her enthusiasms whether artistic, social, metaphysical or ecocultural, and boasted in public about their happy marriage. Baby made do with bronzed young interior decorators and had the house and herself redone more times than was strictly necessary. She frequented hospitals that specialized in cosmetic surgery and Hutchmeyer, arriving home from one of his peripatetic passions, had once failed to recognize her. It was then that the matter of divorce first came up.

'So I don't grab you,' said Baby, 'well you don't grab me either. The last time you had it up was the fall of fifty-five and you were drunk then.'

'I must have been,' said Hutchmeyer and immediately regretted it. Baby pulled the rug from under.

'I've been looking into your affairs,' she said.

'So I have affairs. A man in my position's got to prove his virility. You think I'm going to get financial backing when I need it if I'm too old to screw.'

'You're not too old to screw,' said Baby, 'and I'm not talking about those affairs. I'm talking financial affairs. Now you want a divorce it's all right with me. We split fifty-fifty and the price is twenty million bucks.'

'Are you crazy?' yelled Hutchmeyer. 'No way!'

'Then no divorce. I've done an audit on your books and those are the affairs I'm talking of. Now if you want the Internal Revenue boys and the FBI and the courts to know you've been evading taxes and accepting bribes and handling laundered money for organized crime . . .'

Hutchmeyer didn't. 'You go your way I'll go mine,' he said bitterly.

'And just remember,' said Baby, 'that if anything happens to me like I die suddenly and like unnaturally I've stashed photocopies of all your little misdemeanours with my lawyers and in a bank vault too . . .'

Hutchmeyer hadn't forgotten it. He had an extra seat belt installed in Baby's Lincoln and saw to it she didn't take any risks. The interior decorators returned and so did actors, painters and anyone else Baby fancied. Even MacMordie got dragged one night into the act and was promptly docked a thousand dollars from his salary for what Hutchmeyer lividly called fringe benefits. MacMordie didn't see it that way and had protested to Baby. Hutchmeyer reimbursed him two thousand and apologized.

But for all these side-effects Baby remained unsatisfied. When she wasn't able to find someone or something interesting to do, she read. At first Hutchmeyer had welcomed the move into literacy as an indication that Baby was either growing up or dying down. As usual he was wrong. The strain of self-improvement that had manifested itself in her numerous cosmetic operations combined now with intellectual aspirations to form a fearful hybrid. From being a simple if scarred broad Baby graduated to a well-read woman. The first intimation Hutchmeyer had of this development came when he returned from the Frankfurt Book Fair to find her into *The Idiot*.

'You find it what?' he said when she told him she found it fascinating and relevant. 'Relevant to what?'

'To the spiritual crisis in contemporary society,' said Baby. 'To us.'

'*The Idiot*'s relevant to us?' said Hutchmeyer, scandalized. 'A guy thinks he's Napoleon and icepicks some old dame and that's relevant to us? That is all I need right now. A hole in the head.'

74

'You've got one. That's *Crime and Punishment*, Dummkopf. For a publisher you know but nothing.'

'I know how to sell books. I don't have to read the goddam things,' said Hutchmeyer. 'Books is for people who don't get satisfaction in doing things. Like vicarious.'

'They teach you things,' said Baby.

'Like what? Having apoplectic fits?' said Hutchmeyer who had finally got his bearings on *The Idiot*.

'Epileptic. A sign of genius. Like Mohammed had them.'

'So now I've got an encyclopedia for a wife,' said Hutchmeyer, 'and with Arabs. What are you going to do? Turn this house into a literary Mecca or something?' And leaving Baby with the germ of this idea he had flown hurriedly to Tokyo and the physical pleasures of a woman who couldn't speak English let alone read it. He came back to find Baby had been into Dostoyevsky and out the other side. She was devouring books with as little discrimination as her bears were now devouring blueberry patches. She hit Ayn Rand with as much fervour as Tolstoy, swept amazingly through Dos Passos, lathered in Lawrence, saunaed in Strindberg and then birched herself with Céline. The list was endless and Hutchmeyer found himself married to a biblionut. To make matters worse Baby got into authors. Hutchmeyer loathed authors. They talked about their books and Hutchmeyer under threat from Baby found himself forced to be relatively polite and apparently interested. Even Baby found them disappointing but since the presence of even one novelist in the house sent Hutchmeyer's blood pressure soaring she was generous in her invitations and continued to live in hopes of finding one who lived in the flesh up to his words on paper. And with Peter Piper and *Pause O Men for the Virgin* she felt sure that here at last was a man and his book without discrepancy. She lay on the waterbed and savoured her expectations. It was such a romantic novel. In a significant sort of way. And different.

Hutchmeyer came through from the bathroom wearing a quite unnecessary truss.

'That thing suits you,' said Baby studying the contraption dispassionately. 'You should wear it more often. It gives you dignity.'

Hutchmeyer glared at her.

'No, I mean it,' Baby continued. 'Like it gives you a supportive role.'

'With you to support I need it,' said Hutchmeyer.

'Well, if you've got a hernia you should have it operated on.'

'Seeing what they've done with you I don't need no operations,' Hutchmeyer said. He glanced at *Pause* and went through to his room.

'You still like that book?' he called out presently.

'First good book you've published in years,' said Baby. 'It's beautiful. An idyll.'

'A what?'

'An idyll. You want me to tell you what an idyll is?'

'No,' said Hutchmeyer, 'I can guess.' He climbed into bed and thought about it. An idyll? Well if she said an idyll, an idyll was what it would be to a million other women. Baby was infallible. Still, an idyll?

Chapter 9

There was nothing idyllic about the scene that greeted Piper when the ship berthed in New York. Even the fabulous view of the skyline and the Statue of Liberty, which Sonia had promised would send him, didn't. A heavy mist hung over the river and the great buildings only emerged from it as they moved slowly past the Battery and inched into the berth. By that time Piper's attention had been drawn from the view of Manhattan to a large number of people with visibly different backgrounds and opinions who were gathered on the roadway outside the Customs shed.

'Boy, Hutch has really done you proud,' said Sonia as they went down the gangway. There were shouts from the street and a glimpse of banners some of which said ambiguously, 'Welcome To Gay City', and others even more ominously, 'Go Home, Peipmann'.

'Who on earth is Peipmann?' Piper asked.

'Don't ask me,' said Sonia.

'Peipmann?' said the Customs Officer not bothering to open their bags. 'I wouldn't know. There's a million hags and fags out there waiting for him. Some are for lynching him and others for worse. Have a nice trip.'

Sonia hustled Piper away with their luggage through a barrier to where MacMordie was waiting with a crowd of reporters. 'Pleased to make your acquaintance, Mr Piper,' he said. 'Now if you'll just step this way.'

Piper stepped this way and was immediately surrounded by cameramen and reporters who shouted incomprehensible questions.

'Just say "No comment",' shouted MacMordie as Piper tried to explain that he had never been to Russia. 'That way nobody gets the wrong idea.'

'It's a bit late for that, isn't it?' said Sonia. 'Who the hell told these goons he was in the KGB?'

MacMordie grinned with complicity and the swarm with Piper at its centre moved out into the entrance hall. A squad of cops fought their way through the newsmen and escorted Piper into an elevator. Sonia and MacMordie went down the stairs.

'What in the name of hell gives?' asked Sonia.

'Mr Hutchmeyer's orders,' said MacMordie. 'A riot he asks for, a riot he gets.'

'But you didn't have to say that about him being a hit man for Idi Amin,' said Sonia bitterly. 'Jesus wept!'

At street level it was clear that MacMordie had said a great many other things about Piper, all of them conflicting. A contingent of Survivors of Siberia surged round the entrance chanting, 'Solzhenitsyn Yes. Piperovsky No.' Behind them a band of Arabs for Palestine, acting on the assumption that Piper was an Israeli Minister travelling incognito on an arms-buying mission, battled with Zionists whom MacMordie had alerted to the arrival of Piparfat of the Black September Movement. Farther back a small group of older Jews carried banners denouncing Peipmann but were heavily outnumbered by squads of Irishmen whose information was that O'Piper was a leading member of the IRA.

'Cops are all Irish,' MacMordie explained to Sonia. 'Best to have them on our side.'

'And which goddam side is that?' said Sonia but at that moment the elevator doors opened and an ashen-faced Piper was hustled into public view by his police escort. As the crowd outside surged forward the reporters continued their indefatigable quest for the truth.

'Mr Piper, would you mind just telling us who and what the hell you are?' one of them shouted above the din. But Piper was speechless. His eyes started out of his head and his face was grey.

'Is it true that you personally shot . . .?'

'Can we take it that your government isn't negotiating the purchase of Minutemen rockets?'

'How many people are still in mental . . .'

'I know one who soon will be if you don't do something fast,' said Sonia thrusting MacMordie forward. MacMordie launched himself into the fray.

'Mr Piper has nothing to say,' he yelled gratuitously before being hurled to one side by a cop who had just been hit by a bottle of Seven-Up thrown by an Anti-Apartheid protester for whom Van Piper was a White South African racist. Sonia Futtle shoved past him.

'Mr Piper is a famous British novelist,' she bawled but the time had passed for such unequivocal statements. More missiles rained against the wall of the building, banners disintegrated and were used as weapons, and Piper was dragged back into the hall.

'I haven't shot anyone,' he squawked. 'I've never been to Poland.' But no one heard him. There was a crackle of walkie-talkies and an urgent plea for police reinforcements. Outside the Survivors of Siberia had succumbed to the Gay Liberationists who were fighting for their own. A number of middle-aged dragsters broke through the police cordon and swooped on Piper.

'No, I'm nothing of the kind,' he yelled as they tried to rescue him from the cops. 'I'm simply a normal . . .' Sonia grabbed a pole which had once held a sign saying 'Golden Oldies Love You', and fended off the falsies of one of Piper's captors.

'Oh no he's not,' she shrieked, 'he's mine!' and dewigged another. Then flailing about her she drove the Gay Liberationists out of the lobby. Behind her Piper and the cops cowered while MacMordie shouted encouragement. In the medley outside Arabs For Palestine and Zionists For Israel momentarily united and completed the demolition of Gay Liberation before joining battle again. By that time Sonia had dragged Piper into the elevator. MacMordie joined them and pressed the button. For the next twenty minutes they went up and down while the struggle for Piparfat, O'Piper and Peipmann raged on outside.

'You've really screwed things up now,' Sonia told MacMordie. 'It takes me all my time to get the poor guy over here and you have to arrange Custer's Last Stand for a welcome.'

In the corner the poor guy was sitting on the floor. MacMordie ignored him. 'The product needed exposure and it's sure getting it. This will hit prime time TV. I wouldn't wonder there aren't news flashes going out now.'

'Great,' said Sonia, 'and what have you got laid on for us next? The Hindenburg disaster?'

'So this is going to hit the headlines . . .' MacMordie began but there was a low moan from the corner. Something had already hit Piper. His hand was bleeding. Sonia knelt beside him.

'What happened, honey?' she asked. Piper pointed wanly at a frisbee on which were painted the words Gulag Go. The frisbee was edged with razor blades. Sonia turned on MacMordie.

'I suppose that was your idea too,' she yelled. 'Frisbees with razor blades. You could guillotine someone with a thing like that.'

79

'Me? I didn't have a thing—' MacMordie began but Sonia had stopped the elevator.

'Ambulance! Ambulance,' she shouted, but it was an hour before the police managed to get Piper out of the building. By that time Hutchmeyer's instructions had been carried out. So had a large number of protesters who had been rushed to hospital. The streets were littered with broken glass, smashed banners and tear-gas canisters. As Piper was helped into the ambulance his eyes were streaming tears. He sat nursing his injured hand and the conviction that he had come to a madhouse.

'What did I do wrong?' he asked Sonia pathetically.

'Nothing. Nothing at all.'

'You were great, just great,' said MacMordie appreciatively and studied Piper's wound. 'Pity there's not more blood.'

'What more do you want?' snarled Sonia. 'Two pounds of flesh? Haven't you got enough already?'

'Blood,' said MacMordie. 'Colour TV you can tell the difference from ketchup. This has got to be authentic.' He turned to the nurse. 'You got any whole blood?'

'Whole blood? For a scratch like that you want whole blood?' she said.

'Listen,' said MacMordie, 'this guy's a haemophiliac. You going to let him bleed to death?'

'I am not a haemophiliac,' protested Piper but the siren drowned his voice.

'He needs a transfusion,' shouted MacMordie. 'Give me that blood.'

'Are you out of your fucking mind?' screamed Sonia as MacMordie grappled with the nurse. 'Hasn't he been through enough without you wanting to give him a blood transfusion?'

'I don't want a transfusion,' squeaked Piper frantically. 'I don't need one.'

'Yea but the TV cameras do,' said MacMordie. 'In Technicolor.'

'I will not give the patient . . .' said the nurse but MacMordie had grabbed the bottle and was wrestling with the cap.

'You don't even know his blood group,' the nurse yelled as the cap came off.

'No need to,' said MacMordie and emptied most of the bottle over Piper's head.

80

'Now look what you've done,' bawled Sonia. Piper had passed out.

'Okay so we resuscitate him,' said MacMordie. 'This is going to make Kildare look like nothing,' and he clamped the oxygen mask over Piper's face. By the time Piper was lifted out of the ambulance on a stretcher he looked like death itself. Under the mask and the blood his face had turned purple. In the excitement nobody had thought to turn the oxygen on.

'Is he still alive?' asked a reporter who had followed the ambulance.

'Who knows?' said MacMordie enthusiastically. Piper was carried into Casualty while a bloodstained Sonia tried to calm the nurse who was having hysterics.

'It was too terrible. Never in my whole life have I known such a thing and in my ambulance too,' she screamed at the TV cameras and reporters before being led away after her patient. As the crimson stretcher with Piper's body was lifted on to a trolley and wheeled away, MacMordie wiped his hands with satisfaction. Around him the TV cameras buzzed. The product had got exposure. Mr Hutchmeyer would be pleased.

Mr Hutchmeyer was. He watched the riot on TV with evident satisfaction and all the fervour of a fight enthusiast.

'That's my boy,' he yelled as a young Zionist flattened an innocent Japanese passenger off the ship with a placard saying 'Remember Lod'. A cop tried to intervene and was promptly felled by something in drag. The picture joggled violently as the cameraman was hit from behind. When it finally steadied it was focused on an elderly woman lying bleeding on the ground.

'Great,' said Hutchmeyer, 'MacMordie's done a great job. That boy's got a real talent for action.'

'That's what you think,' said Baby, who knew better.

'What the hell do you mean by that?' said Hutchmeyer, momentarily diverted. Baby shrugged.

'I just don't like violence is all.'

'Violence? So life is violent. Competitive. That's the way the cookie crumbles.'

Baby studied the screen. 'There's two more cookies just crumbled now,' she said.

'Human nature,' said Hutchmeyer, 'I didn't invent human nature.'

'Just exploit it.'

'Make a living.'

'Make a killing if you ask me,' said Baby. 'That woman's not going to make it.'

'Shit,' said Hutchmeyer.

'Took the word out of my mouth,' said Baby. Hutchmeyer concentrated on the screen and tried to ignore Baby. A police posse with Piper came out of Customs.

'That's him,' said Hutchmeyer. 'The motherfucker looks like he's pissing himself.'

Baby looked and sighed. The haunted Piper was just as she had hoped, young, pale, sensitive and intensely vulnerable. Like Keats at Waterloo she thought.

'Who's the fatso with MacMordie?' she asked as Sonia kneed a Ukrainian who had just spat on her dress.

'That's my girl,' shouted Hutchmeyer enthusiastically. Baby looked at him incredulously.

'You've got to be joking. One bounce with that female Russian shotput and you'd bust your truss.'

'Never mind my goddam truss,' said Hutchmeyer, 'I'm just telling you that that baby there is the greatest little saleswoman in the world.'

'Great she may be,' said Baby, 'little she ain't. That Muscovite doubled up with lover's balls knows that. What's her name?'

'Sonia Futtle,' said Hutchmeyer dreamily.

'I could have guessed,' said Baby, 'she's just futtled an Irishman now. He'll never ride again.'

'Jesus,' said Hutchmeyer and retreated to his study to avoid the disillusionment of Baby's commentary. He put a call through to the New York office for a computer forecast on predicted sales of *Pause O Men for the Virgin* in the light of this great new publicity. Then he got through to Production and ordered another half million copies. Finally a call to Hollywood and a demand for another five per cent in TV serial takings. And all the time his mind was busy with wanton thoughts of Sonia Futtle and same natural way of killing what remained of Miss Penobscot 1935 so that he wouldn't have to part with twenty million dollars to get a divorce. Maybe MacMordie could come up with something. Like fucking her to death. That would be natural. And this Piper guy had a hard-on for old women. Could be there was something there.

. . . . .

In the emergency theatre at the Roosevelt Hospital doctors and surgeons struggled to save Piper's life. The fact that appearances led them to suppose he had bled to death from a head wound while his symptoms were those of suffocation made their task more complicated than it might otherwise have been. The hysterical nurse was no help at all.

'He said he was a bleeder,' she told the chief surgeon who could see that already, 'he said he had to have a transfusion. I didn't want to do it and he said he didn't want one and she told him not to and he got at the blood bank and then he passed out and then they put him on resuscitation and —'

'Put her on sedation,' shouted the surgeon as the nurse was dragged out still screaming. On the operating table Piper was bald. In a desperate attempt to find the site of the wound his hair had been clipped.

'So where the fuck's the haemorrhage?' said the surgeon, shining a light down Piper's left ear in the hope of finding some source for this terrible loss of blood. By the time Piper revived they were none the wiser. The scratch on his hand had been cleansed and covered with a Band-Aid and through a needle in his right wrist he was getting the transfusion he had dreaded. Finally they cut off the supply and Piper got off the table.

'You've had a lucky escape,' said the surgeon. 'I don't know what you're suffering from but you want to take it easy for a while. Maybe the Mayo could come up with an answer. We sure as hell can't.'

Piper wobbled out into the corridor bald as a coot. Sonia burst into tears.

'Oh my God what have they done to you, my darling?' she wailed. MacMordie studied Piper's bald head thoughtfully.

'That doesn't look so good,' he said finally and went into the theatre. 'We've got ourselves a problem,' he told the surgeon.

'No need to tell me. Diagnostically I wouldn't know.'

'Yeah,' said MacMordie, 'it's like that. Now what he needs is bandages round his head. I mean he's famous and there's all those TV guys out there and he's going to come out looking like Kojak and he's an author. That isn't going to improve his image.'

'His image is your problem,' said the surgeon, 'mine just happens to be his illness.'

'You cut his hair all off,' said MacMordie. 'Now how about a whole heap of bandages? Like right across his face and all. This guy needs his anonymity till his hair grows back.'

'No way,' said the surgeon, true to his medical principles.

'A thousand dollars,' said MacMordie and went to fetch Piper. He came reluctantly and clutching Sonia's arm pathetically. By the time he emerged and went outside with Sonia on one side and a nurse on the other only two frightened eyes and his nostrils were visible.

'Mr Piper has nothing to say,' said MacMordie quite unnecessarily. Several million viewers could see that. Piper's bandaged face had no mouth. For them he could have been the invisible man. The cameras zoomed in for close-ups and MacMordie spoke.

'Mr Piper has authorized me to say that he had no idea his great novel *Pause O Men for the Virgin* would arouse the degree of public controversy that has marked the start of his lecture tour of this country . . .'

'His what?' demanded a reporter.

'Mr Piper is Britain's greatest novelist. His novel *Pause O Men for the Virgin* published by Hutchmeyer Press and available at seven dollars ninety—'

'You mean his novel caused all this?' said an interviewer.

MacMordie nodded. '*Pause O Men for the Virgin* is the most controversial novel of this century. Read it and see what has caused this terrible sacrifice on Mr Piper's part . . .'

Beside him Piper swayed groggily and had to be helped down the steps to the waiting car.

'Where are you taking him to now?'

'He's being flown to a private clinic for diagnostic treatment,' said MacMordie and the car moved off. In the back seat Piper whimpered through his bandages.

'What's that, darling?' Sonia asked. But Piper's mumble was incomprehensible.

'What was all that about a diagnostic treatment?' Sonia asked MacMordie. 'He doesn't need—'

'Just to throw the press and media off the trail. Mr Hutchmeyer wants you to stay with him at his residence in Maine. We're going to the airport. Mr Hutchmeyer's private plane is waiting.'

'I'll have something to say to Mr Goddam Hutchmeyer when I see him,' said Sonia. 'It's a wonder you didn't get us all killed.'

MacMordie turned in his seat. 'Listen,' he said, 'you try promoting a foreign writer. He's got to have a gimmick like he's won the Nobel

Prize or been tortured in the Lubianka or something. Charisma. Now what's this Piper got? Nothing. So we build him up. We have ourselves a little riot, a bit of blood and all and overnight he's charismatic. And with those bandages he's going to be in every home tonight on TV. Sell a million copies on that face alone.'

They drove to the airport and Sonia and Piper climbed aboard *Imprint One*. Only when they had taken off did Sonia remove the bandages from Piper's face.

'We'll have to leave the rest on till your hair starts to grow again,' she said. Piper nodded his bandaged head.

From Maine Hutchmeyer phoned his congratulations to MacMordie. 'That scene outside the hospital was the greatest,' he said, 'that's going to blow a million viewers' minds. Why we've made a martyr out of him. Like a sacrificial lamb on the altar of great literature. I tell you, MacMordie, for this you get a bonus.'

'It was nothing,' said MacMordie modestly.

'How did he take it?' asked Hutchmeyer.

'Well he seemed a little confused is all,' said MacMordie. 'He'll get over it.'

'All authors have confused minds,' said Hutchmeyer, 'it's natural with them.'

Chapter 10

And Piper spent the flight in a confused state of mind. He still wasn't sure what had hit him or why and his mixed reception as O'Piper, Piparfat, Peipmann, Piperovsky *et al.* added to the problems already confronting him as the supposititious author of *Pause*. And in any case as a putative genius Piper had assumed so many different identities that past personae compounded those of the present. So did shock, MacMordie's bloodbath, suffocation, resuscitation, and the fact that he was wearing a turban of bandages over an unscathed scalp. He stared out of the window and wondered what Conrad or Lawrence or George Eliot would have done in his position. Apart from the certainty that they wouldn't have been in it, he could think of nothing. And Sonia was no great help. Her mind seemed set on making the financial most from his ordeal.

'Either way we've got him over a barrel,' she said as the plane began to descend over Bangor. 'You're too sick to go through with this tour.'

'I absolutely agree,' said Piper.

Sonia crushed his hopes. 'He won't wear that one,' she said. 'With Hutchmeyer it's the contract counts. You could be on an intravenous drip and you'd still have to make appearances. So we sting him for compensation. Like another twenty-five thousand dollars.'

'I think I would rather go home,' said Piper.

'The way I'm going to play it you'll go home with fifty grand.'

Piper raised objections. 'But won't Mr Hutchmeyer be very cross?'

'Cross? He'll blow his top.'

Piper considered the prospect of Mr Hutchmeyer blowing his top and disliked it. It added yet another awful ingredient to a situation that was already sufficiently alarming. By the time the plane landed he was in a state of acute anxiety and it took all Sonia's coaxing to get him down the steps and into the waiting car. Presently they were speeding through pine forests towards the man whom Frensic in an unguarded moment had spoken of as the Al Capone of the publishing world.

86

'Now you leave all the talking to me,' said Sonia, 'and just remember that you're a shy introverted author. Modesty is the line to take.'

The car turned down a drive towards a house that had proclaimed itself by the gate as 'The Hutchmeyer Residence'.

'No one can call that modest,' said Piper staring out at the house. It stood in fifty acres of park and garden, birch and pine, an ornate shingle-style monument to the romantic eclecticism of the late nineteenth century as embodied in wood by Peabody and Stearns, Architects. Sprouting towers, dormer windows, turrets with dovecotes, piazzas with oval windows cut in their latticework, convoluted chimneys and angled balconies, the Residence was awe-inspiring. They drove under a porte-cochère into a courtyard already crammed with cars and got out. A moment later the enormous front door opened and a large red-faced man bounded down the steps.

'Sonia baby,' he bawled and hugged her to his Hawaiian shirt, 'and this must be Mr Piper.' He crunched Piper's hand and stared fiercely into his face. 'This is a great honour, Mr Piper, a very great honour to have you with us,' and still holding Piper's hand he propelled him up the steps and through the door. Inside, the house was as remarkable as the exterior. A vast hall incorporated a thirteenth-century fireplace, a Renaissance staircase, a minstrels' gallery, an excruciatingly ferocious portrait of Hutchmeyer in the pose of J. P. Morgan as photographed by Steichner, and underfoot a mosaic floor depicting a great many stages in the manufacture of paper. Piper stepped cautiously across falling trees, a log jam and a vat of boiling wood pulp and up several more steps at the top of which stood a woman of breathtaking shape.

'Baby,' said Hutchmeyer, 'I want you to meet Mr Peter Piper. Mr Piper, my wife, Baby.'

'Dear Mr Piper,' murmured Baby huskily, taking his hand and smiling as far as the surgeons had permitted, 'I've been just dying to meet you. I think your novel is just the loveliest book I've been privileged to read.'

Piper gazed into the limpid azure contact lenses of Miss Penobscot 1935 and simpered. 'You're too kind,' he murmured. Baby tucked his hand under her arm and together they went into the piazza lounge.

'Does he always wear a turban?' Hutchmeyer asked Sonia as they followed.

'Only when he gets hit with a frisbee,' said Sonia coldly.

87

'Only when he gets hit with a frisbee,' bawled Hutchmeyer roaring with laughter. 'You hear that, Baby. Mr Piper only wears a turban when he gets hit with a frisbee. Isn't that the greatest?'

'Edged with razor blades, Hutch. With goddam razor blades!' said Sonia.

'Yeah, well that's different of course,' said Hutchmeyer deflating. 'With razor blades is different.'

Inside the piazza lounge stood a hundred people. They clutched glasses and were talking at the tops of their voices.

'Folks,' bawled Hutchmeyer and stilled the din, 'I want you all to meet Mr Peter Piper, the greatest novelist to come out of England since Frederick Forsyth.'

Piper smiled inanely and shook his head with unaffected modesty. He was not the greatest novelist to come out of England. Not yet. His greatness lay in the future and it was on the point of his tongue to state this clearly when the crowd closed round him eager to make his acquaintance. Baby had chosen her guests with care. Against their geriatric backdrop her own reconstituted charms would stand out all the more alluringly. Cataracts and fallen arches abounded. So did bosoms, as opposed to breasts, dentures, girdles, surgical stockings and the protruberant tracery of varicose veins. And strung round every puckered neck and blotchy wrist were jewels, an armoury of pearls and diamonds and gold that hung and wobbled and glistened to detract the eye from the lost battle with time.

'Oh, Mr Piper, I just want to say how much pleasure . . .'

'I can't tell you how much it means to me to . . .'

'I think it's fascinating to meet a real . . .'

'If you would just sign my copy . . .'

'You've done so much to bring people together . . .'

With Baby on his arm Piper was swallowed up in the adulating crowd.

'Boy, he's really going over big,' said Hutchmeyer, 'and this is Maine. What's he going to do to the cities?'

'I hate to think,' said Sonia watching anxiously as Piper's turban bobbed among the hairdos.

'Wow them. Zap them. We'll sell two million copies if this is anything to indicate. I got a computer forecast after the welcome he got in New York and—'

'Welcome? You call that riot a welcome?' said Sonia bitterly. 'You could have got us killed.'

'Great copy,' said Hutchmeyer, 'I'm going to give MacMordie a bonus. That boy's got talent. And while we're on the subject let me say I've got a proposition to make to you.'

'I've heard your propositions, Hutch, and the answer is still no.'

'Sure but this is different.' He steered Sonia over to the bar.

By the time he had signed fifty copies of *Pause O Men for the Virgin* and drunk, unthinkingly, four Martinis, Piper's earlier apprehensions had entirely vanished. The enthusiasm with which he was being greeted had the merit that it didn't require him to say anything. He was bombarded from all sides by compliments and opinions. They seemed to come in two sizes. The thin women were intense, the ones with obesity problems cooed. No one expected Piper to contribute more than the favour of his smile. Only one woman broached the subject of his novel and Baby immediately intervened.

'Knock you up, Chloe?' she said. 'Now why should Mr Piper want to do that? He's got a very tight schedule to meet.'

'So not everyone's had the benefit of a pussy lift,' said Chloe with a hideous wink at Piper. 'Now the way I read it Mr Piper's book is about going into the natural in a big way . . .'

But Baby dragged Piper away before he could hear what Chloe had to say about going into the natural in a big way.

'What's a pussy lift?' he asked.

'That Chloe's just a cat,' said Baby, leaving Piper under the happy illusion that pussy lifts were things cats went up and down in. By the time the party broke up Piper was exhausted.

'I've put you in the Boudoir bedroom,' said Baby as she and Sonia escorted him up the Renaissance staircase. 'It's got a wonderful view of the bay.'

Piper went into the Boudoir bedroom and looked around. Originally designed to combine convenience with medieval simplicity, it had been refurbished by Baby with an eye to the supposedly sensual. A heart-shaped bed stood on a carpet of intermingled rainbows which competed for radiance with a furbelowed stool and an Art Deco dressing-table. To complete the ensemble a large and evidently demented Spanish gypsy supported a tasselled lampshade on a bedside table while a black glass chest of drawers gleamed darkly against the Wedgwood blue walls. Piper sat down on the bed and looked up at the great timber rafters. There was a solid craftsmanship about them that contrasted with the ephemeral brilliance of the furnishings.

He undressed and brushed his teeth and climbed into bed. Five minutes later he was asleep.

An hour later he was wide awake again. There were voices coming through the wall behind his quilted bedhead. For a moment Piper wondered where on earth he was. The voices soon told him. The Hutchmeyers' bedroom was evidently next to his and their bathroom had a connecting door. During the next half an hour Piper learnt to his disgust that Hutchmeyer wore a truss, that Baby objected to his use of the washbasin as a urinal, that Hutchmeyer didn't give a damn what she objected to, that Baby's late and unlamented mother, Mrs Sugg, would have done the world a service by having an abortion before Baby was born, and finally that on one traumatic occasion Baby had washed down a sleeping pill with Dentaclene from a glass containing Hutchmeyer's false teeth so would he kindly not leave the things in the medicine cabinet. From these distressing domestic details the conversation veered to personalities. Hutchmeyer thought Sonia mighty attractive. Baby didn't. All Sonia Futtle had got were her hooks into a cute little innocent. It took Piper a moment or two to recognize himself in this description and he was just wondering if he liked being called little and cute when Hutchmeyer riposted by saying he was an asslicking motherfucking Limey who just happened to have written a book that would sell. Piper most definitely didn't like that. He sat up in bed, fumbled with the anatomy of the Spanish Gipsy and switched the light on. But the Hutchmeyers had warred themselves to sleep.

Piper got out of bed and waded across the carpet to the window. Outside in the darkness he could just make out the shapes of a yacht and a large cruiser lying out at the end of a long narrow jetty. Beyond them across the bay a mountain was silhouetted against the starry sky and the lights of a small town shone faintly. Water slapped on the rocky beach below the house and in any other circumstances Piper would have felt the need to muse on the beauties of nature and their possible use in some future novel. Hutchmeyer's opinion of him had driven such thoughts from his mind. He got out his diary and committed to paper his observations that Hutchmeyer was the epitome of everything that was vulgar, debased, stupid and crassly commercial about modern America and that Baby Hutchmeyer was a woman of sensitivity and beauty, and deserved something better than to be married to a coarse brute. Then he got back into bed, read a chapter

90

of *The Moral Novel* to restore his faith in human nature, and fell asleep.

Breakfast next morning proved a further ordeal. Sonia wasn't up and Hutchmeyer was in his friendliest mood.

'What I like about you is you give your readers a good fuck fantasy,' he told Piper who was trying to make up his mind which breakfast cereal to try.

'Wheatgerm is great for Vitamin E,' said Baby.

'That's for potency,' said Hutchmeyer. 'Piper's potent already, eh Piper? What he needs is roughage.'

'I'm sure he'll get all he needs of roughage from you,' said Baby. Piper poured himself a plateful of Wheatgerm.

'Now like I was saying,' Hutchmeyer continued, 'what readers want is—'

'I'm sure Mr Piper knows already what readers want,' said Baby, 'he doesn't have to hear it over breakfast.'

Hutchmeyer ignored her. 'A guy comes home from work what's he to do? Has himself a beer and watches TV, eats and goes to bed too tired to lay his wife so he reads a book—'

'If he's that tired why does he need to read a book?' asked Baby.

'He's too damned tired to sleep. Needs something to send him off. So he picks up a book and has fantasies he's not in the Bronx but in . . . where did you set your book?'

'East Finchley,' said Piper, having trouble with a mouthful of Wheatgerm.

'Devon,' said Baby, 'the book is set in Devon.'

'Devon?' said Hutchmeyer. 'He says it's set in East Finchley, he ought to know for Chrissake. He wrote the goddam thing.'

'It's set in Devon and Oxford,' said Baby stubbornly. 'She has this big house and he—'

'Devon's right,' said Piper, 'I was thinking of my second book.'

Hutchmeyer glowered. 'Yeah, well, wherever. So this guy in the Bronx has fantasies he's in Devon with this old broad who's crazy about him and before he knows it he's asleep.'

'That's a great recommendation,' said Baby, 'and I don't think Mr Piper writes his books with insomniacs in the Bronx in mind. He portrays a developing relationship . . .'

'Sure, sure he does but—'

'The hesitations and uncertainties of a young man whose feelings

91

and emotional responses deviate from the socially accepted norms of his socio-sexual age grouping.'

'Right,' said Hutchmeyer, 'no question about it. He's a deviant and—'

'He is not a deviant,' said Baby, 'he is a very gifted adolescent with an identity problem and Gwendolen . . .'

While Piper munched his Wheatgerm the battle about his intentions in writing *Pause* raged on. Since Piper hadn't written the book and Hutchmeyer hadn't read it, Baby came out on top. Hutchmeyer retreated to his study and Piper found himself alone with a woman who, for quite the wrong reasons, shared his own opinion that he was a great writer. And cute. Piper had reservations about being called cute by a woman whose own attractions were sufficiently at odds with one another to be disturbing. In the dim light of the party the night before he had supposed her to be thirty-five. Now he was less sure. Beneath her blouse her bra-less breasts pointed to the early twenties. Her hands didn't. Finally there was her face. It had a masklike quality, a lack of anything remotely individual, irregular or out of harmony with the faces of the two-dimensional women he had seen staring so fixedly from the pages of women's magazines like *Vogue*. Taut, impersonal and characterless it held a strange fascination for him, while her limpid azure eyes . . . Piper found himself thinking of Yeats' *Sailing to Byzantium* and the artifice of jewelled birds that sang. To steady himself he read the label on the Wheatgerm jar and found that he had just consumed 740 milligrammes of phosphorus, 550 of potassium, together with vast quantities of other essential minerals and every Vitamin B under the sun.

'It seems to have a lot of Vitamin B,' he said, avoiding the allure of those eyes.

'The Bs give you energy,' murmured Baby.

'And As?' asked Piper.

'Vitamin A smooths the mucous membranes,' said Baby and once again Piper was dimly conscious that beneath this dietetic commentary there lurked an undertow of dangerous suggestion. He looked up from the Wheatgerm label and was held once more by that masklike face and limpid azure eyes.

Chapter 11

Sonia Futtle rose late. Never an early riser, she had slept more heavily than usual. The strain of the previous day had taken its toll. She came downstairs to find the house empty apart from Hutchmeyer who was growling into the telephone in his study. She made herself some coffee and interrupted him.

'Have you seen Peter?' she asked.

'Baby's taken him some place. They'll be back,' said Hutchmeyer. 'Now about that proposition I put to you . . .'

'No way. F & F is a good agency. We're doing well. So what would I want to change?'

'It's a Vice-Presidency I'm offering you,' said Hutchmeyer, 'and the offer stays open.'

'The only offer I'm interested in right now,' said Sonia, 'is the one you're going to make my client for all the physical injury and mental suffering and public ridicule he sustained as a result of yesterday's riot you organized at the docks.'

'Physical injury? Mental suffering?' shouted Hutchmeyer incredulously. 'That was the greatest publicity in the world and you want me to make an offer?'

Sonia nodded. 'Compensation. In the region of twenty-five thousand.'

'Twenty-five . . . Are you crazy? Two million I give him for that book and you want to take me for another twenty-five grand?'

'I do,' said Sonia. 'There is nothing in the contract that says my client has to be subjected to violence, assault and the attentions of lethal frisbees. Now you organized that caper—'

'Go jump,' said Hutchmeyer.

'In that case I shall advise Mr Piper to cancel the tour.'

'You do that,' shouted Hutchmeyer, 'and I'll sue for non-fulfilment of contract. I'll take him to the cleaners. I'll goddam . . .'

'Pay up,' said Sonia taking a seat and crossing her legs provocatively.

'Jesus,' said Hutchmeyer admiringly, 'I'll say this for you, you've got nerve.'

'Not all I got,' said Sonia, exposing a bit more, 'I've got Piper's second novel too.'

'And I have the option on it.'

'If he finishes it, Hutch, if he finishes it. You keep this sort of pressure up on him he's likely to Scott Fitzgerald on you. He's sensitive and—'

'I heard all that already. From Baby. Shy, sensitive, my ass. The sort of stuff he writes he ain't sensitive. Got a hide like a fucking armadillo.'

'Which, since you haven't read it . . .' said Sonia.

'I don't have to read it. MacMordie read it and he said it made him almost fetch up and MacMordie don't fetch up easy.'

They wrangled on until lunch, happily embroiled in threat and counter-threat and the financial game of poker which was their real expertise. Not that Hutchmeyer paid up. Sonia had never expected him to, but at least it took his mind off Piper.

The same could not be said for Baby. Their walk along the shore to the studio after breakfast had confirmed her impression that at long last she had met a writer of genius. Piper had talked incessantly about literature and for the most part with an incomprehensibility that Baby found so impressive that she returned to the house feeling that she had undergone a cultural experience of the most profound kind. Piper's impressions were rather different, an amalgam of pleasure at having such an attentive and interested audience and wonder that so perceptive a woman could find the book he was supposed to have written anything less than disgusting. He went up to his room and was about to get out his diary when Sonia entered.

'I hope you've been discreet,' she said. 'That Baby's a ghoul.'

'A ghoul?' said Piper. 'She's a deeply sensitive . . .'

'A ghoul in gold lamé pants. So what's she been doing with you all morning?'

'We went for a walk and she told me about her interest in conservation.'

'Well she didn't have to. You've only got to look at her to see she's done a great job. Like on her face.'

'She's very keen on health foods,' said Piper.

'And sandblasting,' said Sonia. 'Next time she smiles take a look at the back of her head.'

'At the back of her head? What on earth for?'

'To see how far the skin stretches. If that woman laughed she'd scalp herself.'

'Well all I can say is that she's a lot better than Hutchmeyer,' said Piper, who hadn't forgotten what he had been called the night before.

'Hutch I can handle,' said Sonia, 'no problems there. I've got him eating out of my hand so don't foul things up by making goo-goo eyes at his wife and blowing your top about things literary.'

'I am not making goo-goo eyes at Mrs Hutchmeyer,' said Piper indignantly, 'I wouldn't dream of doing such a thing.'

'Well she's making them at you,' said Sonia. 'And another thing, keep that turban on. It suits you.'

'It may suit me, but it's very uncomfortable.'

'It will be a lot more uncomfortable if Hutch finds out you didn't get hit with a frisbee,' said Sonia.

They went down to lunch. Thanks to a call for Hutchmeyer from Hollywood which kept him out of the room for most of the meal it was a lot easier than breakfast. He came in as they were having coffee and looked at Piper suspiciously.

'You heard of a book called *Harold and Maude*?' he asked.

'No,' said Piper.

'Why?' said Sonia.

Hutchmeyer looked at her balefully. 'Why? I'll tell you why,' he said. 'Because *Harold and Maude* just happens to be about an eighteen-year-old who falls in love with an eighty and they've already made the movie. That's why. And I want to know how come no one told me I was buying a novel that had already been written by someone else and—'

'Are you suggesting that Piper's guilty of plagiarism?' said Sonia. 'Because if you are let me—'

'Plagiarism?' yelled Hutchmeyer. 'What plagiarism? I'm saying he stole the goddam story and I've been had for a sucker by some two-bit—'

Hutchmeyer had turned purple and Baby intervened. 'If you're going to stand there and insult Mr Piper,' she said, 'I am not going to sit here and listen to you. Come along, Mr Piper. You and I will leave these two—'

'Stop,' bawled Hutchmeyer, 'I've paid two million dollars and I want to know what Mr Piper has to say about it. Like . . .'

'I assure you I have never read *Harold and Maude*,' said Piper, 'I've never even heard of it.'

'I can vouch for that,' said Sonia. 'Besides, it's quite different. It's not the same at all ...'

'Come, Mr Piper,' said Baby and shepherded him out of the room. Behind them Hutchmeyer and Sonia could be heard shouting. Piper staggered across the piazza lounge and sank ashen-faced into a chair.

'I knew it would go wrong,' he muttered.

Baby looked at him curiously. 'What would go wrong, honey?' she asked. Piper shook his head despondently. 'You didn't copy that book, did you?'

'No,' said Piper, 'I've never even heard of it.'

'Then you've got nothing to worry about. Miss Futtle will sort it out with him. They're two of a kind. Now why don't you go and have a rest?'

Piper went dolefully upstairs with her and into his room. Baby went into her bedroom thoughtfully and shut the door. Her intuition was working overtime. She sat on the bed and thought about his words, 'I knew it would go wrong.' Peculiar. What would go wrong? One thing at least was clear in her mind. He had never heard of *Harold and Maude*. That was sincerity speaking. And Baby Hutchmeyer had lived with insincerity long enough to recognize the truth when she heard it. She waited a while and then went along the passage and quietly opened the door of Piper's room. He was sitting with his back to her at the table by the window. At his elbow was a bottle of ink and in front of him a large leatherbound book. He was writing. Baby watched for a minute and then very gently shut the door and went back to the great waterbed inspired. She had just seen true genius at work. Like Balzac. Downstairs there was the rumble of Hutchmeyer and Sonia Futtle in battle. Baby lay back and stared into space, filled with a terrible sense of her own inutility. In the next room a solitary writer strove to convey to her and millions like her the significance of everything he thought and felt, to create a world enhanced by his imagination which would move into the future a thing of beauty and a joy forever. Downstairs those two word-merchants haggled and fought and ultimately marketed his work. And she did nothing. She was a barren creature without use or purpose, self-indulgent and insignificant. She turned her face to a Tretchikoff and presently fell asleep.

She woke an hour later to the sound of voices from the next room.

They were faint and indistinct. Sonia and Piper talking. She lay and listened but could distinguish nothing. Then she heard Piper's door shut and their voices in the passage. She got off the bed and crossed to the bathroom and unbolted the door. A moment later she was in Piper's room. The leatherbound book was still there on the table. Baby crossed the room and sat down. When she got up half an hour later Baby Hutchmeyer was a different woman. She went back through the bathroom, locked the door again and sat before her mirror filled with a terrible intention.

Hutchmeyer's intentions were pretty terrible too. After his row with Sonia he had retreated to his study to blast hell out of MacMordie for not telling him about *Harold and Maude* but it was Saturday and MacMordie wasn't available for blasting. Hutchmeyer called his home number and got no reply. He sat back fuming and wondering about Piper. There was something wrong with the guy, something he couldn't put his finger on, something that didn't fit in with his idea of an author who had written about screwing old women, something weird. Hutchmeyer's suspicions were aroused. He'd known a lot of authors and none of them had been like Piper. No way. They had talked about their work all the time. But this Piper . . . He'd love to have a talk with him, get him alone and give him a drink or two to loosen him up. But when he came out of his study it was to find Piper screened by women. Baby was down with a fresh dressing of warpaint and Sonia presented him with a book.

'What's that?' said Hutchmeyer recoiling.

'*Harold and Maude*,' said Sonia. 'Peter and I bought it in Bellsworth for you. You can read it and see for yourself—'

Baby laughed shrilly. 'This I must see. Him reading.'

'Shut up,' said Hutchmeyer. He poured a large highball and handed it to Piper. 'Have a highball, Piper.'

'I won't if you don't mind,' said Piper. 'Not tonight.'

'First goddam writer I ever met who doesn't drink,' said Hutchmeyer.

'First real writer you ever met period,' said Baby. 'You think Tolstoy drank?'

'Jesus,' said Hutchmeyer, 'how should I know?'

'That's a lovely yacht out there,' said Sonia to change the subject. 'I didn't know you were a sailing man, Hutch.'

'He isn't,' said Baby before Hutchmeyer could point out that his boat was the finest ocean racer money could buy and that he'd take on any man who said it wasn't. 'It's part of the props. Like the house and the neighbours and—'

'Shut up,' said Hutchmeyer.

Piper left the room and went up to the Boudoir bedroom to confide some more dark thoughts about Hutchmeyer to his diary. When he came down to dinner Hutchmeyer's face was more flushed than usual and his belligerence index was up several points. He had particularly disliked listening to an exposé of his married life by Baby who had, woman-to-woman, discussed with Sonia the symbolic implications of truss-wearing by middle-aged husbands and its relevance to the male menopause. And for once his 'Shut up' hadn't worked. Baby hadn't shut up, she had opened out with further intimate details of his habits so that Hutchmeyer was in the process of telling her to go drown herself when Piper entered the room. Piper wasn't in a mood to put up with Hutchmeyer's lack of chivalry. His years as a bachelor and student of the great novels had infected him with a reverence for Womanhood and very firm views on husbands' attitudes to wives and these didn't include telling them to go drown themselves. Besides, Hutchmeyer's blatant commercialism and his credo that what readers wanted was a good fuck-fantasy had occupied his mind all day. In Piper's opinion what readers wanted was to have their sensibilities extended and fuck-fantasies didn't come into the category of things that extended sensibilities. He went in to dinner determined to make the point. The opportunity occurred early on when Sonia, to change the subject, mentioned *Valley of The Dolls*. Hutchmeyer, glad to escape from the distressing revelations about his private life, said it was a great book.

'I absolutely disagree with you,' said Piper. 'It panders to the public taste for the pornographic.'

Hutchmeyer choked on a piece of cold lobster. 'It does what?' he said when he had recovered.

'It panders to the public taste for pornography,' said Piper, who hadn't read the book but had seen the cover.

'It does, does it?' said Hutchmeyer.

'Yes.'

'And what's wrong with pandering to public taste?'

'It's debasing,' said Piper.

'Debasing?' said Hutchmeyer, eyeing him with mounting fury.

'Absolutely.'

'And what sort of books do you think the public are going to read if you don't give them what they want?'

'Well I think . . .' Piper began before being silenced by a kick under the table from Sonia.

'I think Mr Piper thinks—' said Baby.

'Never mind what you think he thinks,' snarled Hutchmeyer, 'I want to hear what Piper thinks he thinks.' He looked expectantly at Piper.

'I think it is wrong to expose readers to books that are lacking in intellectual content,' said Piper, 'and which are deliberately designed to inflame their imaginations with sexual fantasies that—'

'Inflame their sexual fantasies?' yelled Hutchmeyer, interrupting this quotation from *The Moral Novel*. 'You sit there and tell me you don't hold with books that inflame their readers' sexual fantasies when you've written the filthiest book since *Last Exit*?'

Piper steeled himself. 'Yes, as a matter of fact I do. And as another matter of fact I . . .'

But Sonia had heard enough. With sudden presence of mind she reached for the salt and knocked the waterjug sideways into Piper's lap.

'You ever hear anything like that?' said Hutchmeyer as Baby left the room to fetch a cloth and Piper went upstairs to put on a fresh pair of trousers. 'The guy has the nerve to tell me I got no right to publish . . .'

'Don't listen to him,' said Sonia, 'he's not himself. He's upset. It was that riot yesterday. The blow he got on the head. It's affected him.'

'Affected him? I'll say it has and I'm going to affect the little ass-hole too. Telling me I'm a goddam pornographer. Why I'll show him . . .'

'Why don't you show me your yacht?' said Sonia putting her arms round his neck, a move designed at one and the same time to prevent Hutchmeyer from leaping out of his chair to pursue the retreating Piper and to indicate a new willingness on her part to listen to pro-positions of all kinds. 'Why don't you and me go out and take a cosy little sail around the bay?'

Hutchmeyer succumbed to the soothing influence. 'Who the hell does he think he is anyhow?' he asked with unconscious acumen. Sonia didn't answer. She clung to his arm and smiled seductively. They went out on to the terrace and down the path to the jetty.

Behind them from the piazza lounge Baby watched them thoughtfully. She knew now that in Piper she had found the man she had been waiting for, an author of real merit and one who, without a drink inside him, could stand up to Hutchmeyer and tell him to his face what he thought of him and his books. One too who appreciated her as a sensitive, intelligent and perceptive woman. She had learnt that from Piper's diary. Piper had expressed himself freely on the subject, just as he had given vent to his opinion that Hutchmeyer was a coarse, crass, stupid and commercially motivated moron. On the other hand there had been several references to *Pause* in the diary that had puzzled her and particularly his statement that it was a disgusting book. It seemed a strangely objective criticism for a novelist to make about his own work and while she didn't agree with him it raised him still further in her estimation. It showed he was never satisfied. He was a truly dedicated writer. And so, standing in the piazza lounge staring through limpid azure contact lenses at the yacht moving slowly away from the jetty, Baby Hutchmeyer was herself filled with a sense of dedication, a maternal dedication amounting to euphoria. The days of useless inactivity were over. From now on she would stand between Piper and the harsh insensitivity of Hutchmeyer and the world. She was happy.

Upstairs Piper was anything but. The first flush of his courage in challenging Hutchmeyer had ebbed away leaving him with the horrible feeling that he was in desperate trouble. He took his wet trousers off and sat on the bed wondering what on earth to do. He should never have left the Gleneagle Guest House in Exforth. He should never have listened to Frensic and Sonia. He should never have come to America. He should never have betrayed his literary principles. As the sunset faded Piper got up and was just looking for another pair of trousers when there was a knock at the door and Baby entered.

'You were wonderful,' she said, 'really wonderful.'

'Kind of you to say so,' said Piper interposing the furbelowed stool between his trouserless self and Mrs Hutchmeyer and conscious that if anything more was needed to infuriate Mr Hutchmeyer it was to find the two of them in this compromising situation.

'And I want you to know I appreciate what you have written about me,' continued Baby.

'Written about you?' said Piper groping in the cupboard.

'In your diary,' said Baby. 'I know I shouldn't have . . .'

'What?' squawked Piper from the depths of the cupboard. He found a pair of trousers and struggled into them.

'I just couldn't help it,' said Baby. 'It was lying open on the table and I ...'

'Then you know,' said Piper emerging from the cupboard.

'Yes,' said Baby.

'Christ,' said Piper and slumped on to the stool. 'Are you going to tell him?'

Baby shook her head. 'It's between us two.'

Piper considered this and found it only faintly reassuring. 'It's been a terrible strain,' he said finally. 'I mean not being able to talk to anyone about it. Apart from Sonia of course but she's no help.'

'I don't suppose she is,' said Baby who didn't for one moment suppose that Miss Futtle appreciated being told what a deeply sensitive, intelligent and perceptive person another woman was.

'Well she wouldn't be,' said Piper, 'I mean it was her idea in the first place.'

'It was?' said Baby.

'She said it would work out all right but I knew I would never be able to keep up the pretence,' continued Piper.

'I think that does you great credit,' said Baby trying desperately to imagine what Miss Futtle had had in mind in persuading Piper to pretend that he ... There was something very screwy about all this. 'Look, why don't we go downstairs and have a drink and you can tell me all about it.'

'I've got to talk to someone,' said Piper, 'but won't they be down there?'

'They've gone out on the yacht. We've got all the privacy in the world.'

They went downstairs to a little corner room with a balcony which hung out over rocks and the water lapping the beach.

'It's my hidey hole,' said Baby indicating the rows of books lining the walls. 'Where I can be myself.' She poured two drinks while Piper looked miserably at the titles. They were as confusing as his own situation and seemed to argue an eclecticism he found surprising. Maupassant leant against Hailey who in turn propped up Tolkien, and Piper, whose self was founded upon a few great writers, couldn't imagine how anyone could be themselves in these surroundings. Besides, there were a large number of detective stories and thrillers and Piper held very strong views on such trite works.

101

'Now tell me all about it,' said Baby soothingly and settled herself on a sofa. Piper sipped his drink and tried to think where to begin.

'Well you see I've been writing for ten years now,' he said finally, 'and . . .'

Dusk deepened into night outside as Piper told his story. Beside him Baby sat enthralled. This was better than books. This was life, life not as she had known it but as she had always wanted it to be. Exciting and mysterious and filled with strange, extraordinary hazards which excited her imagination. She refilled their glasses and Piper, intoxicated by her sympathy, spoke on more fluently than he had ever written. He told the story of his life as an unrecognized genius alone in a garret, in any number of garrets looking out on to the windswept sea, struggling through months and years to express with pen and ink and those exquisite curlicues she had so admired in his notebooks the meaning of life and its deepest significance.

Baby gazed into his face and invested it all with a new romance. Pea-soup fogs returned to London. Gas lamps gleamed on the seafronts as Piper took his nightly stroll along the promenade. Baby drew copiously on her fund of half-remembered novels to add these details. Finally there were villains, tawdry rogues out of Dickens, Fagins of the literary world in the form of Frensic & Futtle of Lanyard Lane who lured the genius from his garret with the false promise of recognition. Lanyard Lane! The very name evoked for Baby a legendary London. And Covent Garden. But best of all there was Piper standing alone on a sea wall with the waves breaking below him staring fixedly out across the English Channel, the wind blowing through his hair. And here in front of her was the man himself with his peaked anxious face and tortured eyes, the living embodiment of undiscovered genius as she had visualized it in Keats and Shelley and all those other poets who had died so young. And between him and the harsh relentless reality of Hutchmeyer and Frensic and Futtle there was only Baby herself. For the first time she felt needed. Without her he would be hounded and persecuted and driven to . . . Baby prophesied suicide or madness and certainly a haunted, hunted future, with Piper prey to the commercial rapacity of all those forces which had conspired to compromise him. Baby's imagination raced on into melodrama.

'We can't let it happen,' she said impetuously as Piper ran out of self-pity. He looked at her sorrowfully.

'What can I do?' he asked.

'You've got to get away,' said Baby and turned to the door on to the balcony and flung it open. Piper looked dubiously out into the night. The wind had risen and nature, imitating art or Piper's modicum of art, was hurling waves against the rocks below the house. The gusts caught at the curtains and threw them flapping into the room. Baby stood between them gazing out across the bay. Her mind was inflamed with images from novels. The night escape. The sea lashing at a small boat. A great house blazing in the darkness and two lovers locked in one another's arms. She saw herself in new guises, no longer the disregarded wife of a rich publisher, a creature of habits and surgical artifice, but the heroine of some great novel: *Rebecca, Jane Eyre, Gone With The Wind*. She turned back into the room and Piper was astonished at the intensity of her expression. Her eyes gleamed and her mouth was firm with purpose. 'We will go together,' she said and reached out her hand.

Piper took it cautiously. 'Together?' he said. 'You mean . . .'

'Together,' said Baby. 'You and I. Tonight.' And holding Piper's hand she led the way out into the piazza lounge.

Chapter 12

In the middle of the bay Hutchmeyer wrestled with the helm. His evening had not been a success. It was bad enough to be insulted by one of his own authors, a unique experience for which nothing in twenty-five years in the book trade had prepared him; it was even worse to be out in a yacht in the tail end of a typhoon on a pitch-dark night with a crew that consisted of one cheerfully drunk woman who insisted on enjoying herself.

'This is great,' she shouted as the yacht heaved and a wave broke over the deck, 'England here we come.'

'Oh no we don't,' said Hutchmeyer and put the helm over in order to avoid the possibility that they were heading out into the Atlantic. He stared out into the darkness and then down at the binnacle. At that moment *Romain du Roy* took a terrible turn, water flushed along the rail and into the cockpit. Hutchmeyer clung to the wheel and cursed. Beside him in the darkness Sonia squealed, whether from fear or excitement Hutchmeyer neither knew nor cared. He was wrestling with nautical problems beyond his meagre knowledge. In the dim recesses of his memory he seemed to remember that you shouldn't have sails up in a storm. You rode storms out.

'Hold this,' he yelled to Sonia and waded below into the cabin to find a knife. Another wave broke over the cockpit and into his face as he emerged.

'What are you doing with that thing?' Sonia asked. Hutchmeyer brandished the knife and clung to the rail.

'I'm going to make goddam certain we don't hit land,' he shouted as the yacht scudded forward alarmingly. He crawled along the deck and hacked at every rope he could find. Presently he was writhing in canvas. By the time he had untangled himself they were no longer scudding. The yacht wallowed.

'You shouldn't have done that,' said Sonia, 'I was getting a real high out of that zoom.'

'Well, I wasn't,' said Hutchmeyer, peering into the night. It was impossible to tell where they were. A black sky hung overhead and the lights along both shores seemed to have gone out. Or they had. Out to sea.

'Christ,' said Hutchmeyer dismally. Beside him Sonia played with the wheel happily. There was something exhilarating about being out in a storm on a dark night that appealed to her sense of adventure. It awoke her combative instincts. Something tangible to pit herself against. And besides, Hutchmeyer's despondency was reassuring. At least she had taken his mind off Piper – and off her too. A storm at sea was no scene for seduction. And Hutchmeyer's efforts in that direction had been heavy-handed. Sonia had sought refuge in Scotch. Now as they rose and fell with each successive wave she was cheerfully drunk.

'We'll just have to sit the storm out,' said Hutchmeyer presently but Sonia demanded action.

'Start the motor,' she said.

'What the hell for? We don't know where we are. We could run aground.'

'I want the wind in my hair and the spume in my face,' yelled Sonia.

'Spume?' said Hutchmeyer hoarsely.

'And a man at the helm with his hand on the tiller . . .'

'You got a man at the helm,' said Hutchmeyer taking it from her.

The yacht lurched into the wind and waves sucked at the dragging mainsail. Sonia laughed. 'A real man, a he-man, a seaman. A man with salt in his veins and a sail in his heart. Someone to stir the blood.'

'Stir the blood,' muttered Hutchmeyer. 'You'll get all the blood-stirring you want if we hit a rock. I should never have listened to you. Coming out on a night like this.'

'You should have listened to the weather report,' said Sonia, 'that's what you should have listened to. All I said was . . .'

'I know what you said. You said, "Let's take a sail round the bay." That's what you said.'

'So we're having a little sail. The challenge of the elements. I think it's just wonderful.'

Hutchmeyer didn't. Wet, cold and bedraggled he clutched the wheel and searched the darkness for some sign of the shoreline. It was nowhere to be seen.

'Challenge of the elements my ass,' he thought bitterly, and wondered why it was that women had so little sense of reality.

It was a thought that would have found an echo in Piper's heart. Baby had changed. From being the deeply perceptive intelligent woman he had described in his diary she had become a quite extraordinarily urgent creature hell-bent on getting him out of the house in the middle of a most unsuitably stormy night. To make matters worse she seemed determined to come with him, a course of action calculated in Piper's opinion to put his already strained relations with Mr Hutchmeyer to a test which even flight was hardly likely to mitigate. He made the point to Baby as she led the way through the piazza lounge and into great hall.

'I mean we can't just walk out together in the middle of the night,' he protested standing on a mosaic vat of boiling wood pulp. Hutchmeyer glowered down from his portrait on the wall.

'Why not?' said Baby, whose sense of the melodramatic seemed to be heightened in these grandiose surroundings. Piper tried to think of a persuasive answer and could only come up with the rather obvious one that Hutchmeyer wouldn't like it. Baby laughed luridly.

'Let him lump it,' she said and before Piper could point out that Hutchmeyer's lumping it was going to be personally disadvantageous and that in any case he would prefer the dangers involved in pulling the wool over Hutchmeyer's eyes as to the authorship of *Pause* to the more terrible ones of running off with his wife, Baby had clutched his hand again and was leading him up the Renaissance staircase.

'Pack your things as quickly as you can,' she said in a whisper as they stood outside the door of the Boudoir bedroom.

'Yes but . . .' Piper began whispering involuntarily himself. But Baby had gone. Piper went into his room and switched on the light. His suitcase lay uninvitingly against the wall. Piper shut the door and wondered what on earth to do now. The woman must be demented to think that he was going to . . . Piper staggered across the room to the window trying to rid himself of the notion that all this was really happening to him. There was an awful hallucinatory quality about the experience which fitted in with everything that had taken place since he had stepped ashore in New York. Everyone was stark staring mad. What was more they acted out their madness without a moment's hesitation. 'Shoot you as soon as look at you' was the expression that sprang to mind. It certainly sprang to mind five

106

minutes later when Piper, his case still unpacked, opened the door of the Boudoir bedroom and poked his head outside. Baby was coming down the corridor with a large revolver in her hand. Piper shrank back into his room.

'You'd better pack this,' she said.

'Pack it?' said Piper still glowering at the thing.

'Just in case,' said Baby. 'You never know.'

Piper did. He sidled round the bed and shook his head. 'You've got to understand . . .' he began but Baby had dived into the drawers of the dressing-table and was piling his underclothes on the bed.

'Don't waste time talking. Get the suitcase,' she said. 'The wind's dying down. They could be back at any moment now.'

Piper looked longingly at the window. If only they would come back now before it was too late. 'I really do think we ought to reconsider this,' he said. Baby stopped emptying the drawers and turned to him. Her taut face was alight with unventured dreams. She was every heroine she had ever read, every woman who had gone off happily to Siberia or followed her man across the Sherman-devastated South. She was more, at once the inspiration and protectress of this unhappy youth. This was her one chance of realization and she was not going to let it escape her. Behind was Hutchmeyer, the years of servitude to boredom and artifice, of surgical restoration and constructed enthusiasms; in front Piper, the knowledge that she was needed, a new life filled with meaning and significance in the service of this young genius. And now at this moment of supreme sacrifice, the culmination of so many years of expectation, he was hesitating. Baby's eyes filled with tears and she raised her arms in supplication.

'Don't you understand what this means?' she asked. Piper gaped at her. He understood only too well what it meant. He was alone in an enormous house with the demented wife of America's richest and most powerful publisher and she was proposing that they should run away together. And if he didn't she would almost certainly tell Hutchmeyer the true story of *Pause* or invent some equally frightful tale about how he had tried to seduce her. And finally there was the gun. It lay on the bed where she had dropped it. Piper glanced at the thing and as he did so Baby took a step forward, the tears that had gathered in her eyes ran down her cheeks and carried with them a contact lens. She fumbled for it on the counterpane and encountered the gun. Piper hesitated no longer. He grabbed the suitcase and plumped it on

107

the bed and the next moment was packing it hastily with his shirts and pants. He didn't stop until everything was in, his ledgers and pens and his bottle of Waterman's Midnight Black. Finally he sat on it and fastened the catches. Only then did he turn towards her. Baby was still groping on the bed.

'I can't find it,' she said, 'I can't find it.'

'Leave it, we don't need a thing like that,' said Piper anxious to avoid any further acquaintance with firearms.

'I must have it,' said Baby, 'I can't get along without it.'

Piper humped the suitcase off the bed and Baby found the contact lens. And the gun. Clutching the one while trying to reinsert the other she followed Piper into the corridor. 'Take your bag down and come back for mine,' she told him and went into her own bedroom. Piper went downstairs, encountered the glowering portrait of Hutchmeyer and came back again. Baby was standing by the great waterbed wearing a mink. Beside her were six large travel bags.

'Look,' said Piper, 'are you sure you really want . . .'

'Yes, oh yes,' said Baby. 'It's what I've always dreamt of doing. Leaving all this . . . this falsehood and starting afresh.'

'But don't you think . . .' Piper began again but Baby was not thinking. With a grand final gesture she picked up the gun and fired it repeatedly into the waterbed. Little spurts of water leapt into the air and the room echoed deafeningly with the shots.

'That's symbolic,' she cried and tossed the gun across the room. But Piper didn't hear her. Grabbing three travel bags in each hand he staggered out of the bedroom and dragged them along the corridor, his ears ringing with the sound of gunfire. He knew now that she was definitely out of her mind and the sight of the expiring waterbed had been another awful reminder of his own mortality. By the time he reached the bottom of the stairs he was panting and puffing. Baby followed him, a wraith in mink.

'Now what?' he asked.

'We'll take the cruiser,' she said.

'The cruiser?'

Baby nodded, her imagination once more inflamed with images from novels. The night flight across the water was essential.

'But won't they . . .' Piper began.

'That way they'll never know where we've gone,' said Baby. 'We'll land down the coast and buy a car.'

'Buy a car?' said Piper. 'But I haven't any money.'

'I have,' said Baby and with Piper lugging the travel bags behind her they went through the lounge and down the path to the jetty. The wind had fallen but still the water was choppy and slapped against the wooden piles and the rocks so that drifts of spray sprang up wetly against Piper's face.

'Put the bags aboard,' said Baby, 'I've got to go back for something.'

Piper hesitated for a moment and stared with mixed feelings out across the bay. He wasn't sure whether he wanted Sonia and Hutchmeyer to heave in sight now or not. But there was no sign of them. In the end he dropped the bags down into the cruiser and waited. Baby returned with a briefcase.

'My alimony,' she explained, 'from the safe.' Clutching her mink to her, she clambered down into the cruiser and went to the controls. Piper followed her unsteadily.

'Low on fuel,' she said. 'We'll need some more.' Presently Piper was trudging back and forth between the cruiser and the fuel store at the far side of the courtyard behind the house. It was dark and occasionally he stumbled.

'Isn't that enough?' he asked after the fifth journey as he handed the cans down to Baby in the cruiser.

'We can't afford to make mistakes,' she replied. 'You wouldn't want us to run out of gas in the middle of the bay.'

Piper set off for the store again. There was no doubt in his mind that he had already made a terrible mistake. He should have listened to Sonia. She had said the woman was a ghoul and she was right. A demented ghoul. And what on earth was he doing in the middle of the night filling a cruiser with cans of petrol? It wasn't an activity even vaguely related with being a novelist. Thomas Mann wouldn't have been found dead doing it. Nor would D. H. Lawrence. Conrad might have, just. Even then it was highly unlikely. Piper consulted *Lord Jim* and found nothing reassuring in it, nothing to justify this insane activity. Yes, insane was the word. Standing in the fuel store with two more cans Piper hesitated. There wasn't a single novelist of any merit who would have done what he was doing. They would all have refused to be party to such a scheme. Which was all very well, but then none of them had been in the awful predicament he was in. True, D. H. Lawrence had run off with Mr Somebody-or-other's wife, Frieda, but presumably of his own accord and because he was in love with the woman. Piper was most certainly not in love with Baby and

109

he wasn't doing this of his own accord. Definitely not. Having consulted these precedents Piper tried to think how to live up to them. After all, he hadn't spent the last ten years of his life being the great novelist for nothing. He would take a moral stand. Which was rather easier said than done. Baby Hutchmeyer wasn't the sort of woman who would understand taking a moral stand. Besides there wasn't time to explain. The best thing to do would be to stay where he was and not go down to the boat again. That would put her in a spot when Hutchmeyer and Sonia got back. She'd have her work cut out explaining what she was doing on board the cruiser with her bags packed and ten five-gallon cans of gasolene stashed around the cabin. At least she wouldn't be able to argue that he had forced her to elope with him – if elope was the right word for running away with another man's wife. Not if he wasn't there. On the other hand there was his suitcase on board too. He would have to get that off. But how? Well of course if he didn't go back down there she would come looking for him and in that case . . . Piper peered out of the store and seeing that the courtyard was clear, stole across it to the front door and into the house. Presently he was looking out from behind the lattice of the piazza lounge at the boat. Around him the great wooden house creaked. Piper looked at his watch. It was one o'clock. Where had Sonia and Hutchmeyer got to? They should have been back hours ago.

On board the cruiser Baby was having the same thought about Piper. What was keeping him? She had started the engine and checked the fuel gauge and was ready to go now and he was holding everything up. After ten minutes she became genuinely alarmed.

And with each succeeding minute her alarm grew. The sea was calm now and if he didn't come soon . . .

'Genius is so unpredictable,' she muttered finally and climbed back on to the jetty. She went round the house and across the yard to the fuel store and switched on the light. Empty. Two jerry-cans standing in the middle of the floor were mute testimony to Piper's change of heart. Baby went to the door.

'Peter,' she called, her thin voice dying in the night air. Thrice she called and thrice there was no reply.

'Oh heartless boy!' she cried and this time it seemed there was an answer. It came faintly from the house in the form of a crash and a muffled shout. Piper had tripped over an ornamental vase. Baby headed across the court and up the steps to the door. Once inside she

110

called again. In vain. Standing in the centre of the great hall Baby looked up at the portrait of her detested husband and it seemed to her overwrought imagination that a smile played about those gross arrogant lips. He had won again. He would always win and she would always remain the plaything of his idle hours.

'Never!' she shouted in answer to the clichés that fluttered hysterically about her mind and to the portrait's unspoken scorn. She hadn't come this far to be deprived of her right to freedom and romance and significance by a pusillanimous literary genius. She would do something, something symbolic that would stand as a testimony to her independence. From the ashes of the past she would arise anew like some wild phoenix from the . . . Flames? Ashes? The symbolism drew her on. It would be an act from which there could be no going back. She would burn her boats. Baby, urged on by heroines of several hundred novels, flew back across the courtyard, opened a jerry-can and a moment later was trailing gasolene back to the house. She sloshed it up the steps, over the threshold, across the manifold activities of the mosaic floor, up more steps into the piazza lounge and across the carpet to the study. Then with the reckless abandon that so became her in her new role she seized a table lighter from the desk and lit it. A sheet of flame engulfed the room, scurried into the lounge, hurtled across the hall and out into the night. Then and only then did Baby turn and open the door to the terrace.

Meanwhile Piper, after his brief contretemps with the ornamental vase, was busy on the cruiser. He had heard her call and had seized his opportunity to retrieve his suitcase. He ran down the path to the jetty and clambered aboard. Above him the huge house loomed dark with derived menace. Its towers and turrets, culled from Ruskin and Morris and distilled into shingle through the architectural extravagance of Peabody and Stearns, merged with the lowering sky. Only behind the lattice of the piazza were there lights and these were dim. So was the interior of the cruiser. Piper fumbled about among the travel bags and jerry-cans for his suitcase. Where the hell had it got to? He found it finally under the mink coat and was just disentangling it when he was stopped by a sudden roar from the house and the flicker of flames. Dropping the coat he stumbled to the cabin door and looked out dumbfounded.

The Hutchmeyer Residence was ablaze. Flames shot up across the windows of Hutchmeyer's study. More flames danced behind the latticework. There was a crash of breaking glass as windows shattered in the heat and almost simultaneously from behind the house a mushroom of flame billowed up into the sky followed by the most appalling explosion. Piper gaped, transfixed by the enormity of what was happening. And as he gaped a slim figure detached itself from the shadows of the house and ran across the terrace towards him. It was Baby. The bloody woman must have . . . but Piper had no time to follow this obvious train of thought to its conclusion. As Baby ran towards him another train appeared round the side of the house, a train of flames that danced and skipped, held for a moment and then flickered on along the trail of gasolene Piper had left from the fuel store. Piper watched it coming and then, with a presence of mind that was wholly his own and owed nothing to *The Moral Novel*, he clambered on to the jetty and wrestled with the ropes that held the cruiser.

'We've got to get away before that fire . . .' he yelled to Baby as she rushed along the jetty towards him. Baby looked over her shoulder at the fuse.

'Oh my God,' she shrieked. The dancing flames were scurrying closer. She leapt down into the boat and into the cabin.

'It's too late,' shouted Piper. The flames were licking along the jetty now. They would reach the boat with its cargo of gas and then . . . Piper dropped the line and ran. In the cabin of the cruiser, Baby struggled to find her alimony, grabbed the mink, dropped it again, and finally found the case she was looking for. She turned back towards the door but the flames had reached the end of the jetty and as she looked they leapt the gap. There was no hope. Baby turned to the controls, put the throttle full on, and as the cruiser surged forward, she scrambled out of the cabin and, still clutching the briefcase, dived over the side. Behind her the cruiser gathered speed. Flames flickered somewhere inside to mark its progress and then seemed to die down. Finally it disappeared into the darkness of the bay, the roar of its motor drowned by the much more powerful roar of the blazing house. Baby swam ashore and stumbled up the rocky beach. Piper was standing on the lawn staring in horror at the house. The flames had reached the upper storeys now, they glowed behind windows briefly, there was the crash of breaking glass as more windows splintered and then great gusts of flame shot out to lick up the sides of the shingle. Within minutes the entire façade was ablaze. Baby stood beside Piper proudly.

'There goes my past,' she murmured. Piper turned to look at her.

112

Her hair straggled down her head and her face was naked of its pancake mask. Only her eyes seemed real and in the reflected glow Piper could see that they shone with a demented joy.

'You're out of your tiny mind,' he said with uncharacteristic frankness. Baby's fingers tightened on his arm.

'I did it all for you,' she said. 'You understand that, don't you? We have to plunge into the future unfettered by the past. We have to commit ourselves irrevocably by some free act and make an existential choice.'

'Existential choice?' shrieked Piper. The flames had reached the decorative dovecotes now and the heat was intense. 'You call setting fire to your own house an existential choice? That's not an existential choice, that's a bloody crime, that is.'

Baby smiled happily at him. 'You must read Genet, darling,' she murmured and still gripping his arm pulled him away across the lawn towards the trees. In the distance there came the wail of sirens. Piper hurried. They had just reached the edge of the forest when the night air was split by another series of explosions. Far out across the bay the cruiser had exploded. Twice. And silhouetted against the second ball of flame Piper seemed to glimpse the mast of a yacht.

'Oh my God,' he muttered.

'Oh my darling,' murmured Baby in response and turned her face to his.

Chapter 13

Hutchmeyer was in a foul temper. He had been insulted by an author, he had proved himself an inept yachtsman, had lost his sails, and finally his virility had been put in doubt by Sonia Futtle's refusal to take his overtures seriously.

'O come on now, Hutch baby,' she had said, 'put it away. This is no time to be proving your manhood. Okay, so you're a man and I'm a woman. I heard you. And I don't doubt you. I really don't. You've got to believe me, I don't. Now you just put your clothes back on again and ...'

'They're wet,' said Hutchmeyer. 'They're soaking wet. You want me to catch my death of pneumonia or something?'

Sonia shook her head. 'Let's just get on back to the house and you can be nice and dry in no time at all.'

'Yeah, well you just tell me how I'm going to get us back home with the mainsail in the water. So all we do is go round in circles. That's what we do. Aw come on, honey ...'

But Sonia wouldn't. She went up on deck and looked across the water. In the cabin doorway Hutchmeyer, pinkly naked and shivering, made one last plea. 'You're all woman,' he said, 'you know that. All woman. I got a real respect for you. I mean we've got ...'

'A wife,' said Sonia bluntly, 'that's what you've got. And I've got a fiancé.'

'You've got a what?' said Hutchmeyer.

'You heard me. A fiancé. Name of Peter Piper.'

'That little—' but Hutchmeyer got no further. His attention had been drawn to the shoreline. He could see it now quite clearly. By the light of a blazing house.

'Look at that,' said Sonia, 'somebody's having one hell of a house-warming.'

Hutchmeyer grabbed the binoculars and peered through them. 'What do you mean "somebody"?' he yelled a moment later. 'That's no somebody. That's my house!'

'That was your house,' said Sonia practically, before the full implications of the blaze dawned on her, 'oh my God!'

'You're damn right,' Hutchmeyer snarled and hurled himself at the starter. The marine engine turned over and the yacht began to move. Hutchmeyer wrestled with the wheel and tried to maintain course for the holocaust that had been his home. Over the port gunwale the mainsail acted as a trawl and the *Romain du Roy* veered to the left. Naked and panting, Hutchmeyer fought to compensate but it was no good.

'I'll have to ditch the sail,' he shouted and at that moment a dark shape appeared silhouetted against the blaze. It was the cruiser. Travelling at speed towards them she too had begun to burn. 'My God, the bastard's going to ram us,' he yelled but the next moment the cruiser proved him wrong. She exploded. First the jerry-cans in the cabin blew up and portions of the cruiser cavorted into the air; second what remained of the hull careered towards them and the main fuel tanks blew. A ball of flame ballooned out and from it there appeared a dark oblong lump which arced through the air and fell with a terrible crash through the foredeck of the yacht. The *Romain du Roy* lifted her stern out of the water, slumped back and began to settle. Sonia, clinging to the rail, stared around her. The hull of the cruiser was sinking with a hissing noise. Hutchmeyer had disappeared and a second later Sonia was in the water as the yacht keeled over, tilted and sank. Sonia swam away from the wreckage. Fifty yards away the sea was alight with flaming fuel from the cruiser and by this eerie light she saw Hutchmeyer in the water behind her. He was clinging to a piece of wood.

'Are you okay?' she called.

Hutchmeyer whimpered. It was obvious that he was not okay. Sonia swam over to him and trod water.

'Help, help,' squawked Hutchmeyer.

'Take it easy,' said Sonia, 'just don't panic. You can swim, can't you?'

Hutchmeyer's eyes goggled in his head. 'Swim? What do you mean "swim"? Of course I can swim. What do you think I'm doing?'

'So you're okay,' said Sonia. 'Now all we got to do is swim ashore . . .'

But Hutchmeyer was gurgling again. 'Swim ashore? I can't swim that far. I'll drown. I'll never make it. I'll . . .'

Sonia left him and headed towards the floating wreckage. Maybe

115

she could find a lifejacket. Instead she found a number of empty jerry-cans. She swam back with one to Hutchmeyer.

'Hang on to this,' she told him. Hutchmeyer exchanged his piece of wood for the can and clung to it. Sonia swam off again and collected two more jerry-cans. She also found a piece of rope. Tying the cans together she looped the rope round Hutchmeyer's waist and knotted it.

'That way you can't drown,' she said. 'Now you just stay right here and everything is going to be just fine.'

Hutchmeyer, balancing on his raft of cans, stared at her maniacally. 'Fine?' he shrieked. 'Fine? My house is being burnt, some crazy swine tries to murder me with a fireboat, my beautiful yacht is sunk underneath me and everything is just fine?'

But Sonia was already out of earshot, swimming for the shore with a steady sidestroke that would not tire her. All her thoughts were centred on Piper. He had been in the house when she left and now all that was left of the house . . . She turned over and looked across the water. The house still bulked large upon the horizon, a yellow, ruddy mass from which sparks flew continually upwards, and as she watched a great flame leapt up. The roof had evidently collapsed. Sonia turned on her side and swam on. She had to get back to find out what had happened. Perhaps poor darling Peter had had another of his accidents. She prepared herself for the worst while taking refuge in the maternal excuse that he was accident-prone before recognizing that Piper's accidents had not after all been of his making. It had been MacMordie who had arranged the riot on their arrival in New York. She could hardly blame Piper for that. If anyone was to blame it had been . . .

Sonia shut out the thought of her own culpability by wondering about the boat that had careered out of the darkness at them and exploded. Hutchmeyer had said someone had tried to murder him. It seemed an extraordinary notion but then again it was extraordinary that his house had caught fire. Put these two events together and it argued an organized and premeditated action. In that case Piper was not responsible. Nothing he had ever done had been organized and premeditated. He was plain accident-prone. With this reassuring thought Sonia reached the beach and clambered ashore. For several minutes she lay on the ground to get her strength back and as she lay there another dreadful possibility crossed her mind. If Hutchmeyer

116

had been right and someone had really tried to murder him it was all too likely that finding Piper and Baby alone in the house they had first. . . . Sonia staggered to her feet and set off through the trees towards the fire. She had to find out what had happened. And supposing it had been an accident there was still the chance that the shock of being present when the great house ignited had caused Piper to blurt out to someone that he wasn't the real author of *Pause*. In which case the fat would really be in the fire. If the fat wasn't already. It was the first question she put to a fireman she found dousing a blazing bush in the garden.

'Well if there was he's roasted to a cinder,' he said. 'Some crazy guy loosed off a whole lot of shots when we got here but the roof fell in and he hasn't fired since.'

'Shots?' said Sonia. 'You did say shots?'

'With a machine-gun,' said the fireman, 'from the basement. But like I said the roof fell in and he hasn't fired no more.'

Sonia looked at the glowing mass. Heat waves gusted into her face. Someone firing a machine-gun from the basement? It didn't make sense. Nothing made sense. Unless of course you accepted Hutchmeyer's theory that someone had deliberately set out to murder him.

'And you're quite sure nobody escaped?' she asked.

The fireman shook his head.

'Nobody,' he said. 'We were the first truck to get here and apart from the shooting there hasn't anything come out of there. And the guy who did the shooting just has to be a goner.'

So was Sonia. For a moment she tried to steady herself and then she collapsed. The fireman hoisted her over his shoulder and carried her to an ambulance. Half an hour later Sonia Futtle was fast asleep in hospital. She had been heavily sedated.

Hutchmeyer on the other hand was wide awake. He sat naked except for the jerry-cans in the back of the Coastguard launch that had rescued him and tried to explain what he had been doing in the middle of the bay at two o'clock in the morning. The Coastguard didn't appear to believe him.

'Okay, Mr Hutchmeyer, so you weren't on board your cruiser when she bombed out . . .'

'My cruiser?' yelled Hutchmeyer. 'That wasn't my cruiser. I was on board my yacht.'

The Coastguard regarded him sceptically and pointed to a piece of wreckage on the deck. Hutchmeyer stared at it. The words *Folio Three* were clearly visible, painted on the wood.

'*Folio Three*'s my boat,' he muttered.

'Thought it just might be,' said the Coastguard. 'Still if you say you weren't on her ...'

'On her? On her? Whoever was on that boat is barbecued duck by now. Do I look like I was ...'

Nobody said anything and presently the launch bumped into the shore below what remained of the Hutchmeyer Residence and Hutchmeyer was helped ashore, wrapped in a blanket. In single file they made their way through the woods to the drive where a dozen police cars, fire trucks and ambulances were gathered.

'Found Mr Hutchmeyer floating out there with these,' the Coastguard told the Police Chief and indicated the jerry-cans. 'Thought you might be interested.'

Police Chief Greensleeves looked at Hutchmeyer, at the jerry-cans, and back again. He was obviously very interested.

'And this,' said the Coastguard and produced the piece of wood with *Folio Three* written on it.

Police Chief Greensleeves studied the name. '*Folio Three* eh? Mean anything to you, Mr Hutchmeyer?'

Huddled in the blanket Hutchmeyer was staring at the glowing ruins of his house.

'I said, does *Folio Three* mean anything to you, Mr Hutchmeyer?' the Police Chief repeated and followed Hutchmeyer's gaze speculatively.

'Of course it does,' said Hutchmeyer, 'it's my cruiser.'

'Mind telling us what you were doing out on your cruiser this time of the night?'

'I wasn't on my cruiser. I was on my yacht.'

'*Folio Three* is a cruiser,' said the Coastguard officiously.

'I know it's a cruiser,' said Hutchmeyer. 'What I'm saying is that I wasn't on it when the explosion occurred.'

'Which explosion, Mr Hutchmeyer?' said Greensleeves.

'What do you mean "which explosion"? How many explosions have there been tonight?'

Police Chief Greensleeves looked back at the house. 'That's a good question,' he said, 'a very good question. It's a question I keep asking myself. Like how come nobody calls the Fire Department to say the house is burning until it's too late. And when we get here how come somebody is so anxious we don't put the fire out they open up with a heavy machine-gun from the basement and blast all hell out of a fire truck.'

'Somebody opened fire from the basement?' said Hutchmeyer incredulously.

'That's what I said. With a goddam machine-gun, heavy calibre.'

Hutchmeyer looked unhappily at the ground. 'Well I can explain that,' he began and stopped.

'You can explain it? I'd be glad to hear your explanation, Mr Hutchmeyer.'

'I keep a machine-gun in the romper room.'

'You keep a heavy-calibre machine-gun in the romper room? Like to tell me why you keep a machine-gun in the romper room?'

Hutchmeyer swallowed unhappily. He didn't like to at all. 'For protection,' he muttered finally.

'For protection? Against what?'

'Bears,' said Hutchmeyer.

'Bears, Mr Hutchmeyer? Did I hear you say "bears"?'

Hutchmeyer looked round desperately and tried to think of a reasonable answer. In the end he told the truth. 'You see one time my wife was into bears and I . . .' he tailed off miserably.

Police Chief Greensleeves studied him with even keener interest. 'Mrs Hutchmeyer was into bears? Did I hear you say Mrs Hutchmeyer was into bears?'

But Hutchmeyer had had enough. 'Don't keep asking me if that's what you heard,' he shouted. 'If I say Mrs Hutchmeyer was into bears she was into goddam bears. Ask the neighbours. They'll tell you.'

'We sure will,' said Chief Greensleeves. 'So you go out and buy yourself some artillery? To shoot bears?'

'I didn't shoot bears. I just had the gun in case I had to.'

'And I suppose you didn't shoot up fire trucks either?'

'Of course I didn't. Why the hell should I want to do a thing like that?'

'I wouldn't know, Mr Hutchmeyer, any more than I'd know what you were doing in the middle of the bay in the raw with a heap of empty gas cans tied round you and your house is on fire and nobody has called the Fire Department.'

'Nobody called . . . You mean my wife didn't call . . .' Hutchmeyer gaped at Greensleeves.

'Your wife? You mean you didn't have your wife with you out in the bay on board your cruiser?'

'Certainly not,' said Hutchmeyer, 'I've told you already I wasn't on my cruiser. My cruiser tried to ram me on my yacht and blew up and . . .'

'So where's Mrs Hutchmeyer?'

Hutchmeyer looked around desperately. 'I've no idea,' he said.

'Okay, take him down the station,' said the Police Chief, 'we'll go into this thing more thoroughly down there.' Hutchmeyer was bundled into the back of the police car and presently they were on their way into Bellsworth. By the time they reached the station Hutchmeyer was in an advanced state of shock.

So was Piper. The fire, the exploding cruiser, the arrival of the fire engines and police cars with their wailing sirens and finally the rapid machine-gun fire from the romper room had all served to undermine what little power of self-assertion he had ever possessed. As the firemen ran for cover and the police dropped to the ground he allowed himself to be led away through the woods by Baby. They hurried along a path and came out in the garden of another large house. People were standing outside the front door gazing at the smoke and flames roaring into the air over the trees. Baby hesitated a moment and then, taking advantage of the cover of some bushes, dragged Piper along below the house and into the woods on the other side.

'Where are we going?' Piper asked after another half mile. 'I mean we can't just walk away like this as if nothing had happened.'

'You want to go back?' hissed Baby.

Piper said he didn't.

'Right, so we've got to get some mileage,' said Baby. They went on and passed three more houses. After two miles Piper protested again.

'They're bound to wonder what's become of us,' he said.

'Let them wonder,' said Baby.

'I don't see that's going to do us any good,' said Piper. 'They are going to find out you deliberately set fire to the house and then there's the cruiser. It's got all my things on it.'

'It had all your things on it. Right now they're not on it any more. They're either at the bottom of the bay or they're floating around

120

alongside my mink. When they find them you know what they're going to think?'

'No,' said Piper.

Baby giggled. 'They're going to think we went with them.'

'Went with them?'

'Like we're dead,' said Baby with another sinister giggle. Piper didn't see anything to laugh about. Death even by proxy wasn't a joke and besides he had lost his passport. It had been in the suitcase with his precious ledgers.

'Right, so they'll know you're dead,' said Baby when he pointed this out to her. 'Like I said, we have to make a break with the past. So we've made it. Completely. We're *free*. We can go anywhere and do anything. We've broken the fetters of circumstance.'

'You may see it that way,' said Piper, 'I can't say I do. As far as I'm concerned the fetters of circumstance happen to be a lot stronger than they ever were before all this happened.'

'Oh you're just a pessimist,' said Baby. 'I mean you've got to look on the bright side.'

Piper did. Even the bay was lit up by the conflagration and a number of boats had gathered offshore to watch the blaze.

'And just how do you think you're going to explain all this?' he said, forgetting for the moment that he was free and that there was no going back. Baby turned on him violently.

'Who's to explain to?' she demanded. 'We're dead. Get it, dead. We don't exist in the world where that happened. That's past history. It hasn't got anything to do with us. We belong to the future.'

'Well someone's going to have to explain it,' said Piper, 'I mean you can't just go round burning houses down and exploding boats and hope that people aren't going to ask questions. And what happens when they don't find our bodies at the bottom of the bay?'

'They'll think we floated out to sea or the sharks got us or something. That's not our problem what they think. We've got our new lives to live.'

'Fat chance there's going to be of that,' said Piper, not to be consoled. But Baby was undismayed. Grasping Piper's hand she led the way on through the woods.

'Dual destiny, here we come,' she said gaily. Behind her Piper groaned. Dual destiny with this demented woman was the last thing he wanted. Presently they came out of the woods again. In front of them stood another large house. Its windows were dark and there was no sign of life.

'We'll hole up here until the heat's off,' said Baby using a vernacular that Piper had previously only heard in B-movies.

'What about the people who live here?' he asked. 'Aren't they going to mind if we just move in?'

'They won't know. This is the Van der Hoogens' house and they're away on a world tour. We'll be as safe as houses.'

Piper groaned again. In the light of what had just happened at the Hutchmeyer house the saying seemed singularly inappropriate. They crossed the grass and went round a gravel path to the side door.

'They always leave the key in the glasshouse,' said Baby. 'You just stay here and I'll go get it.' She went off and Piper stood uncertainly by the door. Now if ever was his chance to escape. But he didn't take it. He had lived too long in the shadow of other authors' identities to be able now to act on his own behalf. By the time Baby returned he was shaking. A reaction to his predicament had set in. He wobbled into the house after her. Baby locked the door behind them.

In Hampstead Frensic got up early. It was Sunday, the day before publication, and the reviews of *Pause O Men for the Virgin* should be in the papers. He walked up the hill to the newsagent and bought them all, even the *News of The World* which didn't review books but would be consoling reading if the reviews were bad in the others or, worse still, non-existent. Then, savouring his self-restraint, he strolled back to his flat without glancing at them on the way and put the kettle on for breakfast. He would have toast and marmalade and go through the papers as he ate. He was just making coffee when the telephone rang. It was Geoffrey Corkadale.

'You've seen the reviews?' he asked excitedly. Frensic said he hadn't.

'I've only just got up,' he said, piqued that Geoffrey had robbed him of the pleasure of reading the evidently excellent coverage. 'I gather from your tone that they're good.'

'Good? They're raves, absolute raves. Listen to what Frieda Gormley has to say in *The Times*, "The first serious novel to attempt the disentanglement of the social complicity surrounding the sexual taboo that has for so long separated youth from age. Of its kind *Pause O Men for the Virgin* is a masterpiece." '

122

'Gormless bitch,' muttered Frensic.

'Isn't that splendid?' said Geoffrey.

'It's senseless,' said Frensic. 'If *Pause* is the first novel to attempt the disentanglement of complicity, and Lord alone knows how anyone does that, it can't be "of its kind". It hasn't got any kind. The bloody book is unique.'

'That's in the *Observer*,' said Geoffrey, not to be discouraged, 'Sheila Shelmerdine says, "*Pause O Men* blah blah blah moves us by the very intensity of its literary merits while at the same time demonstrating a compassionate concern for the elderly and the socially isolated. This unique novel attempts to unfathom those aspects of life which for too long have been ignored by those whose business it is to advance the frontiers of social sensibility. A lovely book and one that deserves the widest readership." What do you think of that?'

'Frankly,' said Frensic, 'I regard it as unmitigated tosh but I'm delighted that Miss Shelmerdine has said it all the same. I always said it would be a money-spinner.'

'You did, you most certainly did,' said Geoffrey, 'I have to hand it to you, you've been absolutely right.'

'Well we'll have to see about that,' said Frensic before Geoffrey could become too effusive. 'Reviews aren't everything. People have yet to buy the book. Still, it augurs well for American sales. Is there anything else?'

'There's a rather nasty piece by Octavian Dorr.'

'Oh good,' said Frensic. 'He's usually to the point and I like his style.'

'I don't,' said Geoffrey. 'He's far too personal for my taste and he should stick to the book. That's what he's paid for. Instead he has made some rather odious comparisons. Still I suppose he has given us some quotable quotes for the jacket of Piper's next book and that's the main thing.'

'Quite,' said Frensic and turned with relish to Octavian Dorr's column in the *Sunday Telegraph*, 'I just hope we do as well with the weeklies.'

He put the phone down, made some toast and settled down with Octavian Dorr whose piece was headed 'Permissive Senility'. It began, 'It is appropriate that the publishers of *Pause O Men for the Virgin* by Peter Piper should have printed their first book during the reign of Catherine The Great. The so-called heroine of this their

123

latest has many of the less attractive characteristics of that Empress of Russia. In particular a fondness amounting to sexual mania for the favours of young men and a partiality for indiscretion that was, to say the least, regrettable. The same can be said for the publishers, Corkadales...'

Frensic could see exactly why Geoffrey had hated the review. Frensic found it entirely to his taste. It was long and strident and while it castigated the author, the publisher and the public whose appetite for perverse eroticism made the sale of such novels profitable, and then went on to blame society in general for the decline in literary values, it nevertheless drew attention to the book. Mr Dorr might deplore perverse eroticism but he also helped to sell it. Frensic finished the review with a sigh of relief and turned to the others. Their praise, the presumptuous pap of progressive opinion, earnest, humourless and sickeningly well-meaning, had given *Pause* the imprimatur of respectability Frensic had hoped for. The novel was being taken seriously and if the weeklies followed suit there was nothing to worry about.

'Significance is all,' Frensic murmured and helped his nose to snuff. 'Prime the pump with meaningful hogwash.'

He settled back in his chair and wondered if there was anything he could do to ensure that *Pause* got the maximum publicity. Some nice big sensational story for the daily papers . . .

Chapter 14

In the event Frensic had no need to worry. Five hours to the west the sensational story of Piper's death at sea was beginning to break. So was Hutchmeyer. He sat in the police chief's office and stared at the chief and told his story for the tenth time to an incredulous audience. It was the empty gasolene cans that were fouling things up for him.

'Like I've told you, Miss Futtle tied them to me to keep me afloat while she went to get help.'

'She went to get help, Mr Hutchmeyer? You let a little lady go and get help . . .'

'She wasn't little,' said Hutchmeyer, 'she's goddam large.'

Chief Greensleeves shook his head sorrowfully at this lack of chivalry. 'So you were out in the middle of the bay with this Miss Futtle. What was Mrs Hutchmeyer doing all this time?'

'How the hell would I know? Setting fire to my hou . . .' Hutchmeyer stopped himself.

'That's mighty interesting,' said Greensleeves. 'So you're telling us Mrs Hutchmeyer is an arsonist.'

'No I'm not,' shouted Hutchmeyer, 'all I know is—' He was interrupted by a lieutenant who came in with a suitcase and several articles of clothing, all sodden.

'Coastguards found these out in the wreckage,' he said and held a coat up for inspection. Hutchmeyer stared at it in horror.

'That's Baby's,' he said. 'Mink. Cost a fortune.'

'And this?' asked the lieutenant indicating the suitcase.

Hutchmeyer shrugged. The lieutenant opened the case and removed a passport.

Greensleeves took it from him. 'British,' he said. 'British passport in the name of Piper, Peter Piper. The name mean anything to you?'

Hutchmeyer nodded. 'He's an author.'

'Friend of yours?'

'One of my authors. I wouldn't call him a friend.'

125

'Friend of Mrs Hutchmeyer maybe?' Hutchmeyer ground his teeth.

'Didn't hear that, Mr Hutchmeyer. Did you say something?'

'No,' said Hutchmeyer.

Chief Greensleeves scratched his head thoughtfully. 'Seems like we've got ourselves another little problem here,' he said finally. 'Your cruiser blows out of the water like she's been dynamited and when we go look see what do we find? A mink coat that's Mrs Hutchmeyer's and a bag that belongs to a Mr Piper who just happens to be her friend. You think there's any connection?'

'What do you mean "any connection"?' said Hutchmeyer.

'Like they was on that cruiser when she blew?'

'How the hell would I know where they were? All I know is that whoever was on that cruiser tried to kill me.'

'Interesting you saying that,' said Chief Greensleeves, 'very interesting.'

'I don't see anything interesting about it.'

'Couldn't be the other way round, could it?'

'Could what be the other way round?' said Hutchmeyer.

'That you killed them?'

'I did what?' shouted Hutchmeyer and let go his blanket. 'Are you accusing me of—'

'Just asking questions, Mr Hutchmeyer. There's no need for you getting excited.

But Hutchmeyer was out of his chair. 'My house burns down, my cruiser blows up, my yacht's sunk under me, I'm in the water drowning some hours and you sit there and suggest I killed my . . . why you fat bastard I'll have my lawyers sue you for everything you've got. I'll—'

'Sit down and shut up,' bawled Greensleeves. 'Now you just listen to me. Fat bastard I may be but no New York mobster's going to tell me. We know all about you, Mr Hutchmeyer. We don't just sit on our asses and watch you move in and buy up good real estate with money that could be laundered for the Mafia and we don't know about it. This isn't Hicksville and it isn't New York. This is Maine and you don't carry any weight round here. And we don't like your sort moving in and buying us up. We may be a poor state but we ain't dumb. Now, are you going to tell us what really happened with your wife and her fancy friend or are we going to have to drag the bay and sift the ashes of your house till we find them?'

Hutchmeyer slumped nakedly back into his chair, appalled at the glimpse he had just been given of his social standing in Frenchman's Bay. Like Piper, he knew now that he should never have come to Maine. He was more than ever convinced of his mistake when the lieutenant came in with Baby's travel bags and pocket book.

'There's a whole lot of money in the bag,' he told Greensleeves. The Chief pawed through it and extracted a wad of wet notes. 'Seems like Mrs Hutchmeyer was going some place with a lot of dollars when she died,' he said. 'So now we've really got ourselves a problem. Mrs Hutchmeyer on that cruiser with her friend, Mr Piper. Both got baggage with them and money. And then "Bam" their cruiser explodes just like that. I reckon we're going to have send divers down to see if they can find the bodies.'

'Have to start quick,' said the lieutenant. 'The way the tide's running they could be out to sea by now.'

'So we start now,' said Greensleeves and went out into the lobby where some reporters were waiting.

'Got any theory?' they asked.

Greensleeves shook his head. 'We got two people missing presumed drowned. Mrs Baby Hutchmeyer and a Mr Peter Piper. He's a British author. That's all for now.'

'What about this Miss Futtle?' said the lieutenant. 'She's missing too.'

'And what about the house being burnt down?'

'We're waiting for a report on that,' said Greensleeves.

'But you do suspect deliberate arson?'

Greensleeves shrugged. 'You put all these things together and work out what I suspect,' he said and pressed on. Five minutes later the wires were buzzing with the news that Peter Piper, the famous author, was dead in bizarre circumstances.

In the Van der Hoogen mansion the victims of the tragedy listened to the news of their deaths on a transistor in the gloom of a bedroom on the top floor. Part of the gloom resulted from the shutters on the windows and part, from Piper's point of view, from the prospect that his death opened up before him. It was bad enough being an author by proxy, but being a corpse by proxy was awful beyond belief. Baby on the other hand greeted the news gaily.

'We've made it,' she said, 'they're not even going to come looking for us. You heard what they said. With the tide running the skin-divers aren't expecting to find the bodies.'

Piper looked miserably round the bedroom. 'It's all very well you talking,' he said. 'What you don't seem to understand is that I don't have an identity. I've lost my passport and all my work. How on earth am I going to get back to England? I can't go to the Embassy and ask for another passport. And the moment I appear in public I'm going to be arrested for arson and boat-burning and attempted murder. You've landed us in a ghastly mess.'

'I've freed you from the past. You can be anyone you want to be now.'

'All I want to be is myself,' said Piper.

Baby looked at him dubiously. 'From what you told me last night you weren't yourself before,' she said, 'I mean what sort of self were you being the author of a book you didn't write?'

'At least I knew what I wasn't. Now I don't even know that.'

'You're not a dead body. That's one good thing.'

'I might just as well be,' said Piper looking lugubriously at the sheeted forms of the furniture as if they were so many shrouds cloaking those different authors he had so happily aspired to be. The dim light filtering through the shuttered windows added to the impression that he was sitting in a tomb, the sepulchre of his literary ambitions. A sense of profound melancholy settled on him and with it the imagery of *The Flying Dutchman* doomed to wander the seas until such day . . . but for Piper there would be no release. He had been party to a crime, a whole number of crimes, and even if he went to the police now they wouldn't believe him. Why should they? Was it likely that a rich woman like Baby would burn down her own home and blow up an expensive cruiser and sink her husband's yacht? And even if she admitted that she was to blame for the whole thing, there would still be a trial and Hutchmeyer's lawyers would want to know why his suitcase had been on the boat. And finally the fact that he hadn't written *Pause* would come out and then everyone would suspect . . . not even suspect, they would be certain he was a fraud and after the Hutchmeyer money. And Baby had stolen a quarter of a million dollars from the safe in Hutchmeyer's study. Piper shoook his head hopelessly and looked up to find her watching him with interest.

'No way, baby,' she said evidently reading his mind. 'It's dual destiny for us now. You try anything and I'll turn myself in and say you forced me.'

128

But Piper was past trying anything. 'What are we going to do now?' he asked. 'I mean we can't just sit here in someone else's house for ever.'

'Two days, maybe three,' said Baby, 'then we'll move on.'

'How? Just how are we going to move on?'

'Simple,' said Baby, 'I'll call for a cab and we'll take a flight from Bangor. No problems. They won't be looking for us on dry land . . .'

She was interrupted by a crunch on the drive. Piper went to the shutters and looked down. A police car had stopped outside.

'The cops,' Piper whispered. 'You said they wouldn't be looking for us.'

Baby joined him at the window. A bell chimed eerily two floors below. 'They're merely checking the Van der Hoogens to ask if they heard anything suspicious last night,' she said, 'they'll go away again.' Piper stared down at the two policemen. All he had to do now was to call out and . . . but Baby's fingers tightened on his arm and Piper made no sound. Presently after wandering round outside the house the two cops got back into their car and drove away.

'What did I tell you?' said Baby, 'no problems. I'll go down the kitchen and get us something to eat.'

Left to himself Piper paced the dim room and wondered why he hadn't called out to those two policemen. The simple, obvious reasons no longer sufficed. If he had called out it would have been some proof that he'd had nothing to do with the fire . . . at least an indication of innocence. But he had made no move. Why not? He had had a chance to escape from this mess and he hadn't taken it. Not through fear only but more alarmingly out of a willingness, almost a desire, to remain alone in this empty house with an extraordinary woman. What sort of terrible complicity was it that had prevented him? Baby was mad. He had no doubt in his mind about that and yet she exercised a weird fascination for him. He had never met anyone in his life before like her. She was oblivious of the ordinary conventions that ordered other people's lives and she could look calmly down at the police and say 'They will go away again' as if they were simply neighbours paying a social call. And they had. And he had done what she had expected and would go on doing it, even to the point of being anyone he wanted in this circumscribed freedom she had created round him by her actions. Anyone he wanted? He could only think of other authors but none had been in his predicament, and without a model to guide him Piper was thrown back on his own limited resources. And on Baby's. He would become what she wanted. That was the truth of the matter. Piper glimpsed the attraction she held for him. She knew what he was. She had said so last night before everything had started to go wrong. She had said he was a literary genius and she had meant it. For the first time he had met someone who knew what he really was and having found her he couldn't let her go. Exhausted by this frightening realization Piper lay down on the bed and closed his eyes and when Baby came upstairs with a tray she found him fast asleep. She looked at him fondly and then putting the tray down, took a sheet from a chair and covered him with it. Under the shroud Piper slept on.

In the police station Hutchmeyer would have done the same if they had let him. Instead, still naked beneath the blanket, he was subjected to interminable questions about his relations with his wife and with Miss Futtle and what Piper meant to Mrs Hutchmeyer and finally why he had chosen a particularly stormy night to go sailing in the bay.

'You usually go sailing without checking the weather?'

'Look I told you we just went out for a sail. We weren't figuring on going places, we just got up . . .'

'From the dinner table and said, "Let's just you and me . . ."'

'Miss Futtle suggested it,' said Hutchmeyer.

'Oh she did, did she? And what did Mrs Hutchmeyer have to say about you going sailing with another woman?'

'Miss Futtle isn't another woman. Not that sort of other woman. She's a literary agent. We do business together.'

'Naked on a yacht in the middle of a mini-hurricane you do business together? What sort of business?'

'We weren't doing business on the yacht. It was a social occasion.'

'Kind of thought it was. I mean naked and all.'

'I wasn't naked to begin with. I just got wet so I took my clothes off.'

'You just got wet so you took your clothes off? Are you sure that was the only reason you were naked?'

'Of course I'm sure. Look, no sooner had we got out there than the wind blew up . . .'

'And the house blew up. And your cruiser blew up. And Mrs Hutchmeyer blew up and this Mr Piper . . .' Hutchmeyer blew up.

130

'Okay, Mr Hutchmeyer, if that's the way you want it,' said Greensleeves as Hutchmeyer was pinned back into his chair. 'Now we're really going to get tough.'

He was interrupted by a sergeant who whispered in his ear. Greensleeves sighed. 'You're sure?'

'That's what she says. Been up at the hospital all day.'

Greensleeves went out and looked at Sonia. 'Miss Futtle? You say you're Miss Futtle?'

Sonia nodded. 'Yes,' she said. The police chief could see that Hutchmeyer had been telling the truth after all. Miss Futtle was not a little lady, not by a long way.

'Okay, we'll take your statement in here,' he said and took her into another office. For two hours Sonia made her statement. When Greensleeves came out he had an entirely new theory. Miss Futtle had been most cooperative.

'Right,' he said to Hutchmeyer, 'now we'd like you to tell us just what happened down in New York when Piper arrived. We understand you arranged a kind of riot for him.'

Hutchmeyer looked wildly round. 'Now wait a minute. That was just a publicity stunt. I mean . . .'

'And what I mean,' said Greensleeves, 'is that you set this Mr Piper up for a target for every crazy pressure group going. Arabs, Jews, Gays, the IRA, the blacks, old women, you name it, you let them loose on the guy and you call that a publicity stunt?'

Hutchmeyer tried to think. 'Are you telling me that one of those groups did this thing?' he asked.

'I'm not telling you anything, Mr Hutchmeyer. I'm asking.'

'Asking what?'

'Asking you if you think it was so goddam clever setting Mr Piper up for a target when the poor guy hadn't done anything worse than write a book for you? Doesn't seem you did yourself or him a favour the way things have worked out, does it?'

'I didn't think anything like this . . .'

Greensleeves leant forward. 'Now I'm just telling you something for your own good, Mr Hutchmeyer. You're going to get the hell out of here and not come back. Not if you know what's good for you. And next time you dream up a publicity stunt for one of your authors you'd better get him a goddam bodyguard first.'

Hutchmeyer staggered out of the office.

'I need some clothes,' he said.

131

'Well you're not going to get any back at your house. It's all burnt down.'

On a bench Sonia Futtle was weeping.

'What's the matter with her?' said Hutchmeyer.

'She's all broken up with this Piper's dying,' said Greensleeves, 'and it kind of surprises me you aren't grief-stricken about the late Mrs Hutchmeyer.'

'I am,' said Hutchmeyer, 'I just don't show my feelings is all.'

'So I noticed,' said Greensleeves. 'Well you'd better go comfort your alibi. We'll send out for some clothes.'

Hutchmeyer crossed to the bench in his blanket. 'I'm sorry . . .' he began but Sonia was on her feet.

'Sorry?' she shrieked, 'you murdered my darling Peter and now you say you're sorry?'

'Murdered him?' said Hutchmeyer. 'All I did was . . .'

Greensleeves left them to it and sent out for some clothes. 'We can forget this case,' he told the lieutenant, 'this is Federal stuff. Terrorists in Maine. I mean who the hell would believe it?'

'You don't think it was the Mafia then?'

'What's it matter who it was? We aren't going to get anywhere to solving it is all I know. The FBI can handle this case. I know when I'm out of my depth.'

In the end Hutchmeyer, dressed in a dark suit that didn't fit him properly, and the still inconsolable Sonia were driven to the airport and took the company plane to New York.

They landed to find that MacMordie had laid on the media. Hutchmeyer lumbered down the steps and made a statement.

'Gentlemen,' he said brokenly, 'this has been a double tragedy for me. I have lost the most wonderful, warm-hearted little wife a man ever had. Forty years of happy marriage lie . . .' He broke off to blow his nose. 'It's just terrible. I can't express the full depths of my feelings.'

'What about this Piper?' someone asked. Hutchmeyer drew on his reserves of deep feelings.

'Peter Piper was a young novelist of unsurpassed brilliance. His passing has been a great blow to the world of letters.' He paraded his handkerchief again and was prompted by MacMordie.

'Say something about his novel,' he whispered.

Hutchmeyer stopped sniffling and said something about *Pause O*

132

Men for the Virgin published by Hutchmeyer Press price seven dollars ninety and available at all . . . Behind him Sonia wept audibly and had to be escorted to the waiting car. She was still weeping when they drove off.

'A terrible tragedy,' said Hutchmeyer, still under the influence of his own oratory, 'really terrible.'

He was interrupted by Sonia who was pummelling MacMordie.

'Murderer,' she screamed, 'it was all your fault. You told all those crazy terrorists he was in the KGB and the IRA and a homosexual and now look what's happened !'

'What the hell's going on?' yelled MacMordie, 'I didn't do . . .'

'The fucking cops up in Maine think it was the Symbionese Liberation Army or The Minutemen or someone,' said Hutchmeyer, 'so now we've got another problem.'

'I can see that,' said MacMordie as Sonia blacked his eye. Finally, refusing Hutchmeyer's offer of hospitality, she insisted on being driven to the Gramercy Park Hotel.

'Don't worry,' said Hutchmeyer as she got out, 'I'm going to see that Baby and Piper go to their Maker with all the trimmings. Flowers, a cortège, a bronze casket . . .'

'Two,' said MacMordie, 'I mean they wouldn't fit . . .'

Sonia turned on them. 'They're dead,' she screamed. 'Dead. Doesn't that mean anything to you? Haven't you any consciences? They were real people, real living people and now they're dead and all you can talk about is funerals and caskets and—'

'Well we've got to recover the bodies first,' said MacMordie practically, 'I mean there's no use talking about caskets, we don't have no bodies.'

'Why don't you just shut your mouth?' Hutchmeyer told him, but Sonia had fled into the hotel.

They drove on in silence.

For a while Hutchmeyer had considered firing MacMordie but he changed his mind. After all he had never liked the great wooden house in Maine and with Baby dead . . .

'It was a terrible experience,' he said, 'a terrible loss.'

'It must have been,' said MacMordie, 'all that loveliness gone to waste.'

'It was a showhouse, part of the American heritage. People used to come up from Boston just to look at it.'

'I was thinking of Mrs Hutchmeyer,' said MacMordie. Hutchmeyer looked at him nastily.

'I might have expected that from you, MacMordie. At a time like this you have to think about sex.'

'I wasn't thinking sex,' said MacMordie, 'she was a remarkable woman characterwise.'

'You can say that again,' said Hutchmeyer. 'I want her memory embalmed in books. She was a great book-lover you know. I want a leather-bound edition of *Pause O Men for the Virgin* printed with gold letters. We'll call it the Baby Hutchmeyer Memorial Edition.'

'I'll see to it,' said MacMordie.

And so while Hutchmeyer resumed his role as publisher Sonia Futtle lay weeping on her bed in the Gramercy Park. She was consumed by guilt and grief. The one man who had ever loved her was dead and it was all her fault. She looked at the telephone and thought of calling Frensic but it would be the middle of the night in England. Instead she sent a telegram. PETER PRESUMED DEAD DROWNED MRS HUTCHMEYER DITTO POLICE INVESTIGATING CRIME WILL CALL WHEN CAN SONIA.

Chapter 15

Frensic arrived in Lanyard Lane next morning in fine fettle. The world was a splendid place, the sun was shining, the people would shortly be in the shops buying *Pause* and best of all Hutchmeyer's cheque for two million dollars was nestling happily in the F & F bank account. It had arrived the previous week and all that needed to be done now was to subtract four hundred thousand dollars commission and transfer the remainder to Mr Cadwalladine and his strange client. Frensic would see to it this morning. He collected his mail from the box and stumped upstairs to his office. There he seated himself at his desk, took his first pinch of Bureau for the day and went through the letters in front of him. It was near the bottom of the pile that he came upon the telegram.

'Telegrams, really!' he muttered to himself in criticism of the extravagant hurry of an insistent author and opened it. A moment later Frensic's rosy view of the world had disintegrated, to be replaced by fragmentary and terrible images that rose from the cryptic words on the form. Piper dead? Presumed drowned? Mrs Hutchmeyer ditto? Each staccato message became a question in his mind as he tried to cope with the information. It was a minute before Frensic could realize the full import of the thing and even then he doubted and took refuge in disbelief. Piper couldn't be dead. In Frensic's comfortable little world death was something your authors wrote about. It was unreal and remote, a fabrication, not something that happened. But there, in these few words unadorned by punctuation marks and typed on crooked strips of paper, death intruded. Piper was dead. So was Mrs Hutchmeyer but Frensic accorded her no interest. She wasn't his responsibility. Piper was. Frensic had persuaded him to go to his death. And POLICE INVESTIGATING CRIME robbed him of even the consolation that there had been an accident. Crime and death suggested murder and to be confronted with Piper's murder added to Frensic's sense of horror. He sagged in his chair ashen with shock.

It was some time before he could bring himself to read the telegram again. But it still said the same thing. Piper dead. Frensic wiped his face with his handkerchief and tried to imagine what had happened. This time PRESUMED DROWNED held his attention. If Piper was dead why was there the presumption that he had drowned? Surely they knew how he had died. And why couldn't Sonia call? WILL CALL WHEN CAN added a new dimension of mystery to the message. Where could she be if she couldn't phone straightaway? Frensic visualized her lying hurt in a hospital but if that was the case she would have said so. He reached for the phone to put a call through to Hutchmeyer Press before realizing that New York was five hours behind London time and there would be no one in the office yet. He would have to wait until two o'clock. He sat staring at the telegram and tried to think practically. If the police were investigating the crime it was almost certain they would follow their enquiries into Piper's past. Frensic foresaw them discovering that Piper hadn't in fact written *Pause*. From that it would follow that . . . my God, Hutchmeyer would get to know and there'd be the devil to pay. Or, more precisely, Hutchmeyer. The man would demand the return of his two million dollars. He might even sue for breach of contract or fraud. Thank God the money was still in the bank. Frensic sighed with relief.

To take his mind off the dreadful possibilities inherent in the telegram he went through to Sonia's office and looked in the filing cabinet for the letter from Mr Cadwalladine authorizing Piper to represent the author on the American tour. He took it out and studied it carefully before putting it back. At least he was covered there. If there was any trouble with Hutchmeyer Mr Cadwalladine and his client were party to the deception. And if the two million had to be refunded they would be in no position to grumble. By concentrating on these eventualities Frensic held at bay his sense of guilt and transferred it to the anonymous author. Piper's death was his fault. If the wretched man had not hidden behind a *nom-de-plume* Piper would still be alive. As the morning wore on and he sat unable to work at anything else Frensic's feeling of grievance grew. He had been fond of Piper in an odd sort of way. And now he was dead. Frensic sat miserably at his desk looking out over the roofs of Covent Garden and mourned Piper's passing. The poor fellow had been one of nature's victims, or rather one of literature's victims. Pathetic. A man who couldn't write to save his life . . .

The phrase brought Frensic up with a start. It was too apt. Piper

136

was dead and he had never really lived. His existence had been one long battle to get into print and he had failed. What was it that drove men like him to try to write, what fixation with the printed word held them at their desks year after year? All over the world there were thousands of other Pipers sitting at this very moment in front of blank pages which they would presently fill with words that no one would ever read but which in their naïve conceit they considered to have some deep significance. The thought added to Frensic's melancholy. It was all his fault. He should have had the courage and good sense to tell Piper that he would never be a novelist. Instead he had encouraged him. If he had told him Piper would still be alive, he might even have found his true vocation as a bank clerk or plumber, have married and settled down – whatever that meant. Anyway, he wouldn't have spent those forlorn years in forlorn guest-houses in forlorn seaside resorts living by proxy the lives of Conrad and Lawrence and Henry James, the shadowy ghost of those dead authors he had revered. Even Piper's death had been by way of being a proxy one as the author of a novel he hadn't written. And somewhere the man who should have died was living undisturbed.

Frensic reached for the phone. The bastard wasn't going to go on living undisturbed. Mr Cadwalladine could relay a message to him. He dialled Oxford.

'I'm afraid I've got some rather bad news for you,' he said when Mr Cadwalladine came on the line.

'Bad news? I don't understand,' said Mr Cadwalladine.

'It concerns the young man who went to America as the supposed author of that novel you sent me,' said Frensic.

Mr Cadwalladine coughed uncomfortably. 'Has he ... er ... done something indiscreet?' he asked.

'You could put it like that,' said Frensic. 'The fact of the matter is that we are likely to have some problems with the police.' Mr Cadwalladine made more uncomfortable noises which Frensic relished. 'Yes, the police,' he continued. 'They may be making enquiries shortly.'

'Enquiries?' said Mr Cadwalladine, now definitely alarmed. 'What sort of enquiries?'

'I can't be too certain at the moment but I thought I had better let you and your client know that he is dead,' said Frensic.

'Dead?' croaked Mr Cadwalladine.

'Dead,' said Frensic.

137

'Good Lord. How very unfortunate.'

'Quite,' said Frensic. 'Though from Piper's point of view "unfortunate" seems rather too mild a word, particularly as he appears to have been murdered.'

This time there was no mistaking Mr Cadwalladine's alarm. 'Murdered?' he gasped. 'You did say "murdered"?'

'That's exactly what I said. Murdered.'

'Good God,' said Mr Cadwalladine. 'How very dreadful.'

Frensic said nothing and allowed Mr Cadwalladine to dwell on the dreadfulness of it all.

'I don't quite know what to say,' Mr Cadwalladine muttered finally.

Frensic pressed home his advantage. 'In that case if you will just give me the name and address of your client I will convey the news to him myself.'

Mr Cadwalladine made negative noises. 'There's no need for that. I shall let him know.'

'As you wish,' said Frensic. 'And while you're about it you had also better let him know that he will have to wait for his American advance.'

'Wait for his American advance? You're surely not suggesting . . .'

'I am not suggesting anything. I am merely drawing your attention to the fact that Mr Hutchmeyer was not privy to the substitution of Mr Piper for your anonymous client and, that being the case, if the police should unearth our little deception in the course of their enquiries . . . you take my point?'

Mr Cadwalladine did. 'You think Mr . . . er . . . Hutchmeyer might . . . er . . . demand restitution?'

'Or sue,' said Frensic bluntly, 'in which case it would be as well to be in a position to refund the entire sum at once.'

'Oh definitely,' said Mr Cadwalladine for whom the prospect of being sued evidently held very few attractions. 'I leave the matter entirely in your hands.'

Frensic ended the conversation with a sigh. Now that he had passed some of the responsibility on to Mr Cadwalladine and his damned client he felt a little better. He took a pinch of snuff and was savouring it when the phone rang. It was Sonia Futtle calling from New York. She sounded extremely distressed.

'Oh Frenzy I'm so sorry,' she said, 'it's all my fault. If it hadn't been for me this would never happened.'

138

'What do you mean your fault?' said Frensic. 'You don't mean you ...'

'I should never have brought him over here. He was so happy ...' she broke off and there was the sound of sobs.

Frensic gulped. 'For God's sake tell me what's happened,' he said.

'The police think it was murder,' said Sonia and sobbed again.

'I gathered that from your telegram. But I still don't know what happened. I mean how did he die?'

'Nobody knows,' said Sonia, 'that's what's so awful. They're dragging the bay and going through the ashes of the house and ...'

'The ashes of the house?' said Frensic, trying desperately to square a burnt house with Piper's presumed death by drowning.

'You see Hutch and I went out in his yacht and a storm blew up and then the house caught fire and someone fired at the firemen and Hutch's cruiser tried to ram us and exploded and we were nearly killed and ...'

It was a confused and disjointed account and Frensic, sitting with the phone pressed hard to his ear, tried in vain to form a coherent picture of what had occurred. In the end he was left with a series of chaotic images, an insane jigsaw puzzle in which though the pieces all fitted the final picture made no sense at all. A huge wooden house blazing into the night sky. Someone inside this inferno fending off firemen with a heavy machine-gun. Bears. Hutchmeyer and Sonia on a yacht in a hurricane. Cruisers hurtling across the bay and finally, most bizarre of all, Piper being blown to Kingdom Come in the company of Mrs Hutchmeyer wearing a mink coat. It was like a glimpse of hell.

'Have they no idea who did it?' he asked.

'Only some terrorist group,' said Sonia. Frensic swallowed.

'Terrorist group? Why should a terrorist group want to kill poor Piper?'

'Well because of all the publicity he got in that riot in New York,' said Sonia. 'You see when we landed ...'

She told the story of their arrival and Frensic listened in horror. 'You mean Hutchmeyer deliberately provoked a riot? The man's mad.'

'He wanted to get maximum publicity,' Sonia explained.

'Well he's certainly succeeded,' said Frensic.

139

But Sonia was sobbing again. 'You're just callous,' she wept. 'You don't seem to see what this means . . .'

'I do,' said Frensic, 'it means the police are going to start looking into Piper's background and . . .'

'That we're to blame,' cried Sonia, 'we sent him over and we are the ones—'

'Now hold it,' said Frensic, 'if I'd known Hutchmeyer was going to rent a riot for his welcome I would never have consented to his going. And as for terrorists . . .'

'The police aren't absolutely certain it was terrorists. They thought at first that Hutchmeyer had murdered him.'

'That's more like it,' said Frensic. 'From what you've told me it's nothing more than the truth. He's an accessory before the fact. If he hadn't . . .'

'And then they seemed to think the Mafia could be involved.'

Frensic swallowed again. This was even worse. 'The Mafia? What would the Mafia want to kill Piper for? The poor little sod hadn't . . .'

'Not Piper. Hutchmeyer.'

'You mean the Mafia were trying to kill Hutchmeyer?' said Frensic wistfully.

'I don't know what I mean,' said Sonia, 'I'm telling you what I heard the police say and they mentioned that Hutchmeyer had had dealings with organized crime.'

'If the Mafia wanted to kill Hutchmeyer why did they pick on Piper?'

'Because Hutch and I were out on the yacht and Peter and Baby . . .'

'What baby?' said Frensic desperately incorporating this new and grisly ingredient into an already cluttered crimescape.

'Baby Hutchmeyer.'

'Baby Hutchmeyer? I didn't know the swine had any . . .'

'Not that sort of baby. Mrs Hutchmeyer. She was called Baby.'

'Good God,' said Frensic.

'There's no need to be so heartless. You sound as if you didn't care.'

'Care?' said Frensic. 'Of course I care. This is absolutely frightful. And you say the Mafia . . .'

'No I didn't. I said that's what the police said. They thought it was some sort of attempt to intimidate Hutchmeyer.'

'And has it?' asked Frensic trying to extract a morsel of comfort from the situation.

'No,' said Sonia, 'he's out for blood. He says he's going to sue them.'

Frensic was horrified. 'Sue them? What do you mean "sue them"? You can't sue the Mafia and anyway . . .'

'Not them. The police.'

'Hutchmeyer's going to sue the police?' said Frensic now totally out of his depth.

'Well first off they accused him of doing it. They held him for hours and grilled him. They didn't believe his story that he was out on the yacht with me. And then the gas cans didn't help.'

'Gas can? What gas can?'

'The ones I tied round his waist.'

'You tied gas cans round Hutchmeyer's waist?' said Frensic.

'I had to. To stop him from drowning.'

Frensic considered the logic of this remark and found it wanting. 'I should have thought . . .' he began before deciding there was nothing to be gained by regretting that Hutchmeyer hadn't been left to drown. It would have saved a lot of trouble.

'What are you going to do now?' he asked finally.

'I don't know,' said Sonia, 'I've got to wait around. The police are still making enquiries and I've lost all my clothes . . . and oh Frenzy it's all so horrible.' She broke down again and wept. Frensic tried to think of something to cheer her up.

'You'll be interested to hear that the reviews in the Sunday papers were all good,' he said but Sonia's grief was not assuaged.

'How can you talk about reviews at a time like this?' she said. 'You just don't care is all.'

'My dear I do. I most certainly do,' said Frensic, 'it's a tragedy for all of us. I've just been speaking to Mr Cadwalladine and explaining that in the light of what has happened his client will have to wait for his money.'

'Money? Money? Is that all you think about, money? My darling Peter is dead and . . .'

Frensic listened to a diatribe against himself, Hutchmeyer and someone called MacMordie, all of whom in Sonia's opinion thought only about money. 'I understand your feelings,' he said when she paused for breath, 'but money does come into this business and if Hutchmeyer finds out that Piper wasn't the author of *Pause* . . .'

But the phone had gone dead. Frensic looked at it reproachfully and replaced the receiver. All he could hope now was that Sonia kept

141

her wits about her and that the police didn't carry their investigations too far into Piper's past history.

In New York Hutchmeyer's feelings were just the reverse. In his opinion the police were a bunch of half-wits who couldn't investigate anything properly. He had already been in touch with his lawyers only to be advised that there was no chance of sueing Chief Greensleeves for wrongful arrest because he hadn't been arrested.

'That bastard held me for hours with nothing on but a blanket,' Hutchmeyer protested. 'They grilled me under hot lamps and you tell me I've got no comeback. There ought to be a law protecting innocent citizens against that kind of victimization.'

'Now if you could show they'd roughed you up a bit we could maybe do something but as it is . . .'

Having failed to get satisfaction from his own lawyers Hutchmeyer turned his attention to the insurance company and got even less comfort there. Mr Synstrom of the Claims Department visited him and expressed doubts.

'What do you mean you don't necessarily go along with the police theory that some crazy terrorists did this thing?' Hutchmeyer demanded.

Mr Synstrom's eyes glinted behind silver-rimmed spectacles. 'Three and a half million dollars is a lot of money,' he said.

'Of course it is,' said Hutchmeyer, 'and I've been paying my premiums and that's a lot of money too. So what are you telling me?'

Mr Synstrom consulted his briefcase. 'The Coastguard recovered six suitcases belonging to Mrs Hutchmeyer. That's one. They contained all her jewellery and her best clothing. That's two. Three is that Mr Piper's suitcase was on board that boat and we've checked it contained all his clothes too.'

'So what?' said Hutchmeyer.

'So if this is a political murder it seems peculiar that the terrorists made them pack their bags first and loaded them aboard the cruiser and then set fire to the boat and arsoned the house. That doesn't fit the profile of terrorist acts of crime. It looks like something else again.'

Hutchmeyer glared at him. 'If you're suggesting I blew myself up in my own yacht and bumped my wife and most promising author . . .'

'I'm not suggesting anything,' Mr Synstrom said, 'all I'm saying is that we've got to go into this thing a lot deeper.'

'Yeah, well you do that,' said Hutchmeyer, 'and when you've finished I want my money.'

'Don't worry,' said Mr Synstrom, 'we'll get to the bottom of this thing. With three and a half million at stake we've incentive.'

He got up and made for the door. 'Oh and by the way it may interest you to know that whoever arsoned your house knew exactly where everything was. Like the fuel store. This could have been an inside job.'

He left Hutchmeyer with the uncomfortable notion that if the cops were morons, Mr Synstrom and his investigators weren't. An inside job? Hutchmeyer thought about the words. And all Baby's jewellery on board. Maybe . . . just supposing she *had* been going to run off with that jerk Piper? Hutchmeyer permitted himself the luxury of a smile. If that was the case the bitch had got what was coming to her. Just so long as those incriminating documents she had deposited with her lawyers didn't suddenly turn up. That wasn't such a pleasant prospect. Why couldn't Baby have gone some simpler way, like a coronary?

Chapter 16

In Maine the Van der Hoogens' mansion was shuttered and shrouded and empty. As Baby had promised their departure had passed un-noticed. Leaving Piper alone in the dim twilight of the house she had simply walked into Bellsworth and bought a car, a second-hand estate.

'We'll ditch it in New York and buy something different,' she said as they drove south. 'We don't want to leave any trail behind us.'

Piper, lying on the floor in the back, did not share her confidence. 'That's all very well,' he grumbled, 'but they're still going to be looking for us when they don't find our bodies out in the bay. I mean it stands to reason.'

But Baby drove on unperturbed. 'They'll reckon we were washed out to sea by the tide,' she said. 'That's what would have happened if we had really drowned. Besides I heard in Bellsworth they picked up your passport and my jewels in the bags they found. They've got to believe we're dead. A woman like me doesn't part with pearls and diamonds until the good Lord sends for her.'

Piper lay on the floor and found some sense in this argument. Certainly Frensic & Futtle would believe he was dead and without his passport and his ledgers . . . 'Did they find my notebooks too?' he asked.

'Didn't mention them but if they got your passport, and they did, it's even money your notebooks were with them.'

'I don't know what I'm going to do without my notebooks,' said Piper, 'they contained my life's work.'

He lay back and watched the tops of the trees flashing past and the blue sky beyond, and thought about his life's work. He would never finish *Search for a Lost Childhood* now. He would never be recog-nized as a literary genius. All his hopes had been destroyed in the blaze and its aftermath. He would go through what remained of his existence on earth posthumously famous as the author of *Pause O Men for the Virgin*. It was an intolerable thought and provoked in him a growing determination to put the record straight. There had to be some way of issuing a disclaimer. But disclaimers from beyond

144

the grave were not easy to fabricate. He could hardly write to the *Times Literary Supplement* pointing out that he hadn't in fact written *Pause* but that its authorship had been foisted on to him by Frensic & Futtle for their own dubious ends. Letters signed 'the late Peter Piper' . . . No, that was definitely out. On the other hand it was insufferable to go down in literary history as a pornographer. Piper wrestled with the problem and finally fell asleep.

When he woke they had crossed the state line and were in Vermont. That night they booked into a small motel on the shores of Lake Champlain as Mr and Mrs Castorp. Baby signed the register while Piper carried two empty suitcases purloined from the Van der Hoogen mansion into the cabin.

'We'll have to buy some clothes and things tomorrow,' said Baby. But Piper was not concerned with such material details. He stood at the window staring out and tried to adjust himself to the extraordinary notion that to all intents and purposes he was married to this crazy woman.

'You realize we are never going to be able to separate,' he said at last.

'I don't see why not,' said Baby from the depths of the shower.

'Well for one simple reason I haven't got an identity and can't get a job,' said Piper, 'and for another you've got all the money and if either of us gets picked up by the police we'll go to prison for the rest of our lives.'

'You worry too much,' said Baby. 'This is the land of opportunity. We'll go some place nobody will think of looking and begin all over again.'

'Such as where?'

Baby emerged from the shower. 'Like the South. The Deep South,' she said. 'That's one place Hutchmeyer is never going to come. He's got this thing about the Ku Klux Klan. South of the Mason-Dixon he's never been.'

'And what the hell am I going to do in the Deep South?' asked Piper.

'You could always try your hand at writing Southern novels. Hutch may not go South but he certainly publishes a lot of novels about it. They usually have this man with a whip and a girl cringing on the cover. Surefire bestsellers.'

'Sounds just my sort of book,' said Piper grimly and took a shower himself.

145

'You could always write it under a pseudonym.'

'Thanks to you I'd bloody well have to.'

As night fell outside the cabin Piper crawled into bed and lay thinking about the future. In the twin bed beside him Baby sighed.

'It's great to be with a man who doesn't pee in the washbasin,' she murmured. Piper resisted the invitation without difficulty.

The next morning they moved on again, following back roads and driving slowly and always south. And always Piper's mind nagged away at the problem of how to resume his interrupted career.

In Scranton, where Baby traded the estate for a new Ford, Piper took the opportunity to buy two new ledgers, a bottle of Higgins Ink and an Esterbrook pen.

'If I can't do anything else I can at least keep a diary,' he explained to Baby.

'A diary? You don't even look at the landscape and we eat in McDonalds so what's to put in a diary?'

'I was thinking of writing it retrospectively. As a form of vindication. I would—'

'Vindication? And how can you write a diary retrospectively?'

'Well I'd start with how I was approached by Frensic to come to the States and then work my way forward day by day with the voyage across and everything. That way it would look authentic.'

Baby slowed the car and pulled into a rest area. 'Let's just get this straight. You write the diary backwards . . .'

'Yes, I think it was April the 10th Frensic sent me the telegram . . .'

'Go on. You start 10 April and then what?'

'Well then I'd write how I didn't want to do it and how they persuaded me and promised to get *Search* published and everything.'

'And where would you finish?'

'Finish?' said Piper. 'I wasn't thinking of finishing. I'd just go on and . . .'

'So what about the fire and all?' said Baby.

'Well I would put that in too. I'd have to.'

'And how it started by accident, I suppose?'

'Well, no I wouldn't say that. I mean it didn't did it?'

Baby looked at him and shook her head. 'So you'd put in how I started it and sent the cruiser out to blow up Hutchmeyer and the Futtle? Is that it?'

'I suppose so,' said Piper. 'I mean that's what did happen and . . .'

'And that's what you call vindication. Well you can forget it. No way. You want to vindicate yourself that's fine with me but you don't implicate me at the same time. Dual destiny I said and dual destiny I meant.'

'It's all very well for you to talk,' said Piper morosely, 'you're not lumbered with the reputation of having written that filthy novel and I am . . .'

'I'm just lumbered with a genius is all,' said Baby and started the car again. Piper sat slumped in his seat and sulked.

'The only thing I know how to do is write,' he grumbled, 'and you won't let me.'

'I didn't say that,' said Baby, 'I just said no retrospective diaries. Dead men tell no tales. Not in diaries they don't and anyhow I don't see why you feel so strongly about *Pause*. I thought it was a great book.'

'You would,' said Piper.

'The thing that really has me puzzled is who did write it. I mean they had to have some real good reason for staying under cover.'

'You've only got to read the beastly book to see that,' said Piper. 'All that sex for one thing. And now everyone's going to think I did it.'

'And if you had written the book you would have cut out all the sex?' said Baby.

'Of course. That would be the first thing and then . . .'

'Without the sex the book wouldn't have sold. That much I do know about the book trade.'

'So much the better,' said Piper. 'It debases human values. That is what that book does.'

'In that case you should rewrite it the way you think it ought to have been written . . .' and amazed at this sudden inspiration she lapsed into thoughtful silence.

Twenty miles farther on they entered a small town. Baby parked the car and went into a supermarket. When she returned she was holding a copy of *Pause O Men for the Virgin*.

'They're selling like wild-fire,' she said and handed him the book.

Piper looked at his photograph on the back cover. It had been taken in those halcyon days in London when he had been in love with Sonia and the inane face that smiled up at him seemed to be that of a stranger. 'What am I supposed to do with this?' he asked. Baby smiled.

147

'Write it.'

'Write it?' said Piper. 'But it's already been—'

'Not the way you would have written it, and you're the author.'

'I'm bloody well not.'

'Honey, somewhere out there in the great wide world there is a man who wrote that book. Now he knows it, and Frensic knows it and that Futtle bitch knows it and you and I know it. That's the lot. Hutch doesn't.'

'Thank God,' said Piper.

'Right. And if that's the way you feel, just imagine the way Frensic & Futtle must be feeling now. Two million Hutch paid for that novel. That's a lot of money.'

'It's a ludicrous sum,' said Piper. 'Did you know that Conrad only got—'

'No and I'm not interested. Right now what interests me is what happens when you rewrite this novel in your own beautiful handwriting and Frensic gets the manuscript.'

'Frensic gets . . .' Piper began but Baby silenced him.

'Your manuscript,' she said, 'from beyond the grave.'

'My manuscript from beyond the grave? He'll do his nut.'

'Right first time, and we follow that up with a demand for the advance and full royalties,' said Baby.

'Well, then he'll know I'm still alive,' Piper protested. 'He'll go straight to the police and . . .'

'He does that he's going to have a lot of explaining to do to Hutch and everyone. Hutch will set his legal hound-dogs on him. Yes sir, we've got Messrs Frensic & Futtle right where we want them.'

'You are mad,' said Piper, 'stark staring mad. If you seriously think I'm going to rewrite this awful . . .'

'You were the one who wanted to retrieve your reputation,' said Baby as they drove out of town. 'And this is the only way you can.'

'I wish I could see how.'

'I'll show you,' said Baby. 'Leave it to momma.'

That evening in another motel room Piper opened his ledger, arranged his pen and ink as methodically as they had once been arranged in the Gleneagle Guest House and with a copy of *Pause* propped up in front of him began to write. At the top of the page he wrote 'Chapter One', and underneath, 'The house stood on a knoll.

148

Surrounded by three elms, a beech and a deodar whose horizontal branches gave it the air ...'

Behind him Baby relaxed on a bed with a contented smile. 'Don't make too many alterations this draft,' she said. 'We've got to make it look really authentic.'

Piper stopped writing. 'I thought the whole point of the exercise was to retrieve my lost reputation by rewriting the thing ...'

'You can do that with the second draft,' said Baby. 'This one is to light a fire under Frensic & Futtle. So stay with the text.'

Piper picked up his pen again and stayed with the text. He made several alterations per page and then crossed them out and added the originals from the book. Occasionally Baby got up and looked over his shoulder and was satisfied.

'This is really going to blow Frensic's mind,' she said but Piper hardly heard her. He had resumed his old existence and with it his identity. And so he wrote on obsessively, lost once more in a world of someone else's imagining and as he wrote he foresaw the alterations he would make in the second draft, the draft that would save his reputation. He was still copying at midnight when Baby had gone to bed. Finally at one, tired but vaguely satisfied, Piper brushed his teeth and climbed into bed too. In the morning he would start again.

But in the morning they were on the road again and it was not until late afternoon that Baby pulled into a Howard Johnson's in Beanville, South Carolina, and Piper was able to start work again.

While Piper started his life again as a peripatetic and derivative novelist Sonia Futtle mourned his passing with a passion that did her credit and disconcerted Hutchmeyer.

'What do you mean she won't attend the funeral?' he yelled at MacMordie when he was told that Miss Futtle sent her regrets but was not prepared to take part in a farce simply to promote the sales of *Pause*.

'She says without bodies in the coffins . . .' MacMordie began before being silenced by an apoplectic Hutchmeyer. 'Where the fuck does she think I'm going to get the bodies from? The cops can't get them. The insurance investigators can't get them. The fucking coast-guard divers can't get them. And I'm supposed to go find the things? By this time they're way out in the Atlantic some place or the sharks have got them.'

'But I thought you said they were weighted down like with concrete,' said MacMordie, 'and if they are . . .'

'Never mind what I said, MacMordie. What I'm saying now is we've got to think positive about Baby and Piper.'

'Isn't that a bit difficult? Them being dead and missing and all. I mean . . .'

'And I mean we've got a promotional set-up here that can put *Pause* right up the charts.'

'The computer says sales are good already.'

'Good? Good's not good enough. They've got to be terrific. Now the way I see it we've got an opportunity for building this Piper guy up with a reputation like . . . Who was that bastard got himself knocked off in a car smash?'

'Well there've been so many it's a little difficult to . . .'

'In Hollywood. Famous guy.'

'James Dean,' said MacMordie.

'Not him. A writer. Wrote a great book about insects.'

'Insects?' said MacMordie. 'You mean like ants. I read a great book about ants once . . .'

'Not ants for Chrissake. Things with long legs like grasshoppers. Eat every goddam thing for miles.'

'Oh, locusts. *The Day of The Locust*. A great movie. They had this one scene where there's a guy jumping up and down on this little kid and—'

'I don't want to know about the movie, MacMordie. Who wrote the book?'

'West,' said MacMordie, 'Nathanel West. Only his real name was Weinstein.'

'So who cares what his real name was? Nobody's ever heard of him and he gets himself killed in a pile-up and suddenly he's famous. With Piper we've got it even better. I mean we've got mystery. Maybe mobsters. House burning, boats exploding, the guy's in love with old women and suddenly it's all happening to him.'

'Past tense,' said MacMordie.

'Damn right, and that's what I want on him. His past. A full rundown on him, where he lived, what he did, the women he loved . . .'

'Like Miss Futtle?' said MacMordie tactlessly.

'No,' yelled Hutchmeyer, 'not like Miss Futtle. She won't even come to the poor guy's funeral. Other women. With what he put in that book there've got to be other women.'

150

'With what he put in that book they'll have maybe died by now. I mean the heroine was eighty and he was seventeen. This Piper was twenty-eight, thirty so it's got to have been eleven years ago which would put her up in the nineties and around that age they tend to forget things.'

'Jesus, do I have to tell you everything? Fabricate, MacMordie, fabricate. Call London and speak to Frensic and get the press cuttings. There's bound to be something there we can use.'

MacMordie left the room and put through the call to London. He returned twenty minutes later with the news that Frensic was being uncooperative.

'He says he doesn't know anything,' he told a glowering Hutchmeyer. 'Seems this Piper just sent in the book, Frensic read it, sent it to Corkadales, they liked it and bought and that's about the sum total. No background. Nothing.'

'There's got to be something. He was born some place, wasn't he? And his mother . . .'

'No relatives. Parents dead in a car smash. I mean it's like he never had an existence.'

'Shit,' said Hutchmeyer.

Which was more or less the word that sprang to Frensic's mind as he put the phone down after MacMordie's call. It was bad enough losing an author who hadn't written a book without having demands for background material on his life. The next thing would be the press, some damned woman reporter hot on the trail of Piper's tragic childhood. Frensic went into Sonia's office and hunted through the filing cabinet for Piper's correspondence. It was, as he expected, voluminous. Frensic took the file back to his desk and sat there wondering what to do with the thing. His first inclination to burn it was dissipated by the realization that if Piper had written scores of letters to him from almost as many different boarding-houses over the years, he had replied as often. The copies of Frensic's replies were there in the file. The originals were presumably still in safe keeping somewhere. With an aunt? Or some ghastly boarding-house keeper? Frensic sat and sweated. He had told MacMordie that Piper had no relatives, but what if it turned out that he had an entire lineage of avaricious aunts, uncles and cousins anxious to cash in on royalties? And what about a will? Knowing Piper as well as he did, Frensic thought it unlikely he had made one. In which case the matter of his

151

legacy might well end up in the courts and then . . . Frensic foresaw appalling consequences. On the one hand the anonymous author demanding his advance, and on the other . . . And in the middle the firm of Frensic & Futtle being dragged through the mud, exposed as the perpetrators of fraud, sued by Hutchmeyer, sued by Piper's relatives, forced to pay enormous damages and vast legal costs and finally bankrupted. And all because some demented client of Cadwalladine had insisted on preserving his anonymity.

Having reached this ghastly conclusion Frensic took the file back to the cabinet, re-labelled it Mr Smith as a mild precaution against intruding eyes and tried to think of some defence. The only one seemed to be that he had merely acted on the instructions of Mr Cadwalladine and since Cadwalladine & Dimkins were eminently respectable solicitors they would be as anxious to avoid a legal scandal as he was. And so presumably would the genuine author. It was small consolation. Let Hutchmeyer get a whiff of the impersonation and all hell would be let loose. And finally there was Sonia, who, if her attitude on the phone had been anything to go by, was in a highly emotional state and likely to say something rash. Frensic reached for the phone and dialled International to put through a call to the Gramercy Park Hotel. It was time Sonia Futtle came back to England. When he got through it was to learn that Miss Futtle had already left, and should, according to the desk clerk, be in mid-Atlantic.

' "Is" and "above",' corrected Frensic before realizing that there was something to be said for American usage.

That afternoon Sonia landed at Heathrow and took a taxi straight to Lanyard Lane. She found Frensic in a mood of apparently deep mourning.

'I blame myself,' he said, forestalling her lament, 'I should never have allowed poor Piper to have jeopardized his career by going over in the first place. Our only consolation must be that his name as a novelist has been made. It is doubtful if he would ever have written a better book had he lived.'

'But he didn't write this one,' said Sonia.

Frensic nodded. 'I know. I know,' he murmured, 'but at least it established his reputation. He would have appreciated the irony. He was a great admirer of Thomas Mann you know. Our best memorial to him must be silence.'

Having thus pre-empted Sonia's recriminations Frensic allowed her to work off her feelings by telling the story of the night of the tragedy and Hutchmeyer's subsequent reaction. At the end he was none the wiser.

'It all seems most peculiar,' he said when she had finished. 'One can only suppose that whoever did it made a terrible mistake and got the wrong person. Now if Hutchmeyer had been murdered . . .'

'I would have been murdered too,' said Sonia through her tears.

'We must be grateful for small mercies,' said Frensic.

Next morning Sonia Futtle resumed her duties in the office. A fresh batch of animal stories had come in during her absence and while Frensic congratulated himself on his tactics and sat at his desk silently praying that there would be no further repercussions Sonia busied herself with *Bernie the Beaver*. It needed a bit of rewriting but the story had promise.

Chapter 17

In a cabin in the Smokey Mountains Piper held the same opinion about *Pause*. He sat out on the stoop and looked down at the lake where Baby was swimming and had to admit that his first impression of the novel had been wrong. He had been misled by the passages of explicit sex. But now that he had copied it out word for word he could see that the essential structure of the story was sound. In fact there were large sections of the book which dealt meaningfully with matters of great significance. Subtract the age difference between Gwendolen and Anthony, the narrator, and eradicate the pornography and *Pause O Men for the Virgin* had the makings of great literature. It examined in considerable depth the meaning of life, the writer's role in contemporary society, the anonymity of the individual in the urban collective and the need to return to the values of earlier, more civilized times. It was particularly good on the miseries of adolescence and the satisfaction to be found in the craftsmanship of furniture-making. 'Gwendolen ran her fingers along the gnarled and knotted oak with a sensual touch that belied her years. "The hardiness of time has tamed the wildness of the wood," she said. "You will carve against the grain and give form to what has been formless and insensate." ' Piper nodded approvingly. Passages like that had genuine merit and better still they served as an inspiration to him. He too would cut against the grain of this novel and give form to it, so that in the revised version the grossness of the bestseller would be eliminated, all the sexual addenda which defiled the very essence of the book would be removed and it would stand as a monument to his literary gifts. Posthumously perhaps, but at least his reputation would be retrieved. In years to come critics would compare the two versions and deduce from his deletions that in its earlier uncommercial form the original intentions of the author had been of the highest literary quality and that the novel had subsequently been altered to meet the demands of Frensic and Hutchmeyer and their perverse view of public taste. The blame for the bestseller would lie with them and he would be exonerated. More, he would be acclaimed. He closed the

154

ledger and stood up as Baby came out of the water and walked up the beach to the cabin.

'Finished?' she asked. Piper nodded.

'I shall start the second version tomorrow,' he said.

'While you're doing that I'll take the first down into Ashville and get it copied. The sooner Frensic gets it the sooner we're going to light a fire under him.'

'I wish you wouldn't use that expression,' said Piper, 'lighting fires. And anyway where are you going to mail it from? They could trace us from the postmark.'

'We shan't be here from the day after tomorrow. We rented the cabin for a week. I'll drive down to Charlotte and catch a flight to New York and mail it there. I'll be back tomorrow night and we move on the day after.'

'I wish we didn't have to move all the time,' said Piper, 'I like it here. There's been nobody to bother us and I've had time to write. Why can't we just stay on?'

'Because this isn't the Deep South,' said Baby, 'and when I said Deep I meant it. There are places down Alabama, Mississippi, that just nobody has ever heard of and I want to see them.'

'And from what I've read about Mississippi they aren't partial to strangers,' said Piper, 'they are going to ask questions.'

'You've read too many Faulkners,' said Baby, 'and where we're going a quarter of a million dollars buys a lot of answers.'

She went inside and changed. After lunch Piper swam in the lake and walked along the shore, his mind filled with possible changes he was going to make in *Pause Two*. Already he had decided to change the title. He would call it *Work In Regress*. There was a touch of *Finnegans Wake* about it which appealed to his sense of the literary. And after all Joyce had worked and reworked his novels over and over again with no thought for their commercial worth. And in exile from his native land. For a moment Piper saw himself following in Joyce's footsteps, incognito and endlessly revising the same book, with the difference that he could never emerge from obscurity into fame in his own lifetime. Unless of course his work was of such an indisputable genius that the little matter of the fire and the burning boats and even his apparent death would become part of the mystique of a great author. Yes, greatness would absolve him. Piper turned and hurried back along the shore to the cabin. He would start work at once on *Work in Regress*. But when he got back he found that Baby

155

had already taken the car and his first manuscript and driven into Ashville. There was a note for him on the table. It said simply, 'Gone today. Here tomorrow. Stay with it. Baby.'

Piper stayed with it. He spent the afternoon with a pen going through *Pause* changing all references to age. Gwendolen lost fifty-five years and became twenty-five and Anthony gained ten which made him twenty-seven. And in between times Piper scored out all those references to peculiar sexual activities which had ensured the book's popular appeal. He did this with particular vigour and by the time he had finished was filled with a sense of righteousness which he conveyed to his notebook of Ideas. 'The commercialization of sex as a thing to be bought and sold is at the root of the present debasement of civilization. In my writing I have striven to eradicate the Thingness of sex and to encapsulate the essential relationship of humanity.' Finally he made himself supper and went to bed.

In the morning he was up early and at his table on the stoop. In front of him the first page of his new ledger lay blank and empty waiting for his imprint. He dipped his pen in the ink bottle and began to write. 'The house stood on a knoll. Surrounded by three elms, a beech and a . . .' Piper stopped. He wasn't sure what a deodar was and he had no dictionary to help him. He changed it to 'oak' and stopped again. Did oak have horizontal branches? Presumably some oaks did. Details like that didn't matter. The essential thing was to get down to an analysis of the relationship between Gwendolen and the narrator. Great books didn't bother with trees. They were about people, what people felt about people and what they thought about them. Insight was what really mattered and trees didn't contribute to insight. The deodar might just as well stay where it was. He crossed out 'oak' and put 'deodar' above it. He continued the description for half a page and then hit another problem. How could the narrator, Anthony, be on holiday from school when he was now twenty-seven. Unless of course he was a schoolmaster in which case he would have to teach something and that meant knowing about it. Piper tried to remember his own schooldays and a model on which to base Anthony, but the masters at his school had been nondescript men and had left little impression on him. There was only Miss Pears and she had been a mistress.

Piper put down his pen and thought about Miss Pears. Now if she had been a man . . . or if she were Gwendolen and he was Anthony . . . and if instead of being twenty-seven Anthony had been fourteen . . . or better still if his parents had lived in a house on a knoll surrounded by three elms, a beech and a . . . Piper stood up and paced the stoop, his mind alive with new inspiration. It had suddenly come to him that from the raw material of *Pause O Men for the Virgin* it might be possible to distil the essence of *Search for a Lost Childhood*. Or if not distil, at least amalgamate the two. There would have to be considerable alterations. After all tuberculotic plumbers didn't live on knolls. On the other hand his father hadn't actually had tuberculosis. He had got it from Lawrence and Thomas Mann. And a love affair between a schoolboy and his teacher was a very natural occurrence, provided of course that it didn't become physical. Yes, that was it. He would write *Work In Regress* as *Search*. He sat down at the table and picked up his pen and began to copy. There was no need now to worry about changing the main shape of the story. The deodar and the house on the knoll and all the descriptions of houses and places could remain the same. The new ingredient would be the addition of his troubled adolescence and the presence of his tormented parents. And Miss Pears as Gwendolen, his mentor, adviser and teacher with whom he would develop a significant relationship, meaningfully sexual and without sex.

And so once more the words formed indelibly black upon the page with all the old elegance of shape that had so satisfied him in the past. Below him the lake shone in the summer sunlight and a breeze ruffled the trees around the cabin, but Piper was oblivious to his surroundings. He had picked up the thread of his existence where it had broken in the Gleneagle Guest House in Exforth and was back into *Search*.

When Baby returned that evening from her flight to New York with the copy of his first manuscript now safely mailed to Frensic & Futtle, Lanyard Lane, London, she found Piper his old self. The trauma of the fire and their flight had been forgotten.

'You see, what I am doing is combining my own novel with *Pause*,' he explained as she poured herself a drink. 'Instead of Gwendolen being . . .'

'Tell me about it in the morning,' said Baby. 'Right now I've had a tiring day and tomorrow we've got to be on the road again.'

'I see you've bought another car,' said Piper looking out at a red Pontiac.

'Air-conditioned and with South Carolina plates. Anyone thinks

157

they're going to come looking for us, they're going to have a hard time. I didn't even trade in this time. Sold the Ford in Beanville and took a Greyhound to Charlotte and bought this in Ashville on the way back. We'll change again farther south. We're covering our tracks.'

'Not by sending copies of *Pause* to Frensic, we aren't,' said Piper, 'I mean he's bound to know I haven't died.'

'That reminds me. I sent him a telegram in your name.'

'You did what?' squawked Piper.

'Sent him a telegram.'

'Saying what?'

'Just, quote Transfer advance royalties care of First National Bank of New York account number 478776 love Piper unquote.'

'But I haven't got an account...'

'You have now, honey. I opened one for you and made the first deposit. One thousand dollars. Now when Frensic gets that birthday greeting—'

'Birthday greeting? You send a telegram demanding money and you call that a birthday greeting?'

'Had to delay it somehow till he'd had time to read the original of *Pause*,' said Baby, 'so I said he had a birthday on the 19th and they're holding it over.'

'Christ,' said Piper, 'some damned birthday greeting. I suppose you realize he's got a heart condition? I mean shocks like this could kill him.'

'Makes two of you,' said Baby. 'He's effectively killed you ...'

'He did nothing of the sort. You were the one to sign my death certificate and end my career as a novelist.'

Baby finished her drink and sighed. 'There's gratitude for you. Your career as a novelist is just about to begin.'

'Posthumously,' said Piper bitterly.

'Well, better late than never,' said Baby, and took herself off to bed.

The next morning the red Pontiac left the cabin and wound up the curving mountain road in the direction of Tennessee.

'We'll go west as far as Memphis,' said Baby, 'and ditch the car there and double back by Greyhound to Chattanooga. I've always wanted to see the Choo Choo.'

Piper said nothing. He had just realized how he had met Miss Pears/Gwendolen. It had been one summer holiday when his parents

158

had taken him down to Exforth and instead of sitting on the beach with them he had gone to the public library and there . . . The house no longer stood on a knoll. It was at the top of the hill by the cliffs and its windows stared out to sea. Perhaps that wasn't such a good idea. Not in the second version. No, he would leave it where it was and concentrate on the relationships. In that way there would be more consistency between *Pause* and *Work In Regress,* more authenticity. But in the third revision he would work on the setting and the house would stand on the cliffs above Exforth. And with each succeeding draft he would approximate a little more closely to that great novel on which he had been working for ten years. Piper smiled to himself at this realization. As the author of *Pause O Men for the Virgin* he had been given the fame he had always sought, had had fame forced upon him, and now by slow, persistent rewriting of that book he would reproduce the literary masterpiece that had been his life's work. And there was absolutely nothing Frensic could do about it.

That night they slept in separate motels in Memphis and next morning met at the bus depot and took the Greyhound to Nashville. The red Pontiac had gone. Piper didn't even bother to enquire how Baby had disposed of it. He had more important things on his mind. What, for instance, would happen if Frensic produced the real original manuscript of *Pause* and admitted that he had sent Piper to America as the substitute author?

'Two million dollars,' said Baby succinctly when he put this possibility to her.

'I don't see what they have to do with it,' said Piper.

'That's the price of the risk he took playing people poker with Hutch. You stake two million on a bluff you've got to have good reasons.'

'I can't imagine what they are.'

Baby smiled. 'Like who the real writer is. And don't give me that crap about a guy with six children and terminal arthritis. There's no such thing.'

'There isn't?' said Piper.

'No way. So we've got Frensic willing to risk his reputation as a literary agent for a percentage of two million and an author who goes along with him to preserve his precious anonymity from disclosure. That adds up to one hell of a weird set of circumstances. And Hutch hears what's going on he's going to murder them.'

'If Hutchmeyer hears what we've been doing he isn't going to be exactly pleased,' said Piper gloomily.

'Yes but we aren't there and Frensic is. In Lanyard Lane and by now he's got to be sweating.'

And Frensic was. The arrival of a large packet mailed in New York and addressed Personal, Frederick Frensic, had excited his curiosity only mildly. Arriving early at the office he had taken it upstairs with him and had opened several letters before turning his attention to the package. But from that moment onwards he had sat petrified staring at its contents. In front of him lay, neatly Xeroxed, sheet after sheet of Piper's unmistakable handwriting and just as equally unmistakably the original manuscript of *Pause O Men for the Virgin*. Which was impossible. Piper hadn't written the bloody book. He couldn't have. It was out of the question. And anyway why should anyone send him Xeroxed copies of a manuscript? The manuscript. Frensic rummaged through the pages and noted the corrections. The damned thing *was* the manuscript of *Pause*. And it was in Piper's handwriting. Frensic got up from his desk and went through to the filing cabinet and brought back the file now marked Mr Smith and compared the handwriting of Piper's letters with that of the manuscript. No doubt about it. He even reached for a magnifying glass and studied the letters through it. Identical. Christ. What the hell was going on? Frensic felt most peculiar. Some sort of waking nightmare had taken hold of him. Piper had written *Pause*? The obstacles in the way of such a supposition were insuperable. The little bugger couldn't have written anything and if he had . . . even if he quite miraculously had, what about Mr Cadwalladine and his anonymous client? Why should Piper have sent him the typed copy of the book through a solicitor in Oxford? And anyway the sod was dead. Or was he? No, he was definitely dead, drowned, murdered . . . Sonia's grief had been too real for disbelief. Piper was dead. Which brought him full circle to the question, who had sent this post-mortem manuscript? From New York? Frensic looked at the postmark. New York. And why Xeroxed? There had to be a reason. Frensic grabbed the package and rummaged inside it in the hope that it might contain some clue like a covering letter. But the package was empty. He turned to the outside. The address was typed. Frensic turned the packet over in search of a return address but there was nothing there. He turned back to the pages had read several more. There could be no doubting the authenticity of the writing. The corrections on every page were conclusive. They had been there in exactly the same form in every annual copy of *Search for a Lost Childhood*, a sentence scratched neatly out and a new one written in above. Worst of all, there were even the spelling mistakes. Piper had always spelt necessary with two cs and parallel with two rs, and here they were once again as final proof that the little maniac had actually penned the book which had gone to print with his name on the title page. But the decision to use his name hadn't been Piper's. He had only been consulted when the book had already been sold ...

Frensic's thoughts spiralled. He tried to remember who had suggested Piper. Was it Sonia, or had he himself ...? He couldn't recall and Sonia wasn't there to help him. She had gone down to Somerset to interview the author of *Bernie the* blasted *Beaver* and to ask for amendments in his opus. Beavers, even voluble beavers, didn't say 'Jesus wept' and 'Bloody hell', not if they wanted to get into print as children's bestsellers. Frensic did, several times, as he stared at the pages in front of him. Pulling himself together with an effort, he reached for the phone. This time Mr Cadwalladine was going to come clean about his client. But the telephone beat Frensic to it. It rang. Frensic cursed and picked up the receiver.

'Frensic & Futtle, Literary Agents . . .' he began before being stopped by the operator.

'Is that Mr Frensic, Mr Frederick Frensic?'

'Yes,' said Frensic irritably. He had never liked his Christian name.

'I have a birthday greeting for you,' said the operator.

'For me?' said Frensic. 'But it isn't my birthday.'

But already a taped voice was crooning 'Happy Birthday To You, Happy Birthday, dear Frederick, happy Birthday to you.'

Frensic held the receiver away from his ear. 'I tell you it isn't my bloody birthday,' he shouted at the recording. The operator came back on the line.

'The greetings telegram reads TRANSFER ADVANCE ROYALTIES CARE OF FIRST NATIONAL BANK OF NEW YORK ACCOUNT NUMBER FOUR SEVEN EIGHT SEVEN SEVEN SIX LOVE PIPER. I will repeat that. TRANSFER ...' Frensic sat and listened. He was beginning to shake.

'Would you like that account number repeated once again?' asked the operator.

'No,' said Frensic. 'Yes.' He grabbed a pencil with an unsteady hand and wrote the message down.

'Thank you,' he said without thinking as he finished.

'You're welcome,' said the operator. The line went dead.

'Like hell I am,' said Frensic and put the phone down. He stared for a moment at the word 'Piper' and then groped his way across the room to the cubicle in which Sonia made coffee and washed the cups. There was a bottle of brandy there, kept for emergency resuscitation of rejected authors. 'Rejected?' Frensic muttered as he filled a tumbler. 'More like resurrected.' He drank half the tumbler and went back to his desk feeling little better. The nightmare quality of the manuscript had doubled now with the telegram but it was no longer incomprehensible. He was being blackmailed. 'Transfer advance royalties . . .' Frensic suddenly felt faint. He got out of his chair and lay down on the floor and shut his eyes.

After twenty minutes he got to his feet. Mr Cadwalladine was going to learn that it didn't pay to tangle with Frensic & Futtle. There was no point in phoning the wretched man again. Stronger measures were needed now. He would have the bastard squealing the name of his client and there would be an end to all this talk of professional confidentiality. The situation was desperate and desperate remedies were called for. Frensic went downstairs and out into the street. Half an hour later, armed with a parcel that contained sandals, dark glasses, a lightweight tropical suit and a Panama hat, he returned to the office. All that was needed now was an ambulance-chasing libel lawyer. Frensic spent the rest of the morning going through *Pause* for a suitable identity and then phoned Ridley, Coverup, Makeweight and Jones, Solicitors of Ponsett House. Their reputation as shysters in cases of libel was second to none. Mr Makeweight would see Professor Facit at four.

At five to four Frensic, armed with a copy of *Pause O Men for the Virgin* and peering dimly through his tinted glasses, sat in the waiting-room and looked down at his sandals. He was rather proud of them. If anything distinguished him from Frensic, the literary agent, it was, he felt, those awful sandals.

'Mr Makeweight will see you now,' said the receptionist. Frensic got up and went down the passage to the door marked Mr Make-weight and entered. An air of respectable legal fustiness clung to the room. It didn't to Mr Makeweight. Small, dark and effusive, he was rather too quick for the furnishings. Frensic shook hands and sat

162

down. Mr Makeweight regarded him expectantly. 'I understand you are concerned with a passage in a novel,' he said.

Frensic put the copy of *Pause* on the desk.

'Well, I am rather,' he said hesitantly. 'You see . . . well it's been drawn to my attention by some of my colleagues who read novels – I am not a novel-reader myself you understand – but they have pointed out . . . well I'm sure it must be a coincidence . . . and they have certainly found it very funny that . . .'

'That a character in this novel resembles you in certain ways?' said Mr Makeweight, cutting through Frensic's hesitations.

'Well I wouldn't like to say that he resembles me . . . I mean the crimes he commits . . .'

'Crimes?' said Mr Makeweight, taking the bait. 'A character resembling you commits crimes? In this novel?'

'It's the name you see. Facit,' said Frensic leaning forward to open *Pause* at the page he had marked. 'If you read the passage in question you will see what I mean.'

Mr Makeweight read three pages and looked up with a concern that masked his delight. 'Dear me,' he said, 'I do see what you mean. These are exceedingly serious allegations.'

'Well they are, aren't they?' said Frensic pathetically. 'And my appointment as Professor of Moral Sciences at Wabash has yet to be confirmed and, quite frankly, if it were thought for one moment . . .'

'I take your point,' said Mr Makeweight. 'Your career would be put in jeopardy.'

'Ruined,' said Frensic.

Mr Makeweight selected a cigar happily. 'And I suppose we can take it that you have never . . . that these allegations are quite without foundation. You have never for instance seduced one of your male students?'

'Mr Makeweight,' said Frensic indignantly.

'Quite so. And you have never had intercourse with a fourteen-year-old girl after dosing her lemonade with a barbiturate?'

'Certainly not. The very idea revolts me. And besides I'm not sure I would know how to.'

Mr Makeweight regarded him critically. 'No, I daresay you wouldn't,' he said finally. 'And there is no truth in the accusation that you habitually fail students who reject your sexual overtures?'

'I don't make sexual overtures to students, Mr Makeweight. As a matter of fact I am neither on the examining board nor do I give tutorials. I am not part of the University. I am over here on a sabbatical and engaged in private research.'

'I see,' said Mr Makeweight, and made a note on his pad.

'And what makes it so much more embarrassing,' said Frensic, 'is that at one time I did have lodgings in De Frytville Avenue.'

Mr Makeweight made a note of that too. 'Extraordinary,' he said, 'quite extraordinary. The resemblance would seem to be almost exact. I think, Professor Facit, in fact I do more, I know that . . . provided of course that you haven't committed any of these unnatural acts . . . I take it you have never kept a Pekinese . . . no. Well as I say, provided you haven't and indeed even if you have, I can tell you now that you have grounds for taking action against the author and publishers of this disgraceful novel. I should estimate the damages to be in the region of . . . well to tell the truth I shouldn't be at all surprised if they don't constitute a record in the history of libel actions.'

'Oh dear,' said Frensic, feigning a mixture of anxiety and avarice, 'I was rather hoping it might be possible to avoid a court case. The publicity, you understand.'

Mr Makeweight quite understood. 'We'll just have to see how the publishers respond,' he said. 'Corkadales aren't a wealthy firm of course but they'll be insured against libel.'

'I hope that doesn't mean the author won't have to . . .'

'Oh he'll pay all right, Professor Facit. Over the years. The insurance company will see to that. A more deliberate case of malicious libel I have never come across.'

'Someone told me that the author, Mr Piper, has made a fortune out of the book in America,' said Frensic.

'In that case I think he will have to part with it,' said Mr Makeweight.

'And if you could expedite the matter I would be most grateful. My appointment at Wabash . . .'

Mr Makeweight assured him that he would put the matter in hand at once and Frensic, having given his address as the Randolph Hotel, Oxford, left the office well pleased. Mr Cadwalladine was about to get the shock of his life.

So was Geoffrey Corkadale. Frensic had only just returned to Lanyard Lane and was divesting himself of the disgusting sandals and the tropical suit when the phone rang. Geoffrey was in a state bordering on hysteria. Frensic held the phone away from his ear and listened to a torrent of abuse.

'My dear Geoffrey,' he said when the publisher ran out of epithets. 'What have I done to deserve this outburst?'

'Done?' yelled Corkadale. 'Done? You've done for this firm for one thing. You and that damnable Piper . . .'

'*De mortuis nil nisi . . .*' Frensic began.

'And what about the bloody living?' screamed Geoffrey. 'And don't tell me he didn't speak ill of this Professor Facit knowing full well that the swine was alive because . . .'

'What swine?' said Frensic.

'Professor Facit. The man in the book who did those awful things . . .'

'Wasn't he the character with satyriasis who . . .'

'Was?' bawled Geoffrey. 'Was? The bloody maniac is.'

'Is what?' said Frensic.

'Is! Is! The man's alive and he's filing a libel action against us.'

'Dear me. How very unfortunate.'

'Unfortunate? It's catastrophic. He's gone to Ridley, Coverup, Makeweight and . . .'

'Oh no,' said Frensic, 'but they're absolute rogues.'

'Rogues? They're bloodsuckers. Leeches. They'd get blood out of a stone and with all this filth in the book about Professor Facit they've got a watertight case. They're dunning us for millions. We're finished. We'll never . . .'

'The man you want to speak to is a Mr Cadwalladine,' said Frensic. 'He acted for Piper. I'll give you his telephone number.'

'What good is that going to do? It's deliberate libel . . .'

But Frensic was already dictating Mr Cadwalladine's telephone number and with apologies because he had a client in the room next door he put the phone down on Geoffrey's ravings. Then he changed out of the tropical suit, phoned the Randolph and booked a room in the name of Professor Facit and waited. Mr Cadwalladine was bound to call and when he did Frensic was going to be ready and waiting. In the meantime he sought further inspiration by studying Piper's telegram.'Transfer advance royalties care of account number 478776.' And the little bastard was supposed to be dead. What in God's name was going on? And what on earth was he going to tell Sonia? And where did Hutchmeyer fit into all this? According to Sonia the police had grilled him for hours and Hutchmeyer had come out of the experience a shaken man, and had even threatened to sue the police. That didn't sound like the action of a man who . . . Frensic put the notion of Hutchmeyer kidnapping Piper and demanding his money back by proxy as too improbable for words. If Hutchmeyer had known that Piper hadn't written *Pause* he would have sued. But Piper apparently had written *Pause*. The proof was there in front of him in the copy of the manuscript. Well he would have to screw the truth out of Mr Cadwalladine and with Mr Makeweight in the wings demanding enormous damages, Mr Cadbloodywalladine was going to have to come clean.

He did. 'I don't know who the author of this awful book is,' he admitted in faltering tones when he rang up half an hour later.

'You don't know?' said Frensic, faltering incredulously himself. 'You must know. You sent me the book in the first place. You gave me the authorization to send Piper to the States. If you didn't know you had no right . . .' Mr Cadwalladine made negative noises. 'But I've got a letter here from you saying . . .'

'I know you have,' said Mr Cadwalladine faintly. 'The author gave his consent and . . .'

'But you've just said you don't know who the bloody author is,' shouted Frensic, 'and now you tell me he gave his consent. His written consent?'

'Yes,' said Mr Cadwalladine.

'In that case you've got to know who he is.'

'But I don't,' said Mr Cadwalladine. 'You see I've always dealt with him through Lloyds Bank.'

Frensic's mind boggled. 'Lloyds Bank?' he muttered. 'You did say Lloyds Bank?'

'Yes. Care of the manager. It's such a very respectable bank and I never for one moment supposed . . .'

He left the sentence unfinished. There was no need to end it. Frensic was already ahead of him. 'So what you're saying is that whoever wrote this bloody novel sent the thing to you by way of Lloyds Bank in Oxford and that whenever you've wanted to correspond with him you've had to do so through the bank. Is that right?'

'Precisely,' said Mr Cadwalladine, 'and now that this frightful libel case has come up I think I know why. It puts me in a dreadful situation. My reputation . . .'

'Stuff your reputation,' shouted Frensic, 'what about mine? I've been acting in good faith on behalf of a client who doesn't exist and

166

on your instructions and now we've got a murder on our hands and . . .'

'This terrible libel action,' said Mr Cadwalladine. 'Mr Corkadale told me that the damages are bound to amount to something astronomical.'

But Frensic wasn't listening. If Mr Cadwalladine's client had to correspond with him through Lloyds Bank the bastard must have something to hide. Unless of course it was Piper. Frensic groped for a clue. 'When the novel first came to you there must have been a covering letter.'

'The manuscript came from a typing agency,' said Mr Cadwalladine. 'The covering letter was sent a few days earlier via Lloyd's Bank.'

'With a signature?' said Frensic.

'The signature of the bank manager,' said Mr Cadwalladine.

'That's all I need,' said Frensic. 'What is his name?'

Mr Cadwalladine hesitated. 'I don't think . . .' he began but Frensic lost patience.

'Damn your scruples, man,' he snarled, 'the name of the bank manager and quick.'

'The late Mr Bygraves,' said Mr Cadwalladine sadly.

'The what?'

'The late Mr Bygraves. He died of a heart attack climbing Snowdon at Easter.'

Frensic slumped in his chair. 'He had a heart attack climbing Snowdon,' he muttered.

'So you see, I don't think he's going to be able to help us very much,' continued Mr Cadwalladine, 'and anyway banks are very reticent about disclosing the names of their clients. You have to have a warrant, you know.'

Frensic did know. It was one of the few things about banks he had previously admired. But there was something else that Mr Cadwalladine had said earlier . . . something about a typing agency. 'You said the manuscript came from a typing agency,' he said. 'Have you any idea which one?'

'No. But I daresay I could find out if you'll give me time.' Frensic sat holding the receiver while Mr Cadwalladine found out. 'It's the Cynthia Bogden Typing Service,' he told Frensic at long last. He sounded distinctly subdued.

'Now we're getting somewhere,' said Frensic. 'Ring her up and ask where...'

'I'd rather not,' said Mr Cadwalladine.

'You'd rather not? Here we are in the middle of a libel action which is probably going to cost you your reputation and ...'

'It's not that,' interrupted Mr Cadwalladine. 'You see, I handled the divorce case ...'

'Well that's all right ...'

'I was acting for her ex-husband,' said Mr Cadwalladine. 'I don't think she'd appreciate my ...'

'Oh all right, I'll do it,' said Frensic. 'Give me her number.' He wrote it down, replaced the receiver and dialled again.

'The Cynthia Bogden Typing Service,' said a voice, coyly professional.

'I'm trying to trace the owner of a manuscript that was typed by your agency ...' Frensic began but the voice cut him short.

'We do not divulge the names of our clients,' it said.

'But I'm only asking because a friend of mine ...'

'Under no circumstances are we prepared to confide confidential information of the sort ...'

'Perhaps if I spoke to Mrs Bogden,' said Frensic.

'You are,' said the voice and rang off. Frensic sat at his desk and cursed.

'Confidential information my foot,' he said and slammed the phone down. He sat thinking dark thoughts about Mrs Bogden for a while and then called Mr Cadwalladine again.

'This Bogden woman,' he said, 'how old is she?'

'Around forty-five,' said Mr Cadwalladine, 'why do you ask?'

'Never mind,' said Frensic.

That evening, having left a note on Sonia Futtle's desk saying that urgent business would keep him out of town for a day or two, Frensic travelled by train to Oxford. He was wearing a lightweight tropical suit, dark glasses and a Panama hat. The sandals were in his dustbin at home. He carried with him a suitcase the Xeroxed manuscript of *Pause*, a letter written by Piper and a pair of striped pyjamas. Dressed in the last he climbed into bed at eleven in the Randolph Hotel. His room had been booked for Professor Facit.

Chapter 18

In Chattanooga Baby had fulfilled her ambition. She had seen the Choo Choo. Installed in Pullman Car Number Nine, she lay on the brass bedstead and stared out of the window at the illuminated fountain playing across the tracks. Above the main building of the station tube lighting emblazoned the night sky with with words Hilton Choo Choo and below, in what had once been the waiting-room, dinner was being served. Beside the restaurant there was a crafts shop and in front of them both stood huge locomotives of a bygone era, their cow-catchers freshly painted and their smokestacks gleaming as if in anticipation of some great journey. In fact they were going nowhere. Their fireboxes were cold and empty and their pistons would never move again. Only in the imagination of those who stayed the night in the ornate and divided Pullman cars, now motel bedrooms, was it still possible to entertain the illusion that they would presently pull out of the station and begin the long haul north or west. The place was part museum, part fantasy and wholly commercial. At the entrance to the car park uniformed guards sat in a small cabin watching the television screens on which each platform and each dark corner of the station was displayed for the protection of the guests. Outside the perimeter of the station Chattanooga spread dark and seedy with boarded hotel windows and derelict buildings, a victim of the shopping precincts beyond the ring of suburbs.

But Baby wasn't thinking about Chattanooga or even the Choo Choo. They had joined the illusions of her retarded youth. Age had caught up with her and she felt tired and empty of hope. All the romance of life had gone. Piper had seen to that. Travelling day after day with a self-confessed genius whose thoughts were centred on literary immortality to the exclusion of all else had given Baby a new insight into the monotony of Piper's mind. By comparison Hutch-meyer's obsession with money and power and wheeling and dealing now seemed positively healthy. Piper evinced no interest in the countryside nor the towns they passed through and the fact that they were now in, or at least on the frontier of, the Deep South and that

169

wild country of Baby's soft-corn imagination appeared to mean nothing to him. He had hardly glanced at the locomotives drawn up in the station and seemed only surprised that they weren't travelling anywhere on them. Once that had been impressed on him he had retreated to his stateroom and had started work again on his second version of *Pause*.

'For a great novelist you've just got to be the least observant,' Baby said when they met in the restaurant for dinner. 'I mean don't you ever look around and wonder what it's all about.'

Piper looked around. 'Seems an odd place to put a restaurant,' he said. 'Still, it's nice and cool.'

'That just happens to be the air-conditioning,' said Baby irritably.

'Oh, is that what it is,' said Piper. 'I wondered.'

'He wondered. And what about all the people who have sat right here waiting to take the train north to New York and Detroit and Chicago to make their fortunes instead of scratching a living from a patch of dirt? Doesn't that mean anything to you?'

'There don't seem many of them about,' said Piper looking idly at a woman with an obesity problem and tartan shorts, 'and anyway I thought you said the trains weren't running any more.'

'Oh my God,' said Baby, 'I sometimes wonder what century you're living in. And I suppose it doesn't mean a thing to you that there was a battle here in the Civil War?'

'No,' said Piper. 'Battles don't figure in great literature.'

'They don't? What about *Gone With The Wind* and *War and Peace*? I suppose they aren't great literature.'

'Not English literature,' said Piper. 'What matters in English literature is the relationships people have with one another.'

Baby dug into her steak. 'And people don't relate to one another in battles? Is that it?'

Piper nodded.

'So when one guy kills another that's not relating in a way that matters?'

'Only transitorily,' said Piper.

'And when Sherman's troops go looting and burning and raping their way from Atlanta to the sea and leave behind them homeless families and burning mansions that isn't altering relationships either so you don't write about it?'

'The best novelists wouldn't,' said Piper. 'It didn't happen to them and therefore they couldn't.'

170

'Couldn't what?'

'Write about it.'

'Are you telling me a writer can only write what has really happened to him? Is that what you're saying?' said Baby with a new edge to her voice.

'Yes,' said Piper, 'you see it would be outside the range of his experience and therefore . . .'

He spoke at length from *The Moral Novel* while Baby slowly chewed her way through her steak and thought dark thoughts about Piper's theory.

'In that case you're going to need a lot more experience is all I can say.'

Piper pricked up his ears. 'Now wait a minute,' he said, 'if you think I want to be involved in any more houseburning and boat-exploding and that sort of thing—'

'I wasn't thinking of that sort of experience. I mean things like burning houses don't count do they? It's relationships that matter. What you need is experience in relating.'

Piper ate uneasily. The conversation had taken a distasteful turn. They finished their meal in silence. Afterwards Piper returned to his stateroom and wrote five hundred more words about his tortured adolescence and his feelings for Gwendolen/Miss Pears. Finally he turned out the electric oil lamp that hung above his brass bedstead and undressed. In the next compartment Baby readied herself for Piper's first lesson in relationships. She put on a very little nightdress and a great deal of perfume and opened the door to Piper's stateroom.

'For God's sake,' squawked Piper as she climbed into bed with him.

'This is where it all begins, baby,' said Baby, 'relationshipwise.'

'No, it doesn't,' said Piper. 'It's— '

Baby's hand closed over his mouth and her voice whispered in his ear.

'And don't think you're going to get out of here. They've got TV cameras on every platform and you go hobbling out there in the raw the guards are going to want to know what's been going on.'

'But I'm not in the raw,' said Piper as Baby's hand left his mouth.

'You soon will be, honey,' Baby whispered as her hands deftly untied his pyjamas.

'Please,' said Piper plaintively.

'I aim to, honey, I aim to,' said Baby. She lifted her nightdress and

her great breasts dug into Piper's chest. For the next two hours the
brass bedstead heaved and creaked as Baby Hutchmeyer, *née* Sugg,
Miss Penobscot 1935, put all the expertise of her years to work on
Piper. And in spite of himself and his invocation of the precepts in
The Moral Novel, Piper was for the first time lost to the world of
letters and moved by an inchoate passion. He writhed beneath her,
he pounded on top, his mouth sucked at her silicon breasts and
slithered across the minute scars on her stomach. All the time Baby's
fingers caressed and dug and scratched and squeezed until Piper's
back was torn and his buttocks marked by the curve of her nails and
all the time Baby stared into the dimness of the stateroom dispassionately and wondered at her own boredom. 'Youth must have its
fling,' she thought to herself as Piper hurled himself into her yet
again. But she was no longer young and flinging without feeling was
not her scene. There was more to life than fucking. Much more, and
she was going to find it.

In Oxford Frensic was up and about and finding it when Baby
returned to her own compartment and left Piper sleeping exhaustedly
next door. Frensic had got up early and had breakfasted before eight.
By half past he had found the Cynthia Bogden Typing Service in
Fenet Street. With what he hoped was the expectant look of an
American tourist he haunted the church opposite and sat in one of the
pews staring back through the open door at the entrance to the
Bogden bureau. If he knew anything about middle-aged women who
were divorced and ran their own businesses, Miss Bogden would be
the first to arrive in the morning and the last to leave at night. By
quarter past nine Frensic certainly hoped so. The trail of women he
had seen entering the office were not at all to his taste but at least the
first to arrive had been the most presentable. She had been a large
woman but Frensic's brief glimpse had told him that her legs were
good and that if Mr Cadwalladine had been right about her being
forty-five she didn't look it. Frensic left the church and pondered his
next step. There was no point in going into the Agency and asking
Miss Bogden point blank who had sent her *Pause*. Her tone the
previous day had indicated that more subtle tactics were necessary.
    Frensic made his next move. He found a flower shop and went
inside. Twenty minutes later two dozen red roses were delivered to the
Bogden Typing Service with a note which said simply, 'To Miss
Bogden from an Admirer.' Frensic had thought of adding 'ardent' but

had decided against it. Two dozen expensive red roses argued an ardency by themselves. Miss Bogden or more properly Mrs Bogden, and the reversion indicated a romantic direction to that lady's thoughts, would supply the adjective. Frensic wandered round Oxford, had coffee in the Ship and lunch back at the Randolph. Then, gauging that enough time had elapsed for Miss Bogden to have digested the implications of the roses, he went to Professor Facit's room and phoned the Agency. As before, Miss Bogden answered. Frensic took a deep breath, swallowed and presently heard himself asking with an agony of unaffected coyness if she would do him the honour and privilege of having dinner with him at the Elizabeth. There was a sibilant pause before Miss Bogden replied.

'Do I know you?' she asked archly. Frensic squirmed.

'An admirer,' he murmured.

'Oo,' said Miss Bogden. There was another pause while she observed the proprieties of hesitation.

'Roses,' said Frensic garrottedly.

'Are you quite sure? I mean it's rather unusual . . .'

Frensic silently agreed that it was. 'It's just that . . .' he began and then took the plunge, 'I haven't had the nerve before and . . .' The garrotte tightened.

Miss Bogden on the other hand breathed sympathy. 'Better late than never,' she said softly.

'That's what I thought,' said Frensic who didn't.

'And you did say the Elizabeth?'

'Yes,' said Frensic, 'shall we say eight in the bar?'

'How will I know you?'

'I know you,' said Frensic and giggled involuntarily. Miss Bogden took it as a compliment.

'You haven't told me your name.'

Frensic hesitated. He couldn't use his own and Facit was in *Pause*. It had to be someone else. 'Corkadale,' he muttered finally, 'Geoffrey Corkadale.'

'Not *the* Geoffrey Corkadale?' said Miss Bogden.

'Yes,' stammered Frensic hoping to hell that Geoffrey's epicene reputation hadn't reached her ears. It hadn't. Miss Bogden cooed.

'Well in that case . . .' She left the rest unsaid.

'Till eight,' said Frensic.

'Till eight,' echoed Miss Bogden. Frensic put the phone down and sat limply on the bed.

173

Then he lay down and had a long nap. He woke at four and went downstairs. There was one last thing to do. He didn't know Miss Bogden and there must be no mistake. He made his way to Fenet Street and stationed himself in the church. He was there at five thirty when the trail of awful women came out of the office. Frensic sighed with relief. None of them was carrying a bunch of red roses. Finally the large woman appeared and locked the door. She clutched roses to her ample bosom and hurried off down the street. Frensic emerged from the church and watched her go. Miss Bogden was definitely well-preserved. From her permed head to her pink shoes by way of a turquoise costume there was a tastelessness about the woman that was almost inspired. Frensic went back to the hotel and had a stiff gin. Then he had another, took a bath and rehearsed various approaches that seemed likely to elicit from Miss Bogden the name of the author of *Pause*.

On the other side of Oxford, Cynthia Bogden prepared herself for the evening with the same thoroughness with which she did everything. It had been some years since her divorce and to be asked to dine at the Elizabeth by a publisher augured well. So did the roses, carefully arranged in a vase, and the nervousness of her admirer. There had been nothing brash about the voice on the telephone. It had been an educated voice and Corkadales were most respectable publishers. And in any case Cynthia Bogden was in need of admirers. She selected her most seductive costume, sprayed herself in various places with various aerosols, fixed her face and set out prepared to be wined, dined and, not to put too fine a point on it, fucked. She entered the foyer of the Elizabeth exuding an uncertain hauteur and was somewhat startled when a short baggy man sidled up to her and took her hand.

'Miss Bogden,' he murmured, 'your fond admirer.'

Miss Bogden looked down at her fond admirer dubiously. She was still looking down at him half an hour and three pink gins later as they made their way to the table Frensic had reserved in the farthest corner of the restaurant. He held her chair for her and then, conscious that perhaps he hadn't come as far up to her expectations as he might have done, threw himself into the part of fond admirer with a desperate gallantry and inventiveness that surprised them both.

'I first glimpsed you a year ago when I was up for a conference,' he told her having ordered the wine waiter to bring them a bottle of not

174

too dry champagne, 'I saw you in the street and followed you to your office.'

'You should have introduced yourself,' said Miss Bogden.

Frensic blushed convincingly. 'I was too shy,' he murmured, 'and besides I thought you were . . .'

'Married?' said Miss Bogden helpfully.

'Exactly,' said Frensic, 'or shall we say attached. A woman as . . . er . . . beautiful . . . er . . .'

It was Miss Bogden's turn to blush. Frensic plunged on. 'I was overcome. Your charm, your air of quiet reserve, your . . . how shall I put it . . .' There was no need to put it. While Frensic burrowed into an avocado pear, Cynthia Bogden savoured a shrimp. Baggy this little man might be but he was clearly a gentleman and a man of the world. Champagne at twelve pounds a bottle was a sufficient indication of his honourable intentions. When Frensic ordered a second, Miss Bogden protested feebly.

'Special occasion,' said Frensic wondering if he wasn't overdoing things a bit, 'and besides we have something to celebrate.'

'We do?'

'Our meeting for one thing,' said Frensic, 'and the success of a mutual venture.'

'Mutual venture?' said Miss Bogden, her thoughts veering sharply to the altar.

'Something we both had a hand in,' continued Frensic, 'I mean we don't usually publish that sort of book but I must say it's been a great success.'

Miss Bogden's thoughts turned away from the altar. Frensic helped himself to more champagne. 'We're a very traditional publishing house,' he said, 'but *Pause O Men for the Virgin* is what the public demands these days.'

'It was rather awful, wasn't it?' said Miss Bogden, 'I typed it myself you know.'

'Really?' said Frensic.

'Well I didn't like my girls having to do it and the author was so peculiar about it.'

'Was he?'

'I had to phone up ever so often,' said Miss Bogden. 'But you don't want to hear about that.'

Frensic did but Miss Bogden was adamant. 'We mustn't spoil our first evening talking shop,' she said and in spite of more champagne

175

and a large Cointreau all Frensic's attempts to steer the conversation back to the subject failed. Miss Bogden wanted to hear about Corkadales. The name seemed to appeal to her.

'Why don't you come back to my place?' she asked as they walked beside the river after dinner. 'For a nightcap.'

'That's frightfully kind of you,' said Frensic prepared to pursue his quarry to the bitter end. 'Are you sure I wouldn't be imposing on you?'

'I'd like that,' said Miss Bogden with a giggle and took his arm, 'to be imposed on by you.' She steered him to the carpark and a light blue MG. Frensic gaped at the car. It did not accord with his notion of what a forty-five-year-old head of a typing bureau should drive and besides he was unused to bucket seats. Frensic squeezed in and was forced to allow Miss Bogden to fasten his safety belt. Then they drove rather faster than he liked along the Banbury Road and into a hinterland of semi-detached houses. Miss Bogden lived at 33 Viewpark Avenue, a mixture of pebbledash and Tudor. She pulled up in front of the garage. Frensic fumbled for the catch of his safety belt but Cynthia Bogden was there before him and leaning expectantly. Frensic nerved himself for the inevitable and took her in his arms. It was a long kiss and a passionate one, made even less enjoyable for Frensic by the presence of the gear lever in his right kidney. By the time they had finished and climbed out of the car he was having third and fourth thoughts about the whole enterprise. But there was too much at stake to falter now. Frensic followed her into the house. Miss Bogden switched on the hall light.

'Would you like a drinkie?' she asked.

'No,' said Frensic with a fervour that came largely from the conviction that she would offer him cooking sherry. Miss Bogden took his refusal as a compliment and once more they grappled, this time in the company of a hat stand. Then taking his hand she led the way upstairs.

'The you-know-what's in there,' she said helpfully. Frensic staggered into the bathroom and shut the door. He spent several minutes staring at his reflection in the mirror and wondering why it was that only the most predatory women found him attractive and wishing to hell they didn't and then, having promised himself that he would never again be rude about Geoffrey Corkadale's preferences, he came out and went into the bedroom. Cynthia Bogden's bedroom was pink. The curtains were pink, the carpet pink, the padded and quilted bedhead pink and the lampshade beside it pink. And finally there was a pink Frensic wrestling with the intricacies of Cynthia Bogden's pink underwear while muttering pinkish endearments in her pink ear.

An hour later Frensic was no longer pink. Against the pink sheets he was puce and having palpitations to boot. His efforts to get into her good books among other less savoury things had done something to his circulatory system and Miss Bogden's sexual skills, nurtured in a justifiably broken marriage and gleaned, Frensic suspected, from some frightful manual on how to make sex an adventure, had led him to contortions which would have defied the imaginations of his most sexually obsessed authors. As he lay panting, alternately thanking God it was all over and wondering if he was going to have a coronary, Cynthia bent her permed head over him.

'Satisfied?' she asked. Frensic stared at her and nodded frantically. Any other answer would have invited suicide.

'And now we'll have a little drinkie,' she said and skipping to Frensic's amazement lightly off the bed she went downstairs and returned with a bottle of whisky. She sat down on the edge of the bed and poured two tots.

'To us,' she said. Frensic drank deeply and held out his glass for more. Cynthia smiled and handed him the bottle.

In New York Hutchmeyer was having problems too. They were of a different sort to Frensic's but since they involved three and a half million dollars the effect was much the same.

'What do you mean they aren't prepared to pay?' he yelled at MacMordie who had reported that the insurance company were holding back on compensation. 'They got to pay. I mean why should I insure my property if they aren't going to pay when it's arsonized?'

'I don't know,' said MacMordie, 'I'm just telling you what Mr Synstrom said.'

'Get me Synstrom,' yelled Hutchmeyer. MacMordie got Synstrom. He came up to Hutchmeyer's office and sat blandly regarding the great publisher through steel-rimmed glasses.

'Now I don't know what you're trying to get at—' Hutchmeyer began.

'The truth,' said Mr Synstrom. 'Just the plain truth.'

'That's okay by me,' said Hutchmeyer, 'just so long as you pay up when you've got it.'

'The thing is, Mr Hutchmeyer, we know how that fire started.'

'How?'

'Someone deliberately lit the house with a can of gasolene. And that someone was your wife . . .'

'You know that?'

'Mr Hutchmeyer, we've got analysts who can figure out the nail varnish your wife was wearing when she opened that safe and took out that quarter of a million dollars you had stashed there.'

Hutchmeyer eyed him suspiciously. 'You can?' he said.

'Sure. And we know too she loaded that cruiser of yours with fifty gallons of gasolene. She and that Piper. He carried the cans down and we've got their prints.'

'What the hell would she do that for?'

'We thought you might have the answer to that one,' said Mr Synstrom.

'Me? I was out in the middle of the goddam bay. How should I know what was going on back at my house?'

'We wouldn't know that, Mr Hutchmeyer. Just seems a kind of coincidence you go sailing with Miss Futtle in a storm and your wife is setting out to burn your house down and fake her own death.'

Hutchmeyer paled. 'Fake her own death? Did you say . . .'

Mr Synstrom nodded. 'We call it the Stonehouse syndrome in the trade,' he said. 'It happens every once in a while someone wants the world to think they're dead so they disappear and leave their nearest and dearest to claim the insurance. Now you've put in a claim for three and a half million dollars and we've got no proof your wife isn't alive some place.'

Hutchmeyer stared miserably at him. He was considering the awful possibility that Baby was still around and with her she was carrying all that evidence of his tax evasions, bribes and illegal dealings that could send him to prison. By comparison the forfeiture of three and a half million dollars was peanuts.

'I just can't believe she'd do a thing like that,' he said finally. 'I mean we had a happy marriage. No problems. I gave her everything she asked for . . .'

'Like young men?' said Mr Synstrom.

'No, not like young men,' shouted Hutchmeyer, and felt his pulse.

'Now this Piper writer was a young man,' said Mr Synstrom, 'and from what we've heard Mrs Hutchmeyer had a taste for . . .'

'Are you accusing my wife of . . . My God, I'll . . .'

'We're not accusing anyone of anything, Mr Hutchmeyer. Like I've said we're trying to get at the truth.'

'And are you telling me that my wife, my own dear little Baby, filled that cruiser with gasolene and deliberately tried to murder me by aiming it at my yacht in the middle of—'

'That's exactly what I'm saying. Mind you, that could have been an accident,' said Mr Synstrom, 'the cruiser blowing up where she did.'

'Yeah, well from where I was standing it didn't look like an accident. You can believe it didn't,' said Hutchmeyer. 'You want to have a cruiser come out of the night straight for you before you go round making allegations like you've just done.'

Mr Synstrom got to his feet. 'So you still want us to continue with our investigations?' he said.

Hutchmeyer hesitated. If Baby was still alive the last thing he wanted was investigations. 'I just don't believe my Baby would have done a thing like that is all,' he said.

Mr Synstrom sat down again. 'If she did and we can prove it I'm afraid Mrs Hutchmeyer would stand trial. Arson, attempted murder, defrauding an insurance company. And then there's Mr Piper. He's an accessory. Bestselling author, I hear. I guess he could always get a job in the prison library. Make a sensational trial too. Now if you don't want all of that . . .'

Hutchmeyer didn't want any of that. Sensational trials with Baby in the box pleading that . . . Oh no! Definitely not. And *Pause* was selling by the hundred thousand, had passed the million mark and with the movie of the book in production the computer was overheating with the stupendous forecasts. Sensational trials were out.

'What's the alternative?' he asked.

Mr Synstrom leant forward. 'We could come to an arrangement,' he said.

'We could,' Hutchmeyer agreed, 'but that still leaves the cops . . .'

Mr Synstrom shook his head. 'They're sitting around waiting to see what we come up with. Now the way I see it . . .'

By the time he had finished Hutchmeyer saw it that way too. The insurance company would announce that the claim had been met in full and in return Hutchmeyer would write a disclaimer. Hutchmeyer did. Three and a half million dollars was worth every cent for keeping Baby 'dead'.

'What happens if you're right and she turns up out of the blue?' Hutchmeyer asked as Mr Synstrom got up to leave.

'Then you've really got problems,' he said. 'That's what I'd say.'

He left and Hutchmeyer sat back and considered those problems. The only consolation he could find was that if Baby was still alive she had problems too. Like coming back to life and going to prison. She wasn't fool enough to do that. Which left Hutchmeyer free to go his own way. He could even marry again. His thoughts turned to Sonia Futtle. Now there was a *real* woman.

Chapter 19

Two thousand miles to the south Baby's problems had taken on a new dimension. Her attempt to give Piper the experience he needed relationshipwise had succeeded too well and where before he had thrown himself into *Work In Regress* he now insisted on throwing himself into her as well. The years of his celibacy were over and Piper was making up for them in a hurry. As he lay each night kissing her reinforced breasts and gripping her degreased thighs Piper experienced an ecstasy he could never have found with another woman. Baby's artificiality was entirely to his taste. Lacking so many original parts she had none of those natural physiological disadvantages he had found in Sonia. She had, as it were, been expurgated and Piper, himself in the process of expurgating *Pause*, derived enormous satisfaction from the fact that with Baby he could act out the role he had been assigned as narrator in the book with a woman who if she was much older than him didn't look it. And Baby's response added to his pleasure. She combined lack of fervour with sexual expertise so that he didn't feel threatened by her passion. She was simply there to be enjoyed and didn't interfere with his writing by demanding his constant attention. Finally her intimate knowledge of the novel meant that she could respond word-perfect to his cues. When he murmured, 'Darling, we're being so heuristically creative,' at the penultimate moment of ecstasy, Baby, feeling nothing, could reply, 'Constating, my baby,' in unison with her prototype the ancient Gwendolen on page 185, and thus maintain quite literally the fiction that was the essential core of Piper's being.

But if Baby met Piper's requirements as the ideal lover the reverse was not true. Baby found it unflattering to know that she was merely a stand-in for a figment of his imagination and not even his own imagination but that of the real author of *Pause*. Knowing this, Piper's ardour took on an almost ghoulish quality so that Baby, staring over his shoulder at the ceiling, had the horrid feeling that she might just as well not have been present. At such moments she saw herself as something that had coalesced from the pages of *Pause*, a phantom of the opus which was Piper's pretentious name for what he was now doing in *Work In Regress* and intended to continue in another version. Her future seemed destined to be the recipient of his derived feelings, a sexual artefact compiled from words upon pages to be ejaculated into and then set aside while he put pen to paper. Even the routine of their days had altered. Piper insisted on writing each morning and driving through the heat of the day and stopping early at a motel so that he could read to her what he had written that morning and then relate.

'Can't you just say "fuck" once in a while?' Baby asked one evening at a motel in Tuscaloosa. 'I mean that's what we're doing so why not name it right?'

But Piper wouldn't. The word wasn't in *Pause* and 'relating' was an approved term in *The Moral Novel*.

'What I feel for you . . .' he began but Baby stopped him.

'So I read the original. I don't need to see the movie.'

'As I was saying,' said Piper, 'what I feel for you is . . .'

'Zero,' said Baby, 'absolute zero. You've got more feelings towards that ink bottle you're always sticking your pen in than you have towards me.'

'Well, I like that . . .' said Piper.

'I don't,' said Baby and there was a new note of desperation in her voice. For a moment she thought of leaving Piper there in the motel and going off on her own. But the moment passed. She was tied by the irrevocable act of the fire and her disappearance to this literary mongol whose notion of great writing was to step backwards in time in futile imitation of novelists long dead. Worst of all, she saw in Piper's obsession with past glories a mirror-image of herself. For forty years she too had waged a war with time and had by surgical recession maintained the outward appearance of the foolish beauty who had been Miss Penobscot 1935. They had so much in common and Piper served to remind her of her own stupidity. All that was gone now, the longing to be young again and the sense of knowing she was still sexually attractive. Only death remained and the certainty that when she died there would be no call for the embalmer. She had seen to that in advance.

She had seen to more than that. She had already died by fire, by water, by the bizarre circumstances of her own romantic madness. Which gave her something more in common with Piper. They were both nonentities moving in a limbo of monotonous motels, he with his ledgers and her body but she with nothing more than a sense of meaninglessness and a desperate futility. That night while Piper related, Baby, inanimate beneath him, made up her mind. They would leave the beaten track of motels and drive down dirt roads into the hinterland of the Deep South. What happened to them there would be beyond her choosing.

What was happening to Frensic was definitely beyond his choosing. He sat at the Formica-topped table in Cynthia Bogden's kitchen and tried to eat his cornflakes and forget what had occurred towards dawn. Driven frantic by Cynthia's omnivorous sexuality he had proposed to the woman. It had seemed in his whisky-sodden state the only defence against a fatal coronary and a means of getting her to tell him who had sent her *Pause*. But Miss Bogden had been too overwhelmed to discuss minor matters of that sort in the middle of the night. In the end Frensic had snatched a few hours sleep and had been woken by a radiant Cynthia with a cup of tea. Frensic had staggered through to the bathroom and had shaved with someone else's razor and had come down to breakfast determined to force the issue. But Miss Bogden's thoughts were confined to their wedding day.

'Shall we have a church wedding?' she asked as Piper toyed biliously with a boiled egg.

'What? Oh. Yes.'

'I've always wanted a church wedding.'

'So have I,' said Frensic with as much enthusiasm as if she had suggested a crematorium. He savaged the egg and decided on the direct approach. 'By the way did you ever meet the author of *Pause O Men for the Virgin*?'

Miss Bogden dragged her thoughts away from aisles, altars and Mendelssohn. 'No,' she said, 'the manuscript came by post.'

'By post?' said Frensic, dropping his spoon. 'Isn't that rather unusual?'

'You're not eating your egg,' said Miss Bogden. Frensic took a spoonful of egg into his dry mouth.

'Where did it come from?'

'Lloyds Bank,' said Miss Bogden and poured herself another cup of tea. 'Another cup for you?'

Frensic nodded. He needed something to wash the egg down with.

'Lloyds Bank?' he said finally. 'But there must have been words you couldn't read. What did you do then?'

'Oh I just rang up and asked.'

'You phoned? You mean you phoned Lloyds Bank and they'd ...'

'Oh you are silly, Geoffrey,' said Miss Bogden, 'I didn't phone Lloyds Bank. I had this other number.'

'What other number?'

'The one I had to ring, silly,' said Miss Bogden and looked at her watch. 'Oh look at the time. It's almost nine. You've made me late, you naughty boy.' And she rushed out of the kitchen. When she returned she was dressed for the day. 'You can call a taxi when you're ready,' she said, 'and we'll meet at the office.' She kissed Frensic passionately on his egg-filled mouth and went out.

Frensic got to his feet and spat the egg into the sink and turned the tap on. Then he took a pinch of snuff, helped himself to some more tea and tried to think. A phone number she had to ring? The whole business became more extraordinary the further he delved into it. And for once delved was the right word. In looking for the source of *Pause* he had dug himself ... Frensic shuddered. Dug was the right word too. In the plural it was exact. He went through to the lavatory and sat there miserably for ten minutes trying to concentrate on his next move. A phone number? An author who insisted on making corrections by telephone? There was an insanity about all this that made his own actions over the past few days look positively rational. And there was absolutely nothing rational about proposing to Miss Cynthia Bogden. Frensic finished his business in the lavatory and came out. On a small table in the hall stood a telephone. Frensic crossed to it and looked through Miss Bogden's private list of numbers but there was nothing there to indicate the author. Frensic returned to the kitchen, made himself a cup of instant coffee, took some more snuff and finally telephoned for a taxi.

It came at ten and at half past Frensic shuffled into the Typing Agency. Miss Bogden was waiting for him. So were twelve awful women sitting at typewriters.

'Girls,' Miss Bogden called euphemistically as Frensic peered anxiously into the office, 'I want you all to meet my fiancé, Mr Geoffrey Corkadale.'

The women all rose from the seats and gaggled congratulations on Frensic while Miss Bogden suppurated happiness.

'And now the ring,' she said when the congratulations died down. She led the way out of the office and Frensic followed. The bloody woman would want a ring. Just so long as it wasn't too expensive. It was.

'I think I like the solitaire,' she told the jeweller in the Broad. Frensic flinched at the price and was about to put his entire scheme in jeopardy when he was struck by a brilliant thought. After all, what was five hundred pounds when his entire future was at stake?

'Oughtn't we to have it engraved?' he said as Cynthia put it on her finger and admired its brilliance.

'What with?' she cooed.

Frensic simpered. 'Something secret,' he whispered, 'something we two alone will understand. A *code d'amour.*'

'Oh you are awful,' said Miss Bogden. 'Fancy thinking of something like that.' Frensic glanced at the jeweller uncomfortably and applied his lips to the perm again.

'A code of love,' he explained.

'A code of love?' echoed Miss Bogden. 'What sort of code?'

'A number,' said Frensic, and paused. 'Some number that only we would know had brought us together.'

'You mean . . . ?'

'Exactly,' said Frensic forestalling any alternatives, 'after all, you typed the book and I published it.'

'Couldn't we just have Till Death Do Us Part?'

'Too much like the TV series,' said Frensic who had very much earlier intentions. He was saved by the jeweller.

'You'd never get that inside the ring. Not Till Death Do Us Part. Too many letters.'

'But you could do numbers?' said Frensic.

'Depends how many.'

Frensic looked enquiringly at Miss Bogden. 'Five,' she said after a moment's hesitation.

'Five,' said Frensic. 'Five teeny weeny little numbers that are our code of love, our own, our very own itsy bitsy secret.' It was his last desperate act of heroism. Miss Bogden succumbed. For a moment she had . . . but no, a man who could in the presence of an austere jeweller By Appointment to Her Majesty talk openly about five teeny weeny itsy bitsy numbers that were their code of love, such a man was above suspicion.

'Two oh three five seven,' she simpered.

'Two oh three five seven,' said Frensic loudly. 'You're quite sure? We don't want to make any mistakes.'

'Of course I'm sure,' said Miss Bogden, 'I'm not in the habit of making mistakes.'

'Right,' said Frensic plucking the ring from her finger and handing it to the jeweller, 'stick them on the inside of the thing. I'll be back to collect it this afternoon,' and taking Miss Bogden firmly by the arm he steered her towards the door.

'Excuse me, sir,' said the jeweller, 'but if you don't mind . . .'

'Mind what?' said Frensic.

'I would prefer it if you paid now sir. With engraving, you understand, we have to . . .'

Frensic understood all too well. He released Miss Bogden and sidled back to the counter.

'Er . . . well . . .' he began but Miss Bogden was still between him and the door. This was no time for half-measures. Frensic took out his cheque book.

'I'll be with you in a moment, dear,' he called. 'You just go over the road and look at dresses.'

Cynthia Bogden obeyed her instincts and stayed where she was.

'You do have a cheque card, sir?' said the jeweller.

Frensic looked at him gratefully. 'As a matter of fact, I don't. Not on me.'

'Then I'm afraid it will have to be cash, sir.'

'Cash?' said Frensic. 'In that case . . .'

'We'll go to the bank,' said Miss Bogden firmly. They went to the bank in the High Street. Miss Bogden seated herself while Frensic conferred at the counter.

'Five hundred pounds?' said the teller. 'We'll have to have proof of identity and telephone your own branch.'

Frensic glanced at Miss Bogden and lowered his voice. 'Frensic,' he said nervously, 'Frederick Frensic, Glass Walk, Hampstead but my business account is with the branch in Covent Garden.'

'We'll call you when we have confirmation,' said the teller.

Frensic blanched. 'I'd be grateful if you didn't . . .' he began.

'Didn't what?'

'Never mind,' said Frensic and went back to Miss Bogden. He had to get her out of the bank before that blasted teller started hollering for Mr Frensic.

186

'This is going to take some time, darling. Why don't you toddle back to . . .'

'But I've taken the day off and I thought . . .'

'Taken the day off?' said Frensic. If this sort of stress went on much longer it would take years off. 'But . . .'

'But what?' said Miss Bogden.

'But I'm supposed to be meeting an author for lunch. Professor Dubrowitz. From Warsaw. He's only over for the day and . . .' He hustled her out of the bank promising to come to the office just as soon as he could. Then with a sigh of relief he went back and collected five hundred pounds.

'Now for the nearest telephone,' he said to himself as he pocketed the money and descended the steps. Cynthia Bogden was still there.

'But . . .' Frensic began and gave up. With Miss Bogden there were no buts.

'I thought we'd just go and get the ring first,' she said taking his arm, 'then you can go and have lunch with your boring old professor.'

They went back to the jewellers and Frensic paid £500. Only then did Miss Bogden allow him to escape.

'Call me as soon as you've finished,' she said pecking his cheek. Frensic promised to and hurried off to the main post office. In a foul temper he dialled 23507.

'The Bombay Duck Restaurant,' said an Indian who was unlikely to have written *Pause*. Frensic slammed the phone down and tried another combination of the digits in the ring. This time he got MacLoughlin's Fish Emporium. Then he ran out of change. He went across to the main counter and handed over a five-pound note for a 6½p stamp and returned with a pocketful of coins. The phone booth was occupied. Frensic stood beside it looking belligerent while an apparently sub-normal youth plighted his acned troth to a girl who giggled audibly. Frensic spent the time trying to remember the exact number and by the time the youth had finished he had got it. Frensic went in and dialled 20357. There was a long pause and the sound of the ringing tone before anyone answered. Frensic plunged a coin into the machine.

'Yes,' said a thin querulous voice, 'who is it?'

Frensic hesitated a moment and then coarsened his voice. 'This is the General Post Office, telephone faults department,' he said. 'We are trying to trace a crossed connection in a junction box. If you would just give me your name and address.'

'A fault?' said the voice. 'We haven't had any faults.'

'You soon will have. There's a burst water main and we need your name and address.'

'But I thought you said you had a crossed connection?' said the voice peevishly. 'Now you say there's a water main . . .'

'Madam,' said Frensic officiously, 'the burst water main is affecting the junction box and we need your help to locate it. Now if you will be so good as give me your name and address . . .' There was a long pause during which Frensic gnawed a nail.

'Oh well if you must,' said the voice at long last, 'the name is Dr Louth and the address is 44 Cowpasture Gardens . . . Hullo, are you there?'

But Frensic was miles away in a world of terrible conjecture. Without another word he replaced the receiver and staggered out into the street.

In Lanyard Lane Sonia sat at her typewriter and stared at the calendar. She had returned from Somerset, satisfied that Bernie the Beaver would use less forceful language in future, to find two messages for her. The first was from Frensic saying that he would be out of town on business for a few days and would she mind coping. That was queer enough. Frensic usually left fuller explanations and a telephone number where she could call him in case of emergencies. The second message was even more peculiar and in the shape of a long telegram from Hutchmeyer: POLICE ESTABLISHED DEATHS PIPER AND BABY ACCIDENTAL NO RESPONSIBILITY TERRORISTS RUNNING AWAY WITH EACH OTHER CRAZY ABOUT YOU ARRIVING THURSDAY ALL MY LOVE HUTCHMEYER.

Sonia studied the message and found it at first incomprehensible. Deaths accidental? No responsibility terrorists running away with each other? What on earth did it mean? For a moment she hesitated and then dialled International and was put through to New York and Hutchmeyer Press. She got MacMordie.

'He's in Brasilia right now,' he said.

'What's all this business about Piper's death being accidental?' she asked.

'That's the theory the police have come up with,' said MacMordie, 'like they were eloping some place with all that fuel on board when she blew.'

188

'Eloping? Piper and that bitch eloping? In the middle of the night with a cabin cruiser? Somebody's out of their mind.'

'I wouldn't know,' said MacMordie, 'all I'm saying is what the cops and the insurance company have come up with. And that Piper had this big thing for old women. I mean take his book. It shows.'

'Like hell it does,' said Sonia before recalling that MacMordie didn't know Piper hadn't written it.

'If you don't believe me, call the cops in Maine or the insurers. They'll tell you.'

Sonia called the insurers. They were more likely to come up with the truth. They had money at stake. She was put through to Mr Synstrom.

'And you really believe he was running off with Mrs Hutchmeyer and it was all an accident?' she said when he had given his version of the event. 'I mean you're not having me on?'

'This is the Claims Department,' said Mr Synstrom firmly. 'We don't have people on. It's not our line of business.'

'Well it sounds crazy to me,' said Sonia, 'she was old enough to be his mother.'

'If you want further delineation of the circumstances surrounding the accident I suggest you speak to the Maine State police,' said Mr Synstrom and ended the conversation.

Sonia sat stunned by this new development. That Peter had preferred that awful old hag . . . From being in love with his memory one minute she was out of it the next. Piper had betrayed her and with the knowledge there came a new sense of bitterness and reality. In life, now that she came to think about it, he had been a bit dreary and her love had been less for him as a man than for his aptitude as a husband. Given the chance she could have made something of him. Even before his death she had made him famous as an author and had he lived they would have gone on to greater things. It was not for nothing that Brahms was her favourite composer. There would have been little Pipers, each to be helped towards a suitable career by a woman who was at the same time a mother and a literary agent. That dream had ended. Piper had died with a surgically preserved bitch in a mink coat.

Sonia looked at the telegram again. It had a new message for her now. Piper was not the only man ever to have found her attractive. There was still Hutchmeyer, a widowed Hutchmeyer whose wife had stolen her darling from her. There was a fine irony in the

189

thought that by her action, Baby had made it possible for Hutchmeyer to marry again. And marry her he would. It was marriage or
nothing. There would be no messing.

Sonia reached for a sheet of paper and put it in the typewriter.
Frenzy would have to be told. Poor old Frenzy, she would miss him
but wedlock called and she must respond. She would explain her
reasons and then leave. It seemed the best thing to do. There would
be no recriminations and in a way she was sacrificing herself for him.
But where on earth had he got to, and why?

Chapter 20

Frensic was in Blackwell's bookshop. Half hidden among the stacks of English literary criticism he stood with a copy of *The Great Pursuit* in his hand and *Pause* propped up on the shelf in front of him. *The Great Pursuit* was Dr Sydney Louth's latest, a collection of essays dedicated to F. R. Leavis and a monument to a lifetime's execration of the shallow, the obscene, the immature and the non-significant in English literature. Generations of undergraduates had sat mesmerized by the turgid inelegance of her style while she denounced the modern novel, the contemporary world and the values of a sick and dying civilization. Frensic had been among those undergraduates and had imbibed the truisms on which Dr Louth's reputation as a scholar and a critic had been founded. She had praised the obviously great and cursed the rest and for that simple formula she was known as a great scholar. And all this in language which was the antithesis of the stylistic brilliance of the writers she praised. But it was her anathema which had stuck in Frensic's mind, those bitter graceless curses she had heaped on other critics and those who disagreed with her. By her denunciations she had implanted the inhibitions which had spoilt Frensic and so many others like him who had wanted to write. To appease her he had adopted the grotesque syntax of her lectures and essays. By their style Louthians were instantly recognizable. And by their sterility.

For three decades her influence on English literature had been malignant. And all her imprecations on the present had been hallowed by the great past which had she been a living influence at the time would never have existed. Like some religious fanatic she had consecrated the already sacred and had bred an intellectual intolerance that denied a living to the less than best. There were only saints in Dr Louth's calendar, saints and devils who failed the test of greatness. Hardy, Forster, Galsworthy, Moore and Meredith, even Peacock, consigned to outer darkness and oblivion because they did not measure up to Conrad or Henry James. And what about poor Trollope and Thackeray? More devils. The less than best. And

Fielding . . . The list was endless. And for the present generation the only hope of salvation was to genuflect to her opinions and learn by rote the answers to her literary catechism. And this arid bitch had written *Pause O Men for the Virgin.* Frensic inverted the title and found it wholly appropriate. Dr Louth had given birth to nothing. The stillborn opinions in *The Moral Novel* and now *The Great Pursuit* would moulder and decompose upon the shelves a few more years and be forgotten. And she had known it and had written *Pause* to seek an anonymous immortality. The clues were there to be seen. Frensic wondered how he could have missed them. On page 269 of *Pause* : 'And so inexorably their livingness became lovingness, a rhythmic lovingness that placed them within a new dimension of feeling so that the really real became an . . .' Frensic shut the book before he came to 'apprehended totality'. How many times in his youth had he heard her use those fearful words? And used them himself in his essays for her. That 'placed' too was proof enough but followed by so many meaningless abstractions and a 'really real' it was conclusive. He thrust both books under his arm and went to the counter to pay for them. There were no doubts left, and everything was explained, the obsessive precautions to preserve the author's anonymity, the readiness to allow Piper to act as substitute . . . But now Piper was claiming to have written *Pause.*

Frensic walked more slowly across the Parks deep in thought. Two authors for the same book? And Piper had been a devotee of Dr Louth. *The Moral Novel* was his scripture. In which case he could well have . . . No. Miss Bogden had not been lying. Frensic increased his pace and strode beside the river towards Cowpasture Gardens. Dr Louth was going to learn that she had made a bad mistake in sending her manuscript to one of her former pupils. Because that was what it was all about. In her conceit she had chosen Frensic out of a hundred other agents. The irony of her gesture would have appealed to her. She had never had much time for him. 'A mediocre mind' she had once written at the end of one of his essays. Frensic had never forgiven her. He was going to get his revenge.

He left the parks and entered Cowpasture Gardens. Dr Louth's house stood at the far end, a large Victorian mansion with an air of deliberate desuetude as if the inhabitants were too committed intellectually to notice overgrown borders and untended lawns. And there had been, Frensic recalled, cats.

There were still cats. Two sat on a window-ledge and watched as

192

Frensic walked to the front door and rang the bell. He stood waiting and looked around. If anything the garden had regressed still further towards the pastoral which Dr Louth had so extolled in literature. And the Monkey Puzzle tree stood there as unclimbable as ever. How often had he looked out of the window at that Monkey Puzzle tree while Dr Louth intoned the need for a mature moral purpose in all art. Frensic was about to fall into a nostalgic reverie when the door opened and Miss Christian peered out at him uncertainly.

'If you're from the telephone people . . .' she began but Frensic shook his head.

'My name is . . .' he hesitated as he tried to recall a favoured pupil. 'Bartlett. I was a student of hers in 1955.'

Miss Christian pursed her lips. 'She isn't seeing anyone,' she said.

Frensic smiled. 'I just wanted to pay my respects. I've always regarded her as the greatest influence in my development. Seminal you know.'

Miss Christian savoured 'seminal'. It was the password. 'In 1955?'

'The year she published *The Intuitive Felicity*,' said Frensic to bring out the bouquet of that vintage.

'So it was. It seems so long ago now,' said Miss Christian and opened the door wider. Frensic stepped into the dark hall where the stained-glass windows on the stairs added to the air of sanctity. Two more cats sat on chairs.

'What did you say your name was?' said Miss Christian.

'Bartlett,' said Frensic. (Bartlett had got a First.)

'Ah, yes, Bartlett,' said Miss Christian. 'I'll just go and ask her if she will see you.'

She went away down a threadworn passage to the study. Frensic stood and gritted his teeth against the odour of cats and the almost palpable atmosphere of intellectual high-mindedness and moral intensity. On the whole he preferred the cats.

Miss Christian shuffled back. 'She will see you,' she said. 'She seldom sees visitors now but she will see you. You know the way.'

Frensic nodded. He knew the way. He went down the length of worn carpet and opened the door.

Inside the study it was 1955. In twenty years nothing had changed. Dr Sydney Louth sat in an armchair beside a small fire, a pile of papers on her lap, a cigarette tilted on the lip of an ashtray and a cup of cold half-finished tea on the table at her elbow. She did not look up as Frensic entered. That was an old habit too, the mark of an inner concentration so profound that to disturb it was the highest privilege. A red ballpen wriggled illegibly in the margin of the essay. Frensic took his seat opposite her and waited. There were advantages to be gained from her arrogance. He laid the copy of *Pause*, still in its Blackwell's wrapping, on his knees and studied the bowed head and busy hand. It was all exactly as he had remembered it. Then the hand stopped writing, dropped the ballpen and reached for the cigarette.

'Bartlett, dear Bartlett,' she said and looked up. She stared at him dimly and Frensic stared back. He had been wrong. Things had changed. The face he looked at was not the face he remembered. Then it had been smooth and slightly plump. Now it was swollen and corrugated. A plexus of dropsical wrinkles bagged under the eyes and scored her cheeks, and from the lip of this reticulated mask there hung the cigarette. Only the expression in the eyes remained the same, dimmer but burning with the certainty of her own rightness.

The conviction faded as Frensic watched. 'I thought . . .' she began and looked at him more closely, 'Miss Christian precisely said . . .'

'Frensic. You were my supervisor in 1955,' said Frensic.

'Frensic?' The eyes filled with conjecture now. 'But you said Bartlett . . .'

'A little deceit,' said Frensic, 'to guarantee this interview. I'm a literary agent now. Frensic & Futtle. You won't have heard of us.'

But Dr Louth had. The eyes flickered. 'No. I'm afraid I haven't.'

Frensic hesitated and chose a circuitous approach. 'And since . . . well . . . since you were my supervisor I was wondering, well, if you would consider . . . I mean it would be a great favour to ask . . .' Frensic paraded deference.

'What do you want?' said Dr Louth.

Frensic unwrapped the packet on his lap. 'You see we have a novel and if you would write a piece . . .'

'A novel?' The eyes behind the wrinkles glinted at the wrapping paper. 'What novel?'

'This,' said Frensic, and passed her *Pause O Men for the Virgin*. For a moment Dr Louth stared at the book and the cigarette slouched on her lip. Then she cringed in her chair.

'That?' she whispered. The cigarette dropped from her lip and smouldered on the essay on her lap. 'That?'

Frensic nodded and leaning forward removed the cigarette and put the book down. 'It seemed your sort of book,' he said.

'My sort of book?'

Frensic sat back in his chair. The centre of power had passed to him. 'Since you wrote it,' he said, 'I thought it only fair . . .'

'How did you know?' She was staring at him with a new intensity. There was no high moral purpose in that intensity now. Only fear and hatred. Frensic basked in it. He crossed his legs and looked out at the Monkey Puzzle tree. He had climbed it.

'Mainly through the style,' he said, 'and to be perfectly frank, by critical analysis. You used the same words too often in your books and I placed them. You taught me that, you see.'

There was a long pause while Dr Louth lit another cigarette. 'And you expect me to review it?' she said at last.

'Not really,' said Frensic, 'it's unethical for an author to review her own work. I just wanted to discuss how best we could announce the news to the world.'

'What news?'

'That Dr Sydney Louth, the eminent critic, had written both *Pause* and *The Great Pursuit*. I thought an article in the *Times Literary Supplement* would do to start the controversy raging. After all, it's not every day that a scholar produces a bestseller, particularly the sort of book she has spent her life denouncing as obscene . . .'

'I forbid it,' Dr Louth gasped. 'As my agent . . .'

'As your agent it is my business to see that the book sells. And I can assure you that the literary scandal the announcement will provoke in circles where your name has previously been revered . . .'

'No,' said Dr Louth, 'that must never happen.'

'You're thinking of your reputation?' enquired Frensic gently. Dr Louth did not reply.

'You should have thought of that before. As it is you have placed me in a very awkward situation. I have a reputation to maintain too.'

'Your reputation? What sort of reputation is that?' She spat the words at him.

Frensic leant forward. 'An immaculate one,' he snarled, 'beyond your comprehension.'

Dr Louth tried to smile. 'Grub Street,' she muttered.

'Yes, Grub Street,' said Frensic, 'and proud of it. Where people write without hypocrisy for money.'

'Lucre, filthy lucre.'

Frensic grinned. 'And what did you write for?'

195

The mask looked at him venomously. 'To prove that I could,' she said, 'that I could write the sort of trash that sells. They thought I couldn't. A sterile critic, impotent, an academic. I proved them wrong.' Her voice rose.

Frensic shrugged. 'Hardly,' he said. 'Your name is not upon the title page. Until it is no one will ever know.'

'No one must ever know.'

'But I intend to tell them,' said Frensic. 'It will make fascinating reading. The anonymous author, Lloyds Bank, the Typing Service, Mr Cadwalladine, Corkadales, your American publisher . . .'

'You mustn't,' she whimpered, 'no one must ever know. I tell you I forbid it.'

'It's no longer in your hands,' said Frensic, 'it's in mine and I will not sully them with your hypocrisy. Besides I have another client.'

'Another client?'

'The scapegoat Piper who went to America for you. He has a reputation too, you know.'

Dr Louth sniggered. 'Like yours, immaculate I suppose.'

'In conception, yes,' said Frensic.

'But which he was prepared to put in jeopardy for money.'

'If you like. He wanted to write and he needed the money. You, I take it, don't. You mentioned lucre, filthy lucre. I am prepared to bargain.'

'Blackmail,' snapped Dr Louth and stubbed out her cigarette.

Frensic looked at her with a new disgust. 'For a moral coward who hides behind a *nom de plume* your language is imprecise. Had you come to me in the first place I would not have engaged Piper but since you chose anonymity at the expense of honesty I am now in the position of having to choose between two authors.'

'Two? Why two?'

'Because Piper claims he wrote the book.'

'Let him claim. He accepted the onus, let him bear it.'

'He also claims the money.'

Dr Louth glared at the smouldering fire. 'He has been paid,' she said finally. 'What more does he want?'

'Everything,' said Frensic.

'And you're prepared to let him have it?'

'Yes,' said Frensic. 'My reputation is at stake too. If there's a scandal I will suffer.'

'A scandal,' Dr Louth shook her head. 'There must be no scandal.'

196

'But there will be,' said Frensic. 'You see, Piper is dead.'

Dr Louth shivered suddenly. 'Dead? But you said just now . . .'

'There is the estate to be wound up. It will go to court and with two million dollars . . . Need I say more?'

Dr Louth shook her head. 'What do you want me to do?' she asked.

Frensic relaxed. The crisis was over. He had broken the bitch. 'Write a letter to me denying that you ever wrote the book. Now.'

'Will that suffice?'

'To begin with,' said Frensic. Dr Louth got up and crossed to her desk. For a minute or two she sat there writing. When she had finished she handed Frensic the letter. He read it through and was satisfied.

'And now the manuscript,' he said, 'the original manuscript in your own handwriting and any copies you may have made.'

'No,' she said, 'I will destroy it.'

'We will destroy it,' said Frensic, 'before I leave.'

Dr Louth turned back to the desk and unlocked a drawer and took out a box. She crossed to her chair by the fire and sat down. Then she opened the box and took the pages out. Frensic glanced at the top one. It began 'The house stood on a knoll. Surrounded by three elms, a beech and a deodar whose horizontal branches . . .' He was looking at the original of *Pause*. A moment later the page was on the fire and blazing up into the chimney. Frensic sat and watched as one by one the pages flared up, crinkled to black so that the words upon them stood out like white lace, broke and caught in the draught and were swept up the chimney. And as they blazed Frensic seemed to catch out of the corner of his eye the gleam of tears in the runnels of Dr Louth's cheeks. For a moment he faltered. The woman was cremating her own work. Trash she had called it and yet she was crying over it now. He would never understand writers and the contradictory impulses that were the source of their invention.

As the last page disappeared he got up. She was still huddled over the grate. For a second time Frensic was tempted to ask her why she had written the book. To prove her critics wrong. That wasn't the answer. There was more to it than that, the sex, the ardent love affair . . . He would never learn from her. He left the room quietly and went down the passage to the front door. Outside the air was filled with small black flakes falling from the chimney and near the gate a young cat jumped up clawing at a fragment which danced in the breeze.

Frensic took a deep breath of fresh air and hurried down the road. He had his things to collect from the hotel and then a train to catch to London.

Somewhere south of Tuscaloosa Baby dropped the road map out of the window of the car. It fluttered behind them in the dust and was gone. As usual Piper noticed nothing. His mind was intent on *Work In Regress*. He had reached page 178 and the book was going well. In another fortnight of hard work he would have finished it. And then he would start the third revision, the one in which not only the characters were changed but the setting of every scene. He had decided to call it *Postscript to A Childhood* as a precursor to his final, commercially unadulterated novel *Search for a Lost Childhood* which was to be considered in retrospect as the very first draft of *Pause* by those same critics who had acclaimed that obnoxious novel. In this way his reputation would have been rescued from the oblivion of facile success and scholars would be able to trace the insidious influence of Frensic's commercial recommendations upon his original talent. Piper smiled to himself at his own ingenuity. And after all there could be other yet to be discovered novels. He would go on writing 'posthumously' and every few years another novel would turn up on Frensic's desk to be released to the world. There was nothing Frensic could do about it. Baby was right. By deceiving Hutchmeyer Frensic & Futtle had made themselves vulnerable. Frensic would have to do what he was told. Piper closed his eyes and lay back in his seat contentedly. Half an hour later he opened them again and sat up. The car, a Ford that Baby had bought in Rossville, was lurching on a bad road surface. Piper looked out and saw they were driving along a road built on an embankment. On either side tall trees stood in dark water.

'Where are we?' he asked.

'I've no idea,' said Baby.

'No idea? You've got to know where we are heading.'

'Into the sticks is all I know. And when we get some place we'll find out.'

Piper looked down at the dark water beneath the trees. The forest had a sinister quality to it that he didn't like. Always before they had travelled along homely, cheerful roads with only the occasional stretch of kudzu vine crawling across trees and banks to suggest wild natural growth. But this was different. There were no billboards, no

198

houses, no gas stations, none of those amenities which had signified civilization. This was a wilderness.

'And what happens if when we do get some place there isn't a motel?' he asked.

'Then we'll have to make do with what there is,' said Baby, 'I told you we were coming to the Deep South and this is where it's at.'

'Where what's at?' said Piper staring down at the black water and thinking of alligators.

'That's what I've come to find out,' said Baby enigmatically and braked the car to a standstill at a cross roads. Piper peered through the windshield at a sign. Its faded letters said BIBLIOPOLIS 15 MILES.

'Looks like your kind of town,' said Baby and turned the car on to the side road. Presently the dark water forest thinned and they came out into an open landscape with lush meadows hazy with heat where cattle grazed in long grass and clumps of trees stood apart. There was something almost English about this scenery, an English park-land gone to seed, luxuriant yet immanent with half-remembered possibilities. Everywhere the distance faded into haze blurring the horizon. Piper, looking across the meadows, felt easier in his mind. There was a sense of domesticity here that was reassuring. Occasion-ally they passed a wooden shack part-hidden by vegetation and seemingly unoccupied. And finally there was Bibliopolis itself, a small town, almost a hamlet, with a river running sluggishly beside an abandoned quay. Baby drove down to the riverside and stopped. There was no bridge. On the far side an ancient rope ferry provided the only means of crossing.

'Okay, go ring the bell,' said Baby. Piper got out and rang a bell that hung from a post.

'Harder,' said Baby as Piper pulled on the rope. Presently a man appeared on the far shore and the ferry began to move across.

'You wanting something?' said the man when the ferry grounded.

'We're looking for somewhere to stay,' said Baby. The man peered at the licence plate on the Ford and seemed reassured. It read Georgia.

'There ain't no motel in Bibliopolis,' said the man. 'You'd best go back to Selma.'

'There must be somewhere,' said Baby as the man still hesitated.

'Mrs Mathervitie's Tourist Home,' said the man and stepped aside. Baby drove on to the ferry and got out.

'Is this the Alabama river?' she asked. The man shook his head.

'The Ptomaine River, ma'am,' he said and pulled on the rope.

'And that?' asked Baby, pointing to a large dilapidated mansion that was evidently ante-bellum.

'That's Pellagra. Nobody lives there now. They all died off.'

Piper sat in the car and stared gloomily at the sluggish river. The trees along its bank were veiled with Spanish moss like widows' weeds and the dilapidated mansion below the town put him in mind of Miss Haversham. But Baby, when she got back into the car and drove off the ferry, was clearly elated by the atmosphere.

'I told you this was where it's at,' she said triumphantly. 'And now for Mrs Mathervitie's Tourist Home.'

They drove down a tree-lined street and stopped outside a house. A signboard said Welcome. Mrs Mathervitie was less effusive. Sitting in the shadow of a porch she watched them get out of the car.

'You folks looking for some place?' she asked, her glasses glinting in the sunset.

'Mrs Mathervitie's Tourist Home,' said Baby.

'Selling or staying? Cos if it's cosmetics I ain't in the market.'

'Staying,' said Baby.

Mrs Mathervitie studied them critically with the air of a connoisseur of irregular relationships.

'I only got singles,' she said and spat into the hub of a sun flower, 'no doubles.'

'Praise be the Lord,' said Baby involuntarily.

'Amen,' said Mrs Mathervitie.

They went into the house and down a passage.

'This is yourn,' said Mrs Mathervitie to Piper and opened a door. The room looked out on to a patch of corn. On the wall there was an oleograph of Christ scourging the moneylenders from the temple and a cardboard sign that decreed NO BROWNBAGGING. Piper looked at it dubiously. It seemed a thoroughly unnecessary injunction.

'Well?' said Mrs Mathervitie.

'Very nice,' said Piper who had spotted a row of books on a shelf. He looked at them and found they were all Bibles.

'Good Lord,' he muttered.

'Amen,' said Mrs Mathervitie and went off with Baby down the passage leaving Piper to consider the sinister implications of NO BROWNBAGGING. By the time they returned he was no nearer a solution to the riddle.

'The Reverend and I are happy to accept your hospitality,' said Baby. 'Aren't we, Reverend?'

'What?' said Piper. Mrs Mathervitie was looking at him with new interest.

'I was just telling Mrs Mathervitie how interested you are in American religion,' said Baby. Piper swallowed and tried to think what to say.

'Yes,' seemed the safest.

There was an extremely awkward silence broken finally by Mrs Mathervitie's business sense.

'Ten dollars a day. Seven with prayers. Providence is extra.'

'Yes, well I suppose it would be,' said Piper.

'Meaning?' said Mrs Mathervitie.

'That the good Lord will provide,' interjected Baby before Piper's slight hysteria could manifest itself again.

'Amen,' said Mrs Mathervitie. 'Well which is it to be? With prayers or without?'

'With,' said Baby.

'Fourteen dollars,' said Mrs Mathervitie, 'in advance.'

'Pay now and pray later?' said Piper hopefully.

Mrs Mathervitie's eyes gleamed coldly. 'For a preacher . . .' she began but Baby intervened. 'The Reverend means we should pray without ceasing.'

'Amen,' said Mrs Mathervitie and knelt on the linoleum.

Baby followed her example. Piper looked down at them in astonishment.

'Dear God,' he muttered.

'Amen,' said Mrs Mathervitie and Baby in unison.

'Say the good words, Reverend,' said Baby.

'For Christ's sake,' said Piper fighting for inspiration. He didn't know any prayers and as for good words . . . On the floor Mrs Mathervitie twitched dangerously. Piper found the good words. They came from *The Moral Novel*.

'It is our duty not to enjoy but to appreciate,' he intoned, 'not to be entertained but to be edified, not to read that we may escape the responsibilities of life but that, through reading, we may more properly understand what it is that we are and do and that born anew in the vicarious experience of others we may extend our awareness and our sensibilities and so enriched by how we read we may be better human beings.'

201

'Amen,' said Mrs Mathervitie fervently.

'Amen,' said Baby.

'Amen,' said Piper and sat down on the bed. Mrs Mathervitie got to her feet.

'I thank you for those good words, Reverend,' she said and left the room.

'What the hell was all that about?' said Piper when her footsteps had faded. Baby stood up and raised a finger to her lips.

'No cussing. No brownbagging.'

'And that's another thing . . .' Piper began but Mrs Mathervitie's footsteps came down the passage again.

'Conventicle's at eight,' she said poking her head round the door. 'Doesn't do to be late.'

Piper regarded her biliously. 'Conventicle?'

'Conventicle of the Seventh Day Church of The Servants of God,' said Mrs Mathervitie. 'You said you wanted prayers.'

'The Reverend and I will be right with you,' said Baby. Mrs Mathervitie removed her head. Baby took Piper's arm and pushed him towards the door.

'Good God, you've really landed us—'

'Amen,' said Baby as they went out into the passage. Mrs Mathervitie was waiting on the porch.

'The Church is in the town square,' she said as they climbed into the Ford and presently they were driving down the darkened street where the Spanish moss looked even more sinister to Piper. By the time they stopped outside a small wooden church in the square he was in a state of panic.

'They won't want me to pray again, will they?' he whispered to Baby as they climbed the steps to the church. From inside there came the sound of a hymn.

'We're late,' said Mrs Mathervitie and hurried them down the aisle. The church was crowded but a row of seats at the very front was empty. A moment later Piper found himself clutching a hymn-book and singing an extraordinary hymn called 'Telephoning To Glory'.

When the hymn ended there was a scuffling of feet and the congregation knelt and the preacher launched into prayer.

'Oh Lord we is all sinners,' he declared.

'Oh Lord we is all sinners,' bawled Mrs Mathervitie and the rest of the congregation.

'Oh Lord we is all sinners waiting to be saved,' continued the preacher.

'Waiting to be saved. Waiting to be saved.'

'From the fires of hell and the snares of Satan.'

'From the fires of hell and the snares of Satan.'

Beside Piper Mrs Mathervitie had begun to quiver. 'Hallelujah,' she cried.

When the prayer ended a large black woman who was standing beside the piano began 'Washed In The Blood Of The Lamb' and from there it was but a short step to 'Jericho' and finally a hymn which went 'Servants of The Lord we Pledge our Faith in Thee' with a chorus of 'Faith, Faith, Faith in The Lord, Faith in Jesus is Mightier than the Sword'. Much to his own amazement Piper sang as loudly as anyone and the enthusiasm began to get to him. By this time Mrs Mathervitie was stomping her foot while several other women were clapping their hands. They sang the hymn twice and then went straight into another about Eve and The Apple. As the reverberations died away the preacher raised his hands.

'Brothers and sisters . . .' he began, only to be interrupted.

'Bring on the serpents,' shouted someone at the back.

The preacher lowered his hands. 'Serpents night's Saturday,' he said. 'You know that.'

But the cry 'Bring on the serpents,' was taken up and the large black lady struck up 'Faith in The Lord and the Snakes won't Bite, Them's has Faith is Saved all Right.'

'Snakes?' said Piper to Mrs Mathervitie, 'I thought you said this was Servants of The Lord.'

'Snakes is Saturday,' said Mrs Mathervitie looking decidedly alarmed herself. 'I only come Thursdays. I don't hold with serpentizing.'

'Serpentizing?' said Piper suddenly alive to what was about to happen, 'Jesus Wept.' Beside him Baby was already weeping but Piper was too concerned for his own safety to bother about her. A sack was brought down the aisle by a tall gaunt man. It was a large sack, a large sack which writhed. So did Piper. A moment later he had shot out of his seat and was heading for the door only to find his way blocked by a number of other people who evidently shared his lack of enthusiasm for being confined in a small church with a sackful of poisonous snakes. A hand shoved him aside and Piper fell back into his seat again. 'Let's get the hell out of here,' he shouted to Baby but she was looking with rapt attention at the pianist, a small thin man who was thumping away on the keys with a fervour that was possibly due to what looked like a small boa constrictor which had twined itself round his neck. Behind the piano the large black lady was using two rattlesnakes as maracas and singing 'Bibliopolis we Hold Thee Dear, Snakes Infest us we don't Fear' – which certainly didn't apply to Piper. He was about to make another dash for the door when something slithered across his feet. It was Mrs Mathervitie. Piper sat petrified and moaned. Beside him Baby was moaning too. There was a strange seraphic look on her face. At that moment the man with the sack lifted from it a snake with red and yellow bands across its body.

'The Coral,' someone hissed. The strains of 'Bibliopolis we Hold Thee Dear' faded abruptly. In the silence that followed Baby got to her feet and moved hypnotically forward. By the dim light of the candles she looked majestic and beautiful. She took the snake from the man and held it aloft and her arm became a caduceus, the symbol of medicine. Then, turning to face the congregation, she tore her blouse to the waist and exposed two voluptuously pointed breasts. There was another gasp of horror. Naked breasts were out in Bibliopolis. On the other hand the coral snake was in. As Baby lowered her arm the outraged snake sank its fangs into six inches of plastic silicon. For ten seconds it writhed there before Baby detached it and offered it the other breast. But the coral had had enough. So had Piper. With a groan he joined Mrs Mathervitie on the floor. Baby, triumphantly topless, tossed the coral into the sack and turned to the pianist.

'Launch into the deep, brother,' she cried.

And once again the little church reverberated to the strains of 'Bibliopolis we hold Thee Dear, Snakes Infest us we don't Fear'.

Chapter 21

In his Hampstead flat Frensic lay in his morning bath and twiddled the hot tap with his big toe to maintain an even temperature. A good night's sleep had helped to undo the ravages of Cynthia Bogden's passion and he was in no hurry to go to the office. He had things to think about. It was all very well congratulating himself for his subtlety in unearthing the genuine author of *Pause* and forcing her to renounce all rights in the book but there were still problems to be faced. The first of these concerned the continuing existence of Piper and his inordinate claim to be paid for a novel he hadn't written. On the face of it this seemed a minor problem. Frensic could now go ahead and deposit the two million dollars less his own and Corkadales' commissions in Account Number 478776 in the First National Bank of New York. This seemed at first sight the sensible thing to do. Pay Piper and be rid of the rogue. On the other hand it was succumbing to blackmail and blackmailers tended to renew their demands. Give in once and he would have to give in again and again and in any case transferring the money to New York would necessitate explaining to Sonia that Piper wasn't dead. One whiff of that and she'd be off after him like a scalded cat. Perhaps he might be able to fudge the issue and tell her that Mr Cadwalladine's client had given instructions for the royalties to be paid in this way.

But beyond all these technical problems there lay the suspicion that Piper hadn't come up with this conspiracy to defraud on his own initiative. Ten years of the recurrent *Search for a Lost Childhood* was proof enough that Piper lacked any imagination at all and whoever had dreamt this devious plot up had a remarkably powerful imagination. Frensic's suspicions centred on Mrs Baby Hutchmeyer. If Piper, who was supposed to have died with her, was still alive there was every reason to believe that Baby Hutchmeyer had survived with him. Frensic tried to analyse the psychology of Hutchmeyer's wife. To have endured forty years of marriage to that monster argued either masochism or resilience beyond the ordinary. And then to burn an enormous house to the ground, blow up a cruiser and sink a yacht, all of them belonging to her husband and all in a matter of twenty minutes . . . Clearly the woman was insane and couldn't be relied upon. At any moment she might resurrect herself and drag from his temporary grave the wretched Piper. What would follow this momentous event blew Frensic's mind. Hutchmeyer would go litigiously berserk and sue everyone in sight. Piper would be dragged through the courts and the entire story of his substitution for the real author would be announced to the world. Frensic got out of the bath and dried himself to ward off the spectre of Piper in the witness box.

And as he dressed the problem became more and more complicated. Even if Baby Hutchmeyer didn't decide to go in for self-exhumation there was every chance that she would be discovered by some nosey reporter who might at this very moment be hungrily tracking her down. What the hell would happen if Piper told the truth? Frensic tried to foresee the outcome of his revelations, and was just making himself some coffee when he remembered the manuscript. The manuscript in Piper's handwriting. Or at least the copy. That was the way out. He could always deny Piper's allegation that he hadn't written *Pause* and produce that manuscript copy as proof. And even if the psychotic Baby backed Piper up, nobody would believe her. Frensic sighed with relief. He had found a way out of the dilemma. After breakfast he walked up the hill to the tube station and caught a train in a thoroughly good mood. He was a clever fellow and it would take more than the benighted Piper and Baby Hutchmeyer to put one across him.

He arrived at Lanyard Lane to find the office locked. That was odd. Sonia Futtle should have been back from Bernie the Beaver the previous day. Frensic unlocked the door and went in. No sign of Sonia. He crossed to his desk and there lying neatly separated from the rest of his mail was an envelope. It was addressed in Sonia's handwriting to him. Frensic sat down and opened it. Inside was a long letter which began 'Dearest Frenzy' and ended, 'Your loving Sonia.' In between these endearments Sonia explained with a wealth of nauseating sentimentality and self-deception how Hutchmeyer had asked her to marry him and why she had accepted. Frensic was flabbergasted. And only a week before the girl had been crying her eyes out over Piper. Frensic took out his snuff box and red spotted handkerchief and thanked God he was still a bachelor. The ways and wiles of women were quite beyond him.

．　．　．　．　．

206

They were quite beyond Geoffrey Corkadale too. He was still in a state of nervous agitation over the threatened libel suit of Professor Facit versus the author, publisher and printer of *Pause O Men for the Virgin* when he received a telephone call from Miss Bogden.

'I did what?' he asked with a mixture of total incredulity and disgust. 'And stop calling me darling. I don't know you from a bar of soap.'

'But Geoffrey sweetheart,' said Miss Bogden, 'you were so passionate, so manly . . .'

'I was not !' shouted Geoffrey. 'You've got the wrong number. You can't say these things.'

Miss Bogden could and did. In detail. Geoffrey Corkadale curdled.

'Stop,' he yelled, 'I don't know what the hell has been going on but if you think for one moment that I spent the night before last in your beastly arms . . . dear God . . . you must be out of your bloody mind.'

'And I suppose you didn't ask me to marry you,' screamed Miss Bogden, 'and buy me an engagement ring and . . .'

Geoffrey slammed the phone down to shut out this appalling catalogue. The situation was sufficently desperate on the legal front without demented women claiming he had asked them to marry him. Then, to forestall any resumption of Miss Bogden's accusations, he left the office and made his way to his solicitors to discuss a possible defence in the libel action.

They were singularly unhelpful. 'It isn't as if the defamation of Professor Facit was accidental,' they told him. 'This man Piper evidently set out with deliberate malice to ruin the reputation of the Professor. There can be no other explanation. In our opinion the author is entirely culpable.'

'He also happens to be dead,' said Geoffrey.

'In that case it rather looks as though you are going to have to bear the entire costs of this action and, frankly, we would advise you to settle.'

Geoffrey Corkadale left the solicitors' office in despair. It was all that bloody man Frensic's fault. He should have known better than to have dealt with a literary agent who had already been involved in one disastrous libel action. Frensic was libel-prone. There was no other way of looking at it. Geoffrey took a cab to Lanyard Lane. He was going to tell Frensic what he thought of him. He found Frensic in an unusually affable mood.

'My dear Geoffrey, how very nice to see you,' he said.

'I haven't come to exchange compliments,' said Geoffrey, 'I've come to tell you that you've landed me in the most appalling mess and . . .'

Frensic raised a hand.

'You mean Professor Facit? Oh I shouldn't worry too much . . .'

'Worry too much? I've got every right to worry and as for too much, with bankruptcy staring me in the face just how much is too much?'

'I've been making some private enquiries,' said Frensic, 'in Oxford.'

'You have?' said Geoffrey. 'You don't mean to say he actually did do all those frightful things? That ghastly Pekinese for instance?'

'I mean,' said Frensic pontifically, 'that no one in Oxford has ever heard of a Professor Facit. I've checked with the Lodging House Syndicate and the university library and they have no records of any Professor Facit ever having applied for a ticket to use the library. And as for his statement that he once lived in De Frytville Avenue, it's quite untrue.'

'Good Lord,' said Geoffrey, 'if nobody up there has ever heard of him . . .'

'It rather looks as if Messrs Ridley, Coverup, Makeweight and Jones have just tried to ambulance-chase once too often and are hoist with their own petard.'

'My dear fellow, this calls for a celebration,' said Geoffrey. 'And you mean to say you went up there and found all this out . . .'

But Frensic was modesty itself. 'You see, I knew Piper pretty well. After all he had been sending me stuff for years,' he said as they went downstairs, 'and he wasn't the sort of fellow to set out to libel someone deliberately.'

'But I thought you told me that *Pause* was his first book,' said Geoffrey.

Frensic regretted his indiscretion. 'His first *real* book,' he said. 'The rest was just . . . well, a bit derivative. Not the sort of stuff I could ever have sold.'

They strolled across to Wheeler's for lunch. 'Talking of Oxford,' said Geoffrey when they had ordered, 'I had the most extraordinary phone call this morning from some lunatic woman called Bogden.'

'Really?' said Frensic, spilling dry Martini down his shirt front. 'What did she want?'

'She claimed I'd asked her to marry me. It was absolutely awful.'

'It must have been,' said Frensic, finishing his drink and ordering another. 'Mind you, some women will go to any lengths . . .'

'From what I could gather I was the one to have gone to any lengths. Said I'd bought her an engagement ring.'

'I hope you told her to go to hell,' said Frensic, 'and talking of marriages I've got some news too. Sonia Futtle is going to marry Hutchmeyer.'

'Marry Hutchmeyer?' said Geoffrey. 'But the man's only just lost his wife. You'd think he'd have the decency to wait a bit before sticking his head in the noose again.'

'An apt metaphor,' said Frensic with a smile, and raised his glass.

His worries were over. He had just realized that in marrying Hutchmeyer Sonia had acted more wisely than she knew. She had effectively spiked the enemy's guns. A bigamous Hutchmeyer was no threat, and besides, a man who could find Sonia physically attractive must be besotted and a besotted Hutch would never believe his new wife had once been party to a conspiracy to deceive him. All that remained was to implicate Piper financially. After an excellent lunch Frensic walked back to Lanyard Lane and thence to the bank. There he subtracted Corkadales' 10 per cent and his own commission and despatched one million four hundred thousand dollars to account number 478776 in the First National Bank Of New York. He had honoured his side of the contract. Frensic went home by taxi. He was a rich and happy man.

So was Hutchmeyer. Sonia's whirlwind acceptance of his whirlwind proposal had taken him by surprise. The thighs that had over the years so entranced him were his at last. Her ample body was entirely to his taste. It bore no scars, none of the surgical modifications that in Baby's case had served to remind him of his faithlessness and the artificiality of their relationship. With Sonia he could be himself. There was no need to assert himself by peeing in the washbasin every night or to prove his virility by badgering strange girls in Rome and Paris and Las Vegas. He could relapse into domestic happiness with a woman who had energy enough for both of them. They were married in Cannes and that night as Hutchmeyer lay supine between those hustling thighs he gazed up at her breasts and knew that this was for real. Sonia smiled down at his contented face and was contented herself. She was a married woman at long last.

209

And married to a rich man. The next night Hutchmeyer cele-
brated by losing forty grand at Monte Carlo and then, in memory
of the good fortune that had brought them together, chartered a vast
yacht with an experienced skipper and a competent crew. They
cruised in the Aegean. They explored the ruins of ancient Greece
and, more profitably, a deal involving supertankers which were
going cheap. And finally they flew back to New York for the première
of the film, *Pause*.

There in the darkness, garlanded with diamonds, Sonia finally
broke down and wept. Beside her Hutchmeyer understood. It was a
deeply moving movie with fashionable radicals playing Gwendolen
and Anthony and combined *Lost Horizon, Sunset Boulevard* and
Deep Throat with *Tom Jones*. Under MacMordie's financial tutelage
the critics raved. And all the time the profits from the novel poured in.
The movie boosted sales and there was even talk of a Broadway
musical with Maria Callas in the leading role. To keep sales moving
ever upwards Hutchmeyer consulted the computer and ordered a
new cover for the book with the result that people who had bought
the book before found themselves buying it yet again. After the
musical some would doubtless buy it a third time. The Book Club
sales were enormous and the leather-bound Baby Hutchmeyer
Memorial edition with gold tooling sold out in a week. All over the
country *Pause* left its mark. Elderly women emerged from the
seclusion of bridge clubs and beauty parlours to inveigle young men
into bed. The vasectomy index fell rapidly. And finally, to crown
Hutchmeyer's success, Sonia announced that she was pregnant.

In Bibliopolis, Alabama, things had changed too. The funeral of the
victims of the unscheduled serpentizing took place among the live oaks
that bordered the Ptomaine River. There were seven in all, though
only two from snake bite. Three had been crushed in the stampede for
the door. The Reverend Gideon had succumbed to heart failure, and
Mrs Mathervitie to outraged shock on awakening from her faint to
find Baby standing topless in the pulpit. Out of this terrible infest-
ation Baby had emerged with a remarkable reputation. It was due as
much to the perfection of her breasts as to their immunity; taken
together the two were irresistible. Never before had Bibliopolis witnessed so complete a demonstration of faith, and in the absence of
the late Reverend Gideon Baby was offered the ministry. She
accepted gratefully. It put an end to Piper's sexual depradations,

and besides she had found her forte. From the pulpit she could denounce the sins of the flesh with a relish that endeared her to the womenfolk and excited the men, and having spent so much of her life in Hutchmeyer's company she could speak about hell from experience. Above all she was free to be what remained of herself. And so as the coffins were lowered into the ground the Reverend Hutchmeyer led the congregation in 'Shall we Gather by the River' and the little population of Bibliopolis bowed their heads and raised their voices. Even the snakes, hissing as they were emptied from the sack into the Ptomaine, had benefited. Baby had abolished serpent-izing in a long sermon about Eve and The Apple in which she had pointed out that they were creatures of Satan. The relatives of the deceased tended to agree. And finally there was the problem of Piper. Having found her faith Baby felt obliged to the man who had so fortuitously led her to it.

With the advance royalties from *Pause* she restored Pellagra House to its ante-bellum glory and installed Piper there to continue work on his third version, *Postscript to a Lost Childhood*. As the days passed into weeks and the weeks into months, Piper wrote steadily on and resumed the routine of his life at the Gleneagle Guest House. In the afternoons he walked by the banks of the Ptomaine and in the evening read passages from *The Moral Novel* and the great classics it commended. With so much money at his disposal Piper had ordered them all. They lined the shelves of his study at Pellagra, icons of that literary religion to which he had dedicated his life. Jane Austen, Conrad, George Eliot, Dickens, Henry James, Lawrence, Mann, they were all there to spur him on. His one sorrow was that the only woman he could ever love was sexually inaccessible. As preacher Baby had made it plain she could no longer sleep with him.

'You'll just have to sublimate,' she told him. Piper tried to sub-limate but the yearning remained as constant as his ambition to become a great novelist.

'It's no good,' he said, 'I keep thinking about you all the time. You are so beautiful, so pure, so ... so ...'

'You've too much time on your hands,' said Baby. 'Now if you had something more to do ...'

'Such as?'

Baby looked at the beautiful script upon the page. 'Like you could teach people to write,' she said.

211

'I can't even write myself,' said Piper. It was one of his self-pitying days.

'But you can. Look at the way you form your "f"s and this lovely tail to your "y". If you can't teach people to write, who can?'

'Oh you mean "write",' said Piper, 'I suppose I could do that. But who would want to learn?'

'Lots of people. You'd be surprised. When I was a girl there were schools of penmanship in almost every town. You'd be doing something useful.'

'Useful?' said Piper, attenuating that word with melancholy. 'All I want to do is—'

'Write,' said Baby, hurriedly forestalling his sexual suggestion. 'Well, this way you can combine artistry with education. You can hold classes every afternoon and it will take your mind off yourself.'

'My mind isn't on myself. It's on you. I love you . . .'

'We must all love one another,' said Baby sententiously and left.

A week later the School of Penmanship opened and instead of brooding all afternoon by the sluggish waters of the Ptomaine River, Piper stood in front of his pupils and taught them to write beautifully. The classes were mostly of children but later adults came too and sat there pens in hand and bottles of Higgins Eternal Evaporated Ink at the ready while Piper explained that a diagonal ligature required an upstroke and that a wavy serif was obtrusive. Over the months his reputation grew and with it there came theory. To visitors from as far away as Selma and Meridian Piper expounded the doctrine of the word made perfect. He called it Logosophy, and won adherents. It was as if the process by which he had failed as a novelist had reversed itself in his Writing. In the old days of his obsession with the great novel theory had preceded and indeed pre-empted practice. What *The Moral Novel* had condemned Piper had avoided. With penmanship Piper was his own practitioner and theorist. But still the old ambition to see his novel in print remained and as each newly expurgated version of *Pause* was finished he mailed it to Frensic. At first he sent it to New York to be readdressed and forwarded to Lanyard Lane but as the months passed his confidence in his new life grew and with it forgetfulness and he sent it direct. And every month he ordered *Books & Bookmen* and the *Times Literary Supplement* and scanned the lists of new novels only to be disappointed. *Search for a Lost Childhood* was never there.

Finally, late one night when the moon was full, he decided on a fresh approach and taking up his pen wrote to Frensic. His letter was blunt and to the point. Unless Frensic & Futtle as his literary agents were prepared to guarantee that his novel was published he would be forced to ask some other literary agent to handle his work in future.

'In fact I am seriously considering sending my manuscript direct to Corkadales,' he wrote. 'As you will remember I signed a contract with them to publish my second novel and I can see no good reason why this specific agreement should be negated. Yours sincerely, Peter Piper.'

213

Chapter 22

'The man must be out of his bloody mind,' muttered Frensic a week later. 'I can see no reason why this arrangement should be negated.' Frensic could. 'The sod can't seriously suppose I can go round to Corkadales and force them to publish a book by a corpse.'

But it was evident from the tone of the letter that Piper supposed exactly that. Over the months Frensic had received four Xeroxed and altered drafts of Piper's novel and had consigned them to a filing cabinet which he kept carefully locked. If Piper wanted to waste his own time reworking the damned book until every element that had made *Pause* the least bit readable had been eliminated he was welcome to do so. Frensic felt under no obligation to hawk his rubbish round publishing houses. But the threat to deal direct with Corkadales was, to put it mildly, a different kettle of fish. Piper was dead and buried and he was being well paid for it. Every month Frensic saw that the proceeds from the sale of *Pause* went into account number 478776, and wondered at the extraordinary inefficiency of the American tax system that didn't seem to mind that a taxpayer was supposedly dead. Doubtless Piper paid his taxes promptly or perhaps Baby Hutchmeyer had made complicated accountancy arrangements for his royalties to be laundered. That was none of Frensic's business. He took his commission and paid the rest over. But it was certainly his business when Piper made threats about going to Corkadales or another agent. That arrangement had definitely to be negated.

Frensic turned the letter over and studied the postmark on the envelope. It came from a place called Bibliopolis, Alabama. 'Just the sort of idiotic town Piper would choose,' he thought miserably and wondered how to reply. Or whether he should reply at all. Perhaps the best thing would be to ignore the threat. He certainly had no intention of committing to paper any words that could be used in court to prove that he knew of Piper's continued afterdeath. 'The next thing he'll come up with is a request for me to go and see him

214

and discuss the matter. And fat chance there is of that.' Frensic had had his fill of pursuing phantom authors.

Miss Bogden on the other hand had not given up her pursuit of the man who had asked her to marry him. After the terrible telephone conversation she had had with Geoffrey Corkadale she had wept briefly, had made up her face, and had continued business as usual. For several weeks she had lived in hope that he would phone again, or that another bunch of red roses would suddenly appear, but those hopes had dwindled. Only the diamond solitaire gleaming on her finger kept her spirits up – that and the need to maintain the fiction before her staff that the engagement was still on. To that end she invented long weekends with her fiancé and reasons for the delayed wedding. But as weeks became months Cynthia's disappointment turned to determination. She had been had, and while being had was in some respects better than not being had at all, being made to look foolish in the eyes of her staff was infuriating. Miss Bogden applied her mind to the problem of finding her fiancé. While his disappearance was proof that he hadn't wanted her, the five hundred pounds he had spent on the ring was indication that he had wanted something else. Again Miss Bogden's business sense told her that the favours she had bestowed bodywise on her lover during the night hardly merited the expense of the engagement ring. Only a madman would make such a quixotic gesture and her pride refused the notion that the one man to propose to her since her divorce had been off his head.

No, there had to be another motive and as she recalled the events of those splendid twenty-four hours it slowly dawned on her that the one consistent theme had been the novel *Pause O Men for the Virgin*. In the first place her fiancé had posed as Geoffrey Corkadale, in the second he had reverted to the question of the typescript too frequently for it to be coincidental, and thirdly there had been the *code d'amour*. And the *code d'amour* had been the telephone number she had had to call for information while typing the novel. Cynthia Bogden called the number again but there was no reply, and when a week later she tried again the line had been disconnected. She looked up the name Piper in the phone directory but no one of that name had the number 20357. She called Directory Enquiries and asked for the address and name of the number but was refused the information. Defeated in that direction, she turned to another. Her instructions had been to forward the completed typescript to Cadwalladine & Dimkins, Solicitors and to return the handwritten draft to Lloyds Bank. Miss Bogden phoned Mr Cadwalladine and was puzzled by his apparent inability to remember having received the typescript. 'We may have done,' he said, 'but I'm afraid we handle so much business that . . .'

Miss Bogden pressed him further and was finally told that it was unethical for solicitors to disclose confidential information. Miss Bogden was not satisfied with this answer. With each rebuttal her determination grew and was reinforced by the snide enquiries of her girls. Her mind worked slowly but it worked steadily too. She followed the line from the bank to her typing service and from there to Mr Cadwalladine and from Mr Cadwalladine to Corkadales, the publishers. The secrecy with which the entire transaction had been surrounded intrigued her too. An author who had to be contacted by phone, a solicitor . . . With less flair than Frensic, but with as much perserverance, she followed the trail as far as she could, and late one evening she realized the full implications of Mr Cadwalladine's refusal to tell her where the typescript had been sent. And yet Corkadales had published the book. There had to be someone in between Cadwalladine and Corkadales and that someone was almost certainly a literary agent. That night Cynthia Bogden lay awake filled with a sense of discovery. She had found the missing link in the chain. The next morning she was up early and at the office at half past eight. At nine she telephoned Corkadales and asked to speak to the editor who had handled *Pause*. The editor wasn't in. She called again at ten. He still hadn't arrived. It was only at a quarter to eleven that she got through to him and by then she had had time to devise her approach. It was a straightforward one.

'I run a typing bureau,' she said, 'and I have typed a novel for a friend who is anxious to send it to a good literary agent and I wondered it . . .'

'I'm afraid we can't advise you on that sort of thing,' said Mr Tate.

'Oh I do understand that,' said Miss Bogden sweetly, 'but you published that wonderful novel *Pause O Men for the Virgin* and my friend wanted to send her novel to the same agent. It would be so good of you if you could . . .'

Responding to flattery Mr Tate did.

'Frensic & Futtle of Lanyard Lane?' she repeated.

'Well, Frensic now,' said Mr Tate, 'Miss Futtle is no longer there.'

Nor was Miss Bogden. She had put the phone down and was picking it up to dial Directory Enquiries. A few minutes later she had Frensic's number. Her intuition told her that she was getting close to home. She sat for a while staring into the depths of the solitaire for inspiration. Should she phone or . . . Mr Cadwalladine's refusal to say where the manuscript had gone persuaded her. She got up from her typewriter, asked her senior 'girl' to take over for the day, drove to the station and caught the 11.55 to London. Two hours later she walked down Lanyard Lane to Number 36 and climbed the stairs to Frensic's office.

It was fortunate for Frensic that he was lunching with a promising new author in the Italian restaurant round the corner when Miss Bogden arrived. They came out at two fifteen and walked back to the office. As they climbed the stairs Frensic stopped on the first landing.

'You go on up,' he said, 'I'll be with you in a moment.' He went into the lavatory and shut the door. The promising new author climbed the second flight. Frensic finished his business and came out and he was about to go on up when he heard a voice.

'Are you Mr Frensic?' it asked. Frensic stopped in his tracks.

'Me?' said the promising young author with a laugh. 'No I'm here with a book. Mr Frensic's downstairs. He'll be up in a minute.'

But Frensic wasn't. He shot down to the ground floor again and out into the street. That ghastly woman had tracked him down. What the hell to do now? He went back to the Italian restaurant and sat in a corner. How on earth had she managed to find him? Had that Cadbloodywalladine . . . Never mind how. The thing was what to do about it. He couldn't sit in the restaurant all day and he was no more going to confront Miss Bogden than fly. Fly? The word took on a new significance for him. If he didn't turn up at the office the promising young author would . . . To hell with promising young authors. He had asked that dreadful woman to marry him and . . . Frensic signalled to a waiter.

'A piece of paper please.' He scribbled a note of apology to the author, saying he had been taken ill and handed it with a five pound note to the waiter, asking him to deliver it for him. As the man went out Frensic followed and hailed a taxi. 'Glass Walk, Hampstead,' he said and got in. Not that going home would do him any good. Miss Bogden's tracking powers would soon lead her there. All right, he wouldn't answer the door. But what then? A woman with the perseverance of Miss Bogden, a woman of forty-five who had painstakingly worked her way towards her quarry over the months . . . such a woman held terrors for him. She wouldn't stop now. By the time he reached his flat he was panic-stricken. He went inside and locked and bolted the door. Then he sat down in his study and tried to think. He was interrupted by the phone. Unthinkingly he picked it up. 'Frensic here,' he said.

'Cynthia here,' said that pebbledashed voice. Frensic slammed the phone down. A moment later, to prevent her calling again, he picked it up and dialled Geoffrey's number.

'Geoffrey, my dear fellow,' he said when Corkadale answered, 'I wonder if . . .'

But Geoffrey didn't let him finish. 'I've been trying to get hold of you all afternoon,' he said. 'I've had the most extraordinary manuscript sent to me. You're not going to believe this but there's some lunatic in a place called of all things Bibliopolis . . . I mean can you beat that? Bibliopolis, Alabama . . . Well anyway he calmly announces that he is our late Peter Piper and will we kindly quote fulfil the obligations incurred in my contract unquote and publish his novel, *Search for a Lost Childhood*. I mean it's incredible and the signature . . .'

'Geoffrey dear,' said Frensic lapsing into the affectionate as a prophylactic against Miss Bogden's feminine charms and as a means of preparing Corkadale for the worst, 'I wonder if you would do me a favour . . .'

He spoke fluently for five minutes and rang off. With amazing rapidity he packed two suitcases, telephoned for a taxi, left a note for the milkman cancelling his two pints a day, took his chequebook, his passport and a briefcase containing copies of all Piper's manuscripts, and half an hour later was carrying his belongings into Geoffrey Corkadale's house. Behind him the flat in Glass Walk was locked and when Cynthia Bogden arrived and rang the bell there was no reply. Frensic was sitting in Geoffrey Corkadale's withdrawing-room sipping a large brandy and implicating his host in the plot to deceive Hutchmeyer. Geoffrey stared at him with bulging eyes.

'You mean you deliberately lied to Hutchmeyer and to me for

218

that matter and told him that this Piper madman had written the book?' he said.

'I had to,' said Frensic miserably. 'If I hadn't, the whole deal would have fallen through. Hutchmeyer would have backed out and where would we have been then?'

'We wouldn't be in the ghastly position we are now, that I do know.'

'You'd have gone out of business,' said Frensic. '*Pause* saved you. You've done very nicely out of the book and I've sent you others. Corkadales is a name to be reckoned with now.'

'Well, I suppose that's true,' said Geoffrey, slightly mollified, 'but it's going to be a name that will stink if it gets out that Piper is still alive and didn't write . . .'

'It isn't going to get out,' said Frensic, 'I promise you that.' Geoffrey looked at him doubtfully. 'Your promises . . .' he began.

'You'll just have to trust me,' said Frensic.

'Trust you? After this? You can rest assured that if there's one thing I'm not going to do . . .'

'You'll have to. Remember that contract you signed? The one saying you had paid fifty thousand pounds advance for *Pause*?'

'You tore that up,' said Geoffrey, 'I saw you do it.'

Frensic nodded. 'But Hutchmeyer didn't,' he said. 'He had photo-copies made and if this thing comes to court you're going to have a hard time explaining why you signed two contracts with the same author for the same book. It isn't going to look good, Geoffrey, not good at all.'

Geoffrey could see that. He sat down.

'What do you want?' he asked.

'A bed for the night,' said Frensic, 'and tomorrow morning I shall go to the American Embassy for a visa.'

'I can't see why you've got to spend the night here,' said Geoffrey.

'You would if you saw her,' said Frensic man-to-man. Geoffrey poured him another brandy.

'I'll have to explain to Sven,' he said, 'he's obsessively jealous. By the way, who *did* write *Pause*?' But Frensic shook his head. 'I can't tell you. There are some things it's best for you not to know. Just let's say the late Peter Piper.'

'The late?' said Geoffrey with a shudder. 'It's a curious expression to apply to the living.'

'It's a curious expression to apply to the dead,' said Frensic, 'It seems to suggest that they may yet turn up. Better late than never.'

'I wish I could share your optimism,' said Geoffrey.

Next morning, after a restless night in a strange bed, Frensic went to the American Embassy and got his visa. He visited his bank and he bought a return ticket to Florida. That night he left Heathrow. He spent the crossing in a drunken stupor and boarded the flight from Miami to Atlanta next day feeling hot, ill and filled with foreboding. To delay matters he spent the next night in a hotel and studied a map of Alabama. It was a detailed map but he couldn't find Bibliopolis. He tried the desk clerk but the man had never heard of it.

'You'd best go to Selma and ask there,' he told Frensic. Frensic caught the Greyhound to Selma and enquired at the Post Office.

'The sticks. A wide place in the road over Mississippi way,' he was told. 'Swamp country on the Ptomaine River. Take Route 80 about a hundred miles and go north. Are you from New England?'

'Old England,' said Frensic, 'why do you ask?'

'Just that they don't take too kindly to Northern strangers in those parts. Damn Yankees they call them. They're still living in the past.'

'So is the man I want to see,' said Frensic and went out to rent a car. The man at the office increased his apprehension.

'You're going out along Blood Alley you want to take care,' he said.

'Blood Alley?' said Frensic anxiously.

'That's what they call Route 80 through to Meridian. That road's seen a whole heap of deaths.'

'Isn't there a more direct route to Bibliopolis?'

'You can go through the backwoods but you could get lost. Blood Alley's your best route.'

Frensic hesitated. 'I don't suppose I could hire a driver?' he asked.

'Too late now,' said the man, 'Saturday afternoon this time everyone's gone home and tomorrow being Sunday . . .'

Frensic left the office and drove to a motel. He wasn't going to drive to Bibliopolis along Blood Alley at nightfall. He would go in the morning.

Next day he was up early and on the road. The sun shone down out of a cloudless sky and the day was bright and beautiful. Frensic wasn't. The desperate resolution with which he had left London had faded and with each mile westward it diminished still further. Woods closed in on the road and by the time he reached the sign with the faded inscription BIBLIOPOLIS 15 MILES he almost turned back. But a pinch of snuff and the thought of what would happen if Piper continued his campaign of literary revival gave him the courage he needed. Frensic turned right and followed the dirt road into the woods, trying not to look at the black water and the trees strangled with vines. And, like Piper those many months before, he was relieved when he came to the meadows and the cattle grazing in the long grass. But still the abandoned shacks depressed him and the occasional glimpse of the river, a brown slurry in the distance fringed by veiled trees, did nothing for his morale. The Ptomaine looked aptly named. Finally the road veered down to the left and across the water Frensic looked at Bibliopolis. A wide place in the road, the girl in Selma had called it, but she had quite evidently never seen it. Besides, the road stopped at the river. The little town huddled round the square and looked old and unchanged from some time in the nineteenth century. And the ferry which presently moved towards him with an old man pulling on the rope was from some bygone age. Frensic thought he knew now why Bibliopolis was said to be in the sticks. By the Styx would have done as well. Frensic drove the car carefully on to the ferry and got out.

'I'm looking for a man called Piper,' he told the ferryman.

The man nodded. 'Guessed you might be,' he said. 'They come from all over to hear him preach. And if it isn't him it's the Reverend Baby up at the Church.'

'Preach?' said Frensic, 'Mr Piper preaches?'

'Sure does. Preaching and teaching the good word.'

Frensic raised his eyebrows. Piper as preacher was a new one to him. 'Where will I find him?' he asked.

'Down Pellagra.'

'Down with pellagra?' said Frensic hopefully.

'At Pellagra,' said the old man, 'the house.' He nodded in the direction of a large house fronted by tall white columns. 'There's Pellagra. Used to be the Stopeses place but they all died off.'

'Hardly surprising,' said Frensic, his intellectual compass spinning between vitamin deficiency, advocates of birth control, the Monkey Trial and Yoknapatawpha County. He gave the man a dollar and drove down the drive to an open gate. On one side a sign in large italic said THE PIPER SCHOOL OF PENMANSHIP while on the other an

221

inscribed finger pointed to the CHURCH OF THE GREAT PURSUIT. Frensic stopped the car and stared at the enormous finger. The Church of The Great Pursuit? The Church of . . . There could be no doubting that he had come to the right place. But what sort of religious mania was Piper suffering from now? He drove on and parked beside several other cars in front of the large white building with a wrought-iron balcony extending forward to the columns from the first-floor rooms. Frensic got out and walked up the steps to the front door. It was open. Frensic peered into the hall. A door to the left had painted on it THE SCRIPTORIUM while from a room on the right there came the drone of an insistent voice. Frensic crossed the marble floor and listened. There was no mistaking that voice. It was Piper's, but the old hesitant quality had gone and in its place there was a new strident intensity. If the voice was familiar, so were the words.

'And we must not (the "must" here presupposing explicitly a sustained seriousness of purpose and an undeviating moral duty) allow ourselves to be deluded by the seeming naïvety so frequently ascribed by other less perceptive critics to the presentation of Little Nell. Sentiment not sentimentality as we must understand it is cognizant . . .'

Frensic shyed away from the door. He knew now what the Church of The Great Pursuit had for its gospel. Piper was reading aloud from Dr Louth's essay 'How We Must Approach *The Old Curiosity Shop*'. Even his religion was derived. Frensic found a chair and sat down filled with a mounting anger. 'The unoriginal little sod,' he muttered, and cursed Dr Louth into the bargain. The apotheosis of that dreadful woman, the cause of all his troubles, was taking place here in the heart of the Bible belt. Frensic's anger turned to fury. The Bible belt! Bibliopolis and the Bible. And instead of that magnificent prose, Piper was disseminating her graceless style, her angular inverted syntax, her arid puritanism and her denunciations against pleasure and the joy of reading. And all this from a man who couldn't write to save his soul! For a moment Frensic felt that he was at the heart of a great conspiracy against life. But that was paranoia. There had been no conscious purpose in the circumstances that had led to Piper's missionary zeal. Only the accident of literary mutation which had turned Frensic himself from a would-be novelist into a successful agent and, by the way of *The Moral Novel*, had mutilated what little talent for writing Piper might once have possessed. And now like some carrier of literary death he was passing the infection on. By the time the droning voice stopped and the little congregation filed out, their faces taut with moral intensity, and made their way to the cars, Frensic was in a murderous mood.

He crossed the hall and entered the Church of The Great Pursuit. Piper was putting the book away with all the reverence of a priest handling the Host. Frensic stood in the doorway and waited. He had come a long way for this moment. Piper shut the cupboard and turned. The look of reverence faded from his face.

'You,' he said faintly.

'Who else?' said Frensic loudly to exorcize the atmosphere of sanctity that pervaded the room. 'Or were you expecting Conrad?'

Piper's face paled. 'What do you want?'

'Want?' said Frensic and sat down in one of the pews and took a pinch of snuff. 'Just to put an end to this bloody game of hide-and-seek.' He wiped his nose with a red handkerchief.

Piper hesitated and then headed for the door. 'We can't talk in here,' he muttered.

'Why not?' said Frensic. 'It seems as good a place as any.'

'You wouldn't understand,' said Piper and went out. Frensic blew his nose coarsely and then followed.

'For a horrid little blackmailer you've got a hell of a lot of pretensions,' he said as they stood in the hall, 'all that crap in there about *The Old Curiosity Shop*.'

'It isn't crap,' said Piper, 'and don't call me a blackmailer. You started this. And that's the truth.'

'Truth?' said Frensic with a nasty laugh. 'If you want the truth you're going to get it. That's what I've come here for.' He looked across at the door marked SCRIPTORIUM. 'What's in there?'

'That's where I teach people to write.' said Piper.

Frensic stared at him and laughed again. 'You're joking,' he said and opened the door. Inside the room was filled with desks, desks on which stood bottles of ink and pens, and each desk tilted at an angle. On the walls were framed examples of script and, in front, a blackboard. Frensic glanced round.

'Charming. The Scriptorium. And I suppose you've got a Plagiarium too?'

'A what?' said Piper.

'A special room for plagiarism. Or do you combine the process in here? I mean there's nothing like going the whole hog. How do you

223

go about it? Do you give each student a bestseller to alter and then flog it as your own work?'

'Coming from you, that's a dirty crack,' said Piper. 'I do all my own writing in my study. Down here I teach my students how to write. Not what.'

'How? You teach them how to write?' He picked up a bottle of ink and shook it. The sludge moved slowly. 'Still on the evaporated ink, I see.'

'It gives the greatest density,' said Piper but Frensic had put the bottle down and turned back to the door.

'And where's your study?' he asked. Piper led the way slowly upstairs and opened another door. Frensic stepped inside. The walls were lined with shelves and a big desk stood in front of a window which looked out across the drive towards the river. Frensic studied the books. They were bound in calf. Dickens, Conrad, James . . .

'The old testament,' he said and reached for *Middlemarch*. Piper took it brusquely from him and put it back.

'This year's model?' asked Frensic.

'A world, a universe beyond your tawdry imagination,' said Piper angrily. Frensic shrugged. There was a pathos about Piper's tenseness that was weakening his resolve. Frensic steeled himself to be coarse.

'Bloody cosy little billet you've got yourself here,' he said, seating himself at the desk and putting his feet up. Behind him Piper's face whitened at the sacrilege. 'Curator of a museum, counterfeiter of other people's novels, a bit of blackmail on the side – and what do you do about sex?' He hesitated and picked up a paperknife for safety's sake. If he was going to put the boot in there was no knowing what Piper might do. 'Screw the late Mrs Hutchmeyer?'

There was a hiss behind him and Frensic swung round. Piper was facing him with his pinched face and narrow eyes blazing with hatred. Frensic's grip tightened on the paperknife. He was frightened but the thing had to be done. He had come too far to go back now.

'It's none of my business, I daresay,' he said as Piper stared, 'but necrophilia seems to be your forte. First you rob dead authors, then you put the bite on me for two million dollars, what do you do to the late Mrs Hutch—'

'Don't you dare say it,' shouted Piper, his voice shrill with fury.

'Why not?' said Frensic. 'There's nothing like confession for cleansing the soul.'

224

'It isn't true,' said Piper. His breathing was audible.

Frensic smiled cynically. 'What isn't? The truth will out, as the saying goes. That's why I'm here.' He stood up with assumed menace and Piper shrank back.

'Stop it. Stop it. I don't want to hear any more. Just go away and leave me alone.'

Frensic shook his head. 'And have you send me yet another manuscript and tell me to sell it? Oh no, those days are over. You're going to learn the truth if I have to ram it down your snivelling—'

Piper covered his ears with his hands. 'I won't,' he shouted, 'I won't listen to you.'

Frensic reached in his pocket and took out Dr Louth's letter.

'You don't have to listen. Just read this.'

He thrust the letter forward and Piper took it. Frensic sat down in the chair. The crisis was over. He was no longer afraid. Piper might be mad but his madness was self-directed and held no threat for Frensic. He watched him read the letter with a new sense of pity. He was looking at a nonentity, the archetypal author for whom only words had any reality, and one who couldn't write. Piper finished the letter and looked up.

'What does it mean?' he asked.

'What it doesn't say,' said Frensic. 'That the great Dr Louth wrote *Pause*. That's what it means.'

Piper looked down at the letter again. 'But it says here she didn't.'

Frensic smiled. 'Quite. And why should she have written that? Ask yourself that question. Why deny what nobody had ever supposed?'

'I don't understand,' said Piper, 'it doesn't make sense.'

'It does if you accept that she was being blackmailed,' said Frensic.

'Blackmailed? But by whom?'

Frensic helped himself to snuff. 'By you. You threatened me and I threatened her.'

'But . . .' Piper wrestled with this incomprehensible sequence. It was beyond his simple philosophy.

'You threatened to expose me and I passed the message on,' said Frensic. 'Dr Sydney Louth paid two million dollars not to be revealed as the author of *Pause*. The price of her sacred reputation.'

Piper's eyes were glazed. 'I don't believe you,' he muttered.

'Don't,' said Frensic. 'Believe what you bloody well like. All you've

225

got to do is resurrect yourself and tell Hutchmeyer you're still alive and kicking and the media will do the rest. It will all come out. My role, your role, the whole damned story and at the end of it, your Dr Louth with her reputation as a critic in ruins. The bitch will be the laughing-stock of the literary world. Mind you, you'll be in prison. And I dare say I'll be bankrupt too, but at least I won't have to put up with the impossible task of trying to sell your rotten *Search for a Lost Childhood*. That'll be some compensation.'

Piper sat down limply in a chair.

'Well?' said Frensic, but Piper simply shook his head. Frensic took the letter from him and turned to the window. He had called the little sod's bluff. There would be no more threats, no more manuscripts. Piper was broken. It was time to leave. Frensic stared out at the dark river and the forest beyond, a strange foreign landscape, dangerously lush, and far from the comfortable little world he had come to protect. He crossed to the door and went down the broad staircase and across the hall. All that was needed now was to get home as quickly as possible.

But when he got into his rented car and drove down the drive to the ferry it was to find the pontoon on the far side of the river and no one to bring it across. Frensic rang the bell but nobody answered. He stood in the bright sunlight and waited. There was a stillness in the air and only the sound of the black river slurping against the bank below him. Frensic got back into the car and drove into the square. Here too there was nobody in sight. Dark shadows under the tin roofs that served as awnings to the shop fronts, the white-painted church, a wooden bench at the foot of a statue in the middle of the square, blank windows. Frensic got out of his car and looked round. The clock on the courthouse stood at midday. Presumably everyone was at lunch, but there was still a sense of unnatural desolation which disturbed him and back beyond the river the forest, an undomesticated tangle of trees and underbush, made a close horizon above which the sky was an empty blue. Frensic walked round the square and then got back into the car. Perhaps if he tried the ferry again . . . But it was still there across the water and when Frensic tried to pull on the rope there was no movement. He rang the bell again. There was no echo and his sense of unease redoubled. Finally leaving the car in the road he walked along the bank of the river following a little path. He would wait a while until the lunch hour was over and then try again. But the path led under live oaks hung with Spanish moss and ended in the cemetery. Frensic looked for a moment at the grave-stones and then turned back.

Perhaps if he drove west he would find a road out of town on that side which would lead him back to Route 80. Blood Alley had an almost cheerful ring to it now. But he had no map in the car and after driving down a number of side streets that ended in cul-de-sacs or uninviting tracks into the woods he turned back. Perhaps the ferry would be open now. He looked at his watch. It was two o'clock and people would be out and about again.

They were. As he drove into the little square a group of gaunt men standing on the sidewalk outside the courthouse moved across the road. Frensic stopped the car and stared unhappily through the windshield. The gaunt men had holsters on their belts and the gauntest of them all wore a star on his chest. He walked round the car to the side window and leant in. Frensic studied his yellow teeth.

'Your name Frensic?' he asked. Frensic nodded. 'Judge wants to see you,' continued the man. 'You going to come quietly or . . .?' Frensic came quietly and with the little group behind him climbed the steps to the courthouse. Inside it was cool and dark. Frensic hesitated but the tall man pointed to a door.

'Judge is in chambers,' he said. 'Go on in.'

Frensic went in. Behind a large desk sat Baby Hutchmeyer. She was dressed in a long black robe and above it her face, always un-naturally taut, was now unpleasantly white. Frensic, staring down at her, had no doubt about her identity.

'Mrs Hutchmeyer . . .' he began, 'the late Mrs Hutchmeyer?'

'Judge Hutchmeyer to you,' said Baby, 'and we won't have any-thing more about the late unless you want to end up the late Mr Frensic right soon.'

Frensic swallowed and glanced over his shoulder. The sheriff was standing with his back against the door and the gun on his belt glinted obtrusively.

'May I ask what the meaning of this is?' he asked after a moment's significant silence. 'Bringing me here like this and . . .'

The judge looked across at the sheriff. 'What have you got on him so far?' she asked.

'Uttering threats and menaces,' said the sheriff. 'Possession of an unauthorized firearm. Spare tyre stashed with heroin. Blackmail. You name it, Judge, he's got it.'

Frensic groped for a chair. 'Heroin?' he gasped. 'What do you mean heroin? I haven't a single grain of heroin.'

'You think not?' said Baby. 'Herb'll show you, won't you, Herb?'

Behind Frensic the sheriff nodded. 'Got the automobile round at the garage dismantling it right now,' he said, 'you want proof we'll show it to you.'

But Frensic was in no need of proof. He sat stunned in the chair and stared at Baby's white face. 'What do you want?' he asked finally.

'Justice,' said Baby succinctly.

'Justice,' muttered Frensic, 'you talk about justice and . . .'

'You want to make a statement now or reserve your defence for court tomorrow?' said Baby.

Frensic glanced over his shoulder again. 'I'd like to make a statement now. In private,' he said.

Baby nodded to the sheriff. 'Wait outside, Herb,' she said, 'and stay close. Any trouble in here and . . .'

'There won't be any trouble in here,' said Frensic hastily, 'I can assure you of that.'

Baby waved his assurances and Herb aside. As the door closed Frensic took out his handkerchief and mopped his face.

'Right,' said Baby, 'so you want to make a statement.'

Frensic leant forward. It was in his mind to say 'You can't do this to me,' but the cliché culled from so many of his authors didn't seem appropriate. She *could* do this to him. He was in Bibliopolis and Bibliopolis was off the map of civilization.

'What do you want me to do?' he asked faintly.

Judge Baby swung her chair and leant back. 'Coming from you, Mr Frensic, that's an interesting question,' she said. 'You come into this little town and you start uttering threats and menaces against one of our citizens and you want me to tell you what I want you to do.'

'I didn't utter threats and menaces,' said Frensic, 'I came to tell Piper to stop sending me his manuscripts. And if anyone's been uttering threats it's him, not me.'

Baby shook her head. 'If that's your defence I can tell you right off nobody in Bibliopolis is going to believe you. Mr Piper is the most peaceful non-violent citizen around these parts.'

'Well, he may be around these parts,' said Frensic, 'but from where I'm sitting in London . . .'

228

'You ain't sitting in London now,' said Baby, 'you're sitting right here in my chambers and shaking like a hound dog pissing peach pits.'

Frensic considered the simile and found it disagreeable. 'You'd be shaking if you'd just been accused of having a spare tyre filled with heroin,' he said.

Baby nodded. 'You could be right at that,' she said. 'I can give you life for that. Throw in the threats and menaces, the firearm and the blackmail and it could all add up to life plus ninety-nine years. You had better consider that before you say anything more.'

Frensic considered it and found he was shaking even harder. Hound dogs having problems with peach pits were no comparison. 'You can't mean it,' he gasped.

Baby smiled. 'You'd better believe I mean it. The warden of the penitentiary's a deacon in my church. You wouldn't have to do the ninety-nine years. Like life would be three months and you wouldn't last in the chain gang. They got snakes and things to make it natural death. You've seen our little cemetery?'

Frensic nodded. 'So we've got a little plot marked out already,' said Baby. 'It wouldn't have no headstone. No name like Frensic. Just a little mound and nobody would ever know. So that's your choice.'

'What is?' said Frensic when he could find his voice.

'Like life plus ninety-nine or you do what I tell you.'

'I think I'll do what you tell me,' said Frensic for whom this was no choice at all.

'Right,' said Baby, 'so first you make a full confession.'

'Confession?' said Frensic. 'What sort of confession?'

'Just that you wrote *Pause O Men for the Virgin* and palmed it off on Mr Piper and hoodwinked Hutch and instigated Miss Futtle to arsonize the house and—'

'No,' cried Frensic, 'never. I'd rather . . .' He stopped. He wouldn't rather. There was a look on Baby's face that told him that. 'I don't see why I've got to confess to all those things,' he said.

Baby relaxed. 'You took his good name away from him. Now you're going to give it back to him.'

'His good name?' said Frensic.

'By putting it on the cover of that dirty novel,' said Baby.

'He didn't have any sort of name till we did that,' said Frensic, 'he had never published anything and now he's so-called dead he isn't going to.'

'Oh yes, he is,' said Baby leaning forward. 'You're going to give him your name. Like *Search for a Lost Childhood* by Frederick Frensic.'

Frensic stared at her. The woman was mad as a March hare. '*Search* by me?' he said. 'You don't understand. I've hawked that blasted book round every publisher in London and no one wants to know. It's unreadable.'

Baby smiled. Unpleasantly.

'That's your problem. You're going to get it published and you're going to get all his future books published under your own name. Its that or the chain gang.'

She glanced significantly out of the window at the horizon of trees and the empty sky and Frensic following her glance gazed into a terrible future and an early death. He'd have to humour her. 'All right,' he said, 'I'll do my best.'

'You'll do better than that. You'll do exactly what I say.' She took a sheet of paper from a drawer and handed him a pen. 'Now write,' she said.

Frensic hitched his chair forward and began to write very shakily. By the time he had finished he had confessed to having evaded British income tax by paying two million dollars plus royalties into Account Number 478776 in the First National Bank of New York and to having incited his partner, the former Miss Futtle, to arsonize the Hutchmeyer residence. The whole statement was such an amalgam of things he had done and things he hadn't that, cross-examined by a competent lawyer, he would never be able to disentangle himself. Baby read it through and witnessed his signature. Then she called Herb in and he witnessed it too.

'That should keep you on the straight and narrow,' she said as the sheriff left the room. 'One squeak out of you and one attempt to evade your obligation to publish Mr Piper's novels and this goes straight to Hutchmeyer, the insurance company, the FBI and the tax authorities, and you can wipe that smile off your face.' But Frensic wasn't smiling. He had developed a nervous tic. 'Because if you think you can worm your way out of this by going to the authorities yourself and telling them to look me up in Bibliopolis you can forget it. I've got friends round here and no one talks if I say no. You understand that?'

230

Frensic nodded. 'I quite understand,' he said.

Baby stood up and took off her robe. 'Well, just in case you don't, you're going to be saved,' she said. They went out into the hall where the group of gaunt men waited.

'We've got a convert, boys,' she said. 'See you all in Church.'

Frensic sat in the front row of the little Church of The Servants of The Lord. Before him, radiant and serene, Baby conducted the service. The church was packed and Herb sat next to Frensic and shared his hymnbook with him. They sang 'Telephoning to Glory' and 'Rock of Ages' and 'Shall we Gather by the River', and with Herb's nudging Frensic sang as loudly as the rest. Finally Baby delivered a virulent sermon on the text 'Behold a man gluttonous, and a winebibber, a friend of publishers and sinners,' her gaze fixed pointedly on Frensic throughout, and the congregation launched into 'Bibliopolis we Hold Thee Dear.' It was time for Frensic to be saved. He moved shakily forward and knelt. Snakes might no longer infest Bibliopolis, but Frensic was still petrified. Above him Baby's face was radiant. She had triumphed once again.

'Swear by the Lord to keep the covenant,' she said. And Frensic swore.

He was still swearing an hour later as he sat in his car and the ferry crossed the river. Frensic glanced across at Pellagra. The light was burning on the upper floor. Piper was doubtless at work on some terrible novel that Frensic would have to sell under his own name. He drove off the ferry recklessly and the hired car bucketed down the dirt road and the headlights picked out the dark water gleaming beneath the entwined trees. After Bibliopolis the grim landscape held no menace for him. It was a natural world full of natural dangers and Frensic could cope with them. With Baby Hutchmeyer there had been no coping. Frensic swore again.

In his study in Pellagra Piper sat silently at his desk. He was not writing. He was looking at the guarantee Frensic had written promising to publish *Search for a Lost Childhood* even at his own expense. Piper was going to be published at long last. Never mind that the name on the cover would be Frensic. One day the world would learn the truth. Or better still, perhaps, would be an un-answered question. After all who knew who Shakespeare was or who had written *Hamlet*? No one.

Chapter 23

Nine months later *Search for a Lost Childhood* by Frederick Frensic, published by Corkadales, price £3.90, came out in Britain. In America it was published by Hutchmeyer Press. Frensic had had to apply some direct pressure in both directions and it was only the threat of exposure that had persuaded Geoffrey to accept the book. Sonia had been influenced by feelings of loyalty, and Hutchmeyer had needed no urging. The sound of a familiar female voice on the telephone had sufficed. And so the review copies had gone out with Frensic's name on the title-page and the dust jacket. A short biography at the back said he had once been a literary agent. He was one no longer. The name on the door of the office in Lanyard Lane still lingered but the office was empty and Frensic had moved from Glass Walk to a cottage in Sussex without a telephone.

There, safe from Mrs Bogden, he was Piper's amanuensis. Day after day he typed out the manuscripts Piper sent him and night after night lurked in the corner of the village pub and drowned his sorrows. His friends in London saw him seldom. From necessity he visited Geoffrey and occasionally went out to lunch with him. But for the most part he spent his days at his typewriter, cultivated his garden and went for long walks sunk in melancholy thought.

Not that his thoughts were always depressed. There remained a deep core of deviousness in Frensic which nagged at the problem of his predicament and sought ways to escape. But none came to mind. His imagination had been anaesthetized by his terrible experience and each day Piper's dreary prose reinforced the effect. Distilled from so many sources, it acted on Frensic's literary nerve and kept him in a state of disorientation so that he had no sooner recognized a sentence from Mann than he was flung a chunk of Faulkner to be followed by a *mot* from Proust or a slice of *Middlemarch*. After such

232

a paragraph Frensic would get up and reel into the garden to escape his associations by mowing the lawn. At night before going to sleep he would excise the memory of Bibliopolis by reading a page or two of *The Wind in the Willows* and wish he could potter about in boats like the Water Rat. Anything to escape the ordeal he had been set.

And now it was Sunday and the reviews of *Search* would be in the papers. In spite of himself Frensic was drawn to the little shop in the village to buy the *Sunday Times* and the *Observer*. He bought them both and didn't wait until he got home to read the worst. It was best to get the agony over and done with. He stood in the lane and opened the *Sunday Times Review* and turned to the book page and there it was. At the top of the list. Frensic leant against a gatepost and read the review and as he read his world turned topsy turvy once again. Linda Gormley 'loved' the book and devoted two columns to its praise. She called it 'the most honest and original appraisal of the adolescent trauma I have read for a very long time'. Frensic stared at the words in disbelief. Then he rummaged in the *Observer*. It was the same there. 'For a first novel it has not only freshness but a deeply intuitive insight into family relationships . . . a masterpiece . . .' Frensic shut the paper hurriedly. A masterpiece? He looked again. The word was still there, and further down there was even worse. 'If one can say of a novel that it is a work of genius . . .' Frensic clutched the gatepost. He felt weak. *Search for a Lost Childhood* was being acclaimed. He staggered on up the lane with a fresh sense of loss. His nose, his infallible nose, had betrayed him. Piper had been right all along. Either that or the plague of *The Moral Novel* had spread and the days of the novel of entertainment were over, supplanted by the religion of literature. People no longer read for pleasure. If they liked *Search* they couldn't. There wasn't an ounce of enjoyment to be got from the book. Frensic had painstakingly (and the word was precise) typed the manuscript out page by ghastly page and from those pages there had emanated a whining self-pity, an arrogantly self-directed sycophancy that had sickened him. And this wretched puke of words was what the reviewers called originality and freshness and a work of genius. Genius! Frensic spat the word. It had lost all meaning.

And as he lumbered up the lane the full portent of the book's success hit him. He would have to go through life bearing the stigma of being known as the author of a book he hadn't written. His friends would congratulate him . . . For one awful moment Frensic contemplated suicide but his sense of irony saved him. He knew now how Piper had felt when he had discovered what Frensic had foisted on him with *Pause*. 'Hoist with his own petard' sprang to mind and he acknowledged Piper's triumphant revenge. The thought brought Frensic to a standstill. He had been made to look a fool and if the world now considered him a genius, one day they would learn the truth and the laughter would never cease. It was a threat he had used against Dr Louth and it had been turned against him. Frensic's fury at the thought spurred his deviousness to work. Standing in the lane between the hedgerows he saw his escape. He would turn the tables on them yet. Out of the accumulated experience of the thousand commercially successful novels he had sold he could surely concoct a story that would contain every ingredient Piper and his mentor, Dr Louth, would most detest. It would have sex, violence, sentimentality, romance – and all this without an ounce of significance. It would be a rattling good yarn, a successor to *Pause*, and on the dust jacket in bold type there would be Peter Piper's name. No, that was wrong. Piper was a mere pawn in the game. Behind him there lay a far deadlier enemy to literature, Dr Sydney Louth.

Frensic quickened his pace and hurried across the little wooden bridge that led to his cottage. Presently he was sitting at his typewriter and had inserted a sheet of paper. First he needed a title. His fingers hammered on the keys and the words appeared. AN IMMORAL NOVEL by DR SYDNEY LOUTH. CHAPTER ONE. Frensic typed on and his mind flickered with fresh subtleties. He would incorporate her graceless style. And her ideas. It would be a grotesque pastiche of everything she had ever written and with it all there would be a story so sickly and vile as to deny every precept of *The Moral Novel*. He would stand the bitch on her head and shake her till her teeth rattled. And there was nothing she could do about it. As her agent, Frensic was safe. Only the truth could hurt him and she was in no position to tell the truth. Frensic stopped typing at the thought and stared into the distance. There was no need to concoct a story. The truth was far more deadly. He would tell the history of The Great Pursuit just as it had happened. His name would be mud but it was mud already in his own eyes with the success of *Search*, and besides he owed a duty to English literature. To hell with English literature. To Grub Street and all those writers without pretensions who wrote for a living. A living? The ambiguity of the word held him for a moment. Who wrote for a living and the living too. Frensic tore the sheet from the typewriter and started again.

He would call it THE GREAT PURSUIT. A TRUE STORY by Frederick Frensic. The living deserved the truth, and a story, and he would give them both. He would dedicate the book to Grub Street. It had a good old eighteenth-century ring to it. Frensic's nose twitched. He knew he had just begun to write a book that would sell. And if they wanted to sue, let them. He would publish and be damned.

In Bibliopolis the publication of *Search* made no impression on Piper. He had lost his faith. It had gone with Frensic's visit and the revelation that Dr Sydney Louth had written *Pause*. It had taken some time for the truth to sink in and he had gone on writing and rewriting for a few months almost automatically. But in the end he knew that Frensic had not lied. He had written to Dr Louth and had had no reply. Piper closed the Church of The Great Tradition. Only the School of Penmanship remained and with it the doctrine of logosophy. The age of the great novel was over. It remained only to commemorate it in manuscript. And so while Baby preached the need to imitate Christ, Piper too returned to traditional virtues in everything. Already he had abolished pens and his pupils had moved back to quills. They were more natural than nibs. They needed cutting, they were the original tools of his craft and they stood as reminders of that golden age when books were written by hand and to be a copyist was to belong to an honourable profession.

And so that Sunday morning Piper sat in the Scriptorium and dipped his quill in Higgins Eternal Evaporated Ink and began to write : 'My fathers' family name being Pirrip, and my Christian name being Philip, my infant tongue could make of both names nothing longer or more explicit than Piper . . .' He stopped. That wasn't right. It should have been Pip. But after a moment's hesitation he dipped his quill again and continued.

After all in a thousand years who the dickens would care who had written *Great Expectations*? Only a few scholars who could still read English. The printed works would have perished by then. Only Piper's own parchment manuscripts bound in the thickest leather and filled with his perfect hieroglyphic handwriting and gold illuminated lettering would stand the test of time and lie in the museums of the world, mute testimony to his dedication to literature, and to his craftsmanship. And when he had finished Dickens, he would start on Henry James and write *his* novels out in longhand too. There was a lifetime's work ahead of him just copying the great tradition out in Higgins Eternal Ink. The name of Piper would be literally immortal yet...